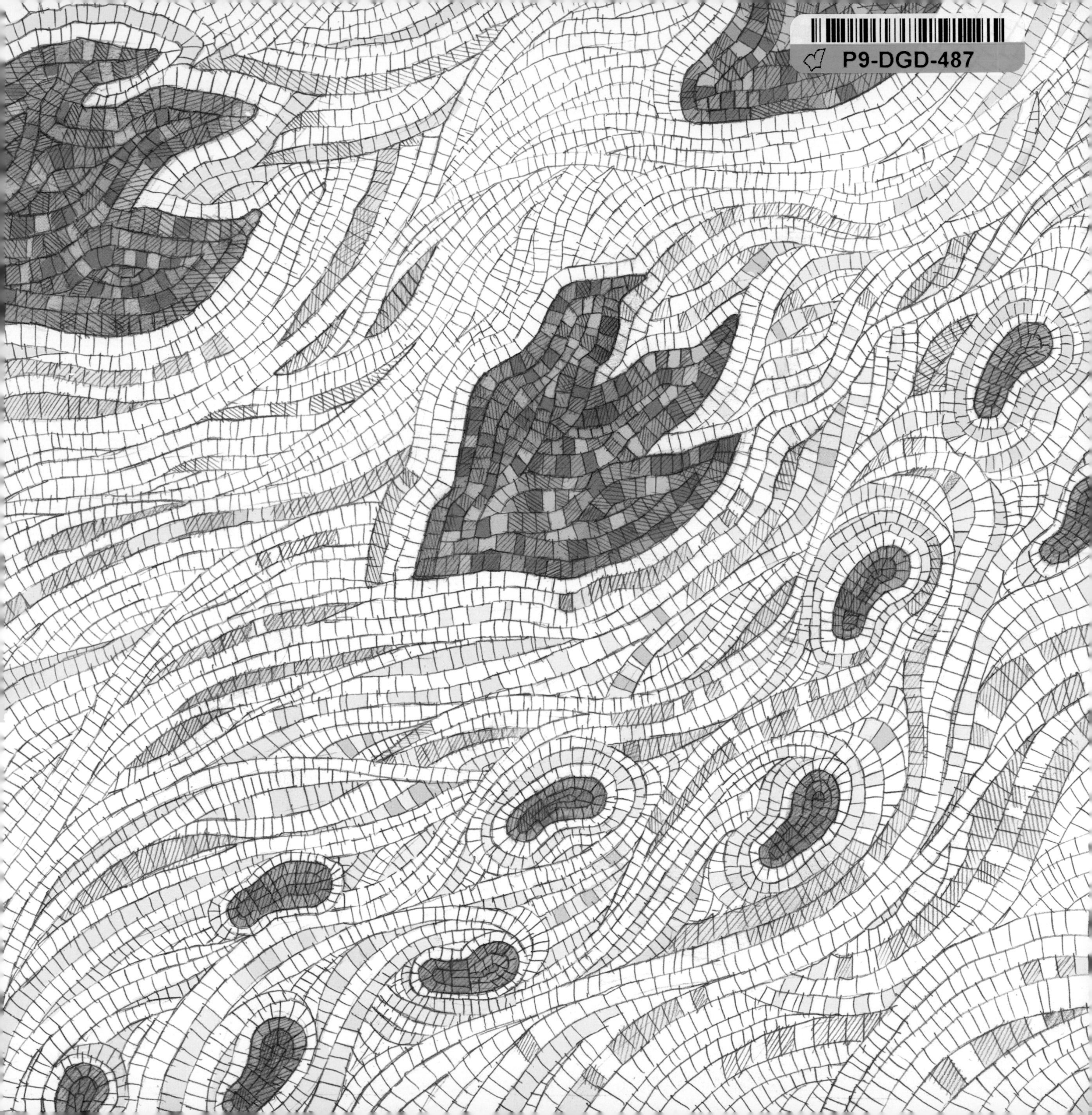

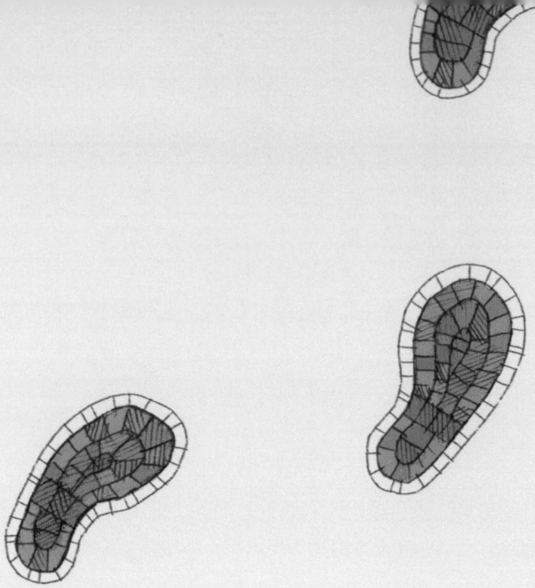

BOLIVAR™

Published by
ARCHAIA™

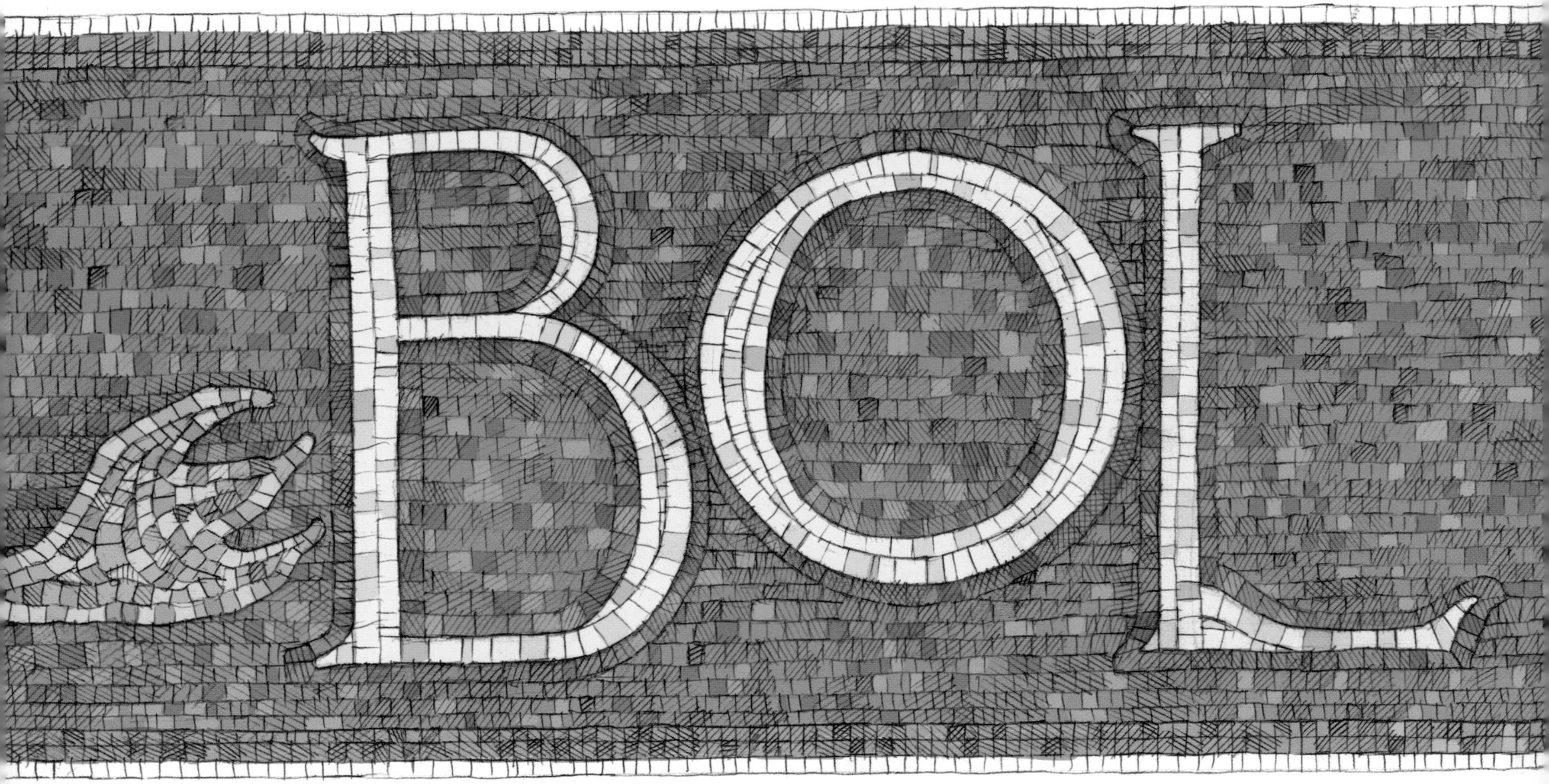
BOL

ARCHAIA • LOS ANGELES, CALIFORNIA

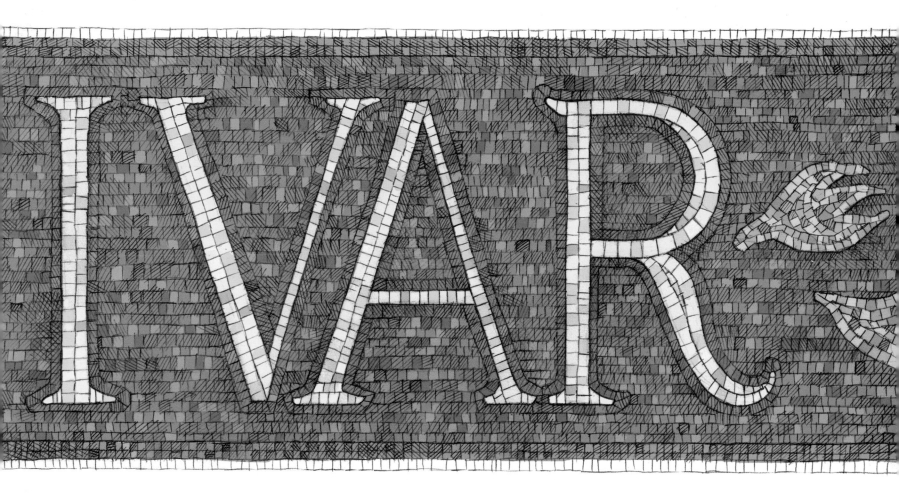

IVAR

written and illustrated by

SEAN RUBIN

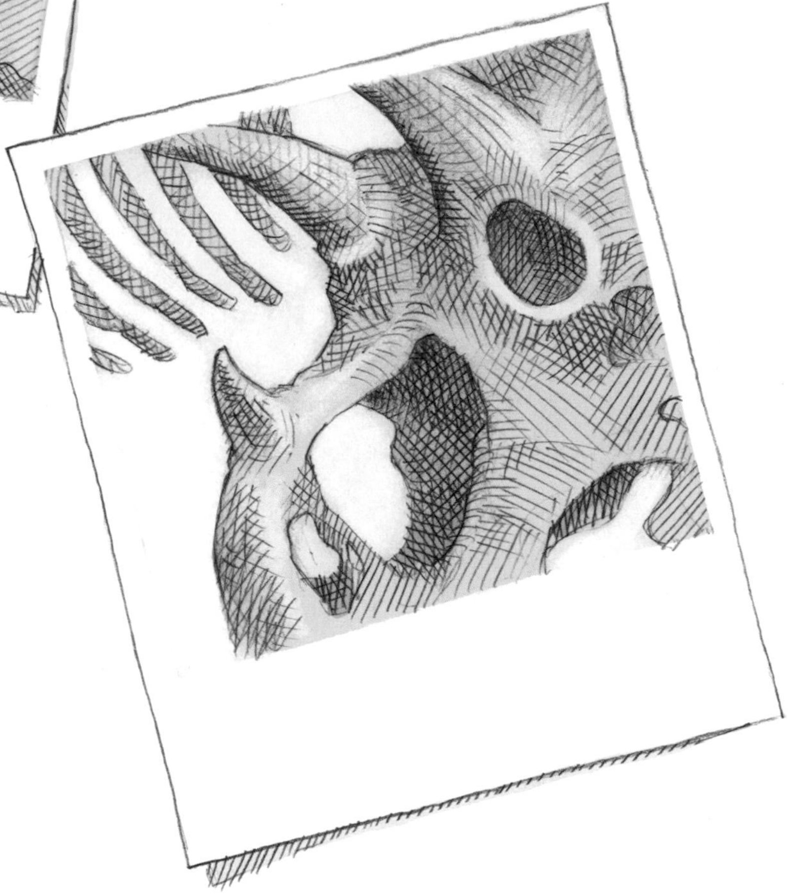

Designers **Scott Newman** and **Chelsea Roberts**
Editors **Whitney Leopard** and **Sierra Hahn**

Special Thanks to **Rebecca Taylor**, **Stephen Christy**, and **Paul Morrissey**

ROSS RICHIE CEO & Founder
MATT GAGNON Editor-in-Chief
FILIP SABLIK President of Publishing & Marketing
STEPHEN CHRISTY President of Development
LANCE KREITER VP of Licensing & Merchandising
PHIL BARBARO VP of Finance
ARUNE SINGH VP of Marketing
BRYCE CARLSON Managing Editor
MEL CAYLO Marketing Manager
SCOTT NEWMAN Production Design Manager
KATE HENNING Operations Manager
SIERRA HAHN Senior Editor
DAFNA PLEBAN Editor, Talent Development
SHANNON WATTERS Editor
ERIC HARBURN Editor
WHITNEY LEOPARD Editor
CAMERON CHITTOCK Editor
CHRIS ROSA Associate Editor
MATTHEW LEVINE Associate Editor

SOPHIE PHILIPS-ROBERTS Assistant Editor
AMANDA LaFRANCO Executive Assistant
KATALINA HOLLAND Editorial Administrative Assistant
JILLIAN CRAB Production Designer
MICHELLE ANKLEY Production Designer
KARA LEOPARD Production Designer
MARIE KRUPINA Production Designer
GRACE PARK Production Design Assistant
CHELSEA ROBERTS Production Design Assistant
ELIZABETH LOUGHRIDGE Accounting Coordinator
STEPHANIE HOCUTT Social Media Coordinator
JOSÉ MEZA Event Coordinator
HOLLY AITCHISON Operations Coordinator
MEGAN CHRISTOPHER Operations Assistant
RODRIGO HERNANDEZ Mailroom Assistant
MORGAN PERRY Direct Market Representative
CAT O'GRADY Marketing Assistant
LIZ ALMENDAREZ Accounting Administrative Assistant
CORNELIA TZANA Administrative Assistant

ARCHAIA™

BOLIVAR, March 2018. Published by Archaia, a division of Boom Entertainment, Inc. Bolivar is ™ & © 2018 Sean Rubin. All Rights Reserved. Archaia™ and the Archaia logo are trademarks of Boom Entertainment, Inc., registered in various countries and categories. All characters, events, and institutions depicted herein are fictional. Any similarity between any of the names, characters, persons, events, and/or institutions in this publication to actual names, characters, and persons, whether living or dead, events, and/or institutions is unintended and purely coincidental.

BOOM! Studios, 5670 Wilshire Boulevard, Suite 400, Los Angeles, CA 90036-5679.
Printed in China. Second Printing.

ISBN: 978-1-68415-069-4, eISBN: 978-1-61398-795-7

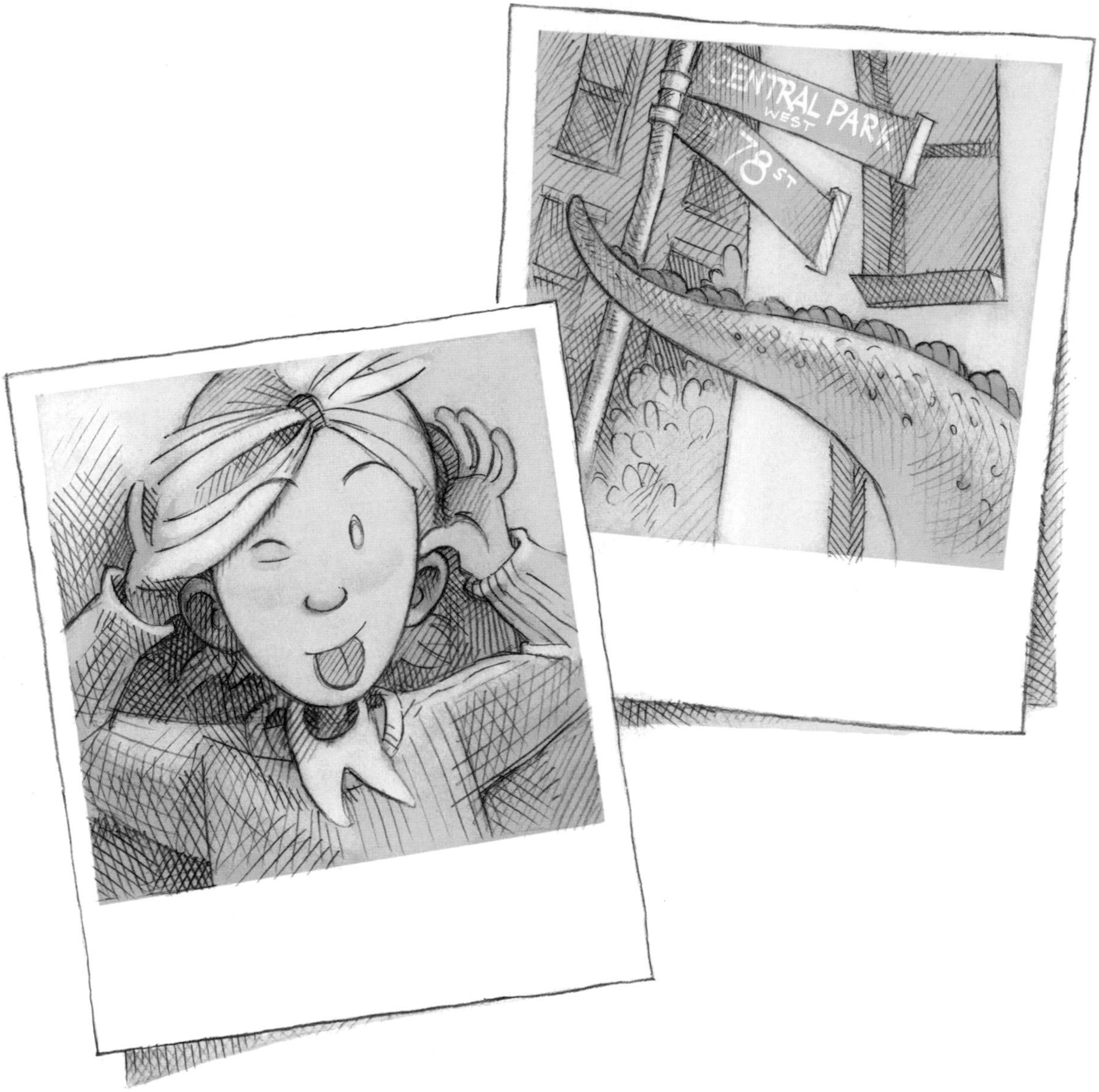
CENTRAL PARK
WEST
78 ST

(For Uncle Eddie)

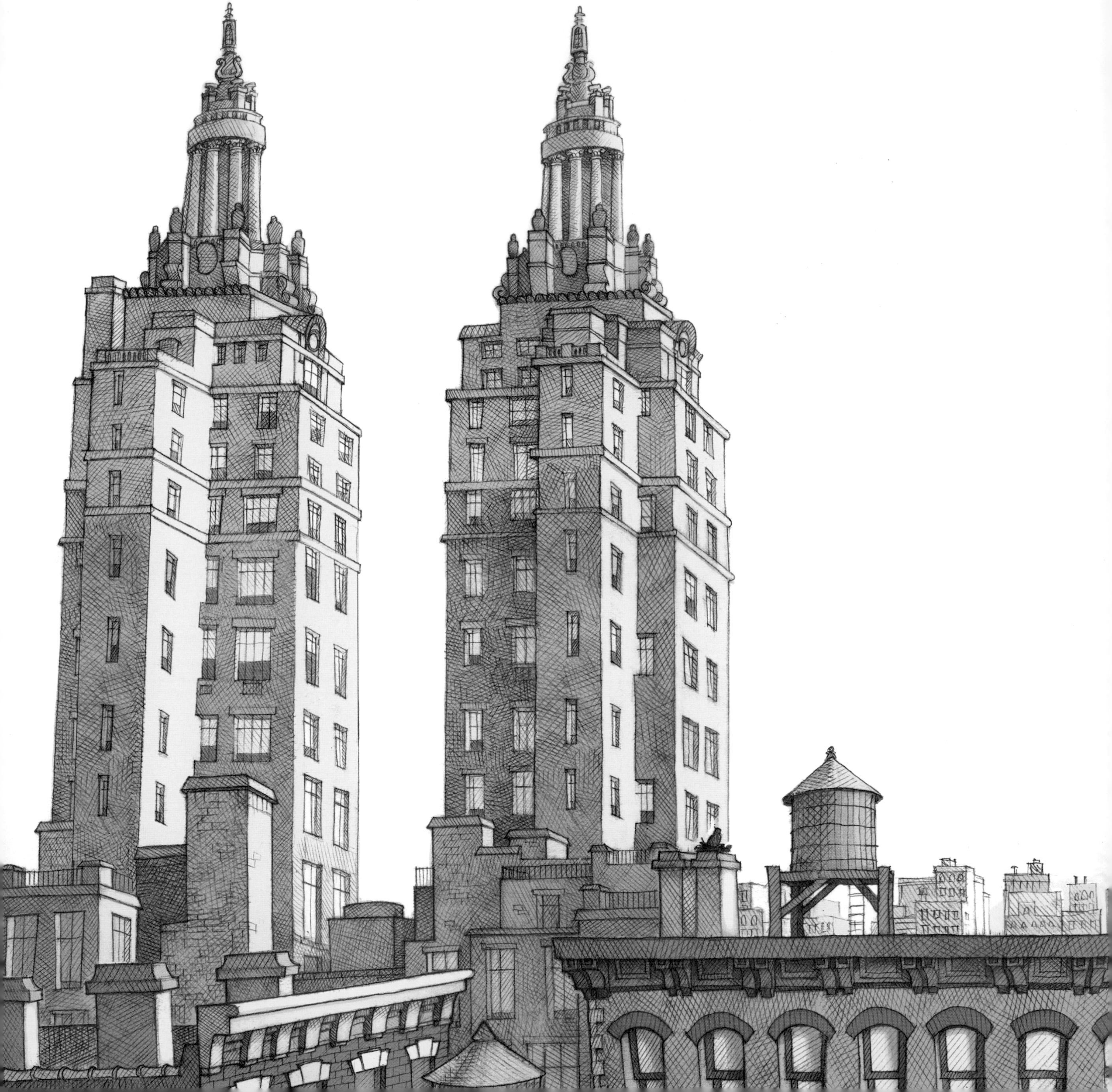

CHAPTER 1

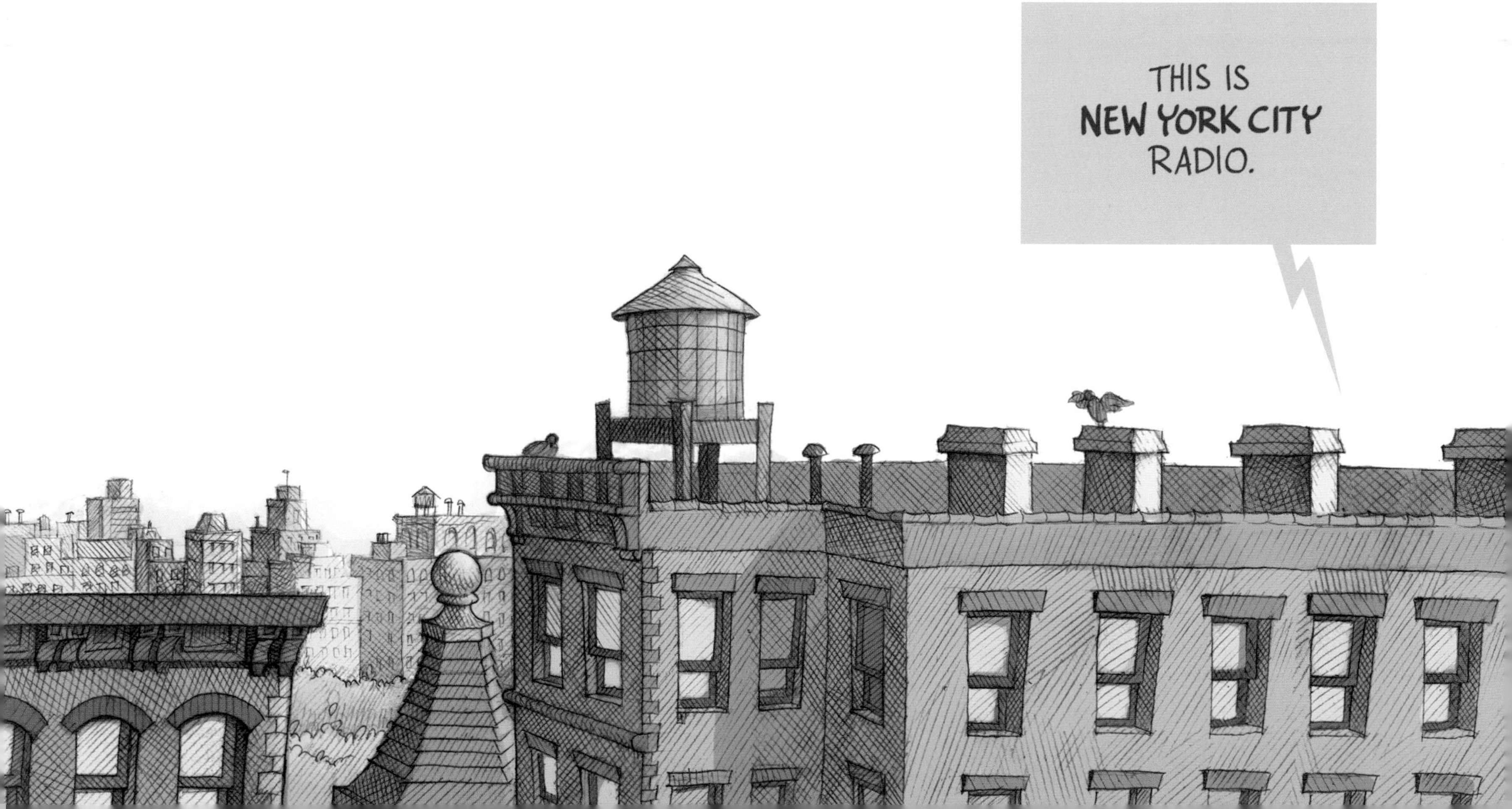
THIS IS
NEW YORK CITY
RADIO.

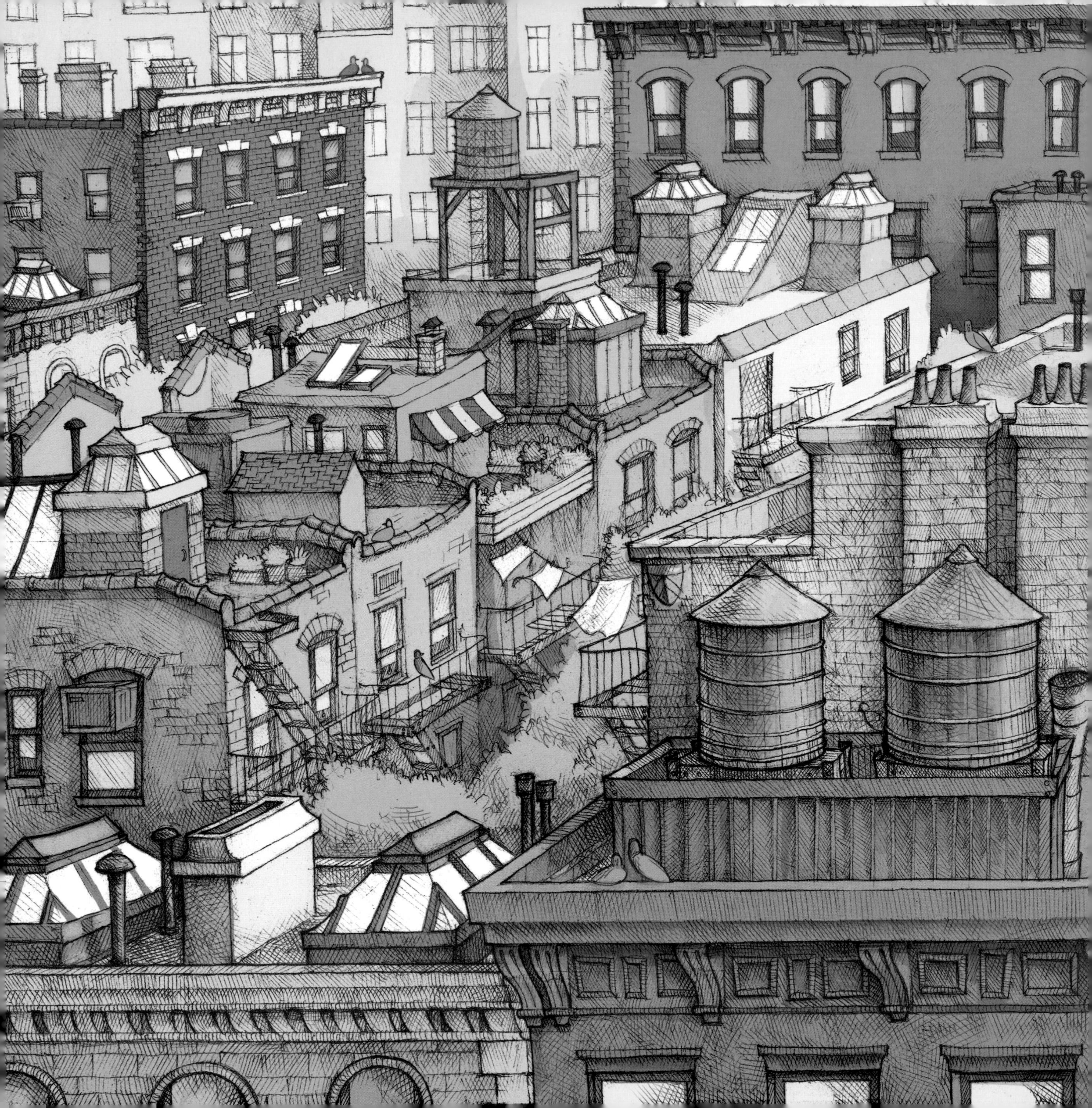

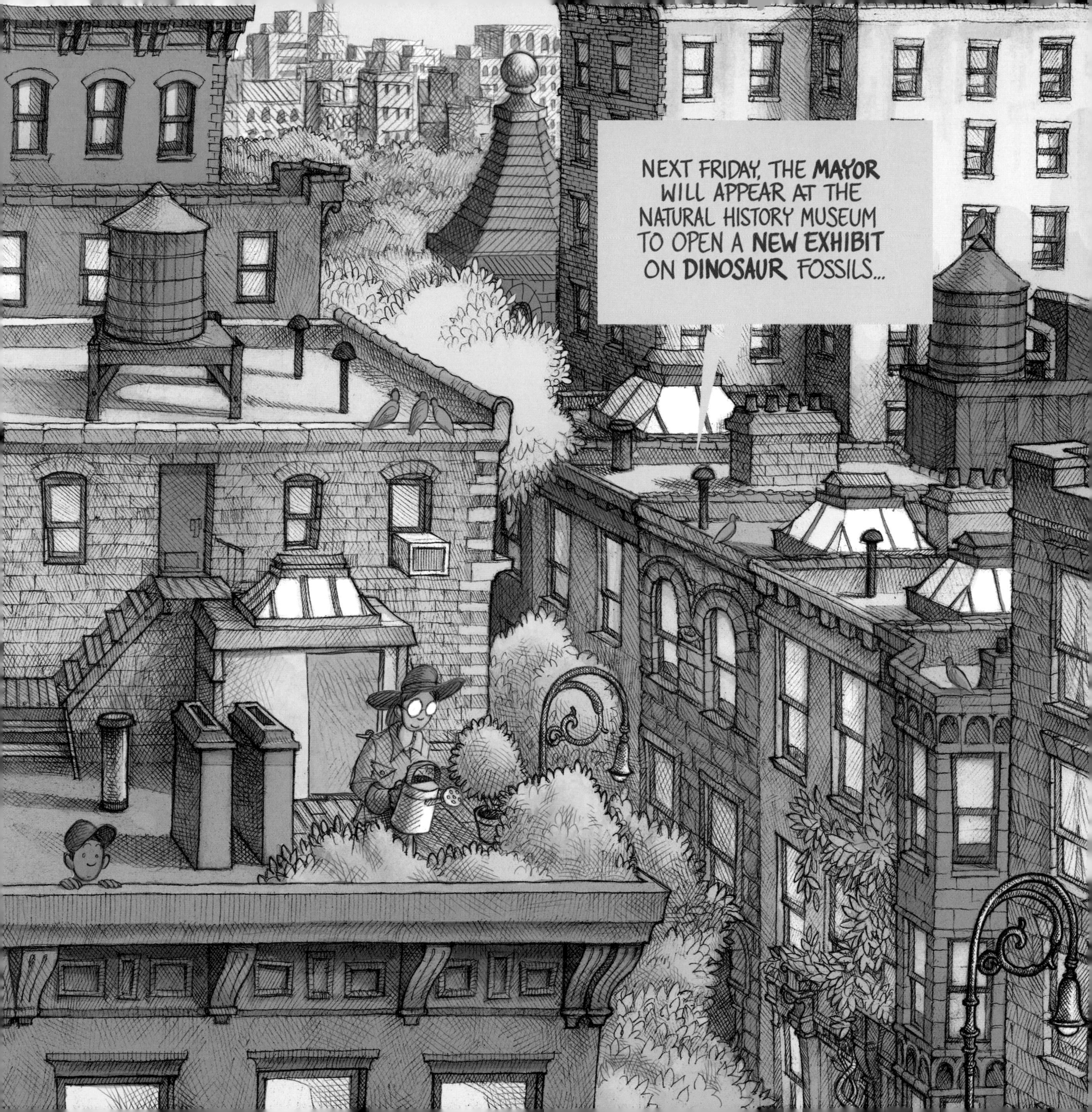
NEXT FRIDAY, THE MAYOR WILL APPEAR AT THE NATURAL HISTORY MUSEUM TO OPEN A NEW EXHIBIT ON DINOSAUR FOSSILS...

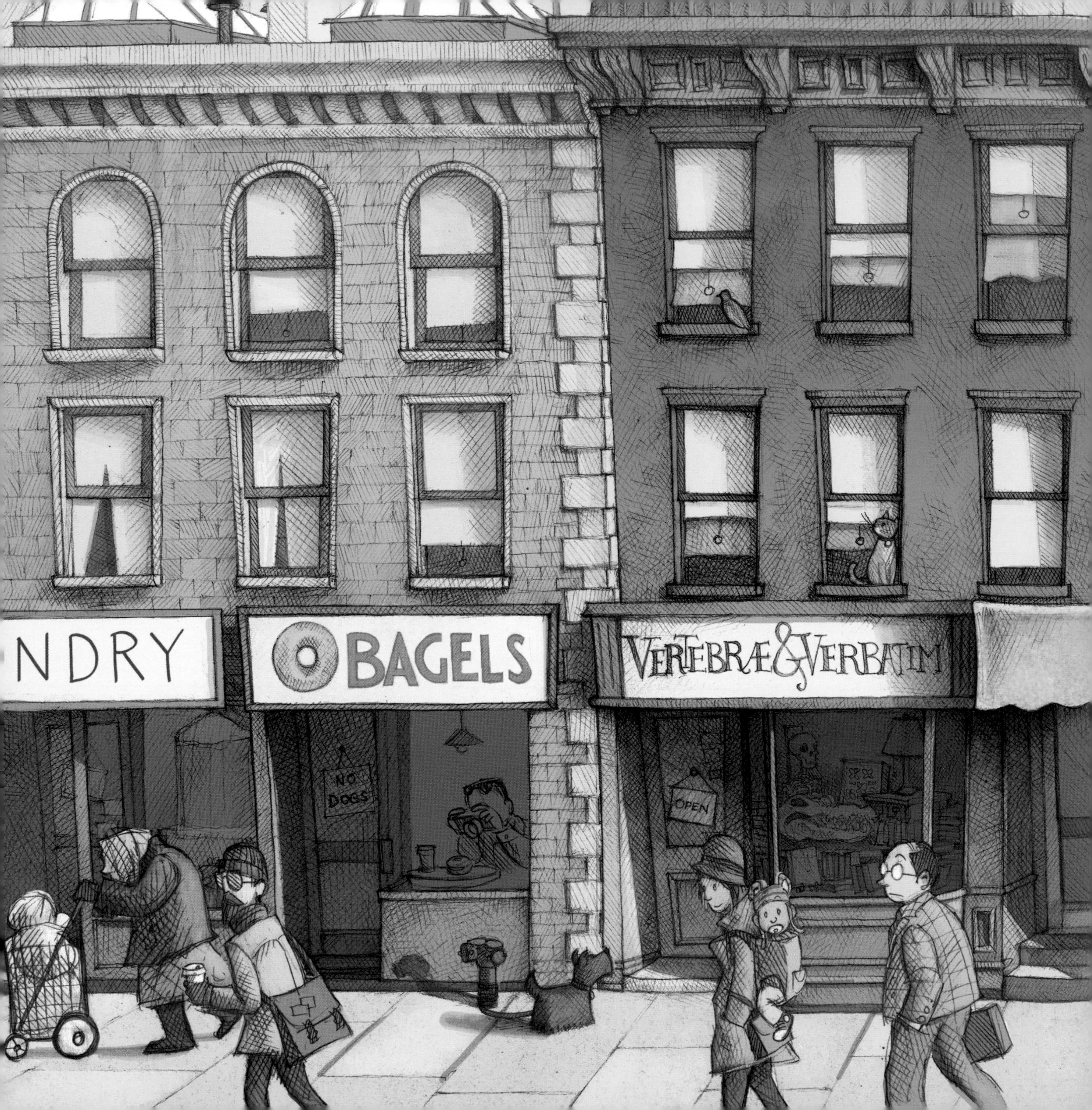
NDRY
BAGELS
VERTEBRÆ & VERBATIM
NO DOGS
OPEN

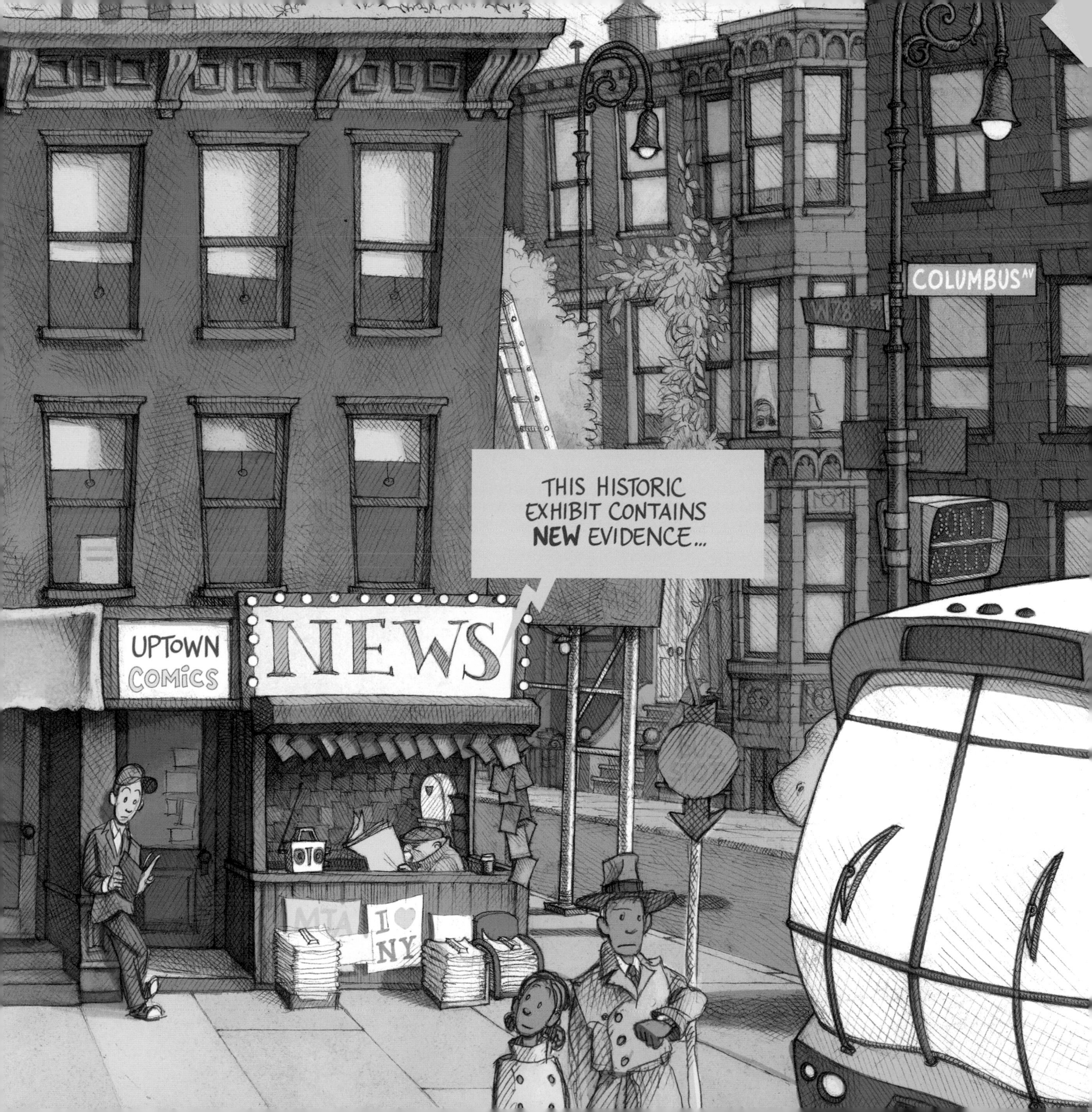
THIS HISTORIC
EXHIBIT CONTAINS
NEW EVIDENCE...
UPTOWN
COMICS
NEWS
COLUMBUS AV
MTA
I ♥ NY

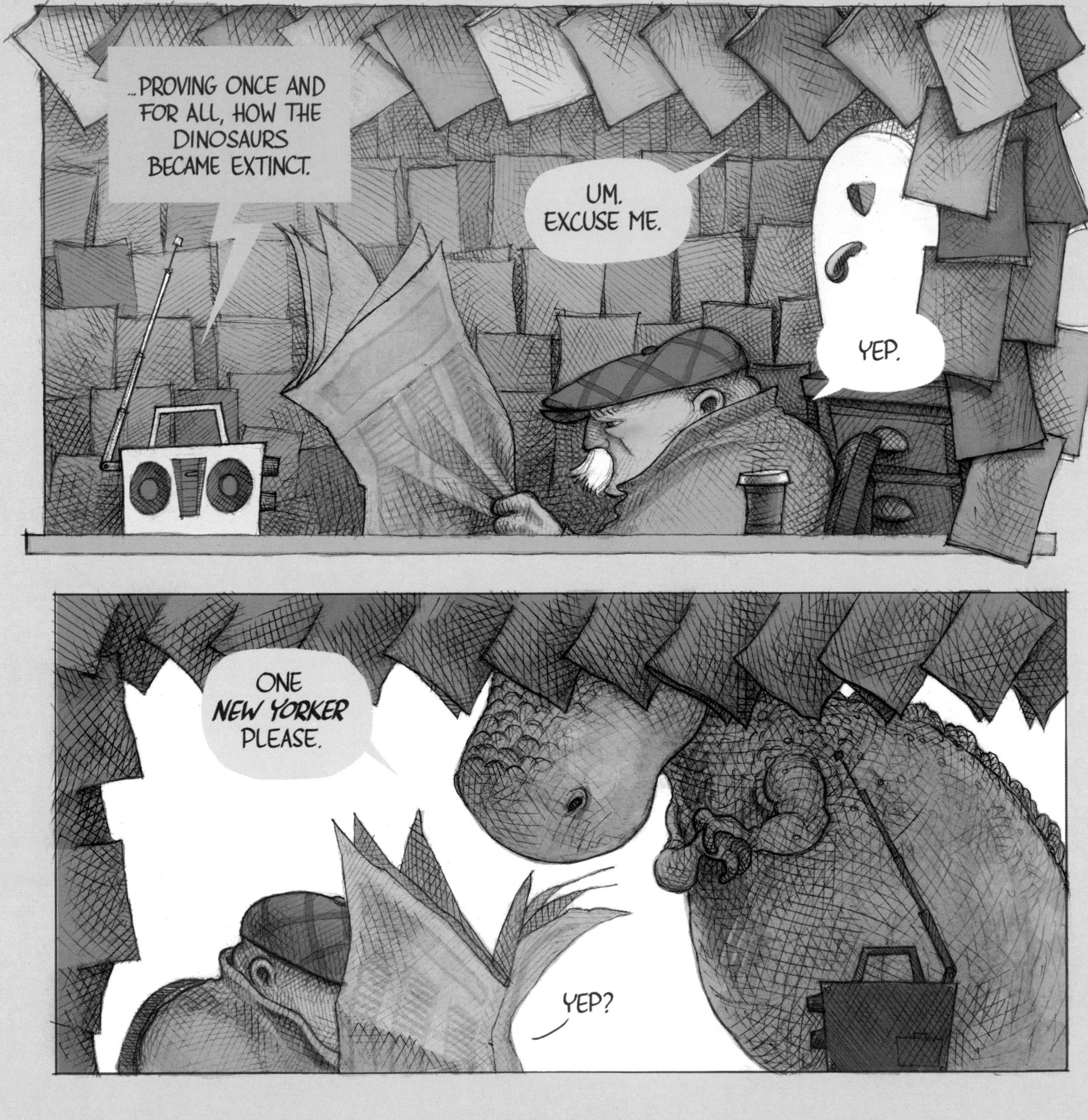

...PROVING ONCE AND FOR ALL, HOW THE DINOSAURS BECAME EXTINCT.
UM. EXCUSE ME.
YEP.
ONE *NEW YORKER* PLEASE.
YEP?

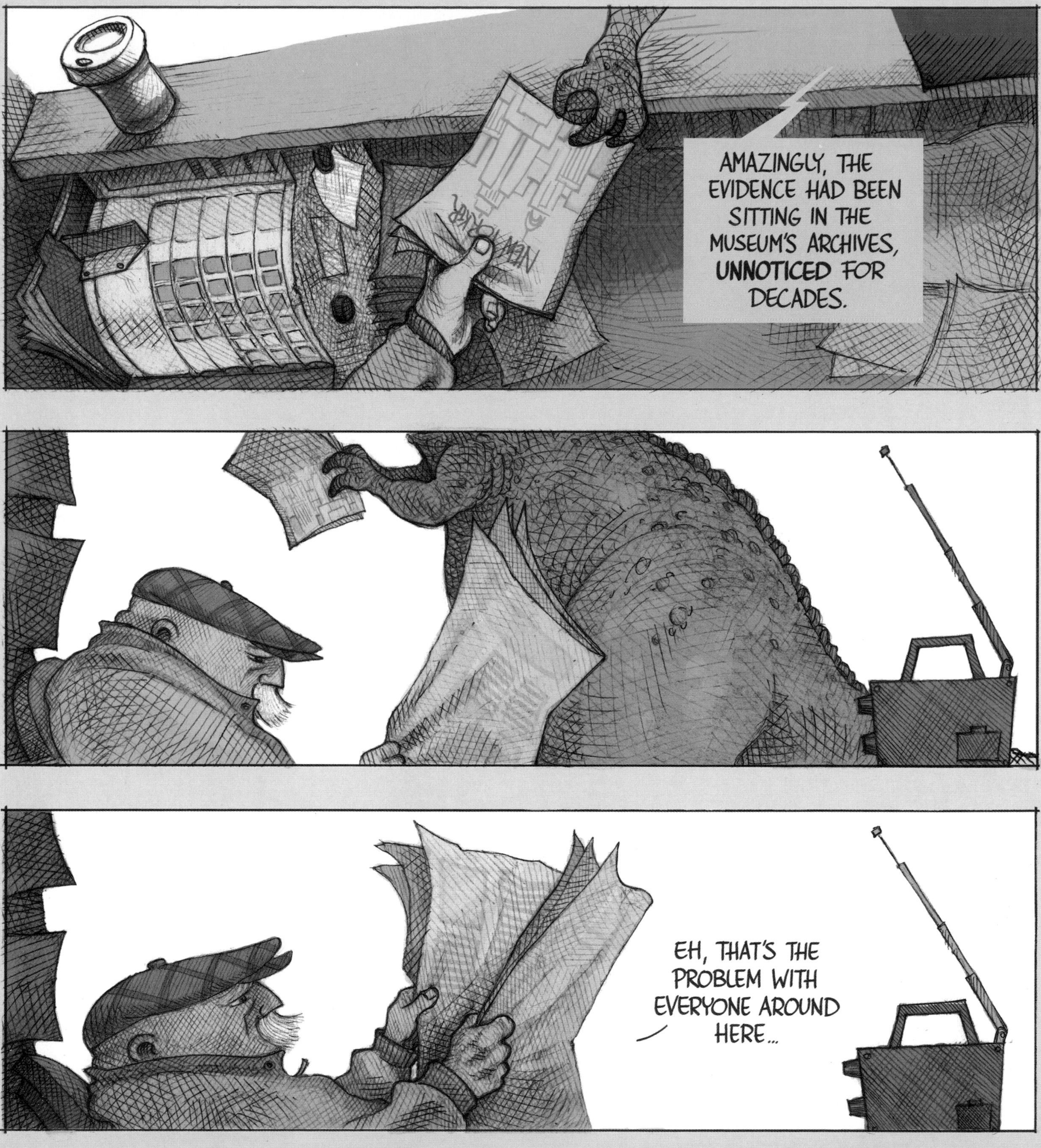
AMAZINGLY, THE EVIDENCE HAD BEEN SITTING IN THE MUSEUM'S ARCHIVES, **UNNOTICED** FOR DECADES.
EH, THAT'S THE PROBLEM WITH EVERYONE AROUND HERE...

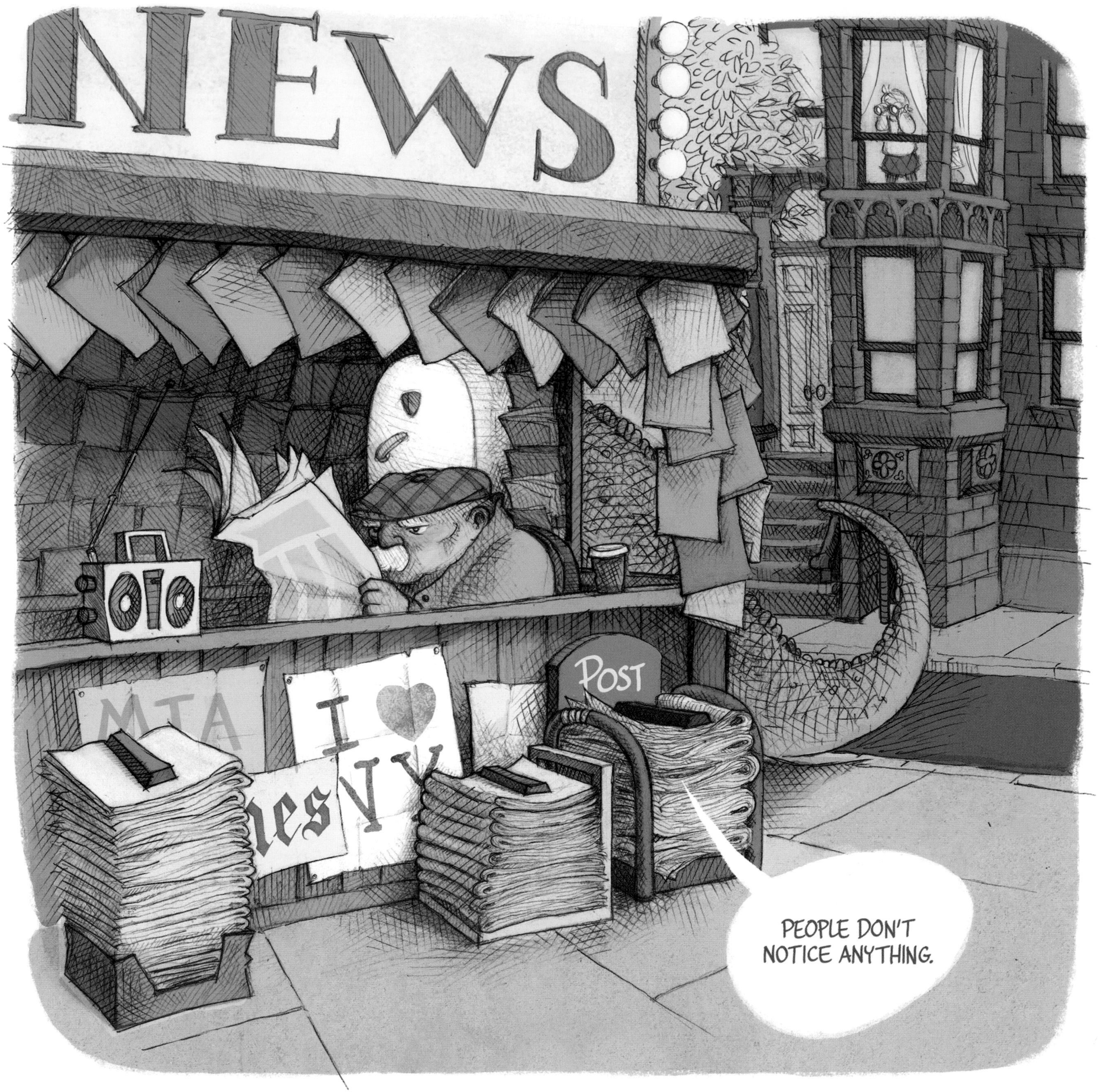
NEWS
MTA
I ♥ NY
nes
POST
PEOPLE DON'T NOTICE ANYTHING.

Bolivar was a dinosaur. He was the last dinosaur left anywhere.

Sure, he heard stories about the Loch Ness Monster, and sure, he'd watched the old sea creature movies, but Bolivar knew they were a bunch of baloney.

Real dinosaurs didn't like attention. They didn't want anyone to see them.

That's why Bolivar lived in the
busiest city in the world.

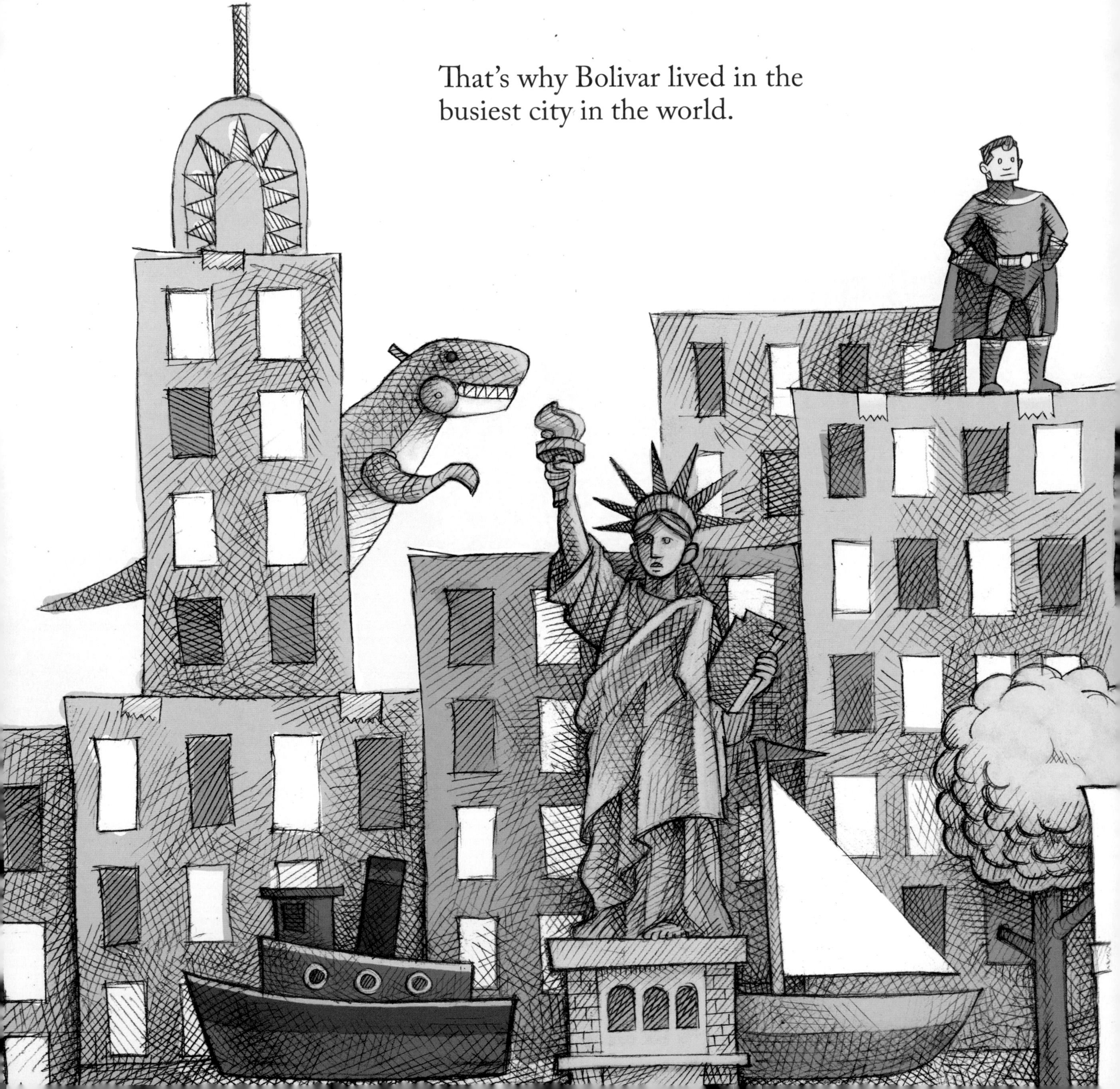

MOM!

HE'S **BACK!**

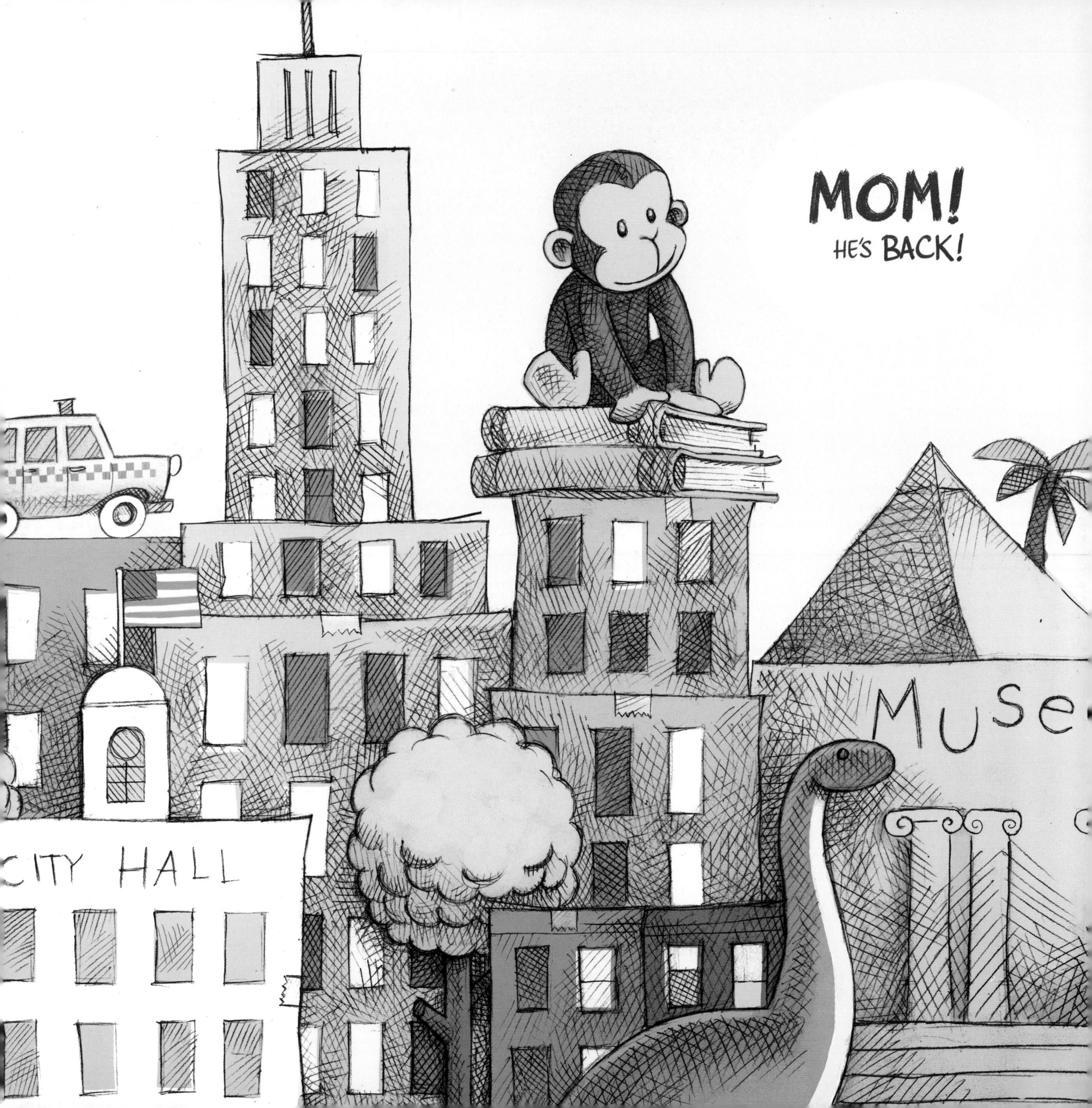
CITY HALL
Muse

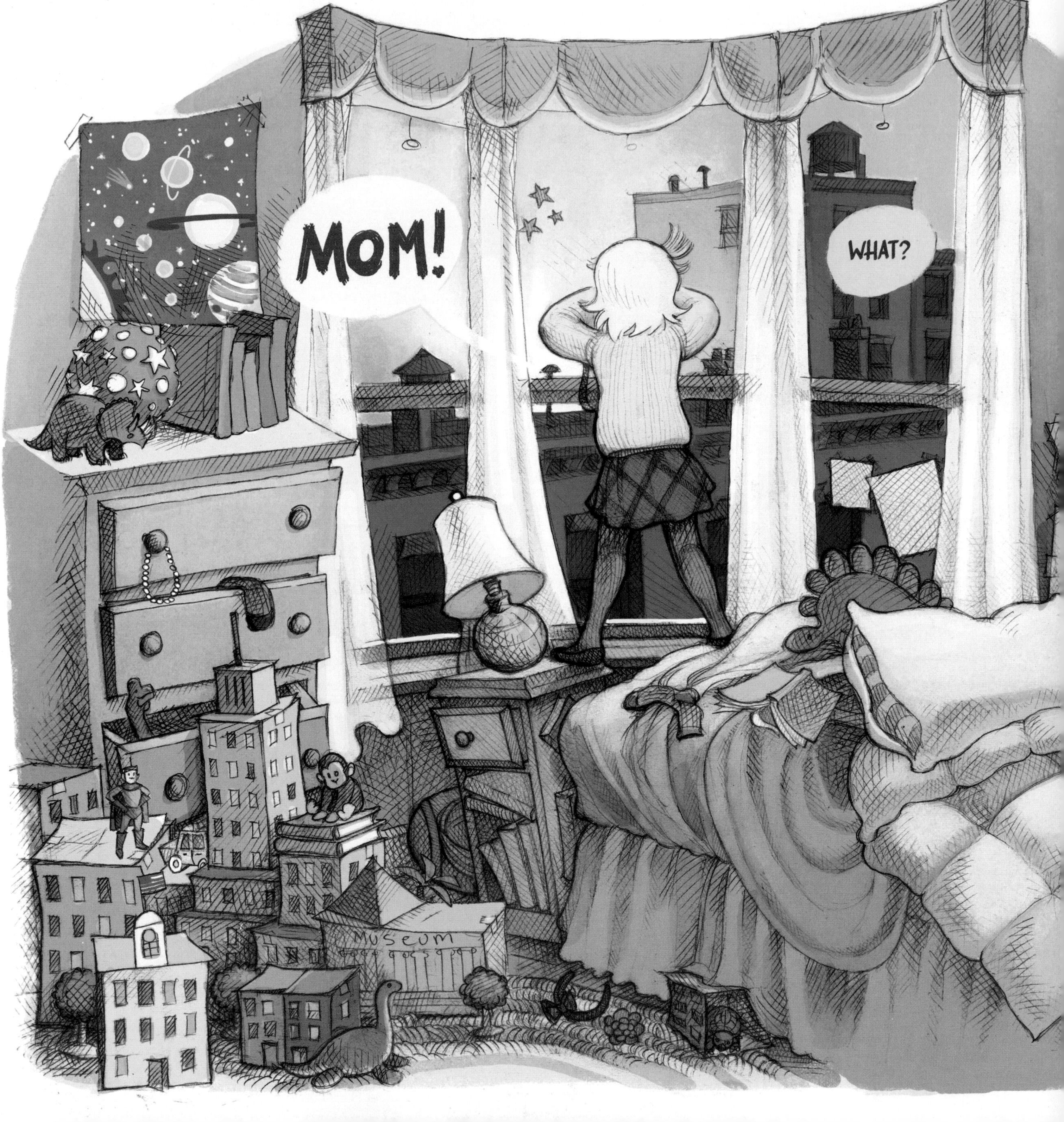
MOM!
WHAT?
MUSEUM

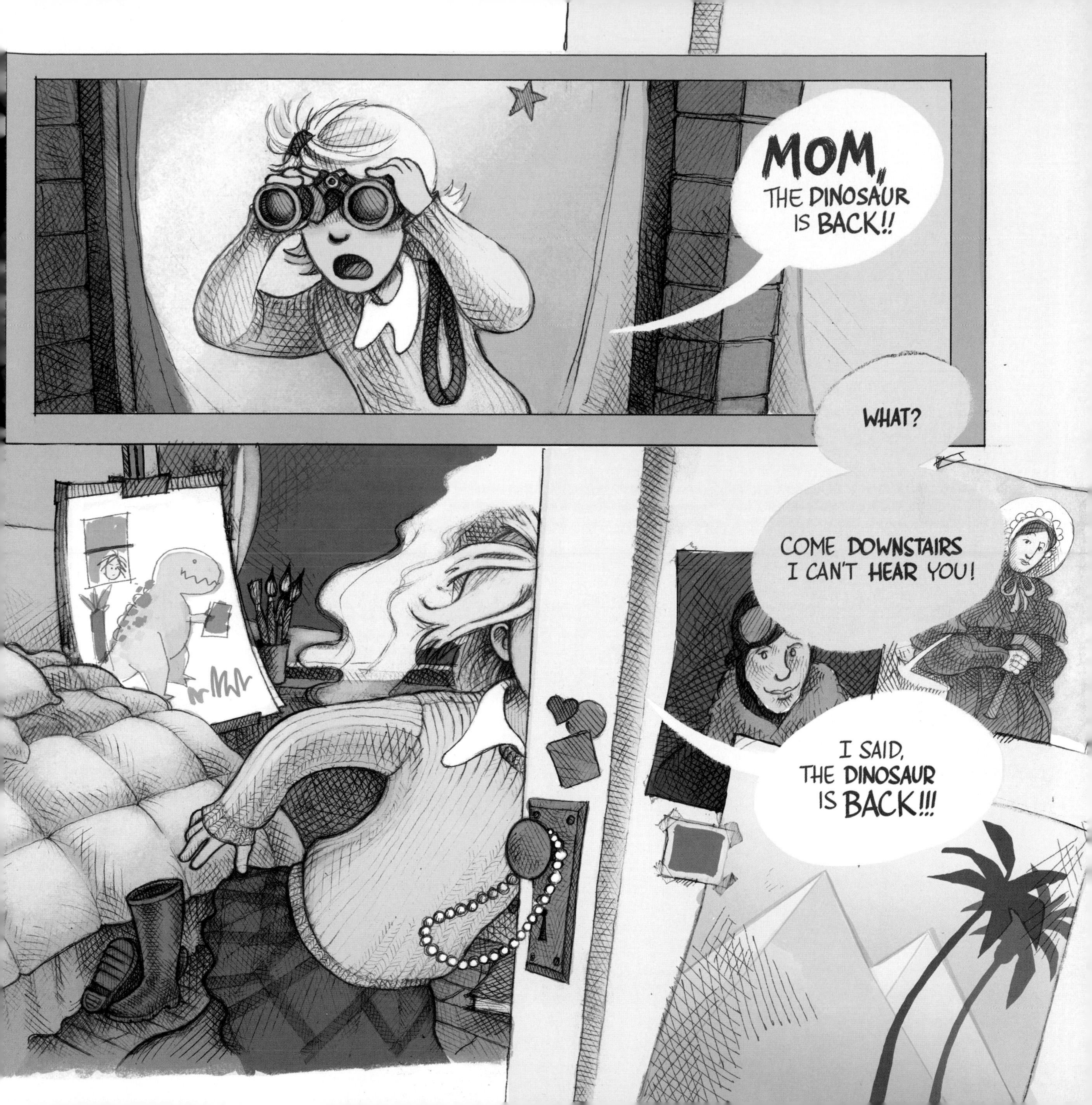
MOM, THE DINOSAUR IS BACK!!
WHAT?
COME DOWNSTAIRS I CAN'T HEAR YOU!
I SAID, THE DINOSAUR IS BACK!!!

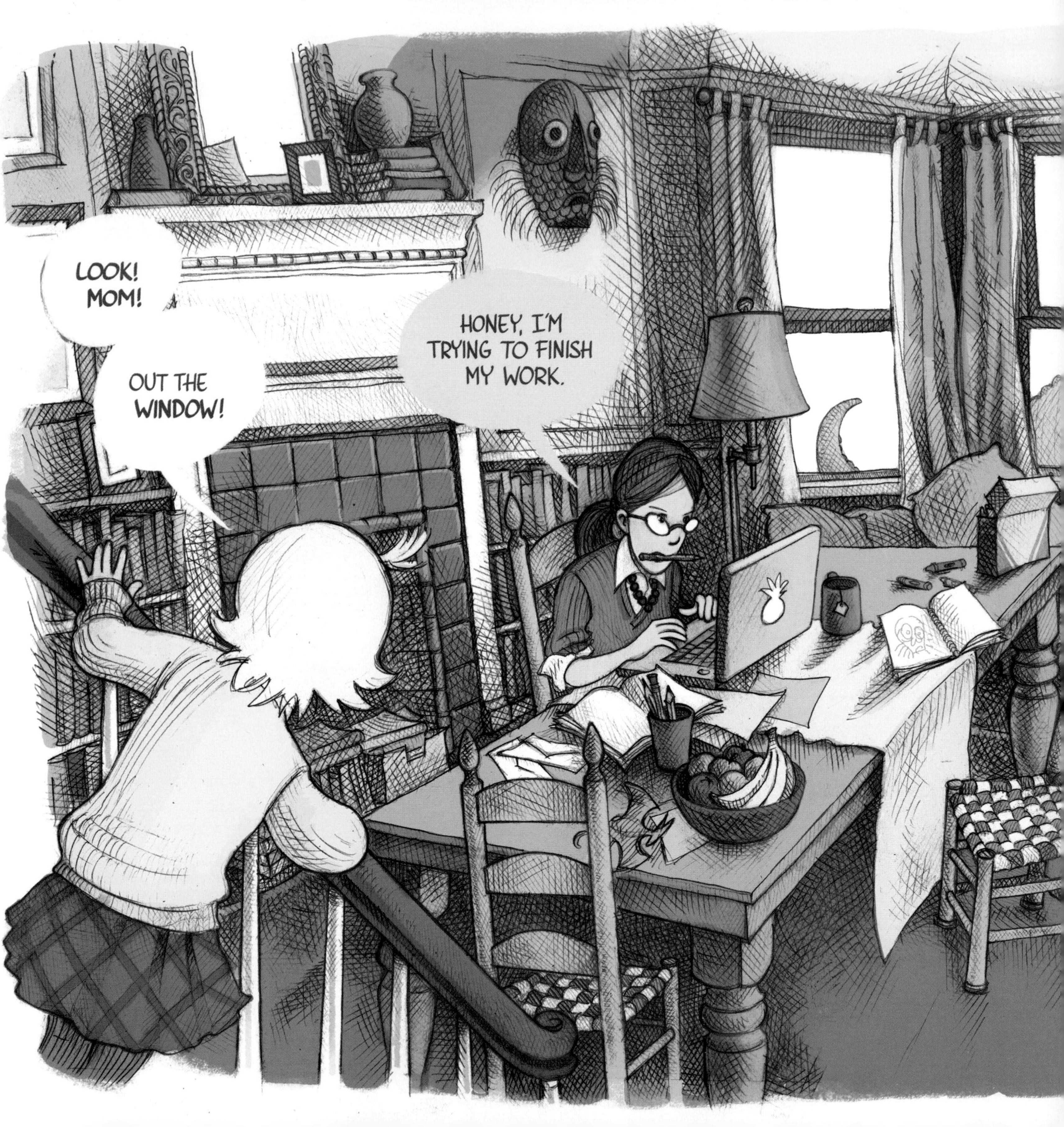
LOOK! MOM!
OUT THE WINDOW!
HONEY, I'M TRYING TO FINISH MY WORK.

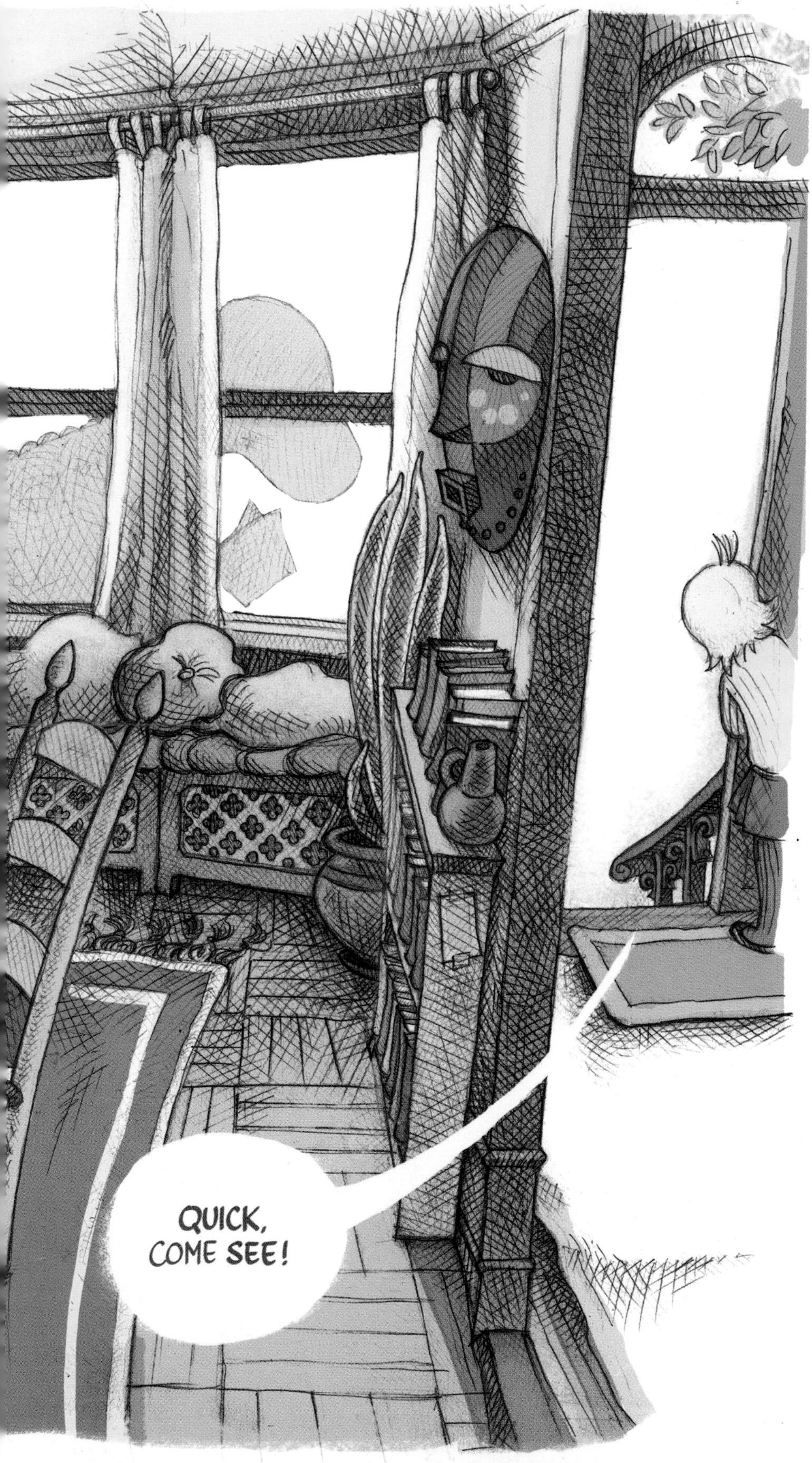
QUICK, COME SEE!

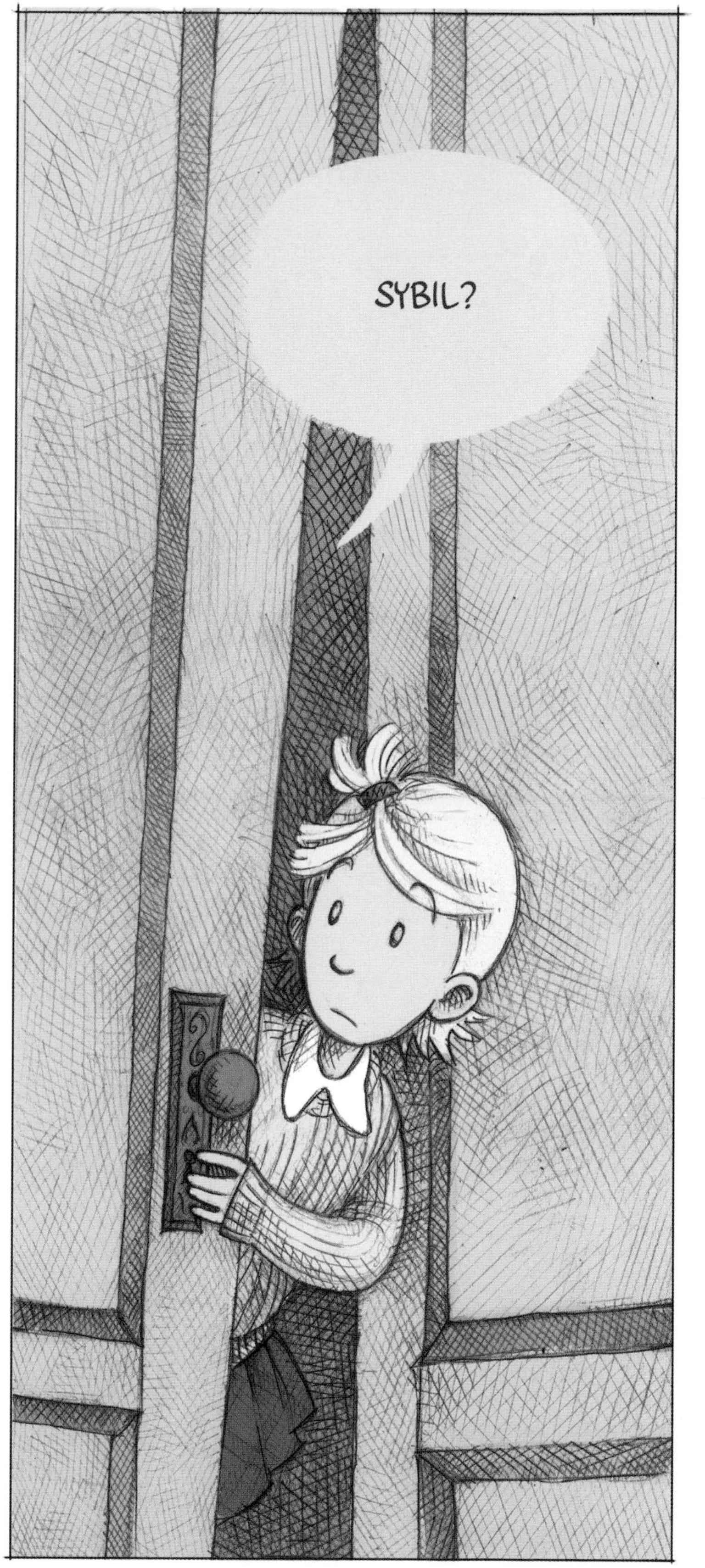
SYBIL?

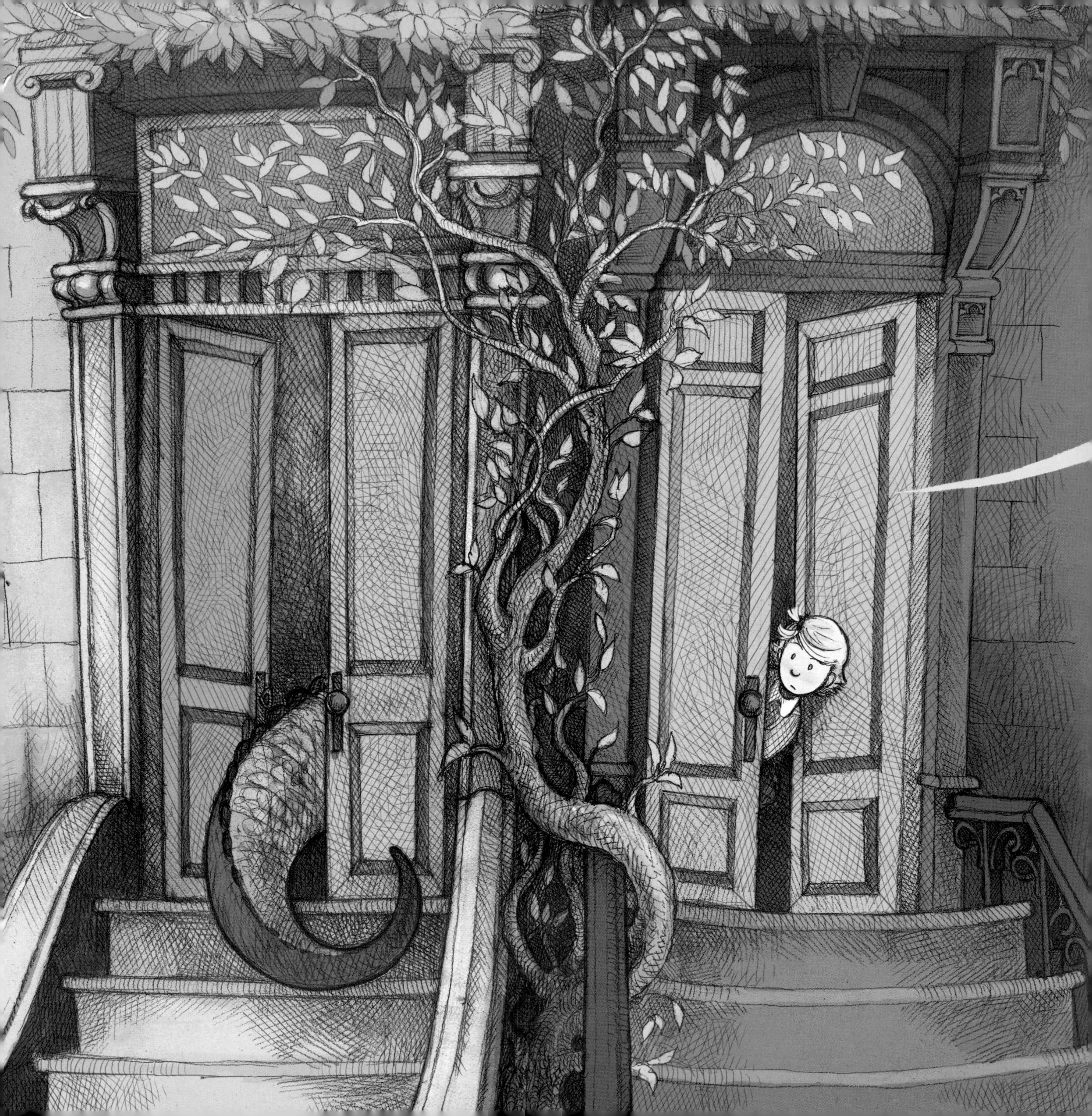

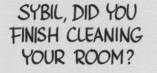

SYBIL, DID YOU FINISH CLEANING YOUR ROOM?

When Bolivar had first moved into his apartment, the landlord was much too busy to even notice he was a dinosaur. The landlord just gave Bolivar some forms to sign.

The forms said you couldn't have any dogs or cats in the apartment. Bolivar didn't have dogs or cats, so he was allowed to live there.

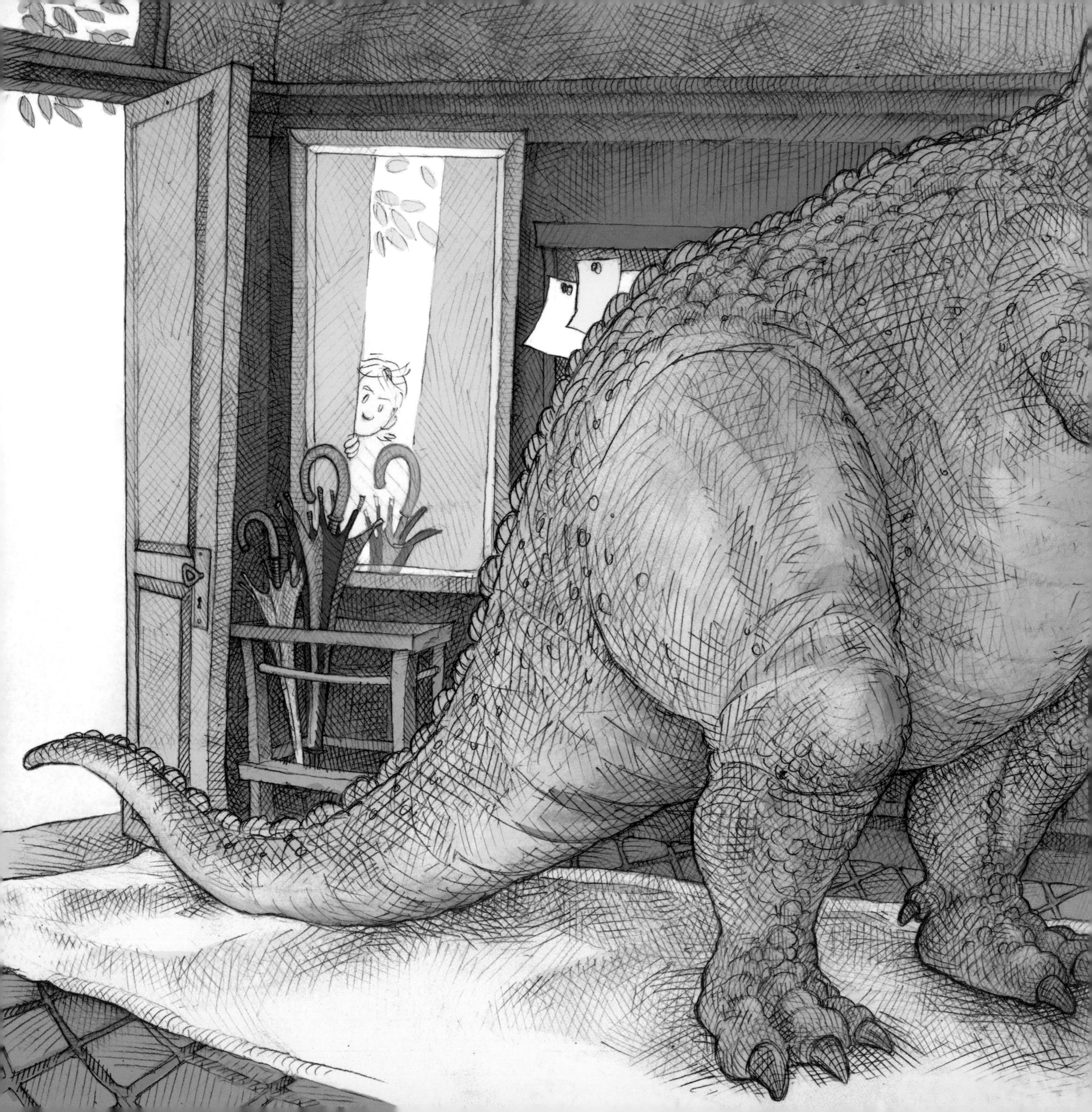

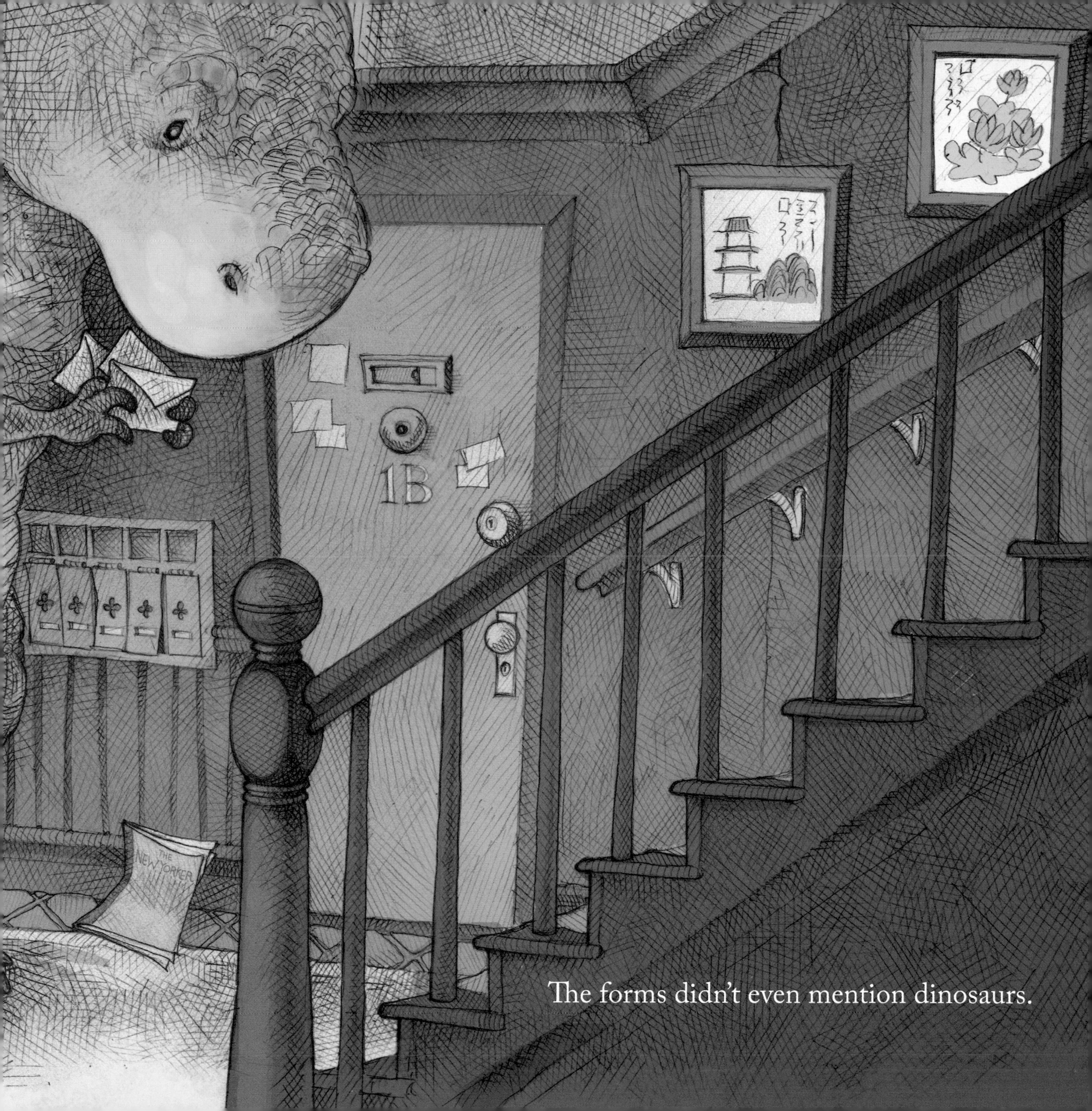
1B
THE NEW YORKER

The forms didn't even mention dinosaurs.

Like most dinosaurs,
Bolivar lived on corned beef
sandwiches and tonic water,
which he drank with lime.

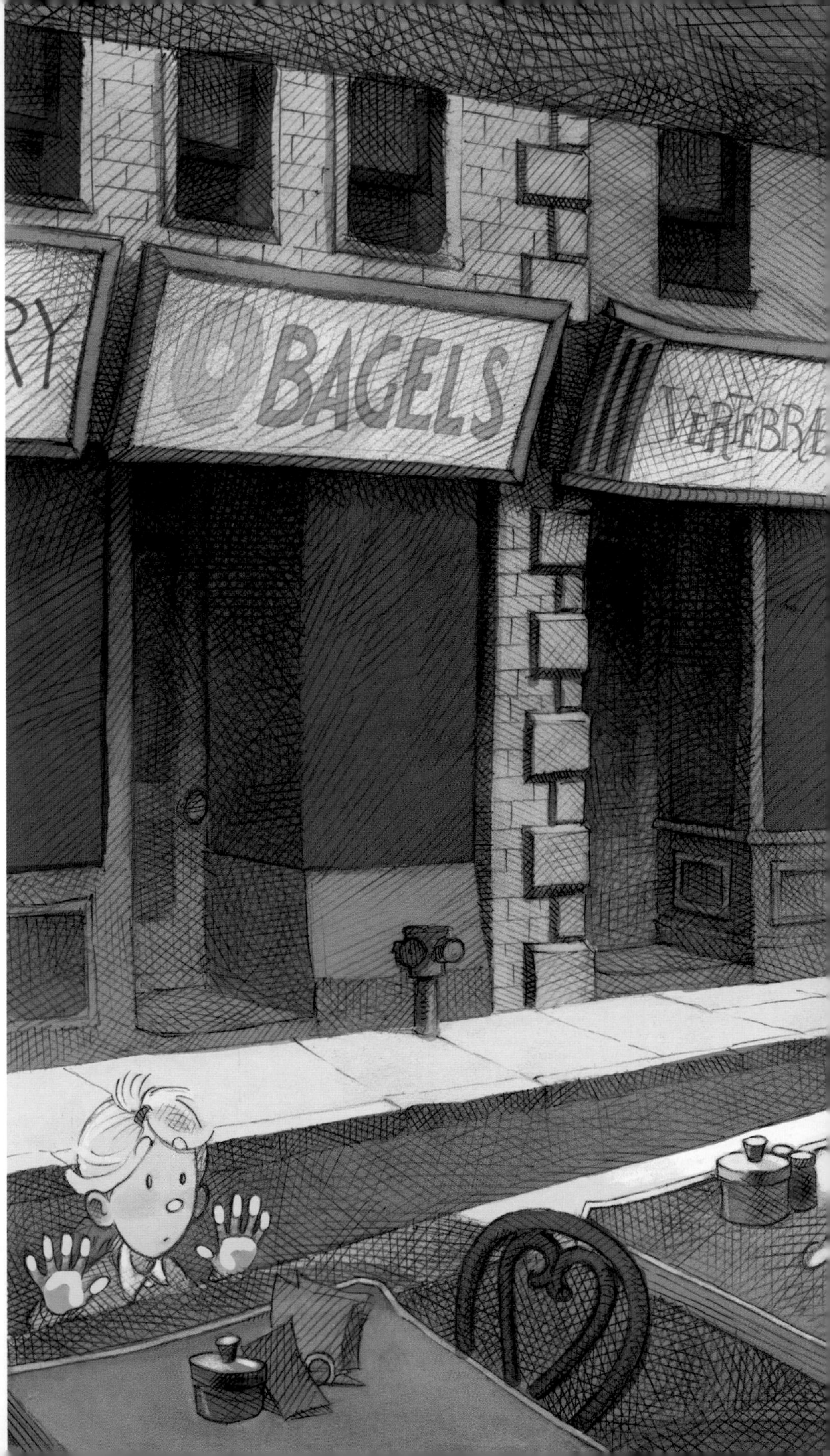
RY
BAGELS
VERTEBRA

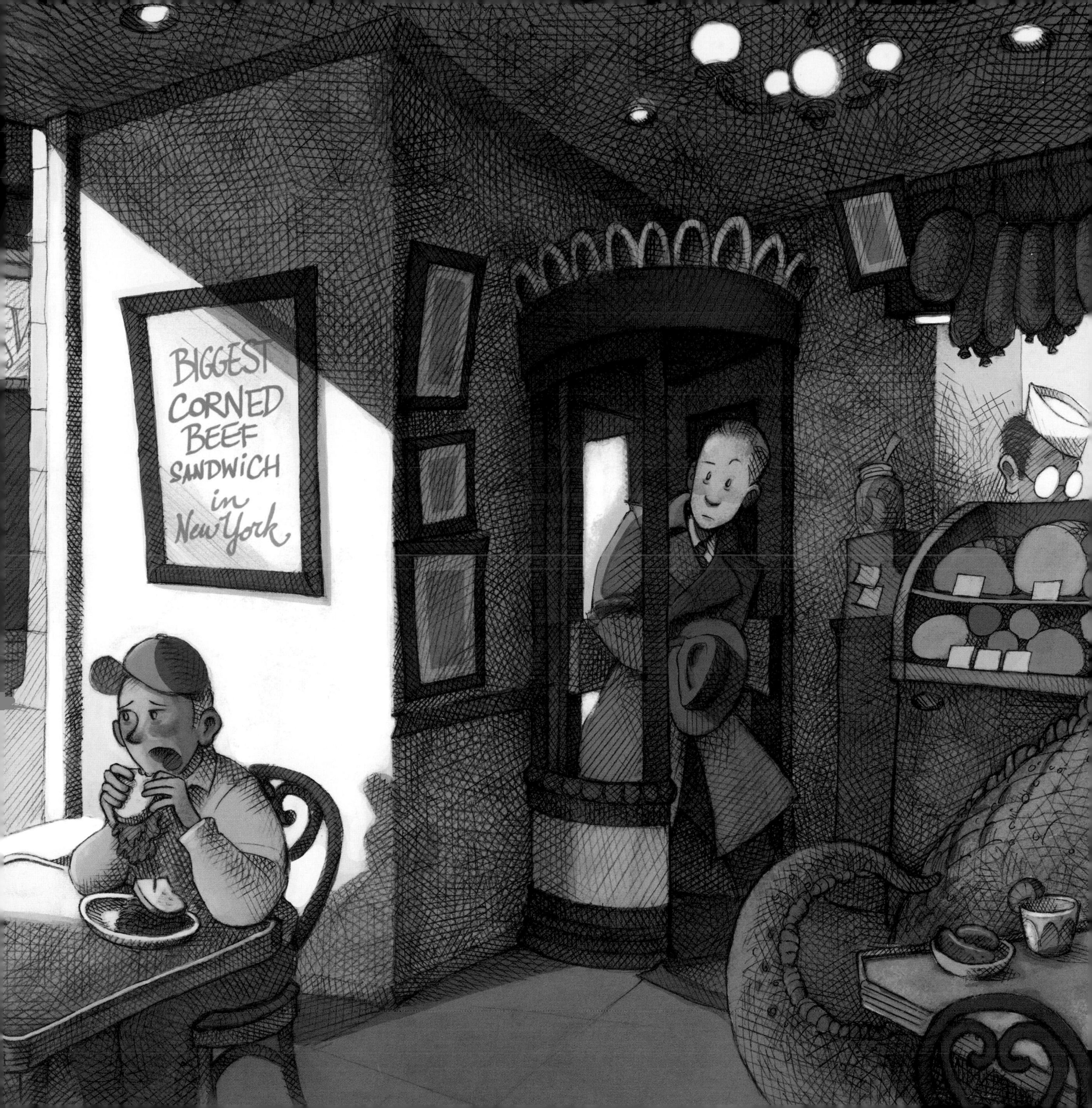
BIGGEST
CORNED
BEEF
SANDWICH
in
New York

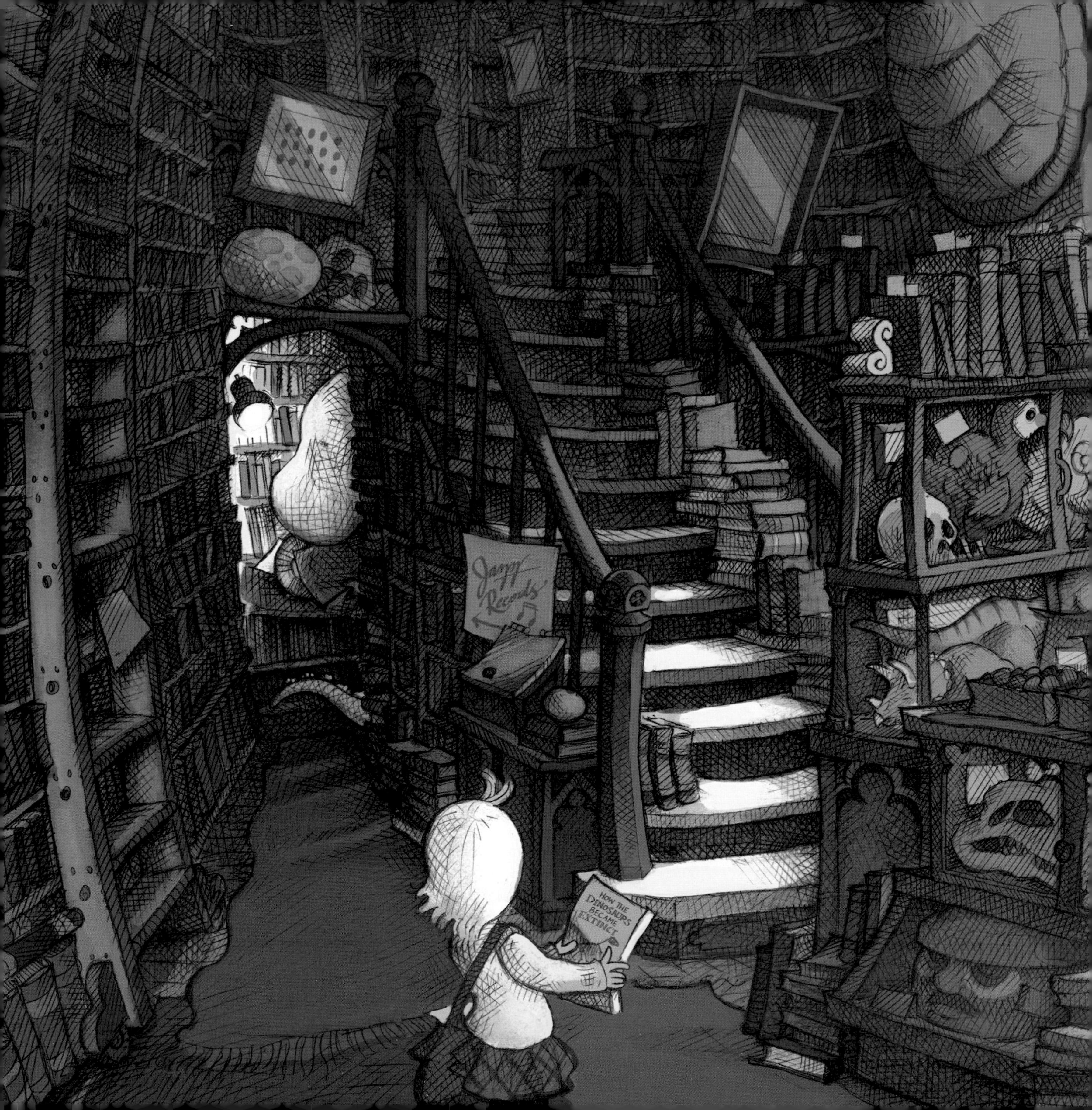
Jazz Records
HOW THE DINOSAURS BECAME EXTINCT

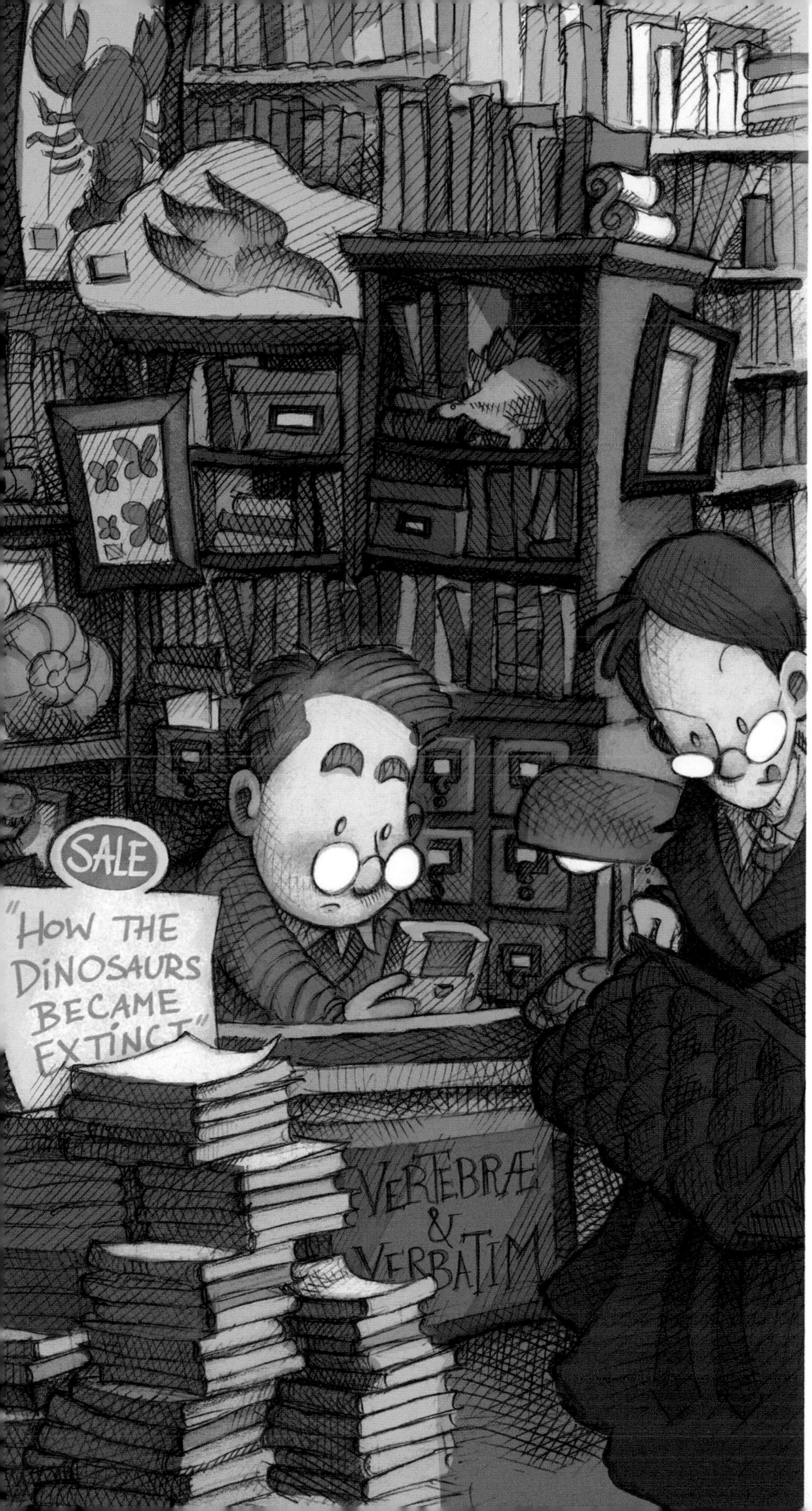
SALE
"HOW THE DINOSAURS BECAME EXTINCT"
VERTEBRÆ & VERBATIM

He liked collecting used books and rummaging through old records.

So long as Bolivar paid his rent (he did) and stayed quiet after 10 o'clock at night (he did that too), no one ever bothered him.

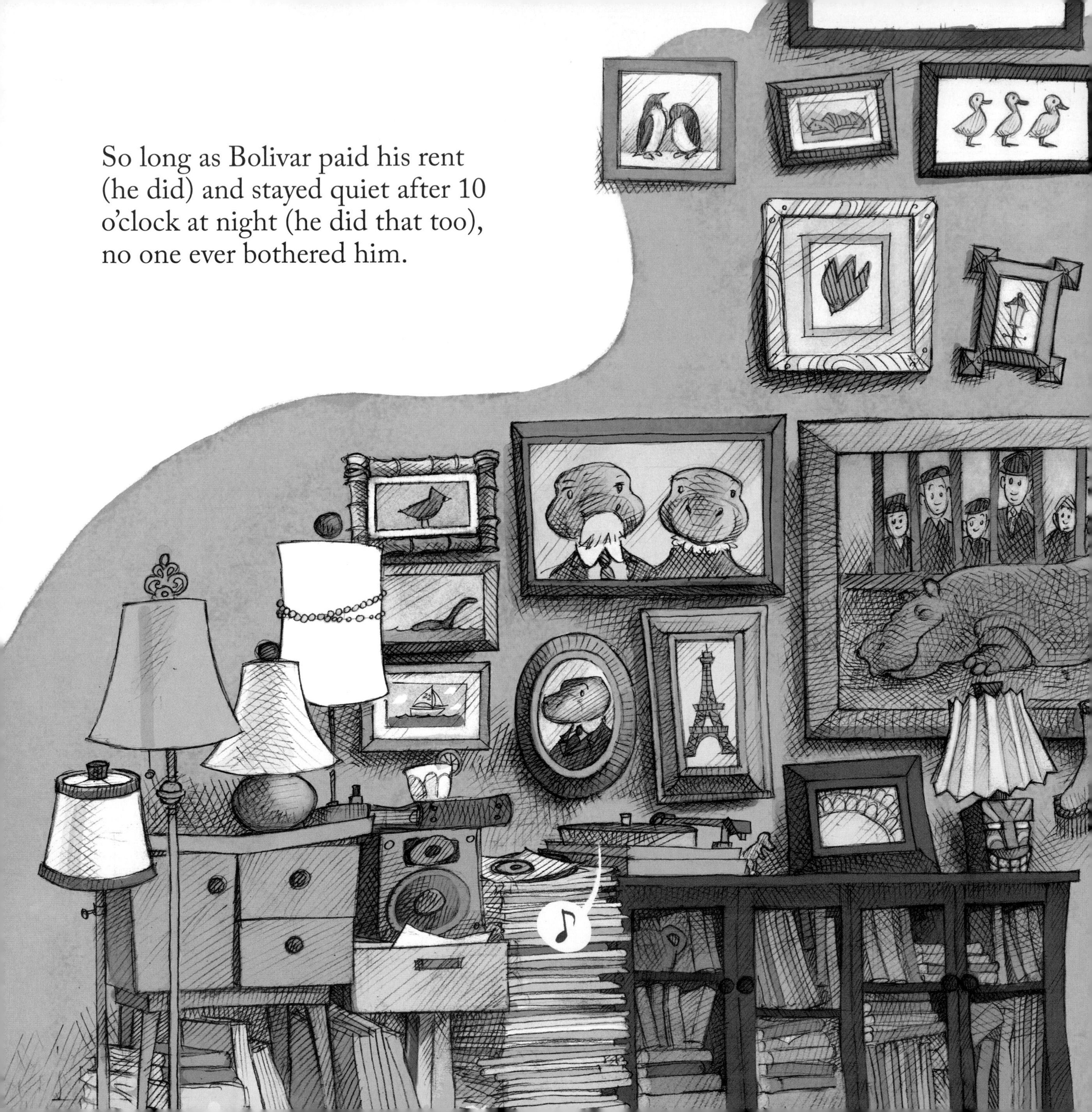

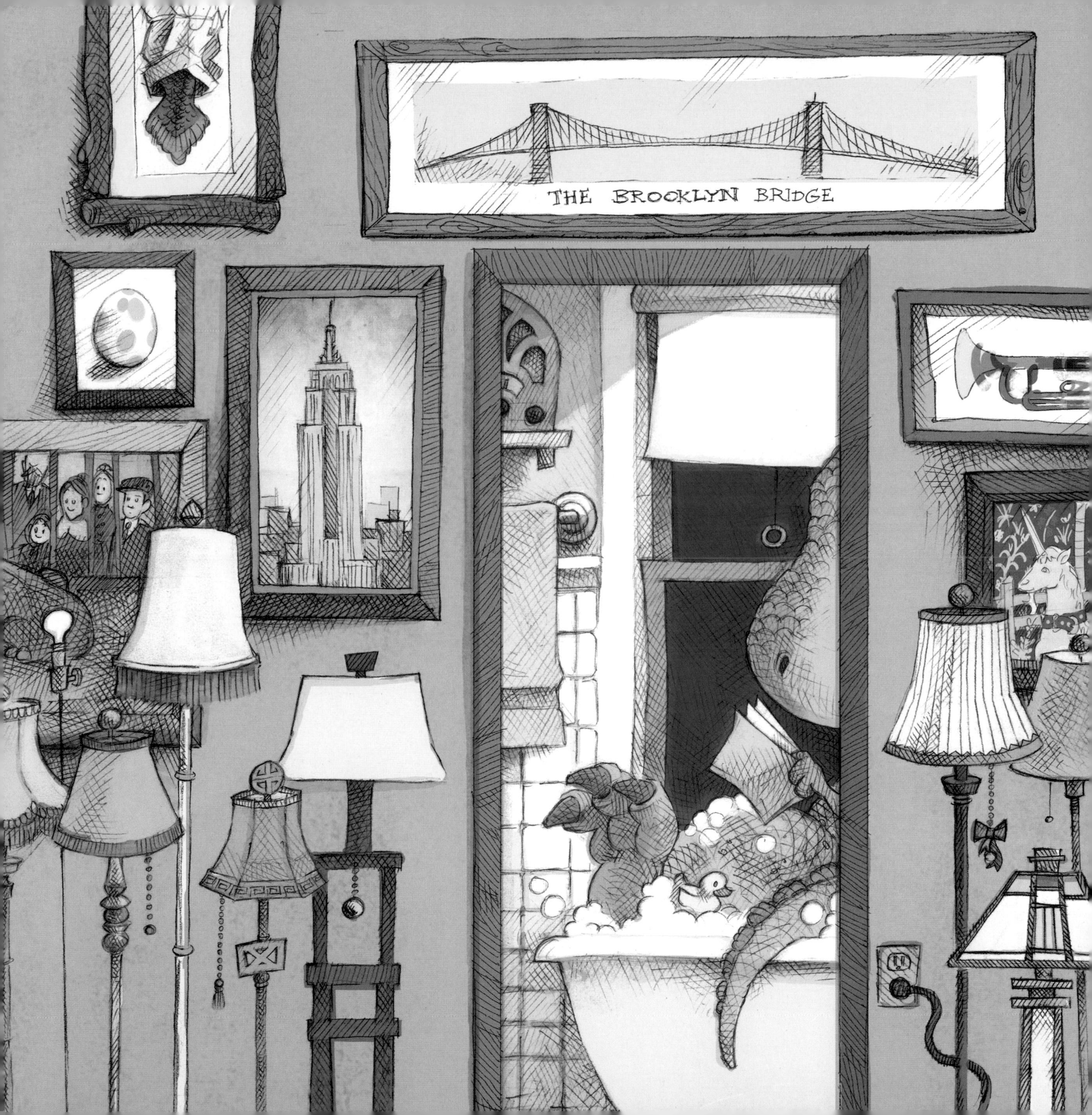
THE BROOKLYN BRIDGE

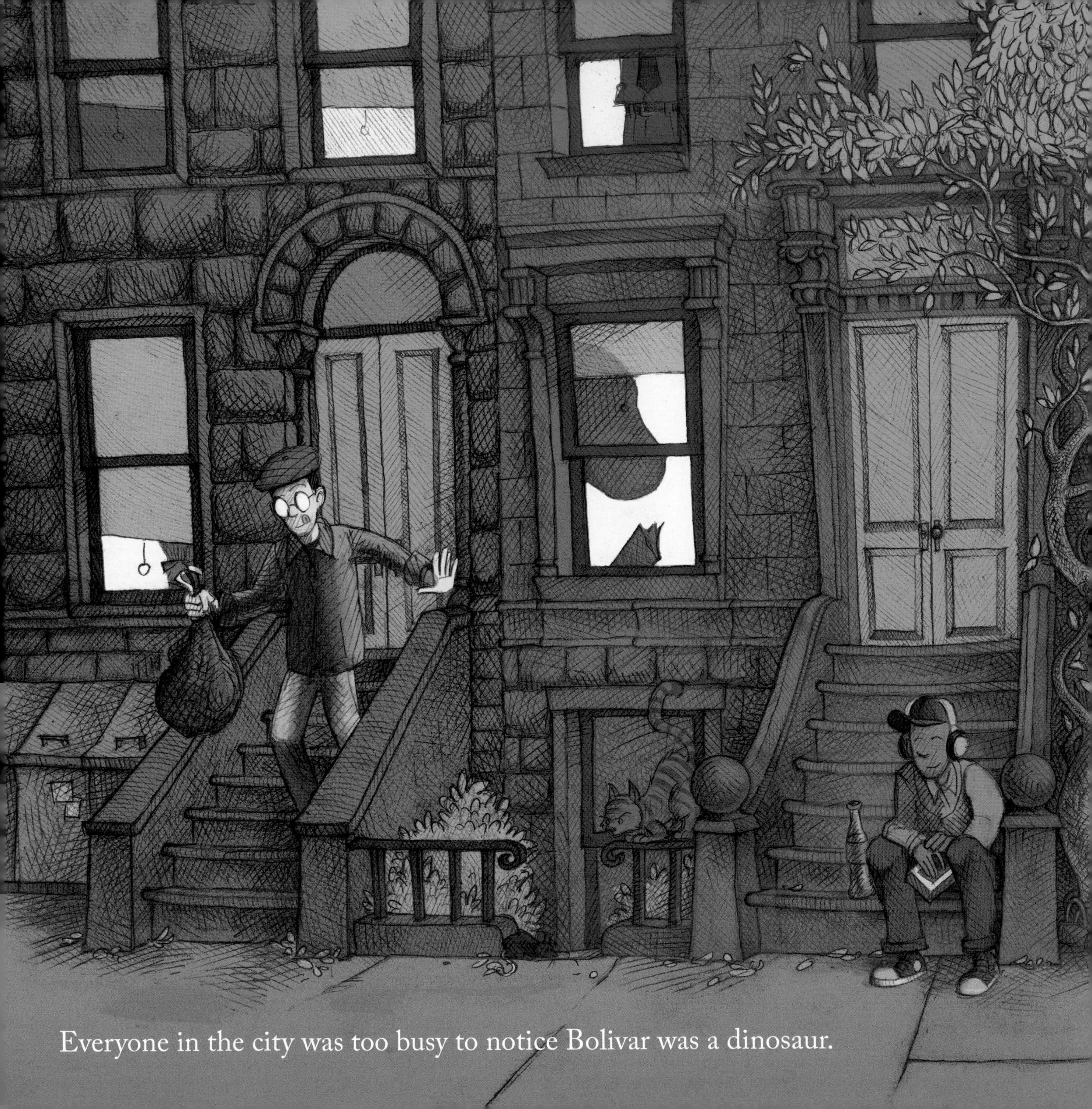

Everyone in the city was too busy to notice Bolivar was a dinosaur.

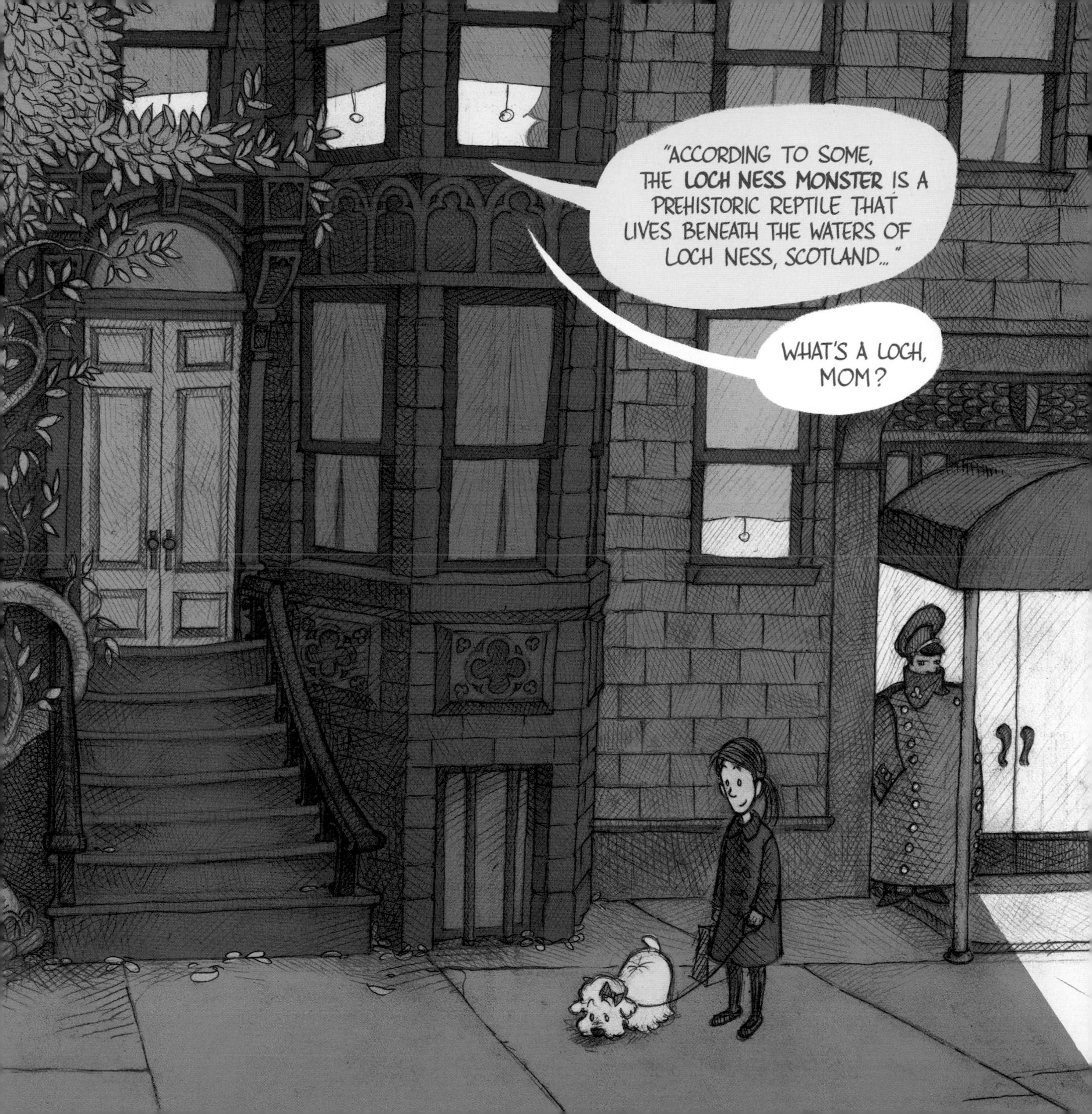
"ACCORDING TO SOME, THE **LOCH NESS MONSTER** IS A PREHISTORIC REPTILE THAT LIVES BENEATH THE WATERS OF LOCH NESS, SCOTLAND..."
WHAT'S A LOCH, MOM?

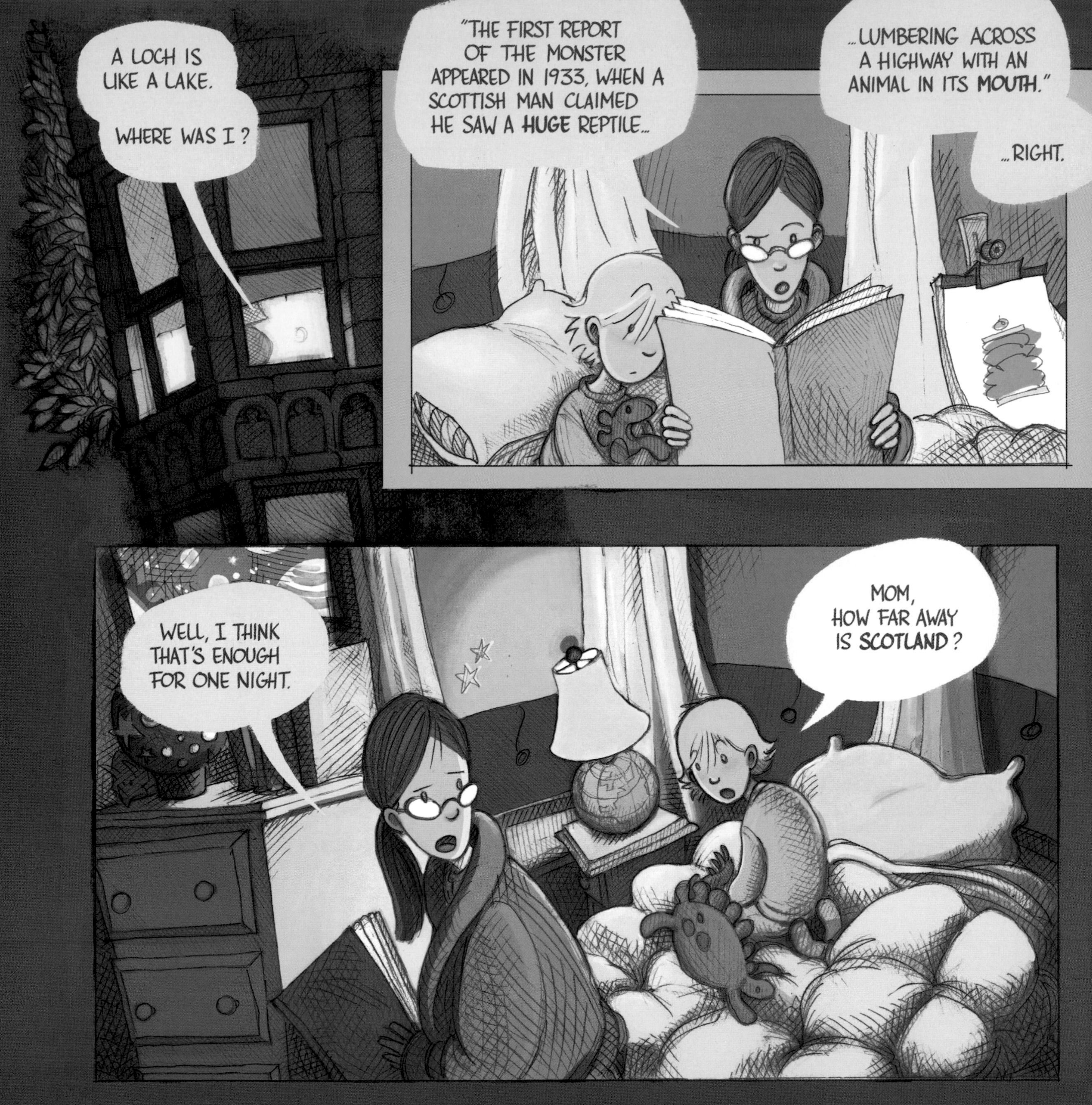
A LOCH IS LIKE A LAKE.
WHERE WAS I?
"THE FIRST REPORT OF THE MONSTER APPEARED IN 1933, WHEN A SCOTTISH MAN CLAIMED HE SAW A **HUGE** REPTILE...
...LUMBERING ACROSS A HIGHWAY WITH AN ANIMAL IN ITS **MOUTH**."
...RIGHT.
WELL, I THINK THAT'S ENOUGH FOR ONE NIGHT.
MOM, HOW FAR AWAY IS **SCOTLAND**?

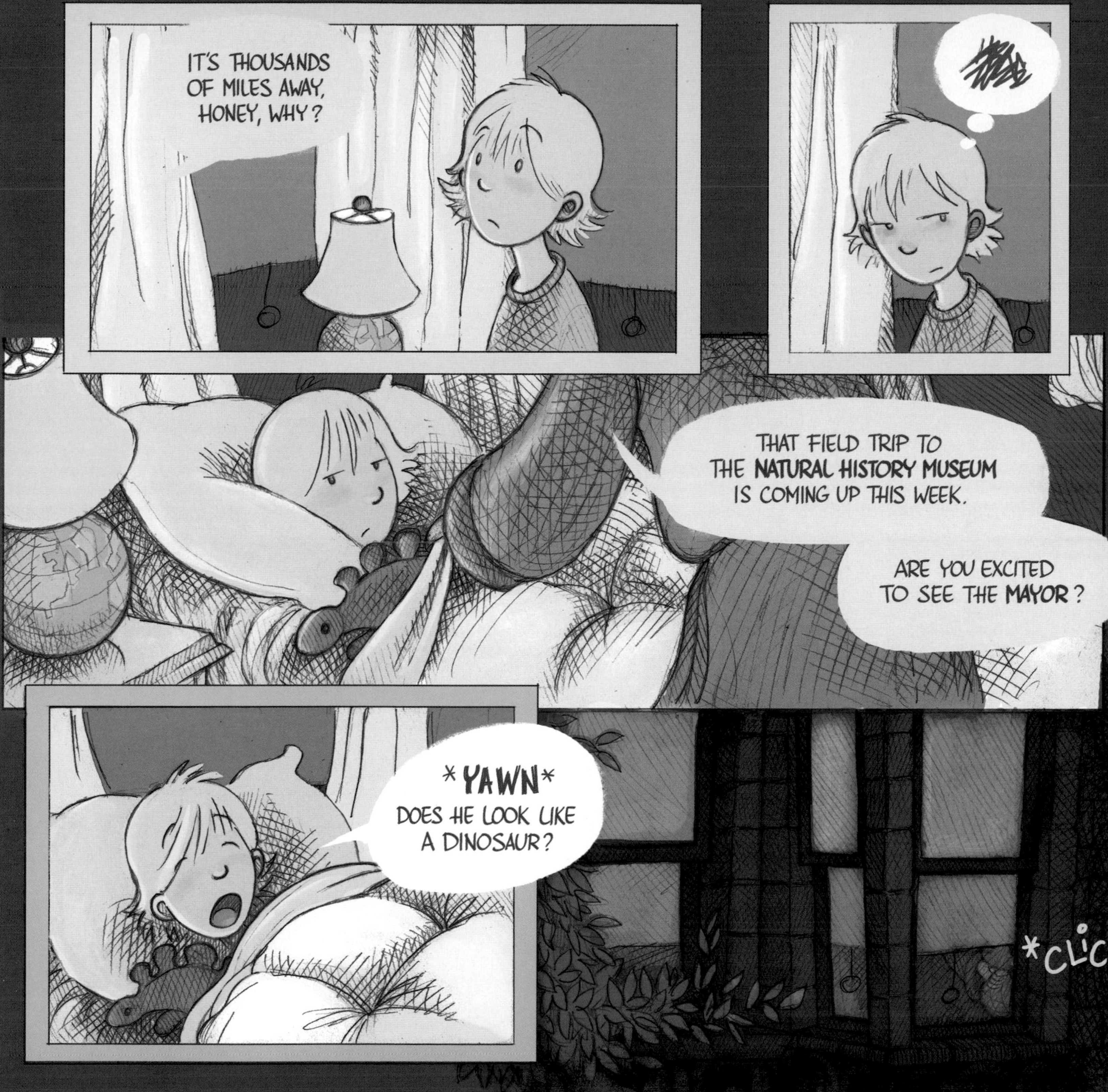
IT'S THOUSANDS OF MILES AWAY, HONEY, WHY?
THAT FIELD TRIP TO THE NATURAL HISTORY MUSEUM IS COMING UP THIS WEEK.
ARE YOU EXCITED TO SEE THE MAYOR?
YAWN DOES HE LOOK LIKE A DINOSAUR?
CLICK!

And so long as everyone was too busy to notice Bolivar, everyone in New York City thought dinosaurs were extinct.

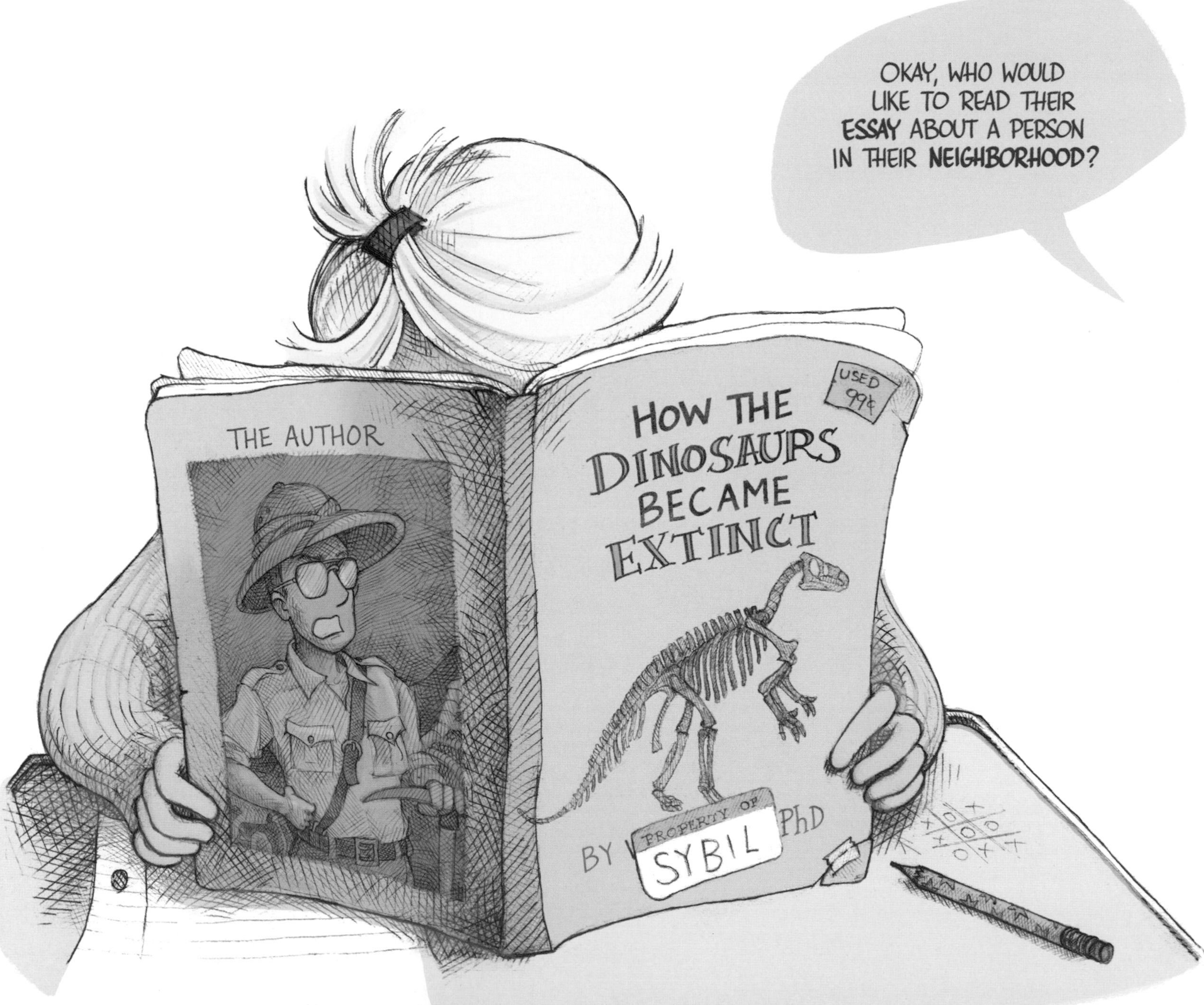
OKAY, WHO WOULD LIKE TO READ THEIR **ESSAY** ABOUT A PERSON IN THEIR **NEIGHBORHOOD**?
THE AUTHOR
HOW THE DINOSAURS BECAME EXTINCT
USED 99¢
BY
PhD
PROPERTY OF
SYBIL

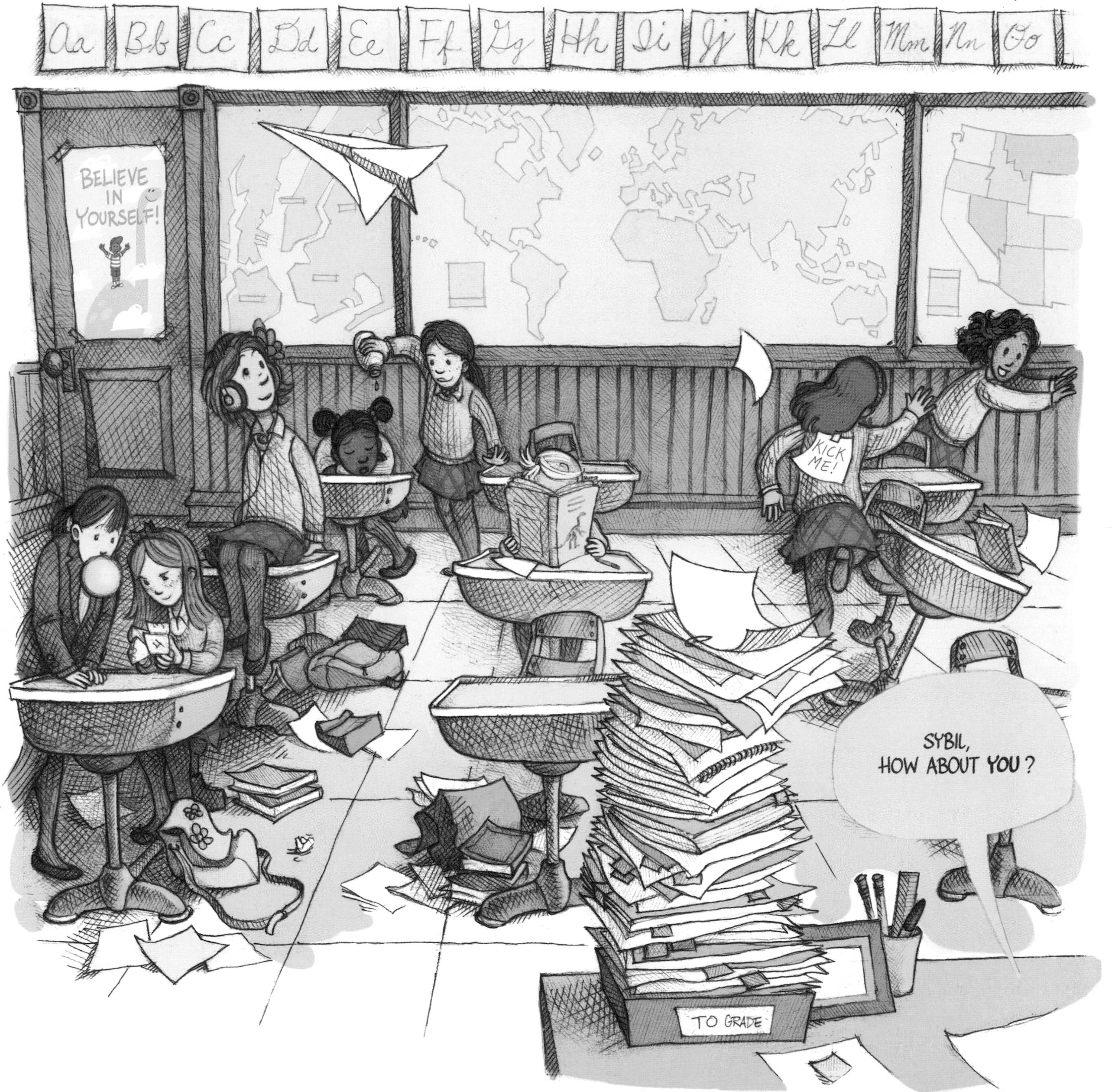
Aa Bb Cc Dd Ee Ff Gg Hh Ii Jj Kk Ll Mm Nn Oo
BELIEVE IN YOURSELF!
KICK ME!
SYBIL, HOW ABOUT YOU?
TO GRADE

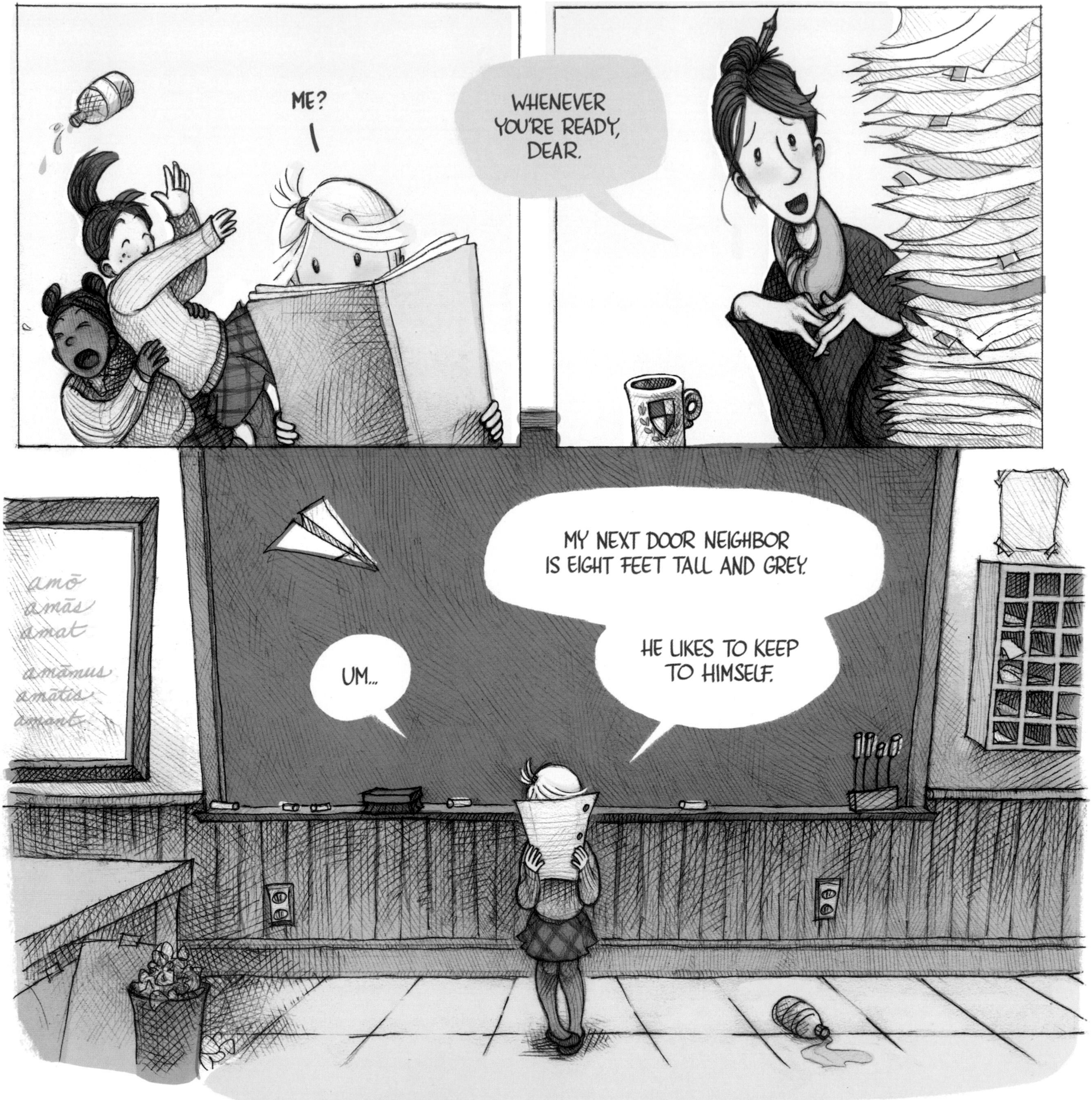
ME?
WHENEVER YOU'RE READY, DEAR.
amō
amās
amat
amāmus
amātis
amant
UM...
MY NEXT DOOR NEIGHBOR IS EIGHT FEET TALL AND GREY.
HE LIKES TO KEEP TO HIMSELF.

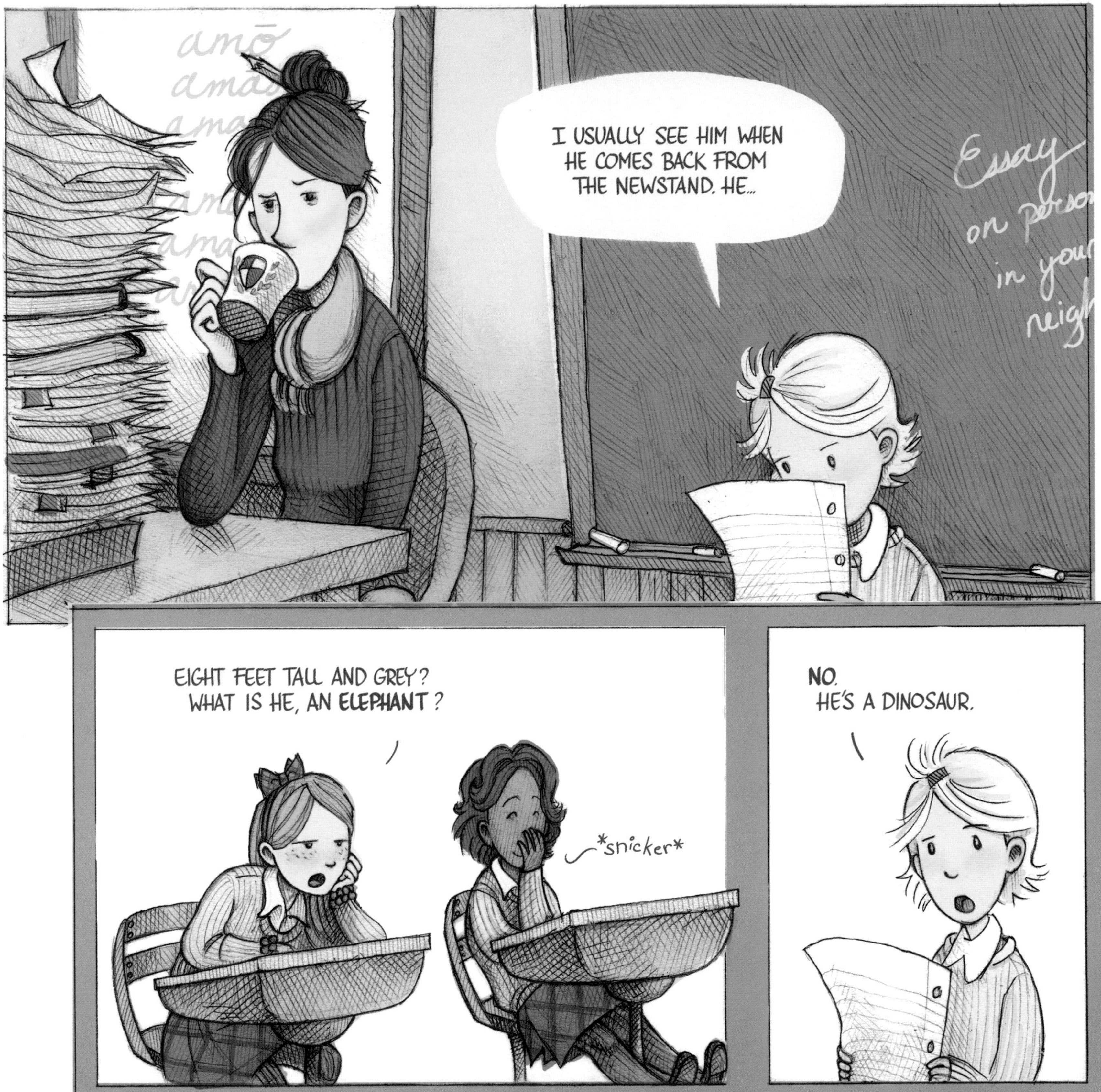
I USUALLY SEE HIM WHEN HE COMES BACK FROM THE NEWSTAND. HE...
EIGHT FEET TALL AND GREY? WHAT IS HE, AN **ELEPHANT**?
snicker
NO. HE'S A DINOSAUR.

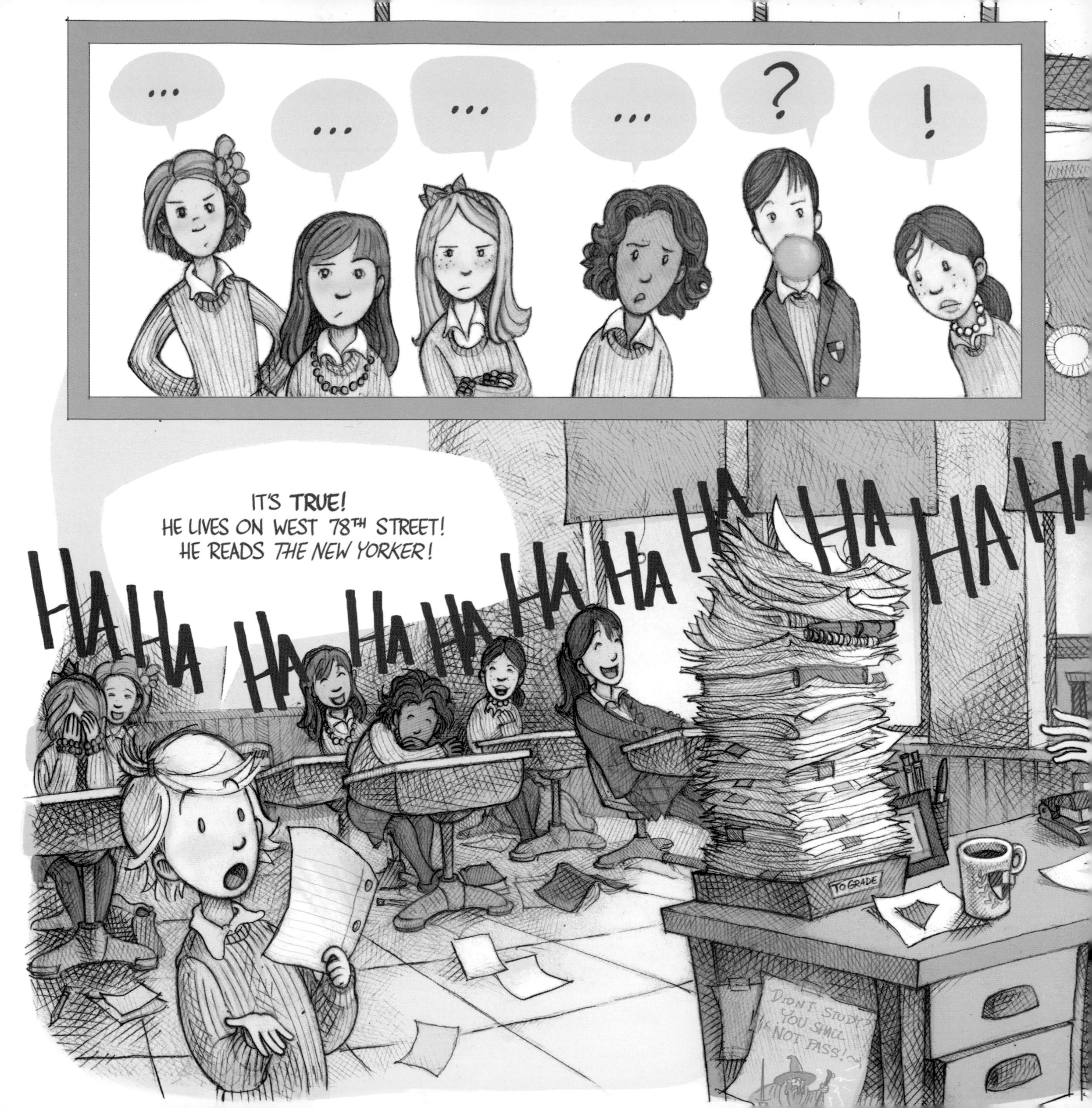
...
...
...
...
?
!
IT'S TRUE!
HE LIVES ON WEST 78TH STREET!
HE READS THE NEW YORKER!
HA HA HA HA HA HA HA HA HA HA HA HA HA HA
TO GRADE
DIDN'T STUDY? YOU SHALL NOT PASS!

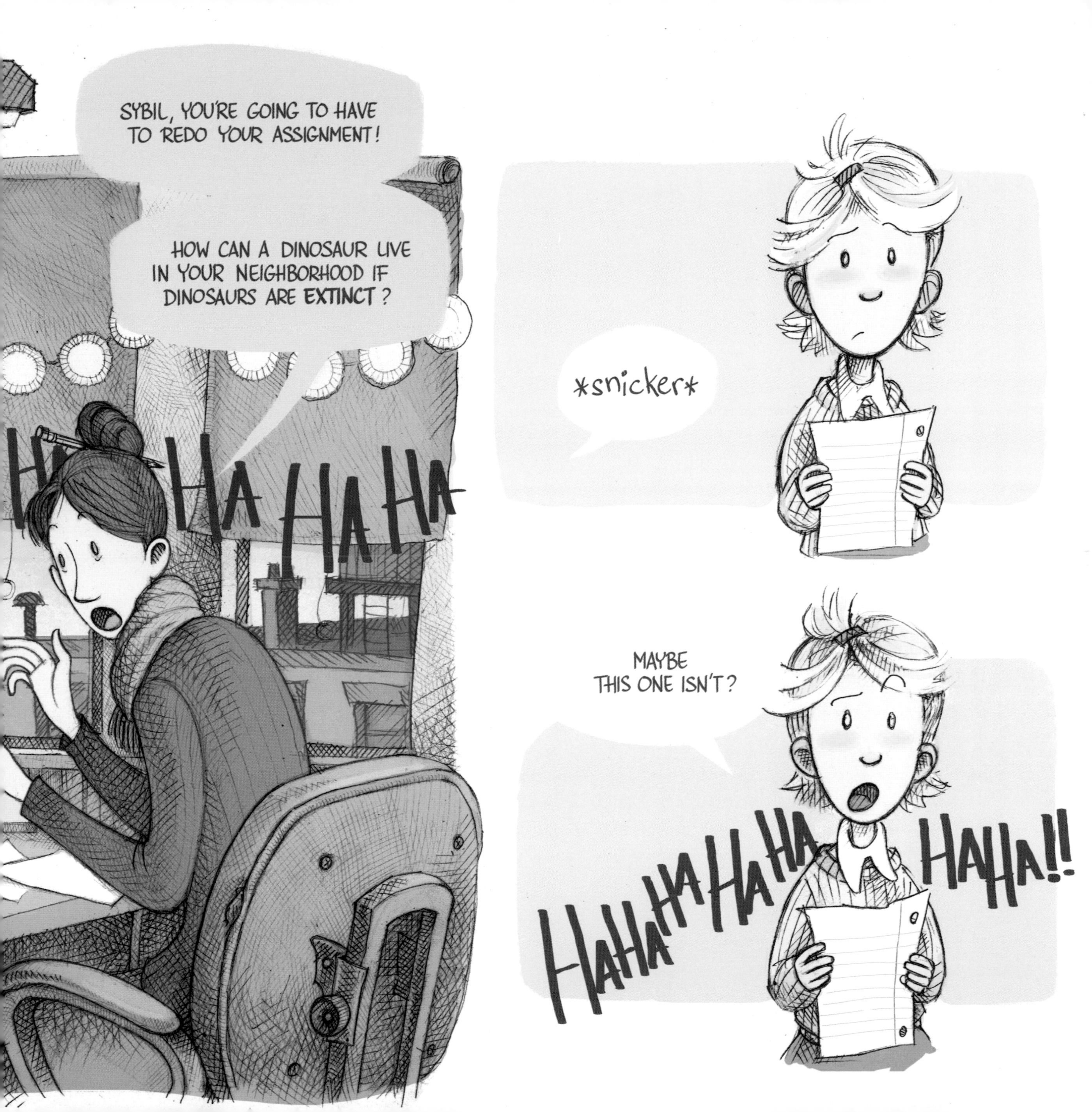
SYBIL, YOU'RE GOING TO HAVE TO REDO YOUR ASSIGNMENT!
HOW CAN A DINOSAUR LIVE IN YOUR NEIGHBORHOOD IF DINOSAURS ARE **EXTINCT**?
HA HA HA HA HA
snicker
MAYBE THIS ONE ISN'T?
HAHAHAHAHAHA HAHAHA!!

CHAPTER 2

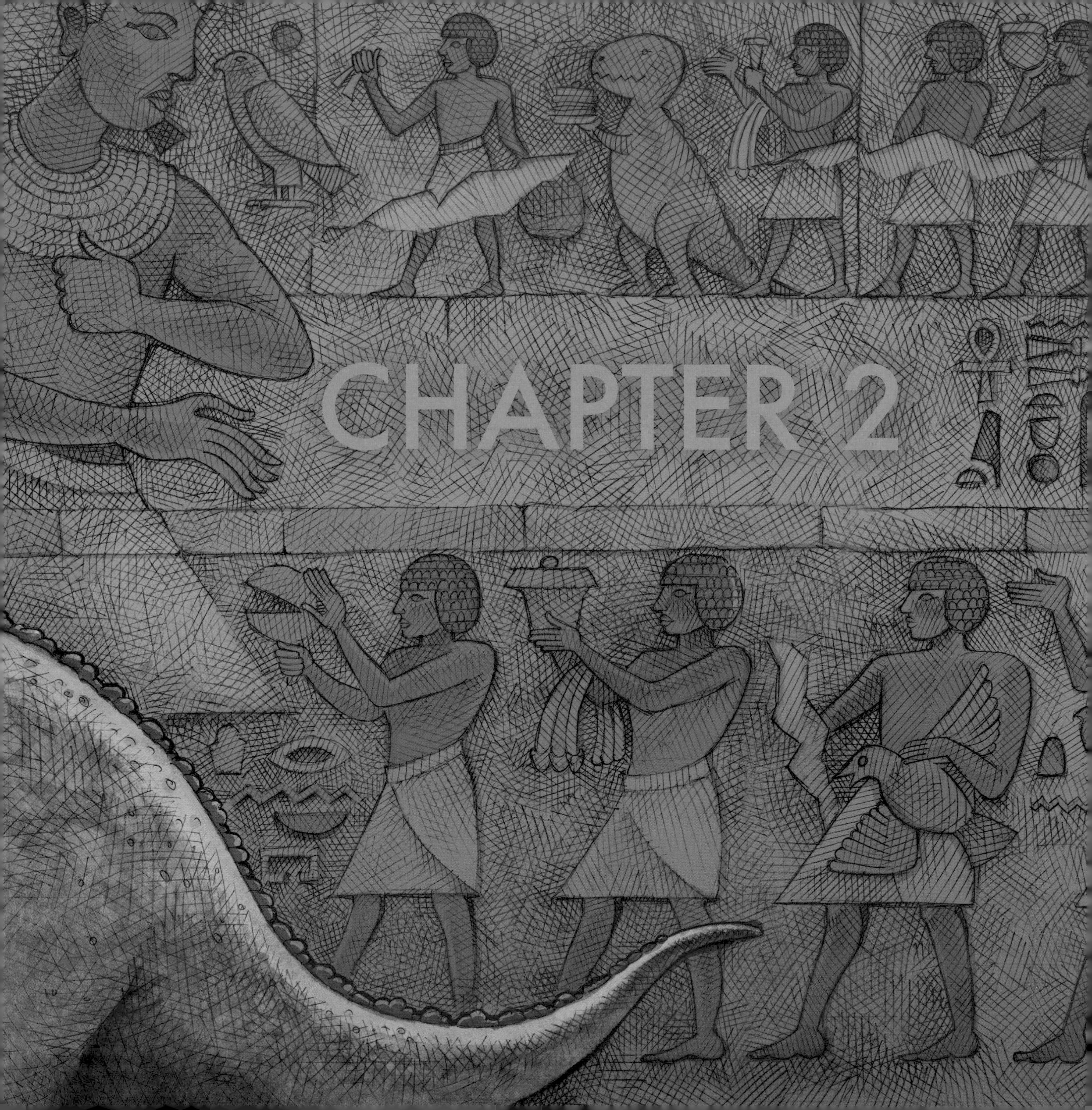

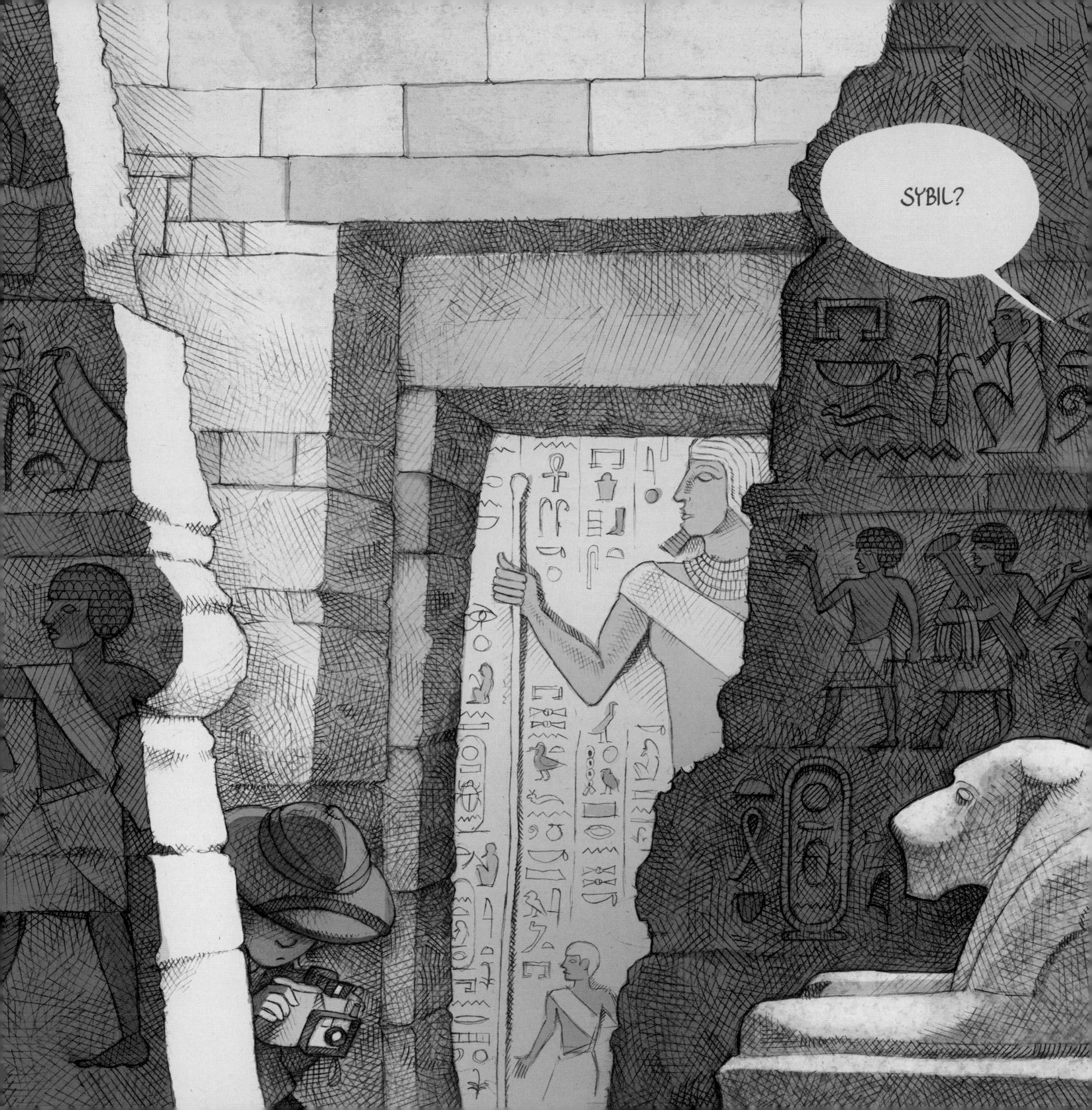
SYBIL?

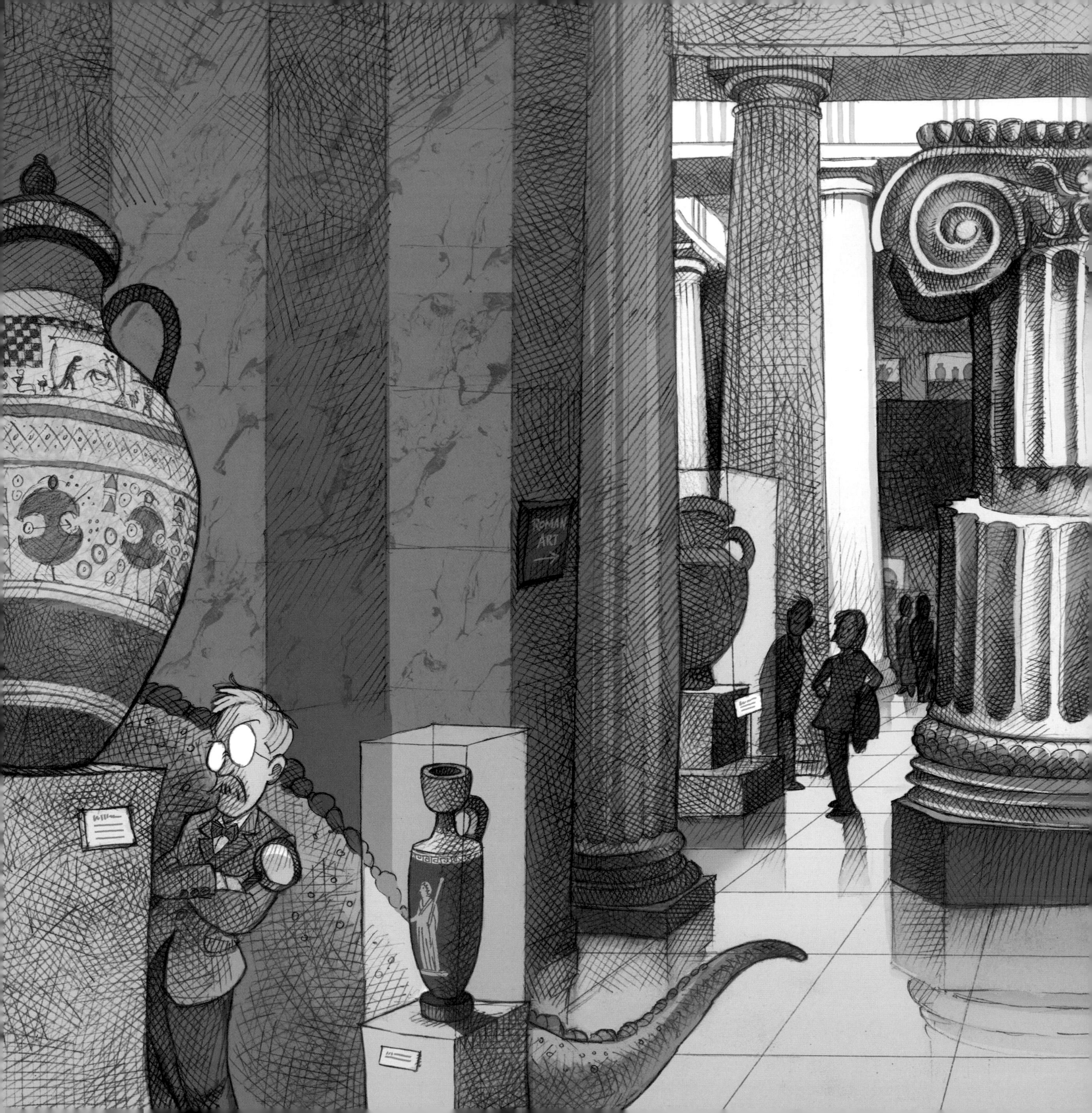
ROMAN
ART

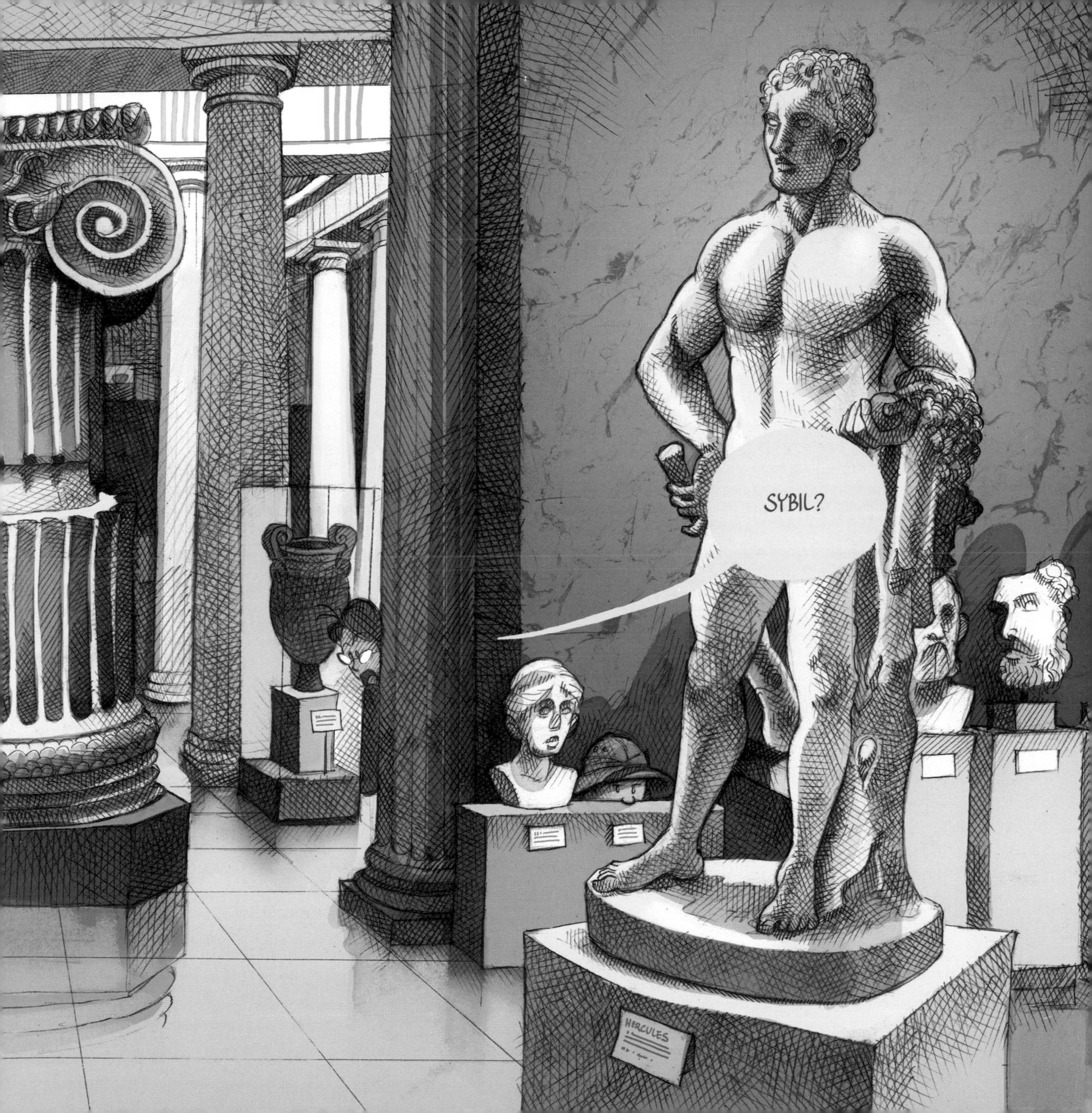
SYBIL?
HERCULES

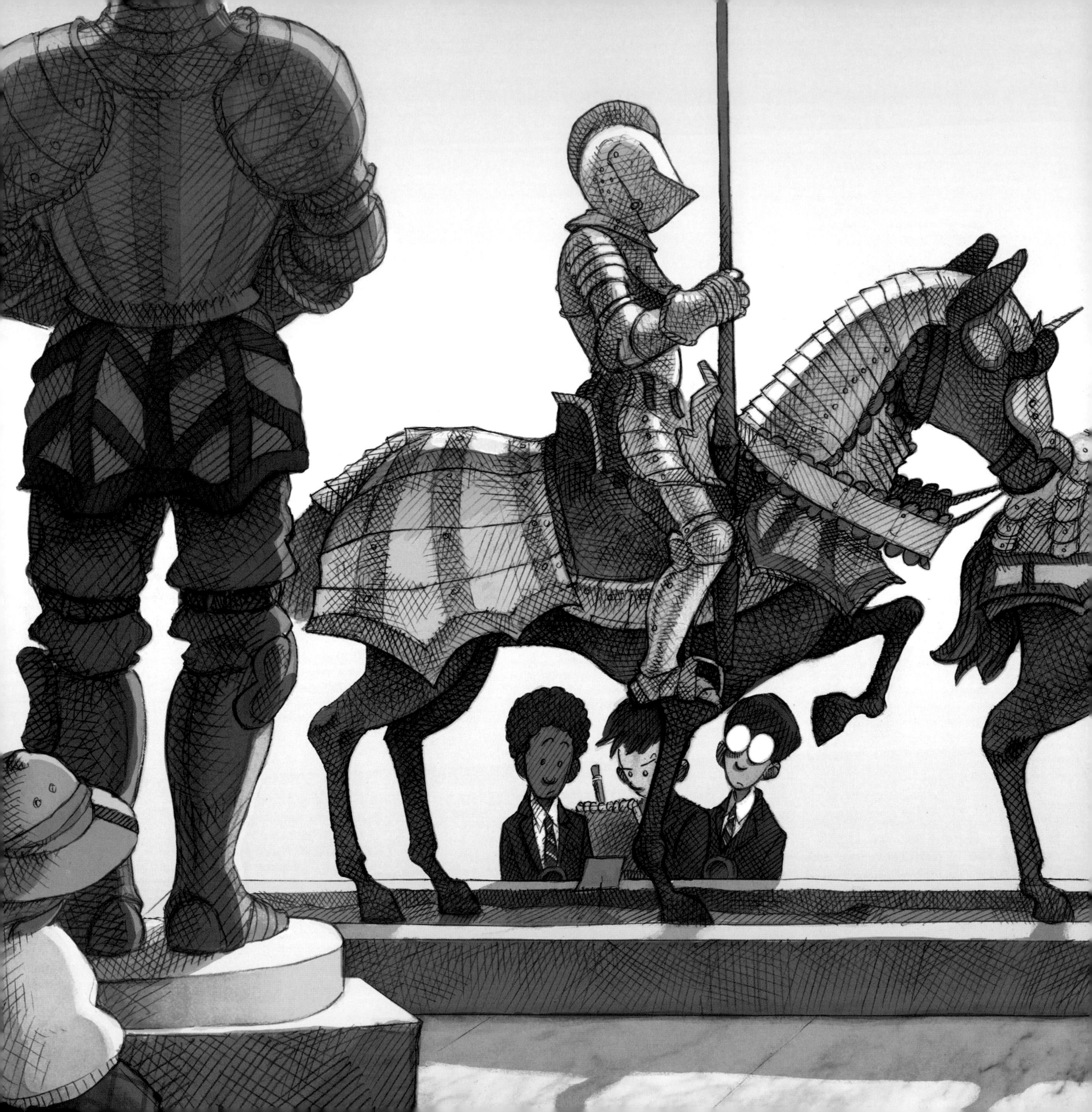

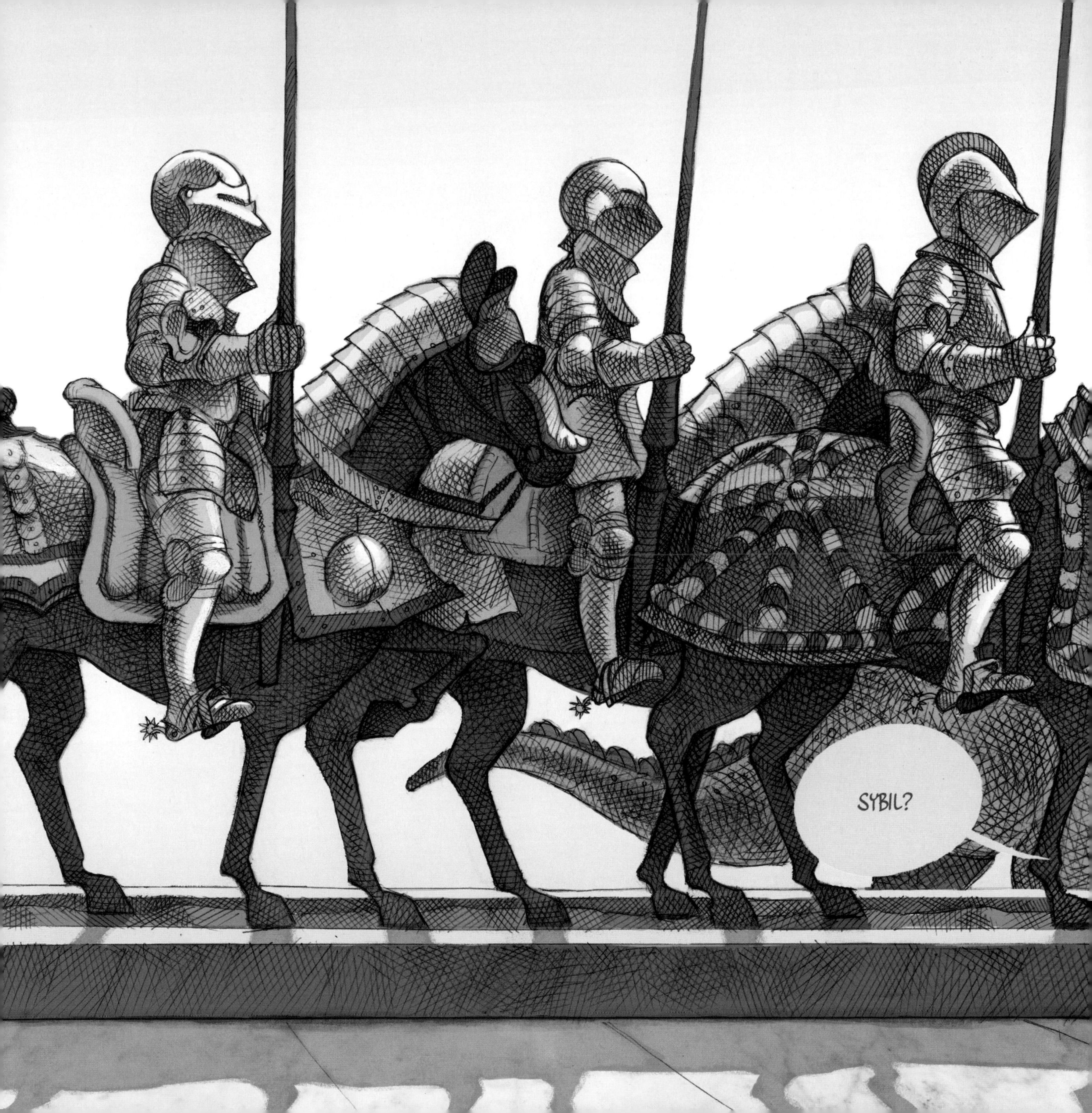
SYBIL?

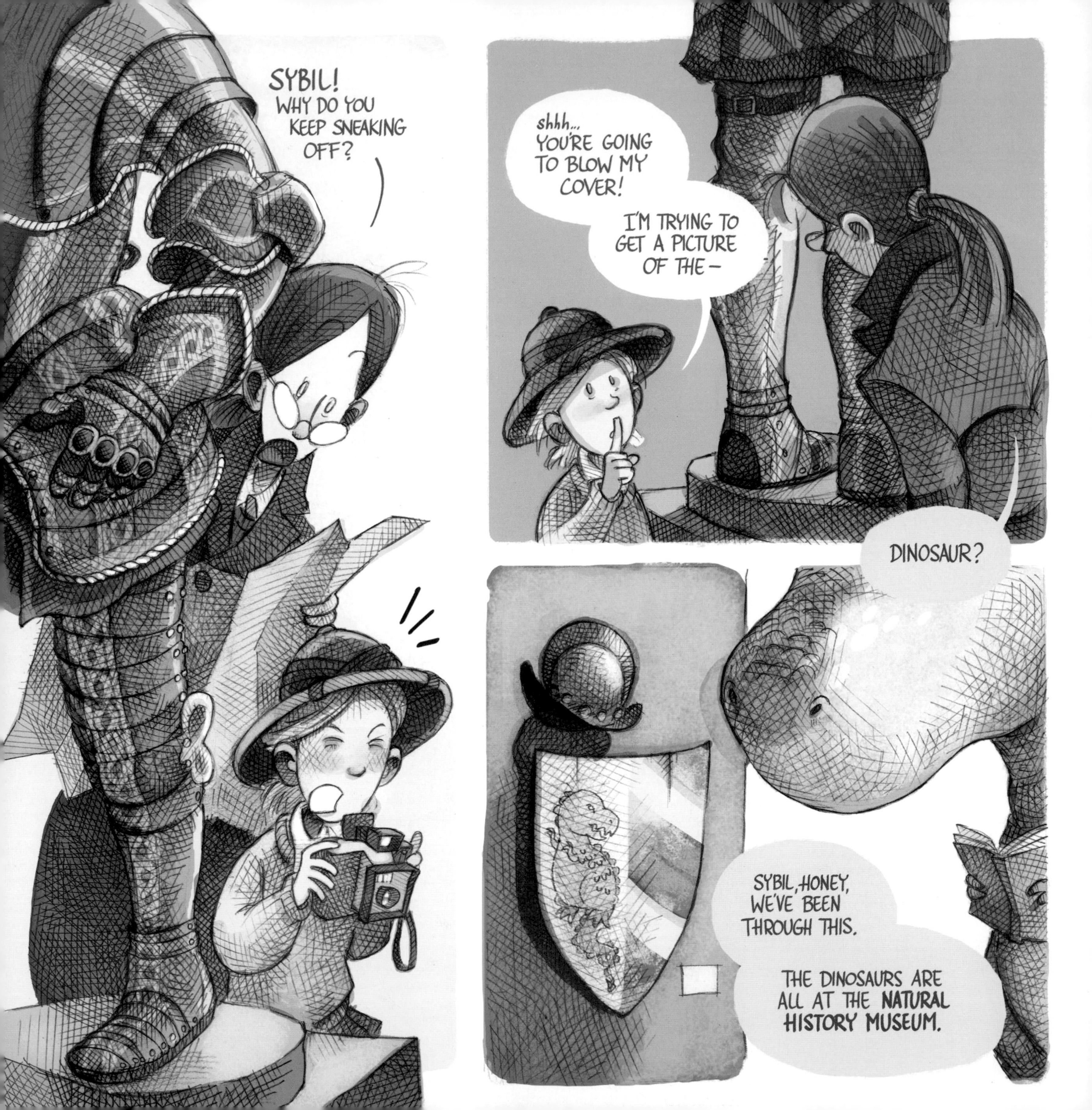
SYBIL! WHY DO YOU KEEP SNEAKING OFF?
shhh... YOU'RE GOING TO BLOW MY COVER!
I'M TRYING TO GET A PICTURE OF THE—
DINOSAUR?
SYBIL, HONEY, WE'VE BEEN THROUGH THIS.
THE DINOSAURS ARE ALL AT THE NATURAL HISTORY MUSEUM.

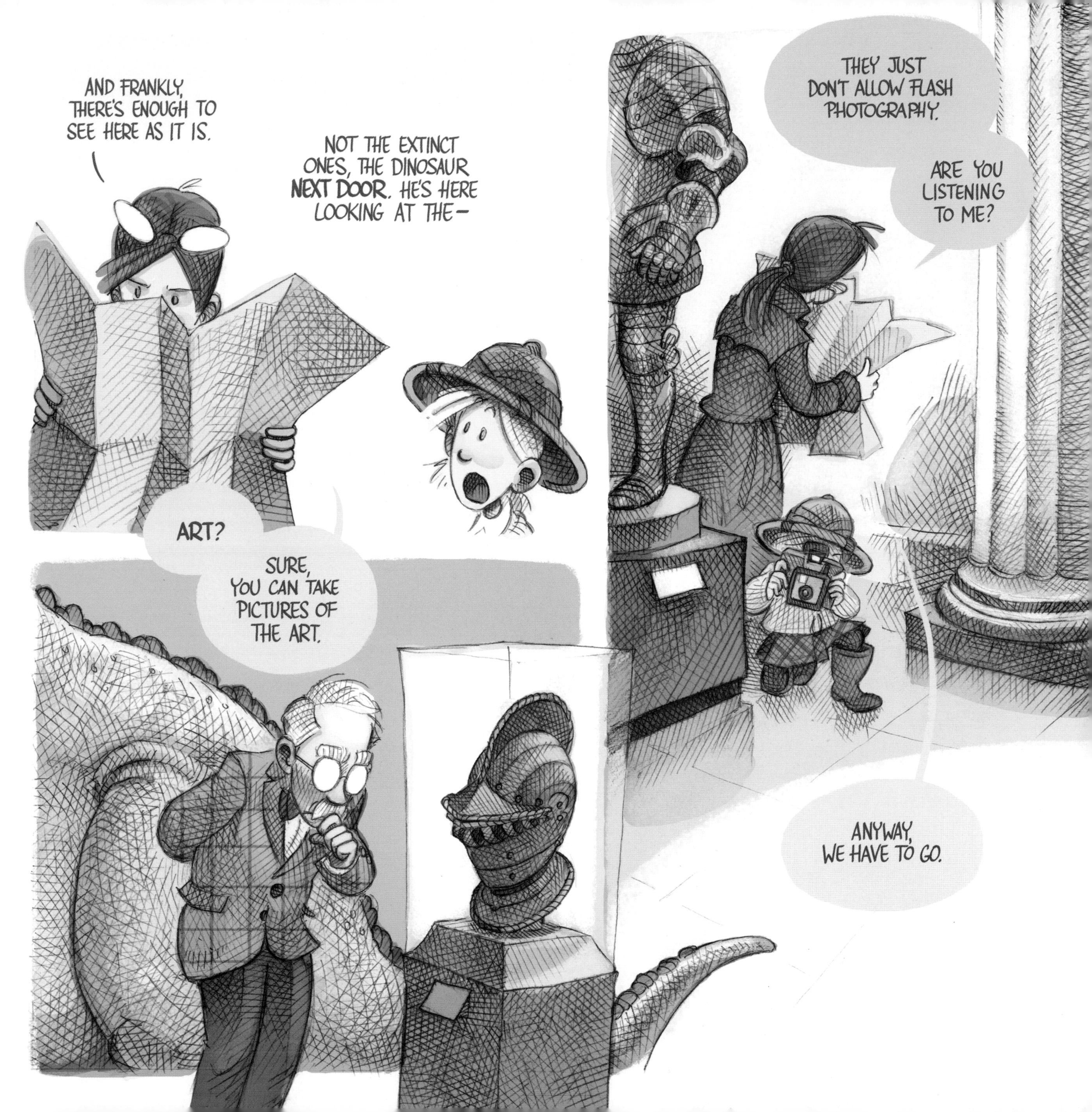
AND FRANKLY, THERE'S ENOUGH TO SEE HERE AS IT IS.
NOT THE EXTINCT ONES, THE DINOSAUR **NEXT DOOR**. HE'S HERE LOOKING AT THE—
ART?
SURE, YOU CAN TAKE PICTURES OF THE ART.
THEY JUST DON'T ALLOW FLASH PHOTOGRAPHY.
ARE YOU LISTENING TO ME?
ANYWAY, WE HAVE TO GO.

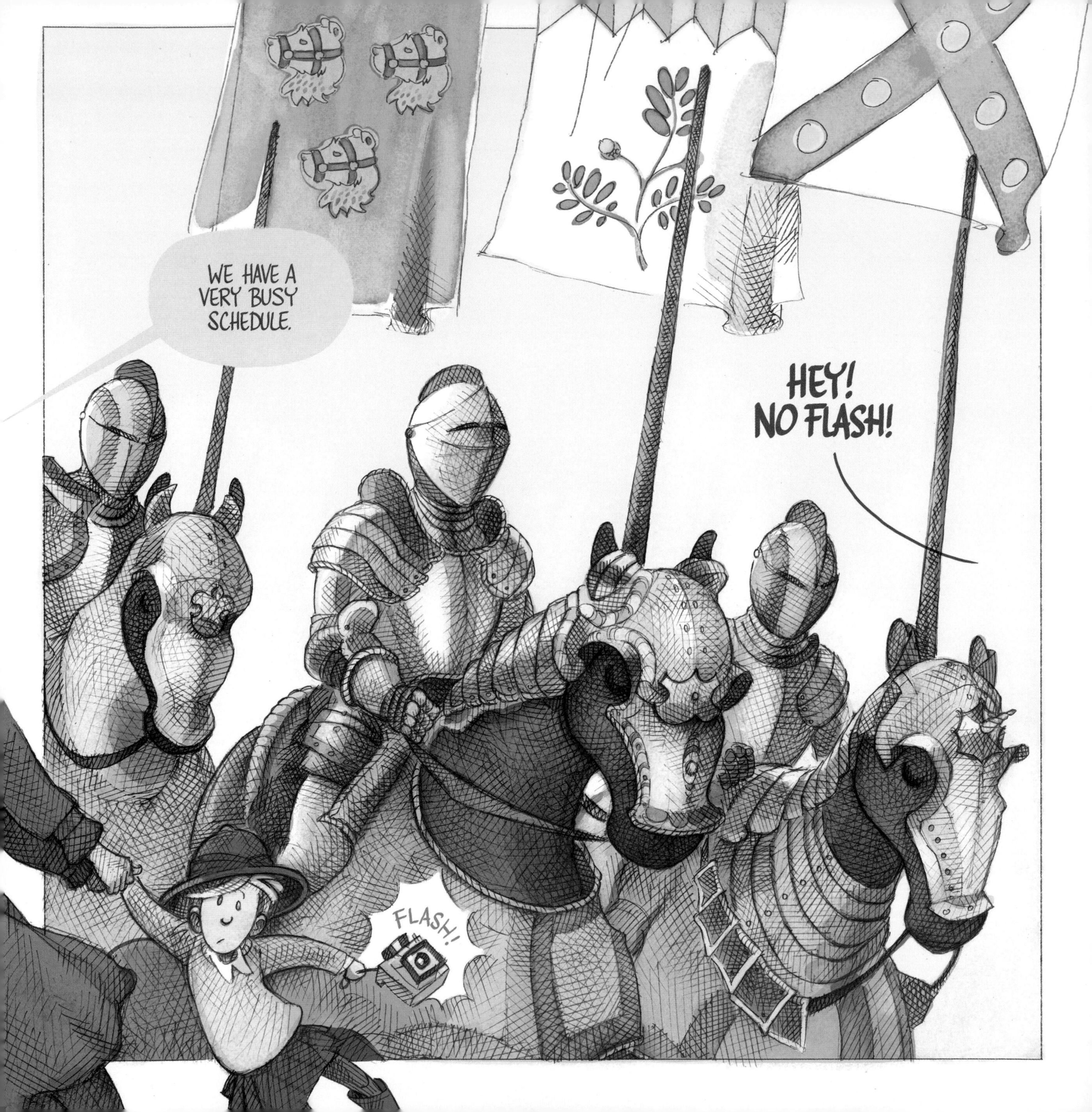
WE HAVE A VERY BUSY SCHEDULE.
HEY! NO FLASH!
FLASH!

Like most New Yorkers, Bolivar had a very busy schedule.
In the mornings, he liked to visit the big art museum on Fifth Avenue.

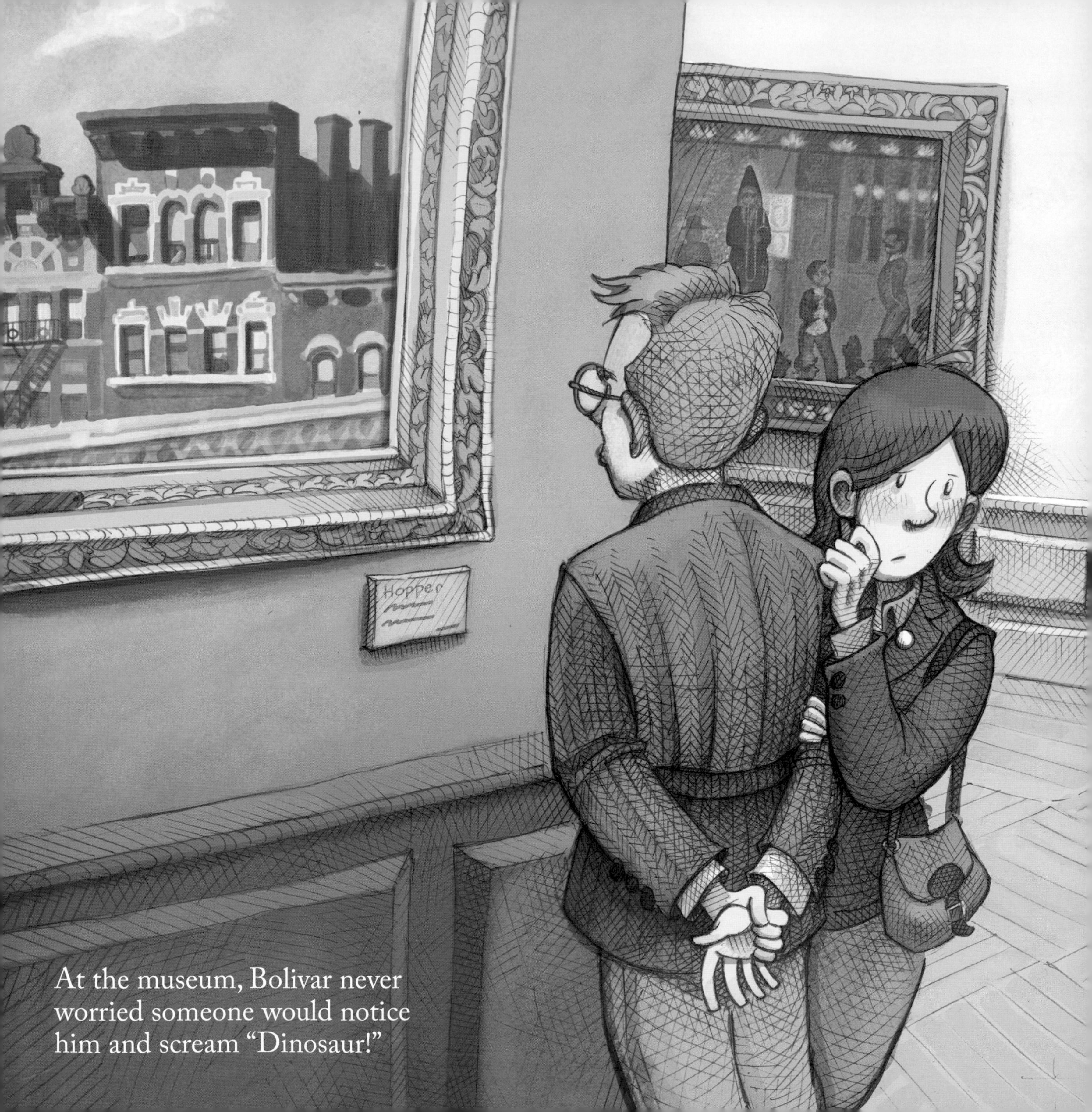
Hopper

At the museum, Bolivar never worried someone would notice him and scream "Dinosaur!"

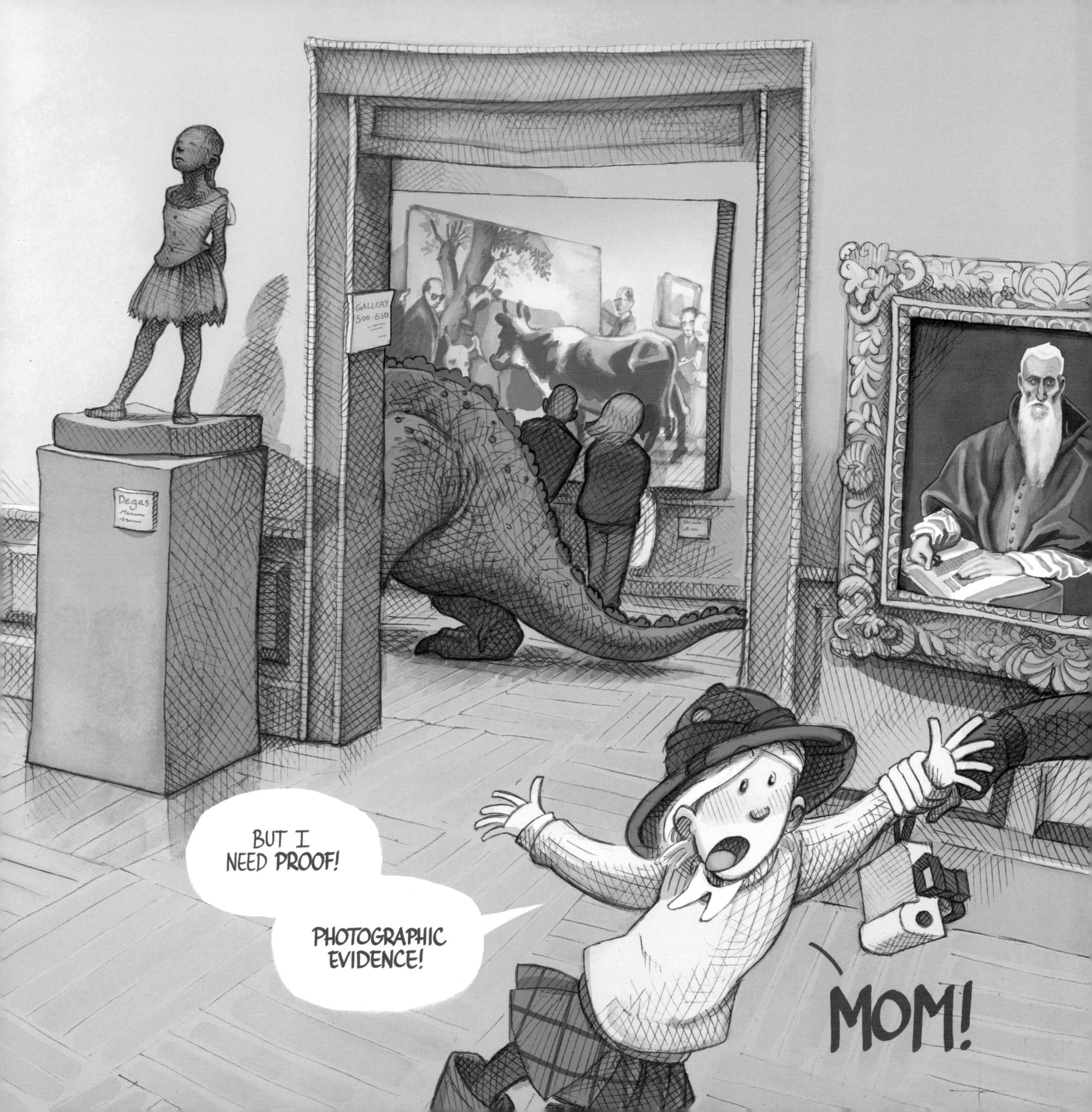

GALLERY 500-550
Degas
BUT I NEED PROOF!
PHOTOGRAPHIC EVIDENCE!
MOM!

They were much too busy looking at the art.

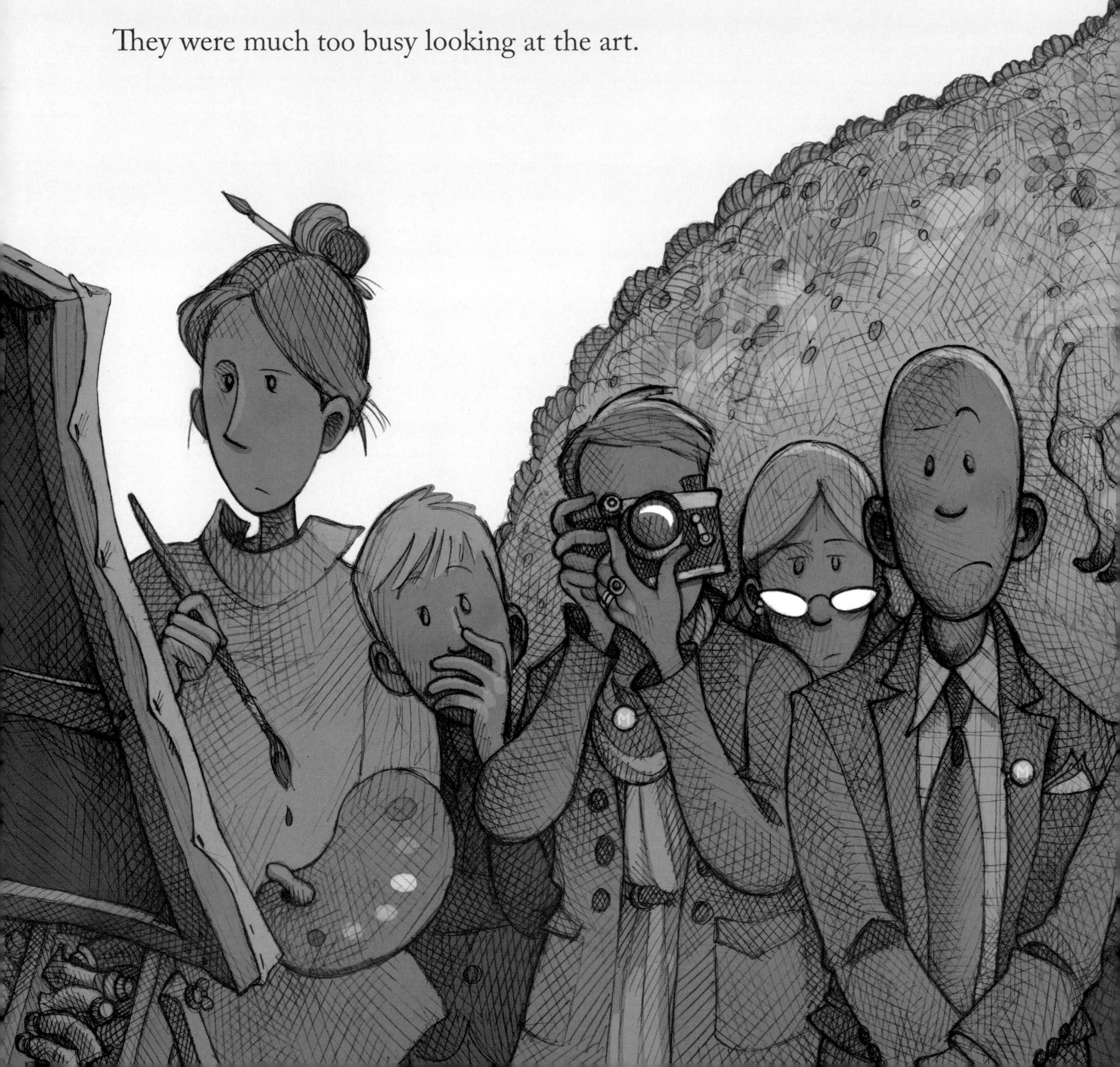

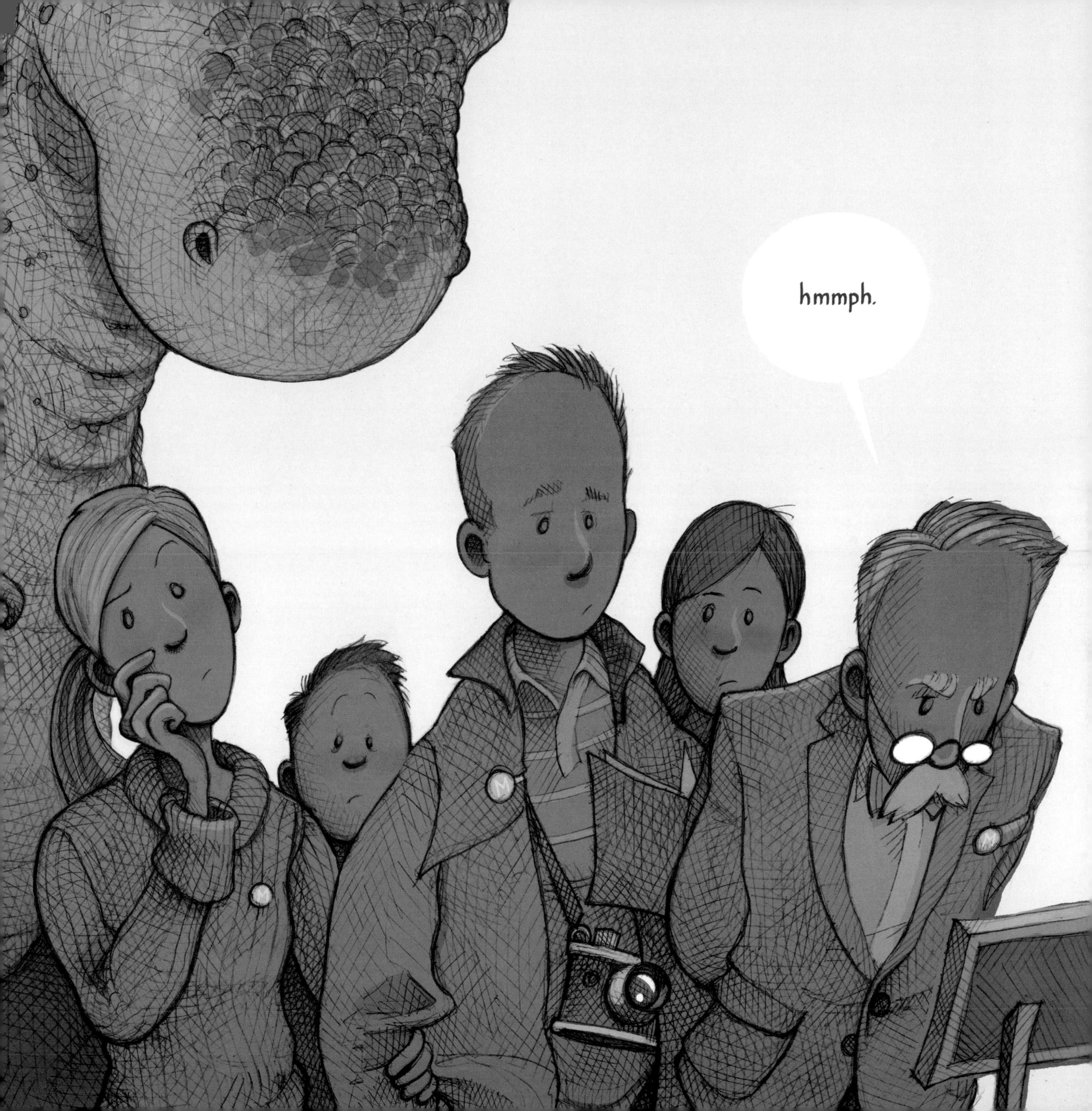
hmmph.

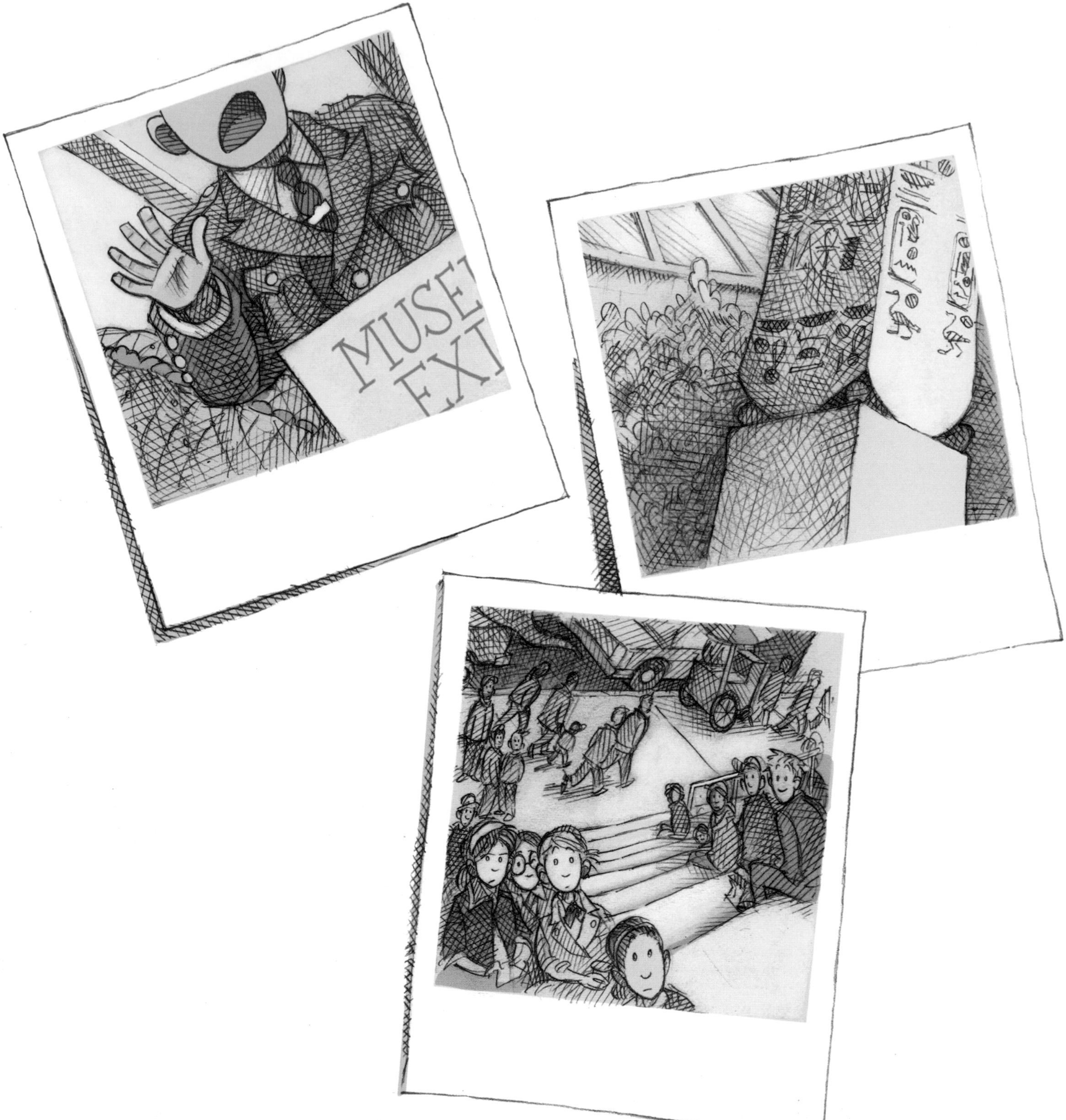
MUSE
EX

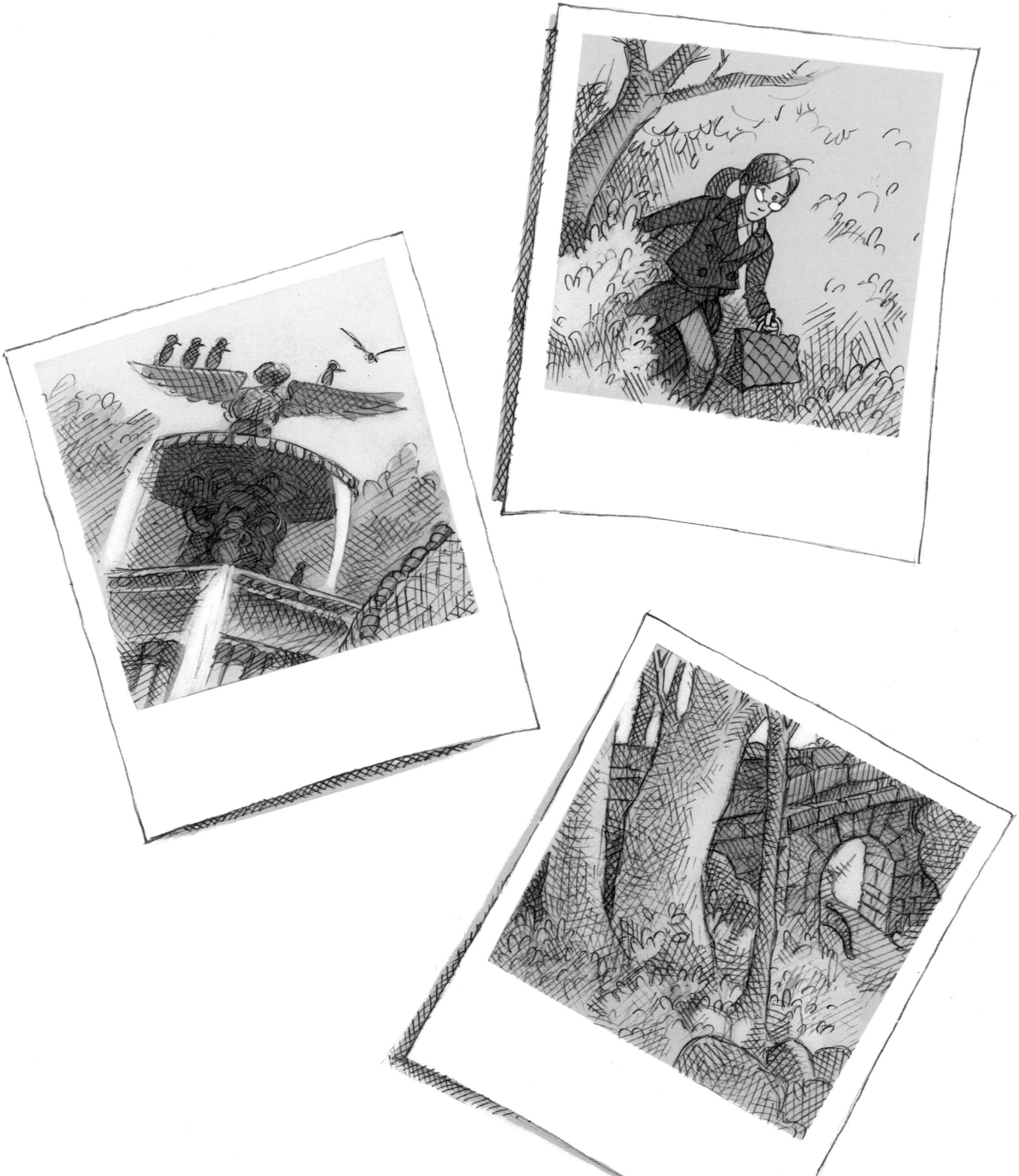

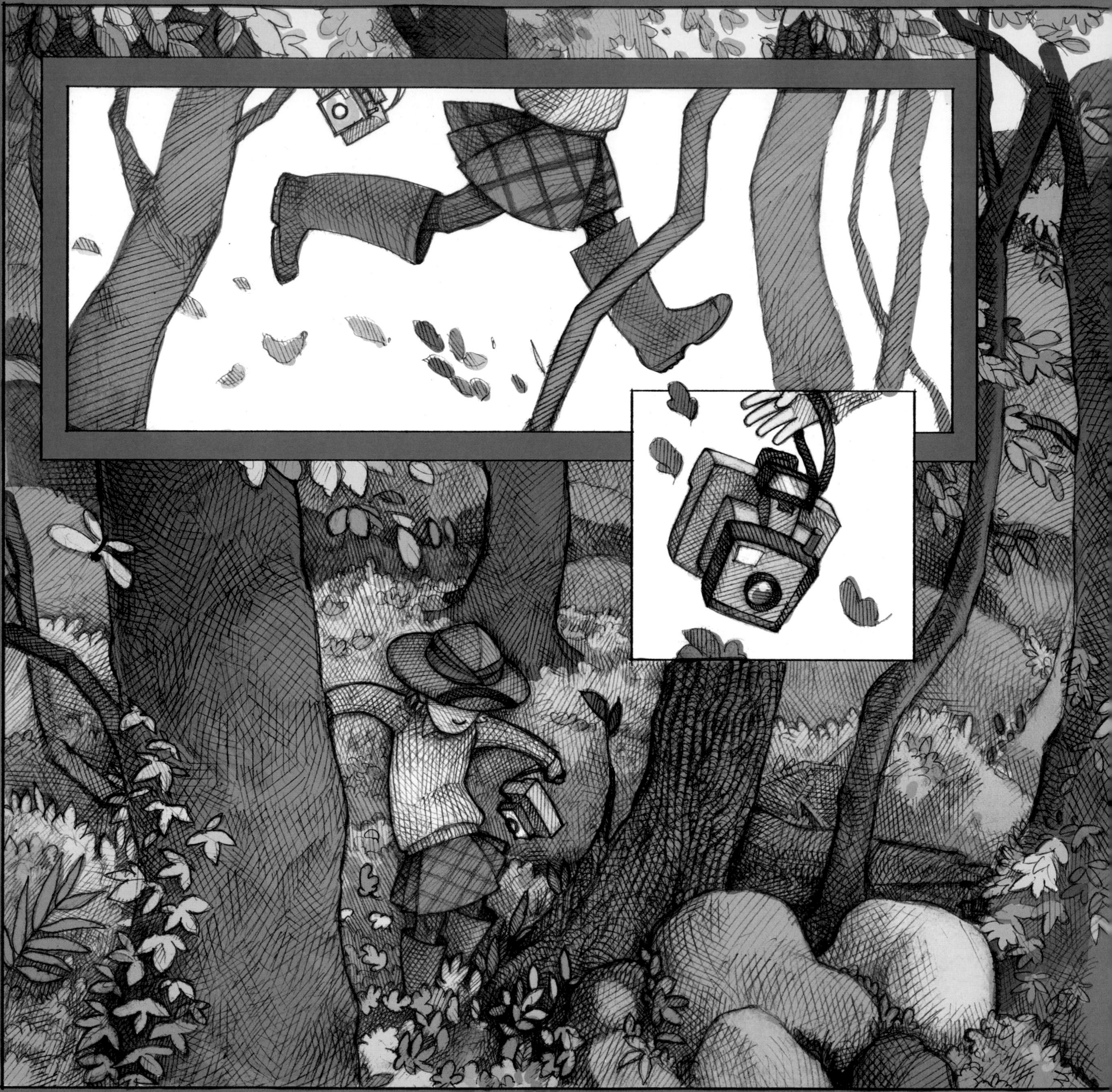

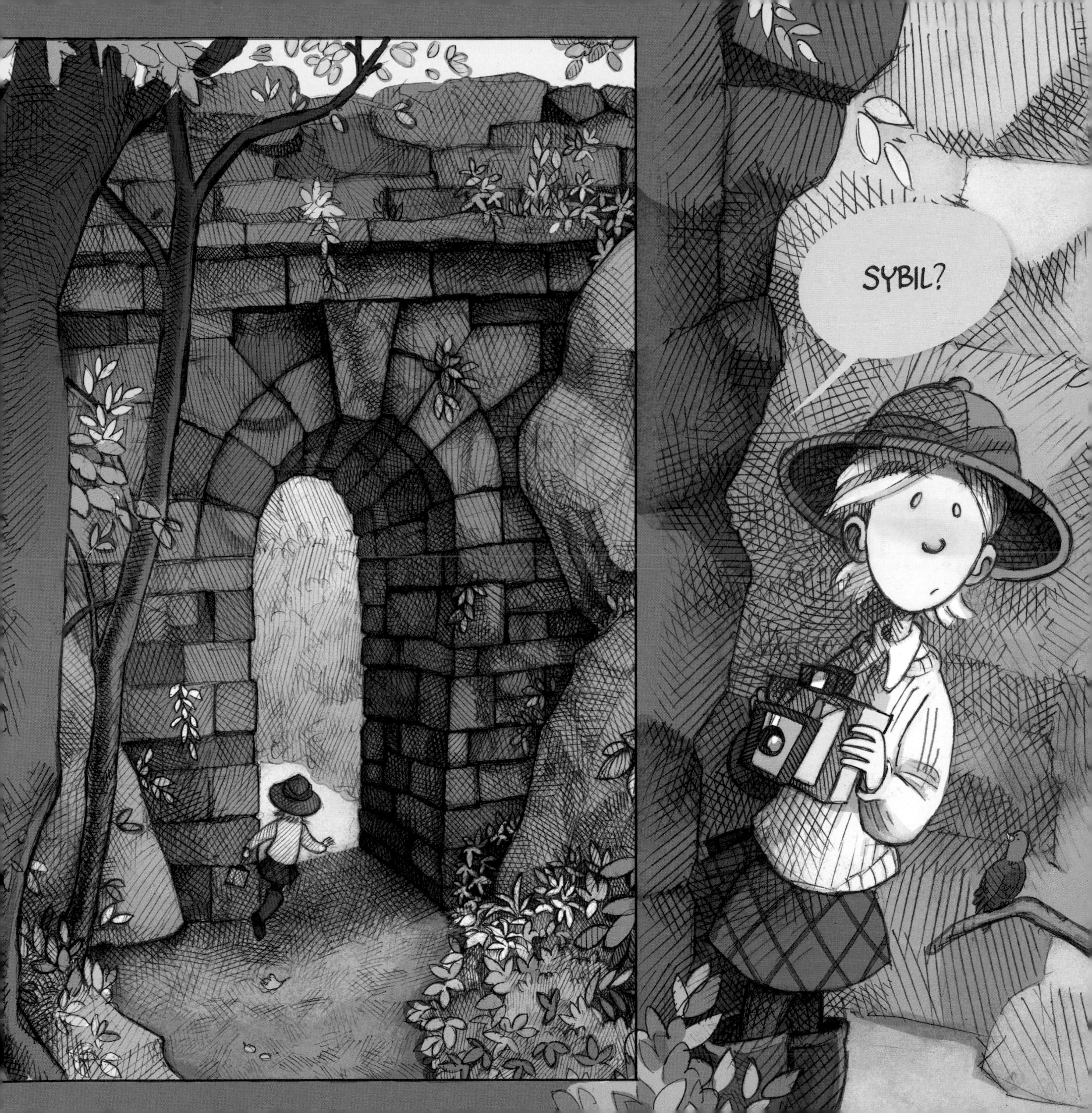
SYBIL?

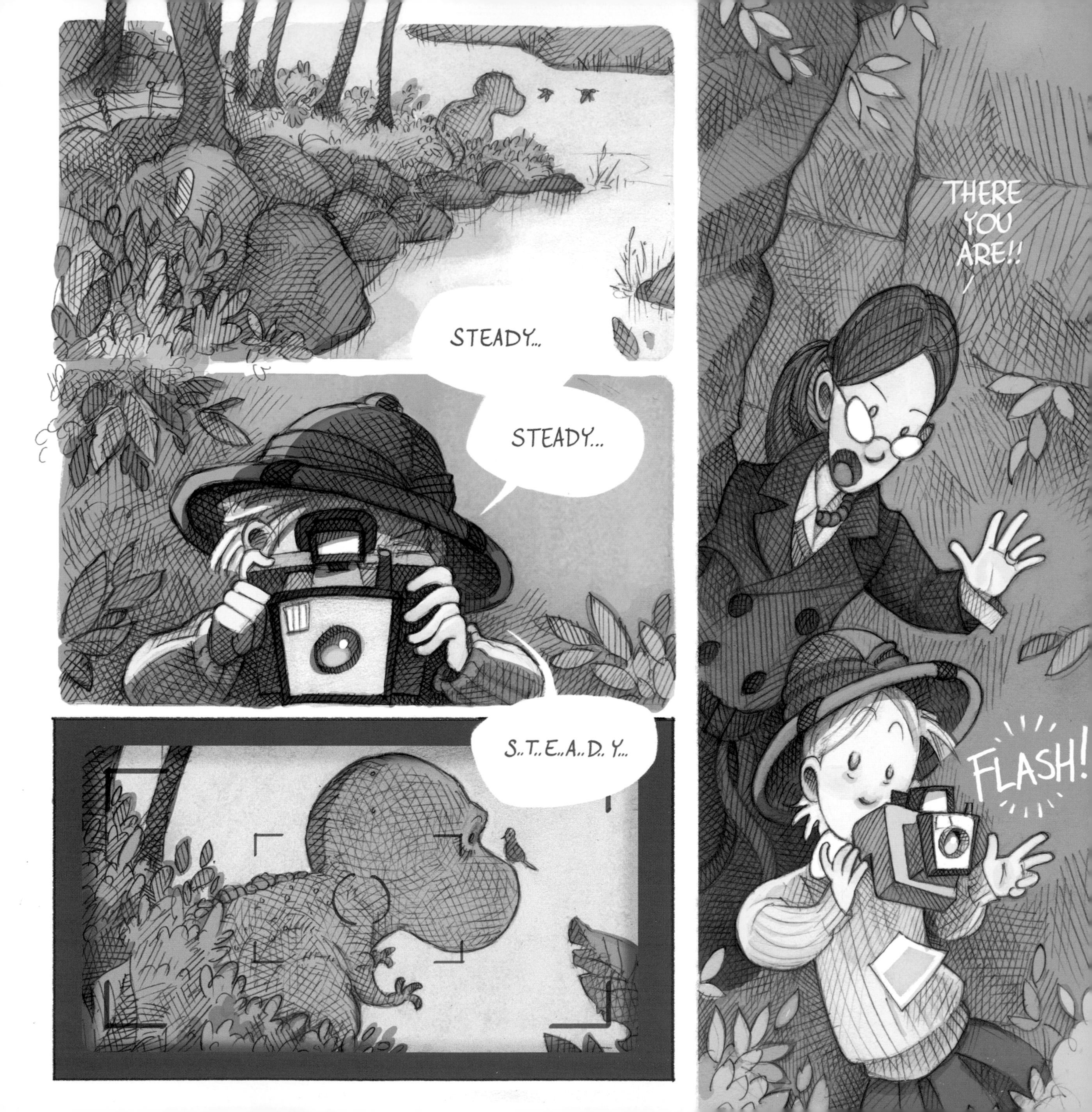
STEADY...
STEADY...
S..T..E..A..D..Y...
THERE YOU ARE!!
FLASH!

In the afternoon, Bolivar liked to
ramble through Central Park.

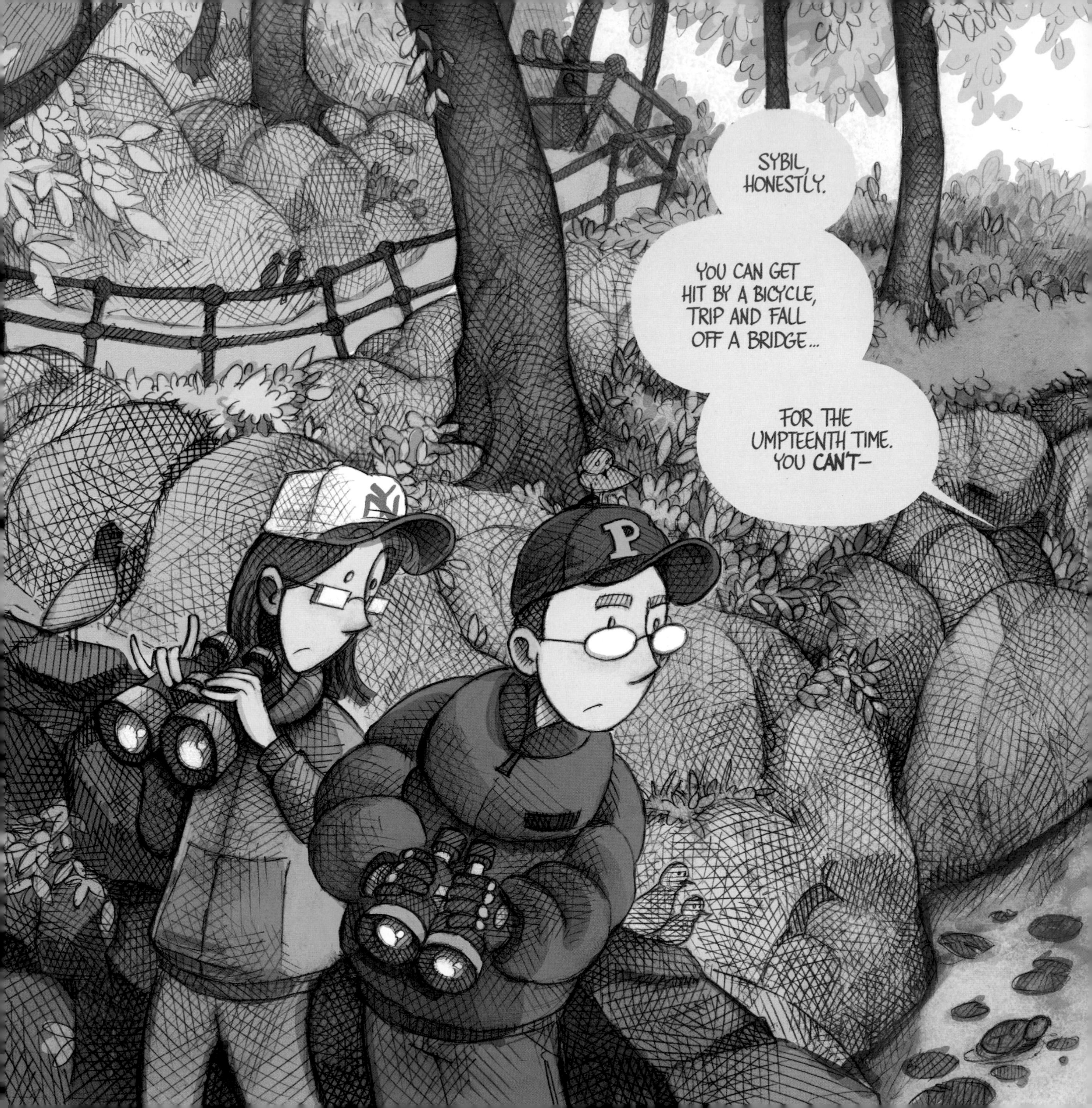
SYBIL, HONESTLY.
YOU CAN GET HIT BY A BICYCLE, TRIP AND FALL OFF A BRIDGE...
FOR THE UMPTEENTH TIME. YOU **CAN'T**–

At the park, Bolivar never worried that someone would notice him and scream "Dinosaur!"

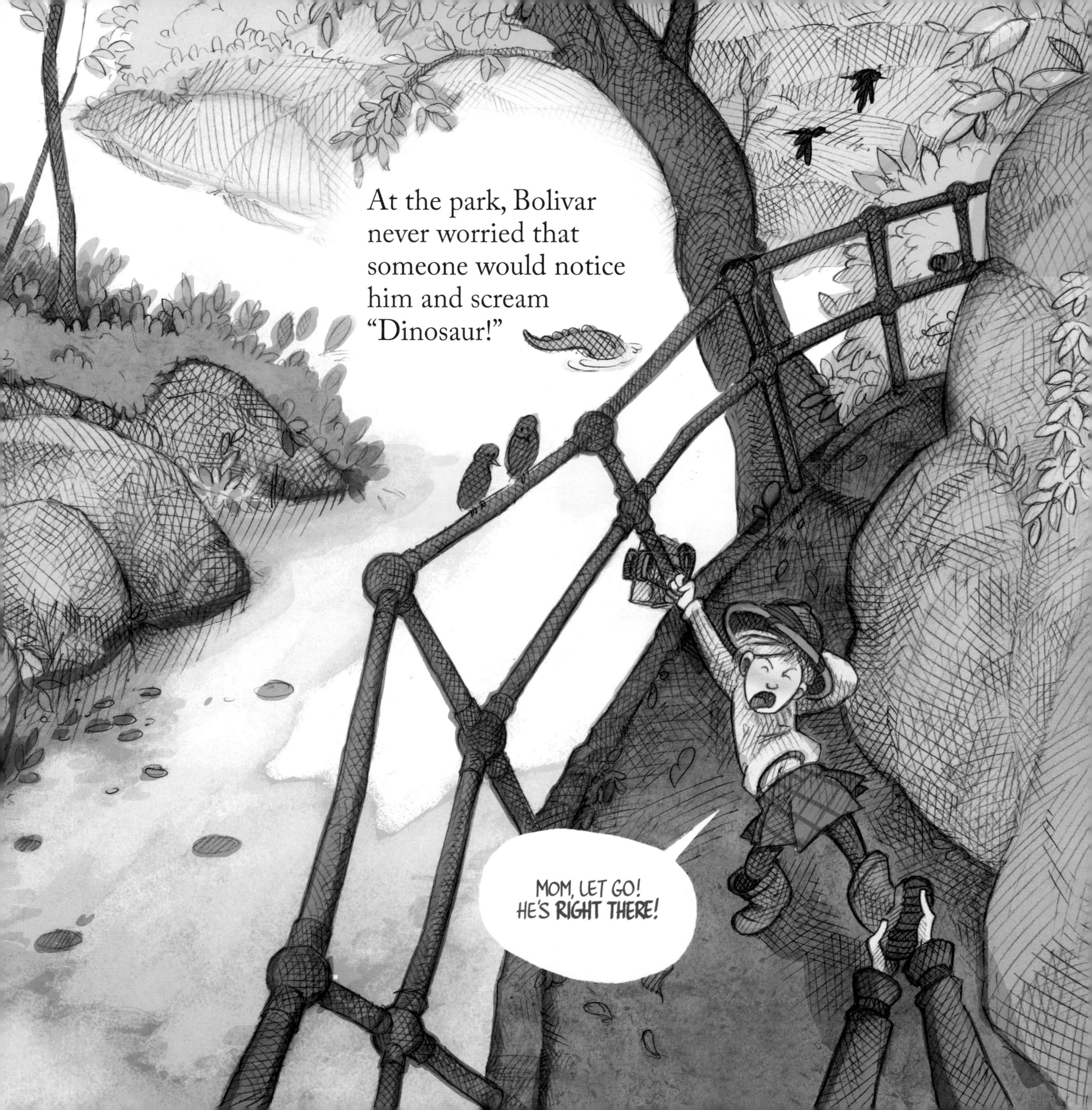
MOM, LET GO!
HE'S **RIGHT THERE!**

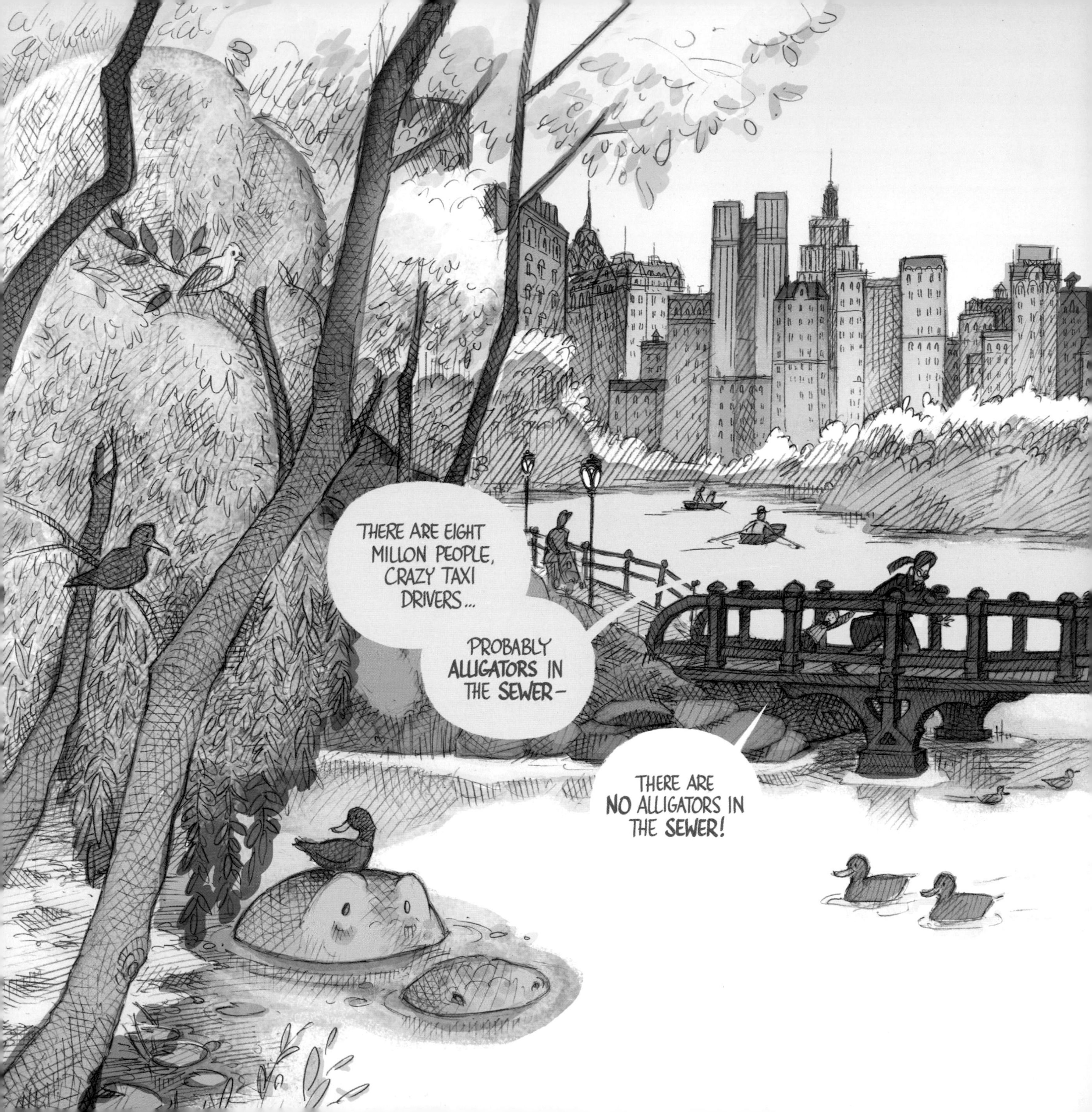
THERE ARE EIGHT MILLON PEOPLE, CRAZY TAXI DRIVERS...
PROBABLY ALLIGATORS IN THE SEWER–
THERE ARE NO ALLIGATORS IN THE SEWER!

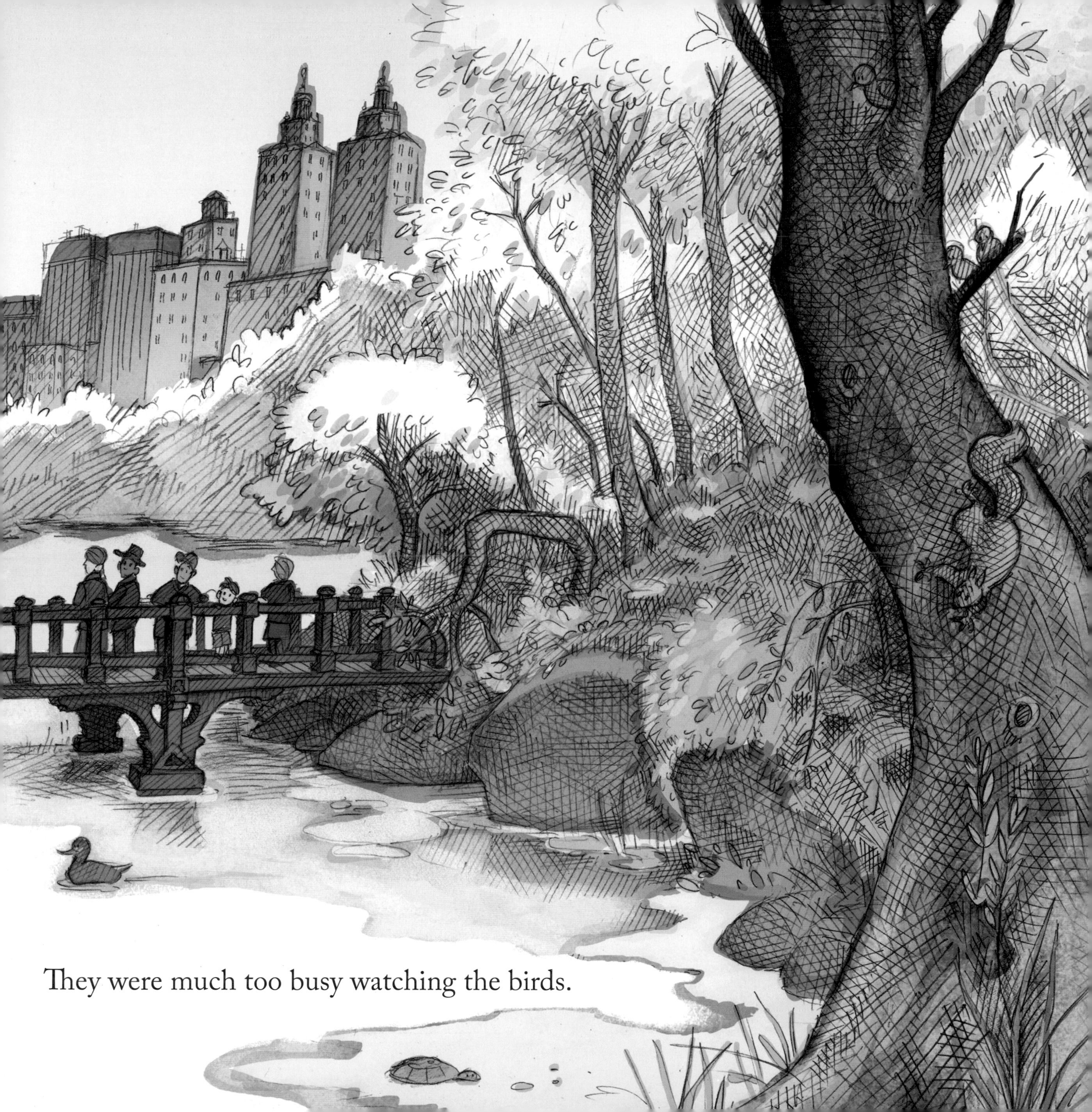

They were much too busy watching the birds.

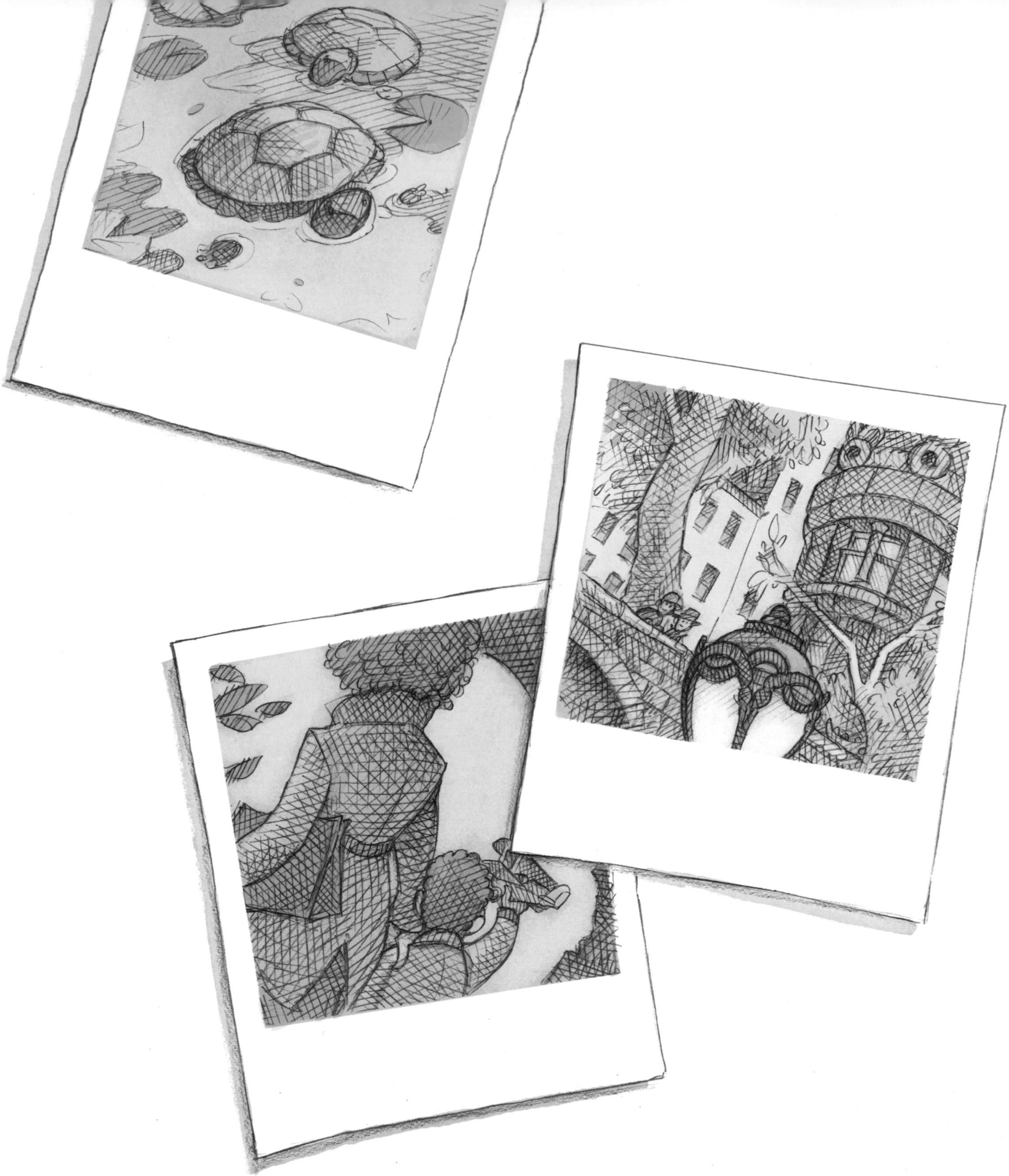

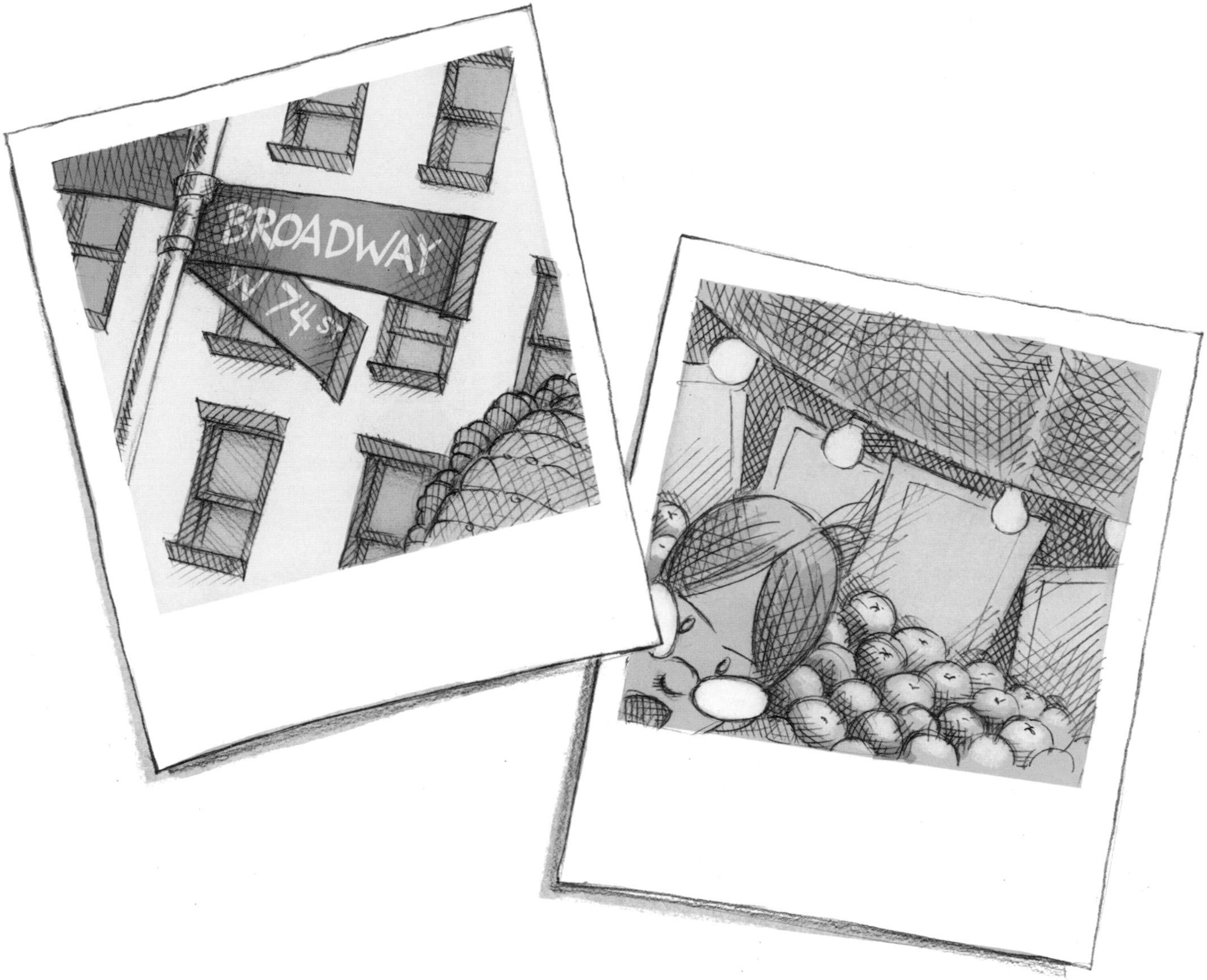
BROADWAY
W 74 ST

No one noticed Bolivar in the evening,
when he went grocery shopping.

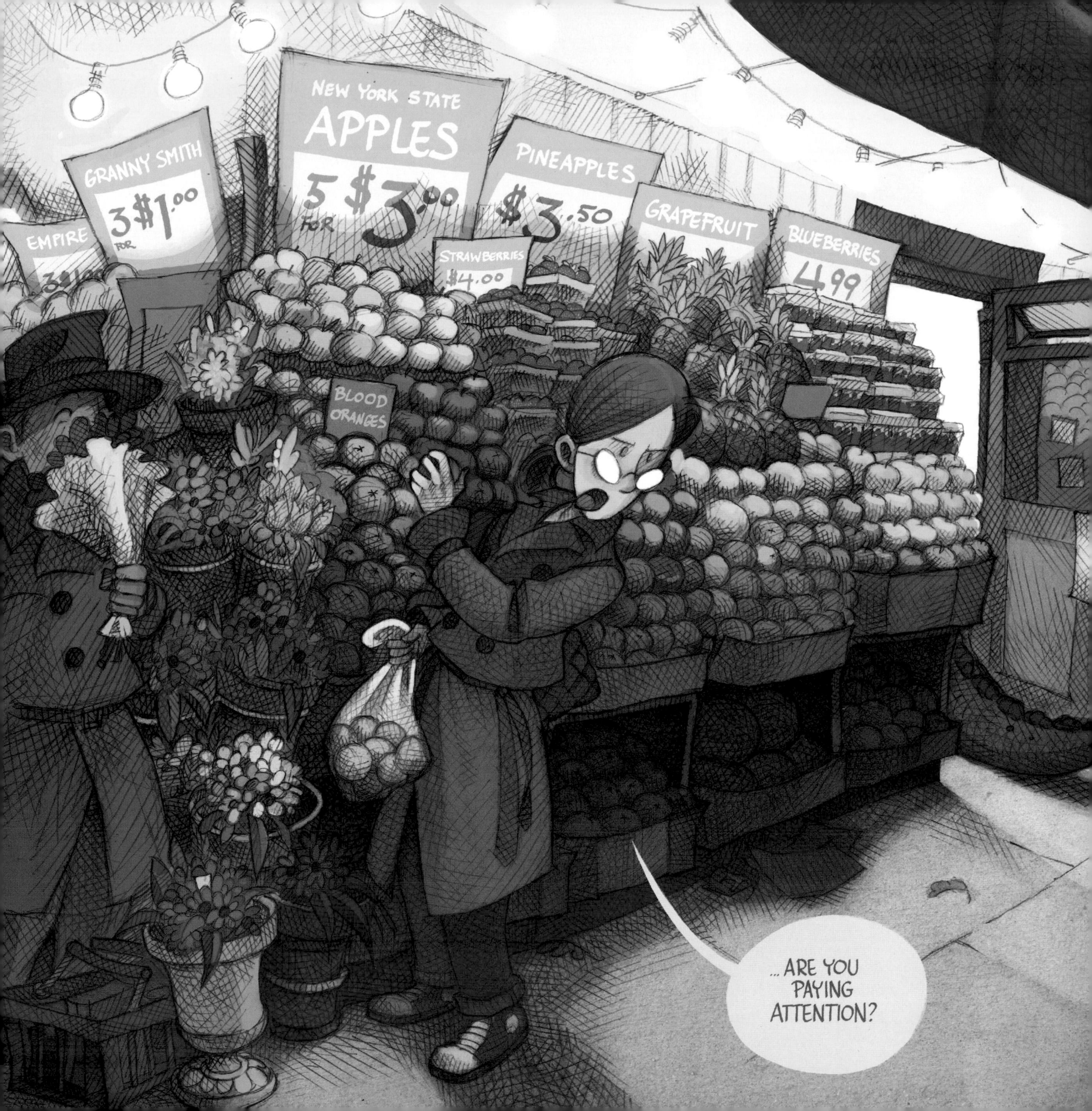
EMPIRE
GRANNY SMITH
3 FOR $1.00
NEW YORK STATE
APPLES
5 FOR $3.00
PINEAPPLES
$3.50
STRAWBERRIES
$4.00
GRAPEFRUIT
BLUEBERRIES
4.99
BLOOD ORANGES
... ARE YOU PAYING ATTENTION?

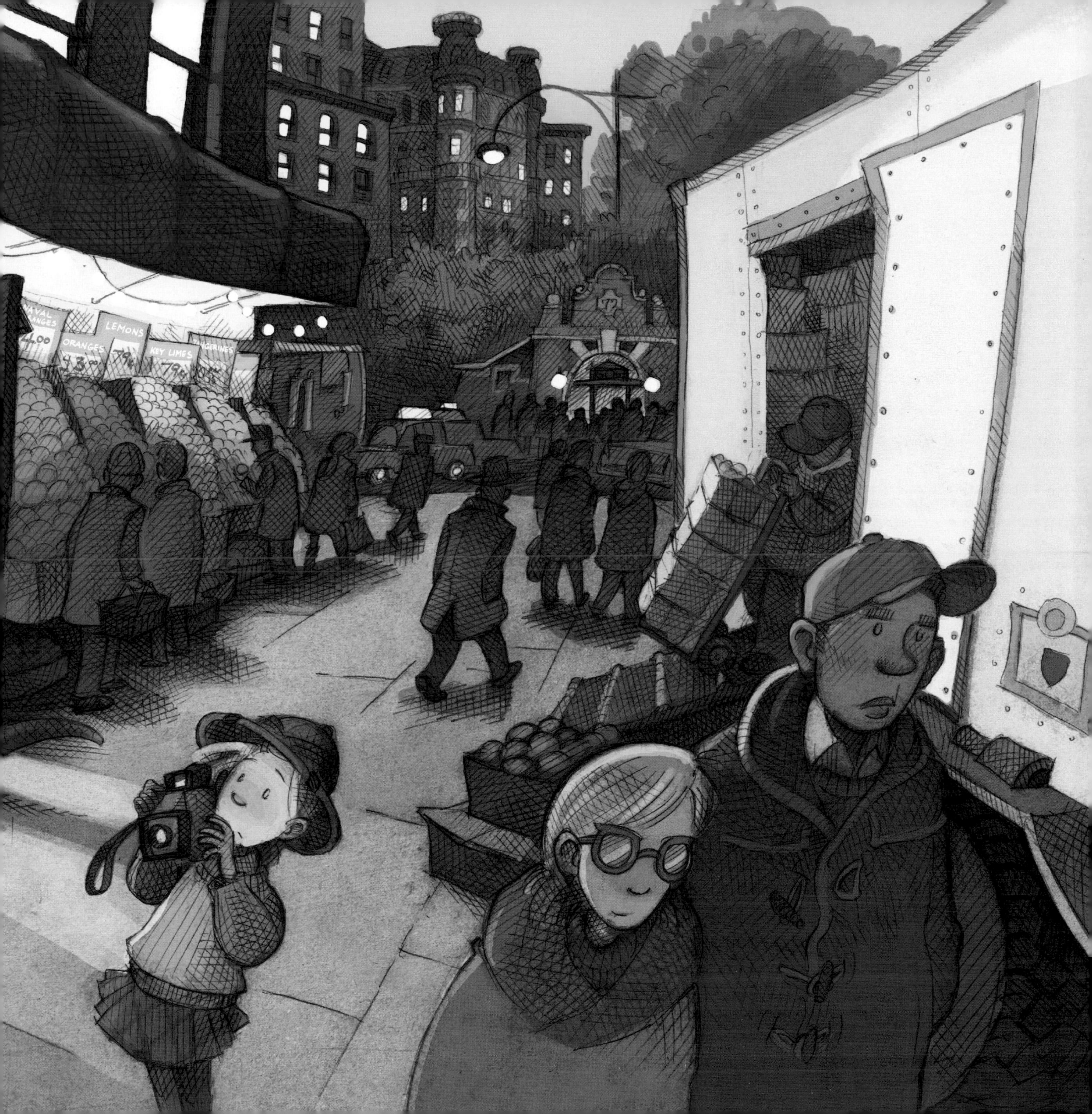

NAVAL
4.00
ORANGES
LEMONS
79¢
KEY LIMES
79¢
TANGERINES
72

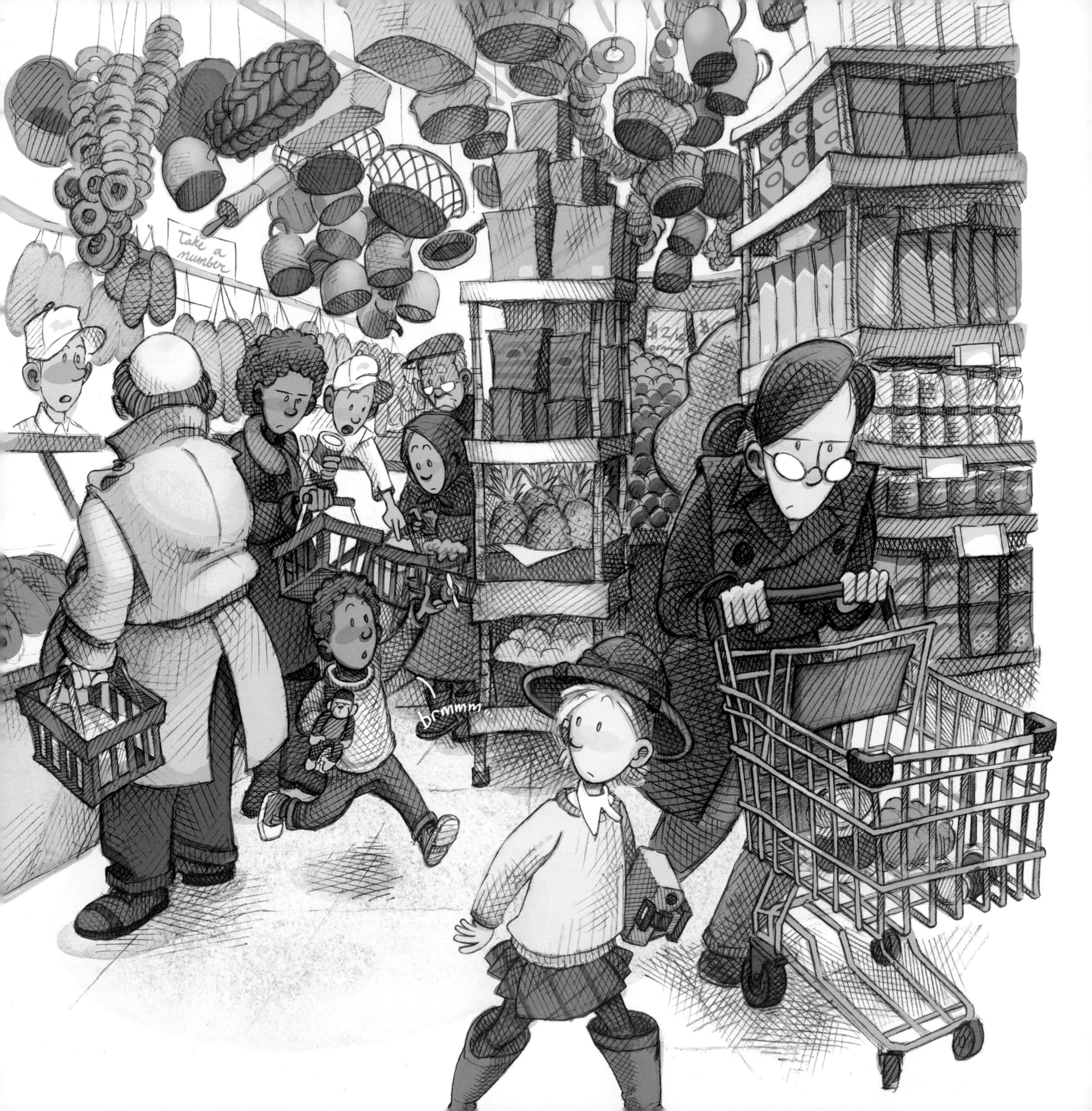
Take a number
brmmm

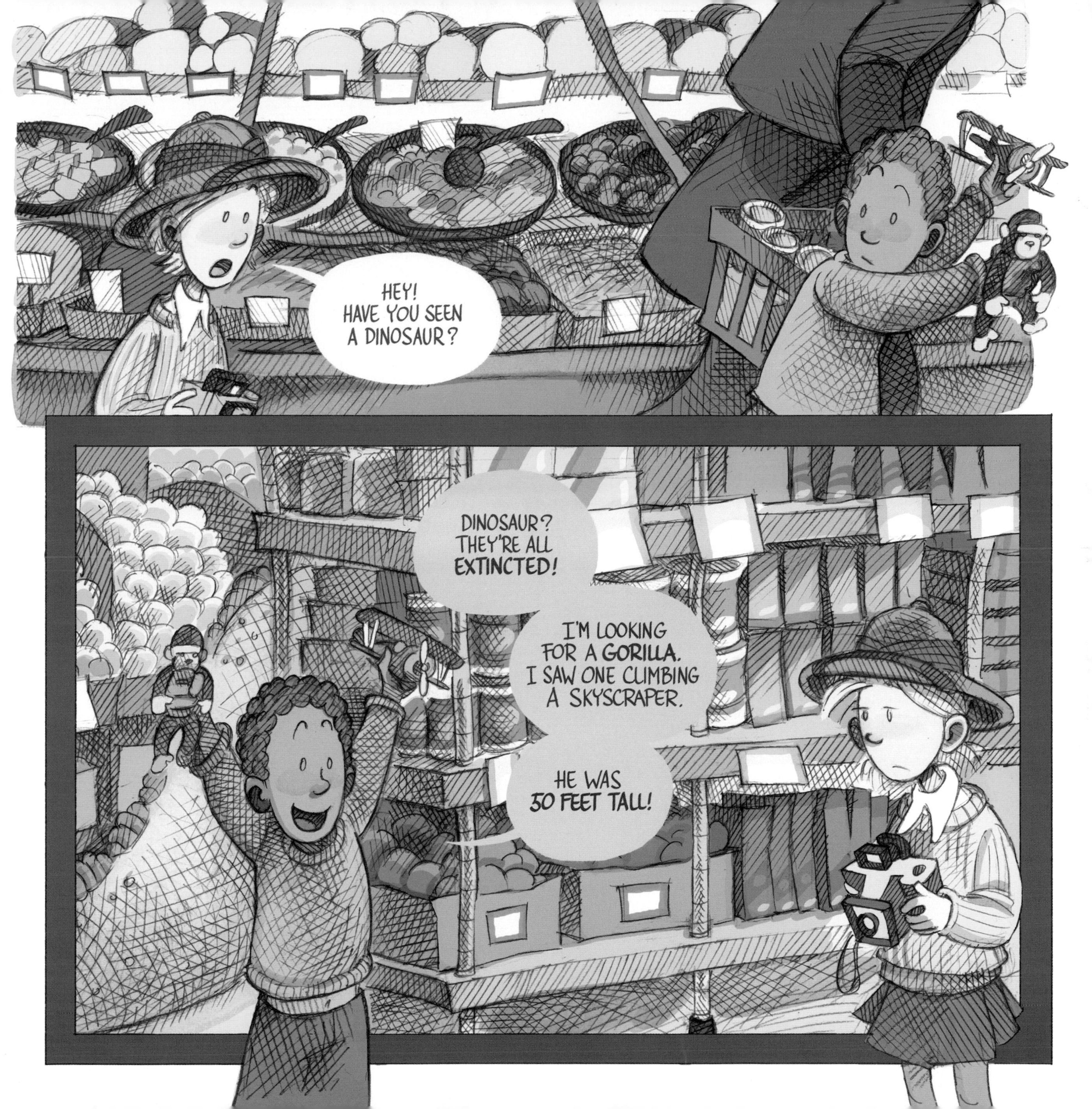
HEY! HAVE YOU SEEN A DINOSAUR?
DINOSAUR? THEY'RE ALL **EXTINCTED!**
I'M LOOKING FOR A **GORILLA.** I SAW ONE CLIMBING A SKYSCRAPER.
HE WAS **50 FEET TALL!**

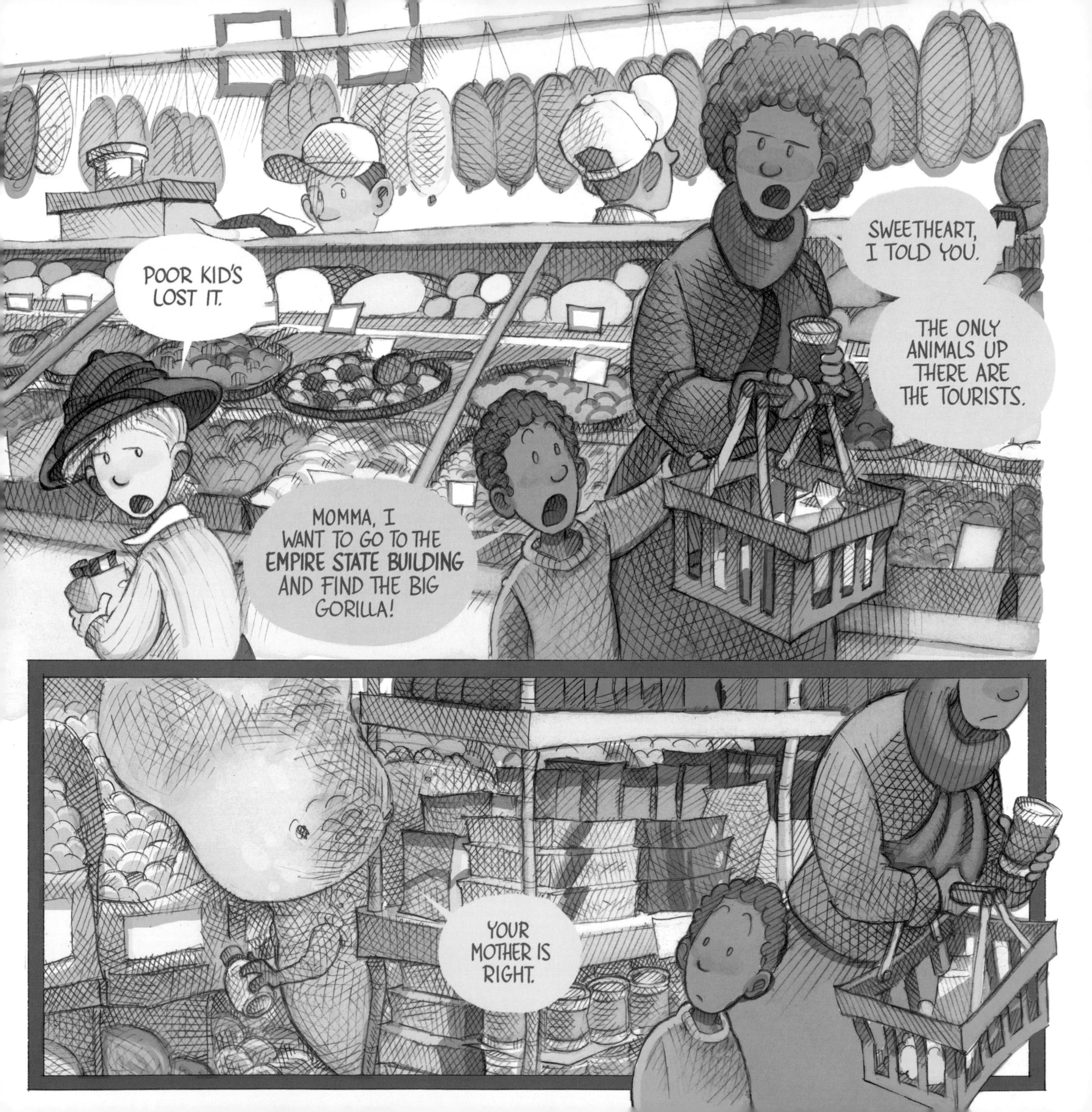
POOR KID'S LOST IT.
MOMMA, I WANT TO GO TO THE EMPIRE STATE BUILDING AND FIND THE BIG GORILLA!
SWEETHEART, I TOLD YOU.
THE ONLY ANIMALS UP THERE ARE THE TOURISTS.
YOUR MOTHER IS RIGHT.

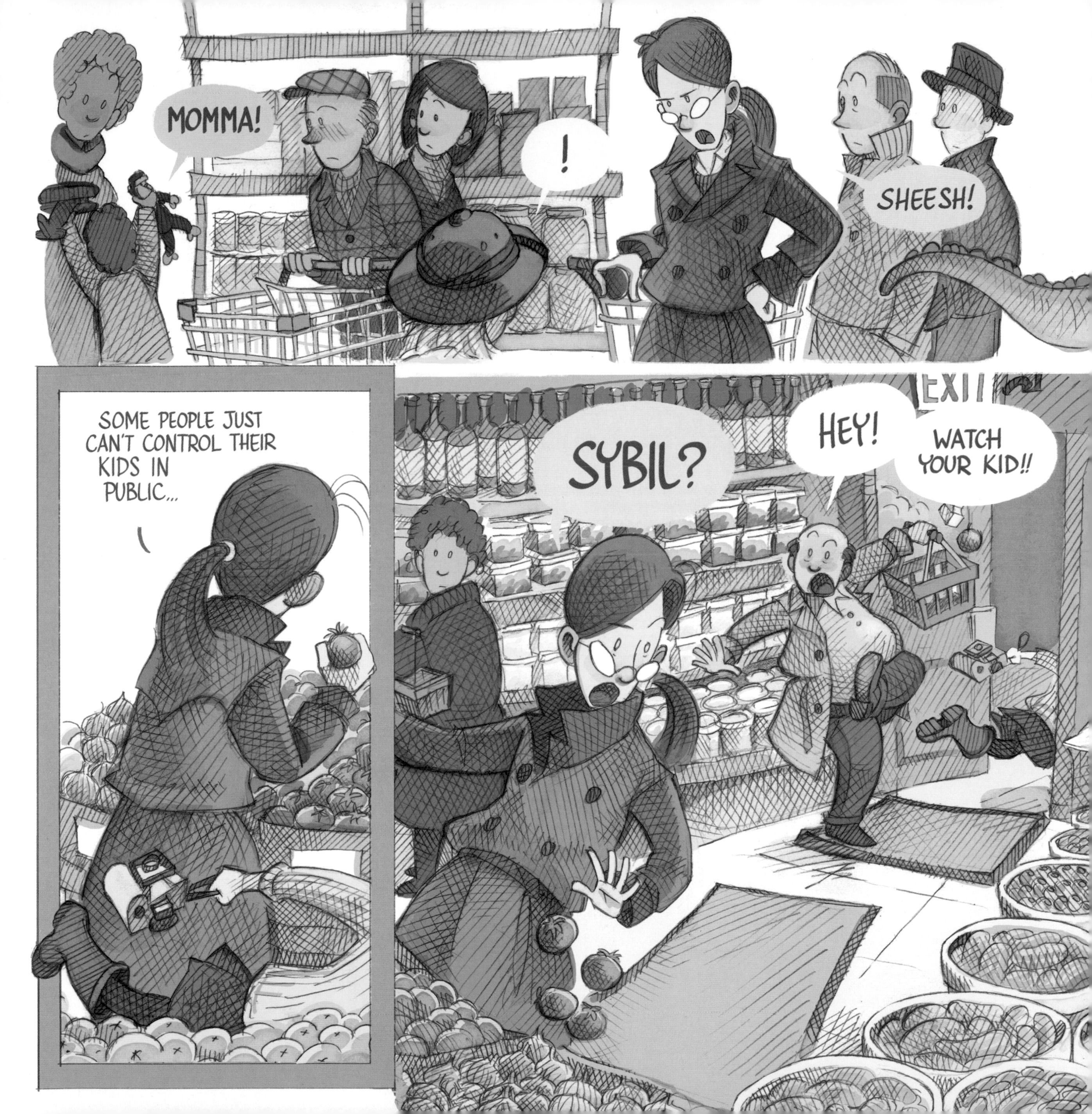
MOMMA!
!
SHEESH!
SOME PEOPLE JUST CAN'T CONTROL THEIR KIDS IN PUBLIC...
SYBIL?
HEY!
WATCH YOUR KID!!
EXIT

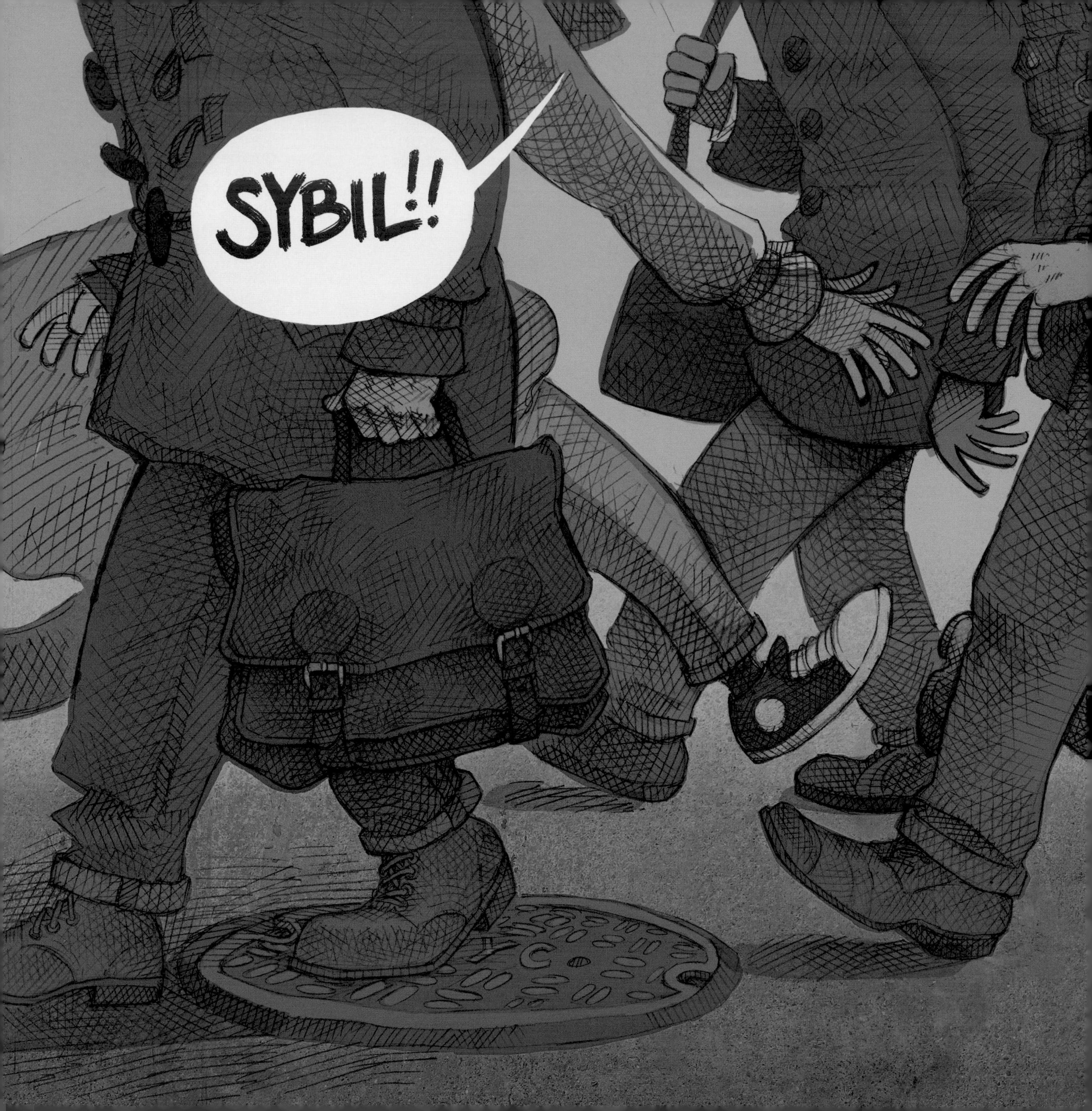
SYBIL!!

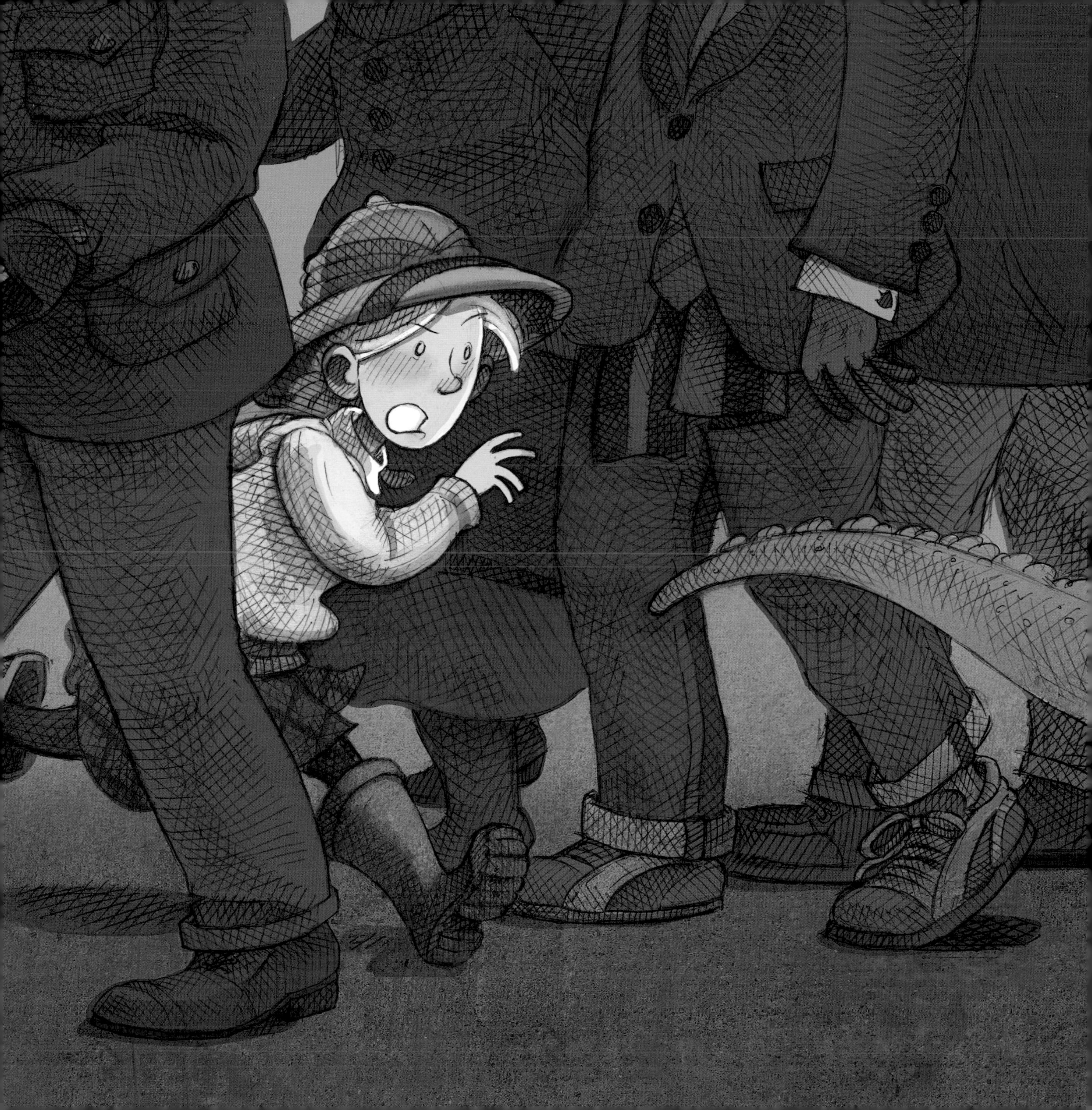

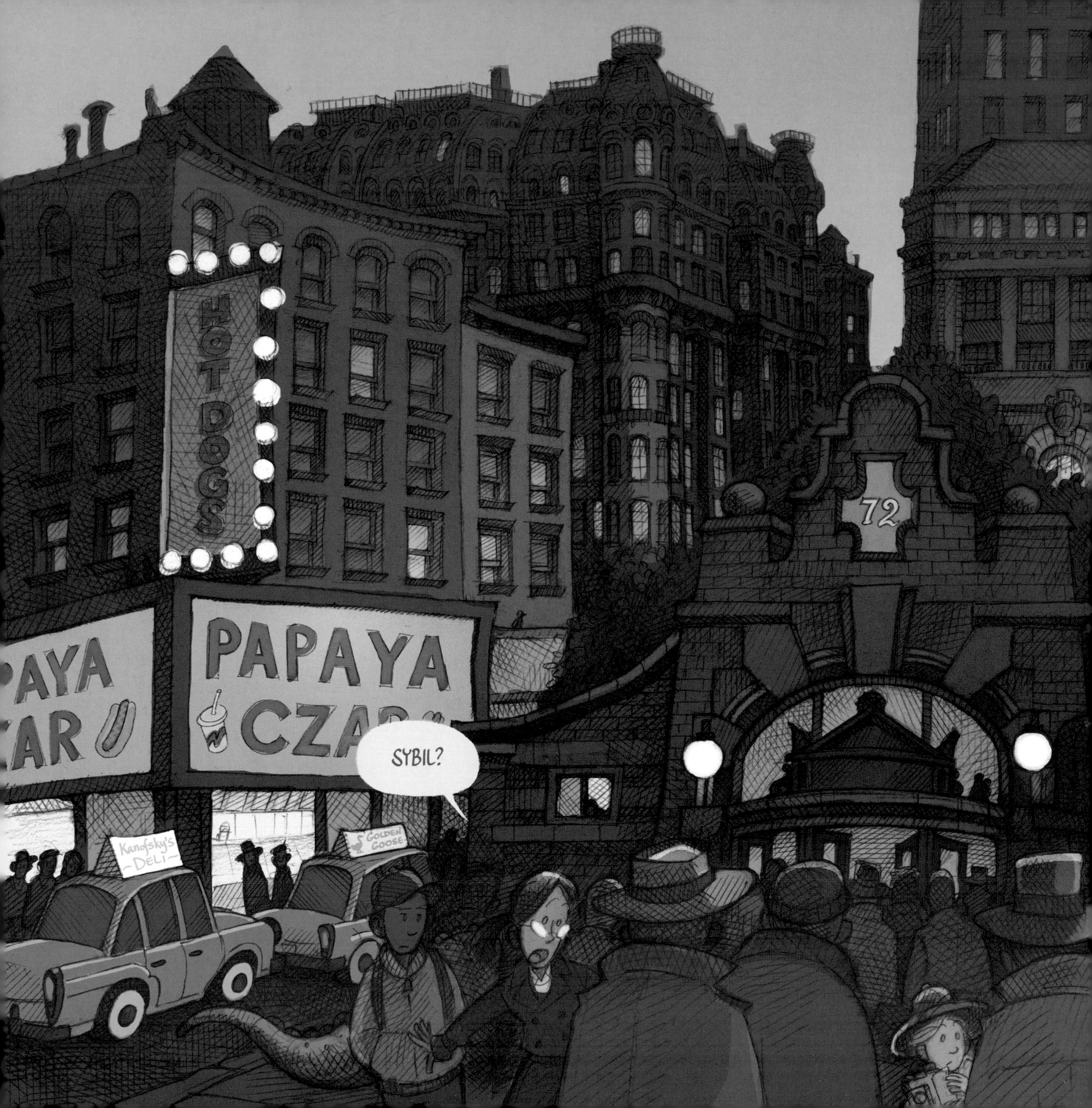
HOT DOGS
PAYA
ZAR
PAPAYA
CZAR
SYBIL?
72
Kanofsky's
DELI
GOLDEN
GOOSE

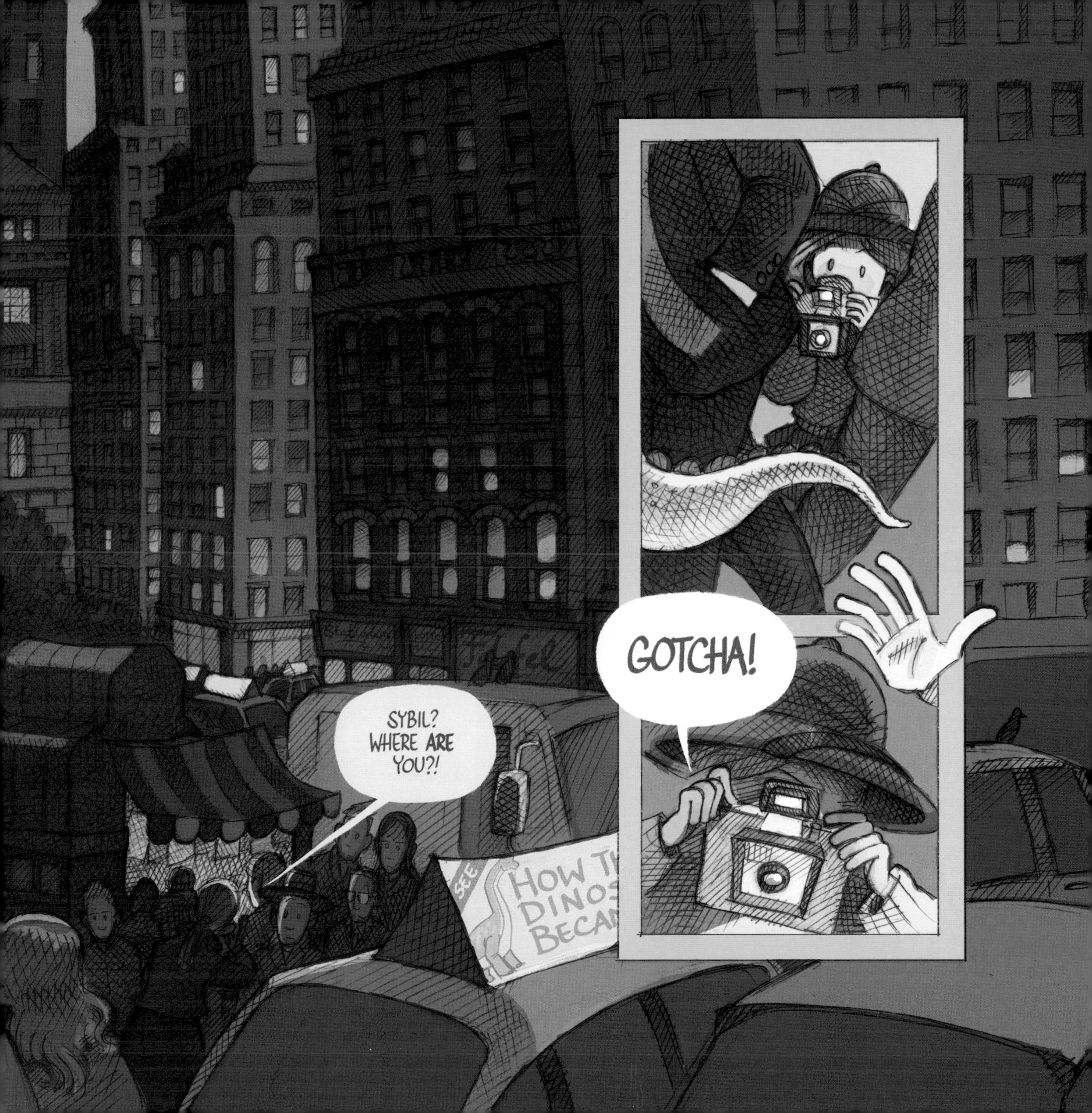
SYBIL? WHERE ARE YOU?!
GOTCHA!

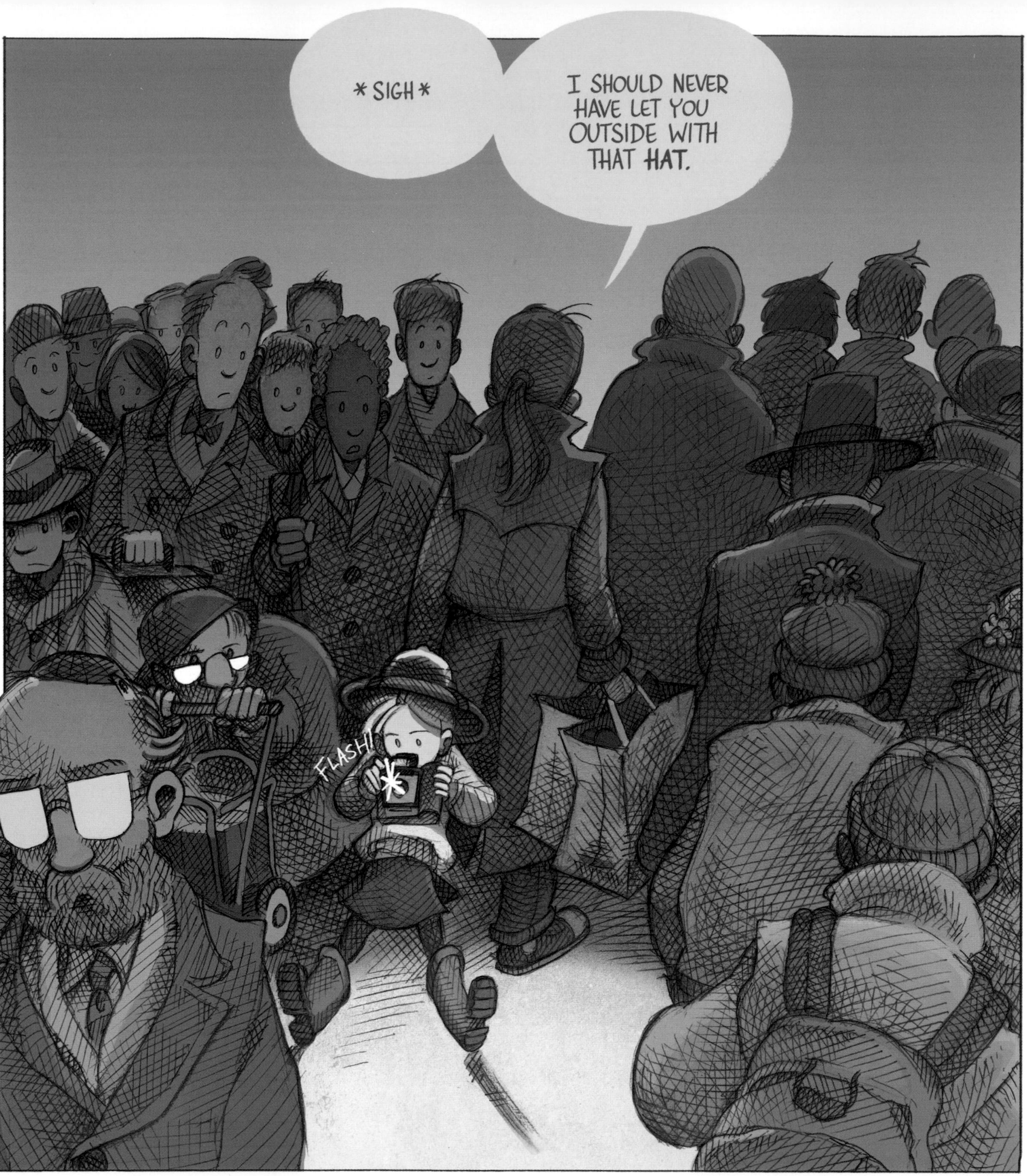
SIGH
I SHOULD NEVER HAVE LET YOU OUTSIDE WITH THAT HAT.
FLASH!

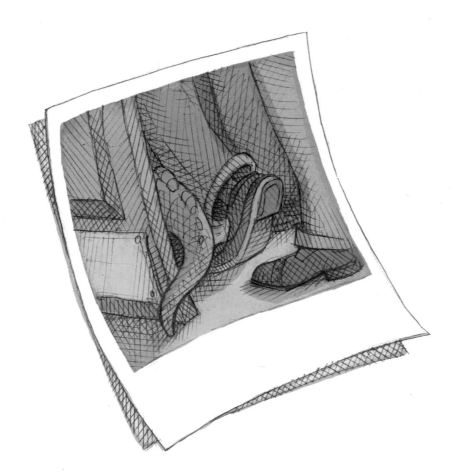

And no one noticed Bolivar at night, when he took the subway downtown to listen to music.

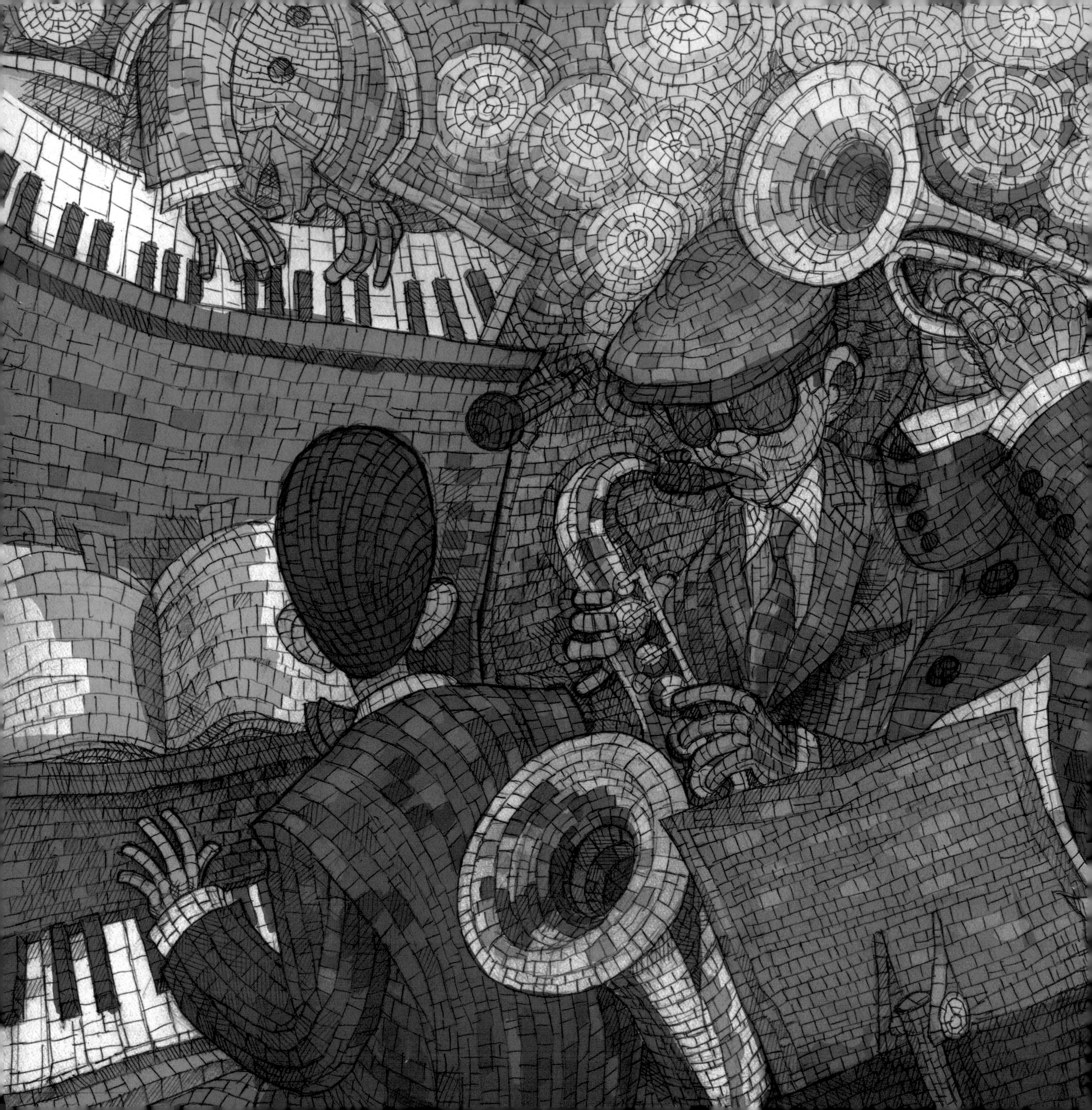

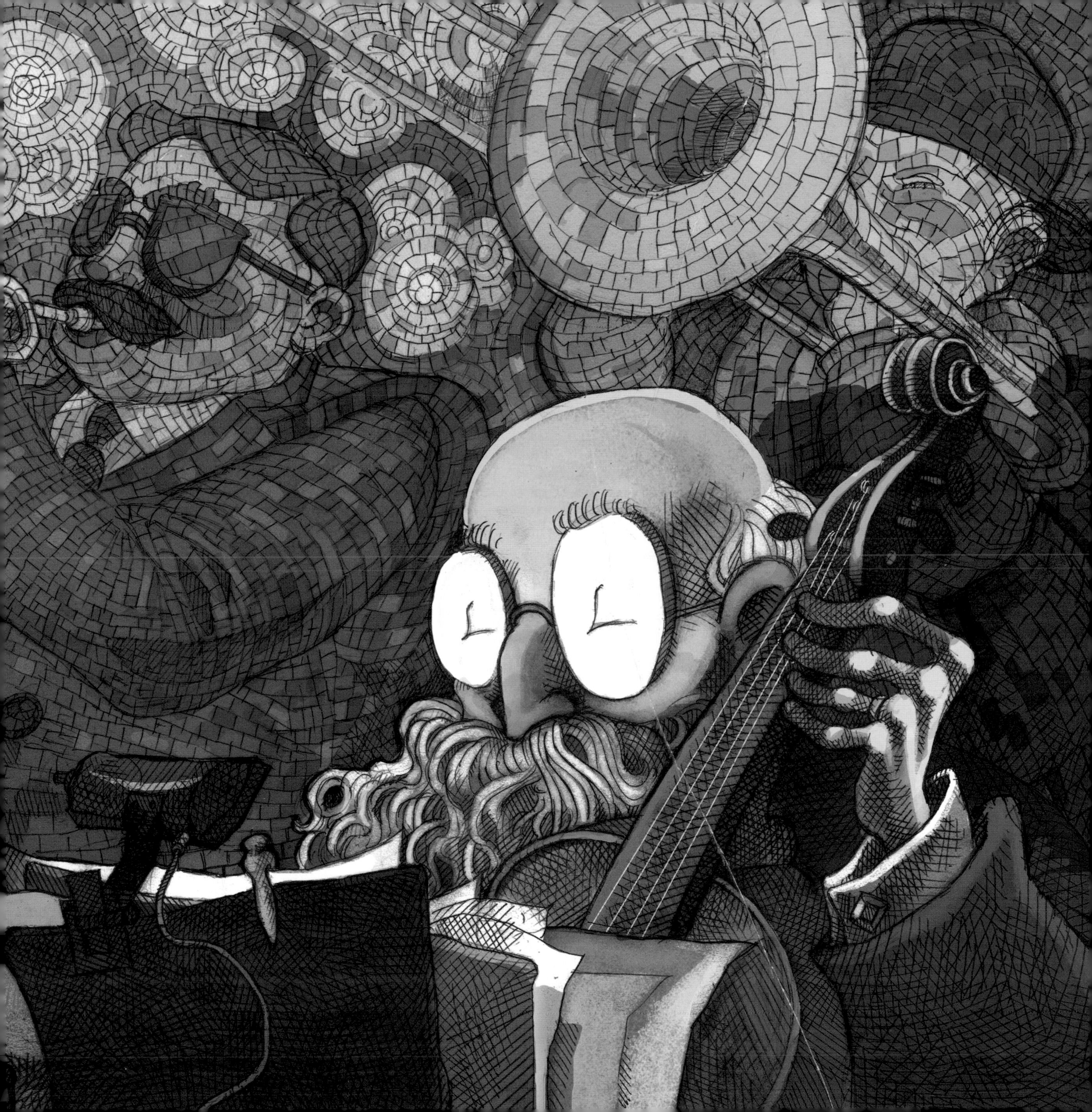

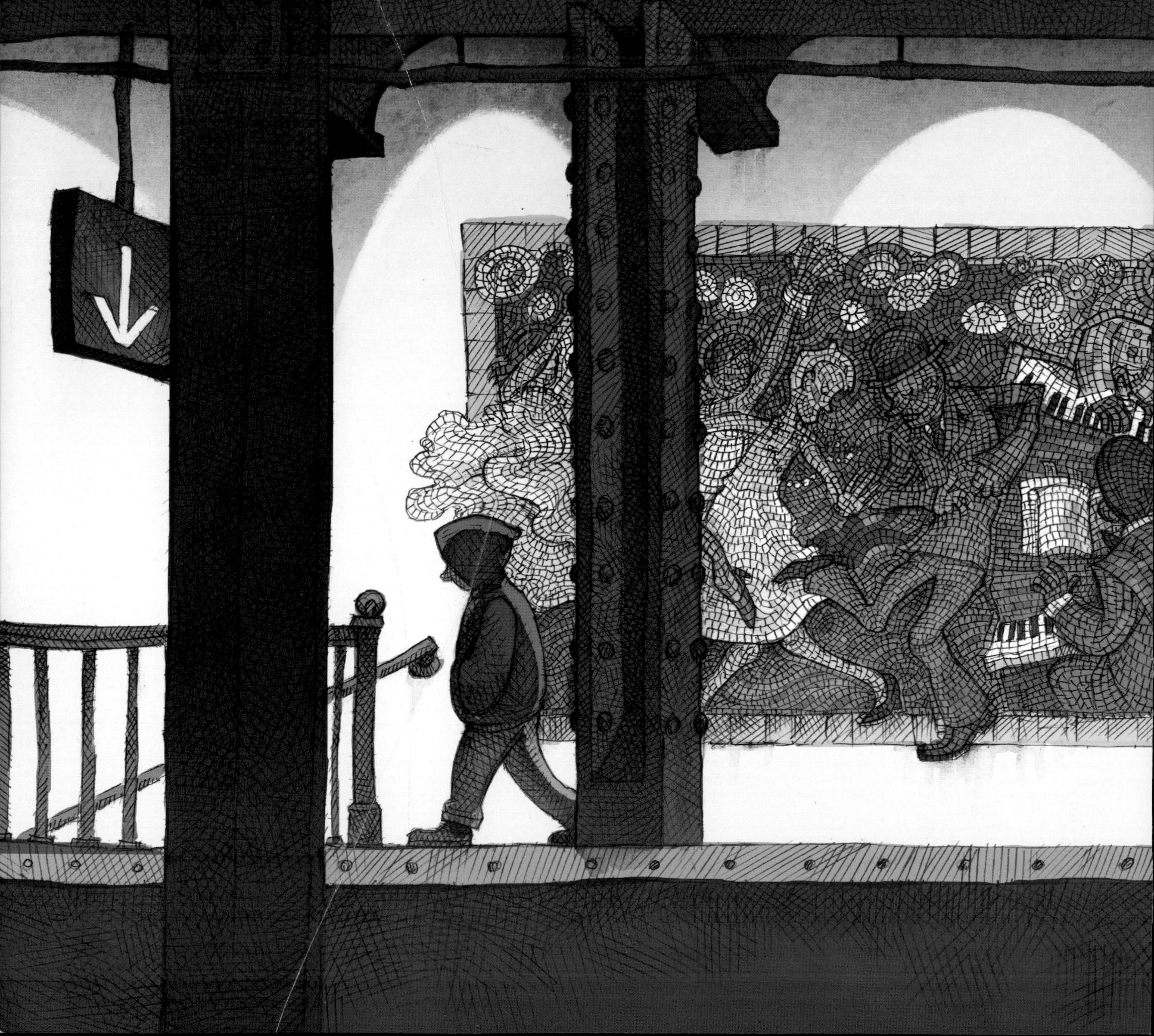

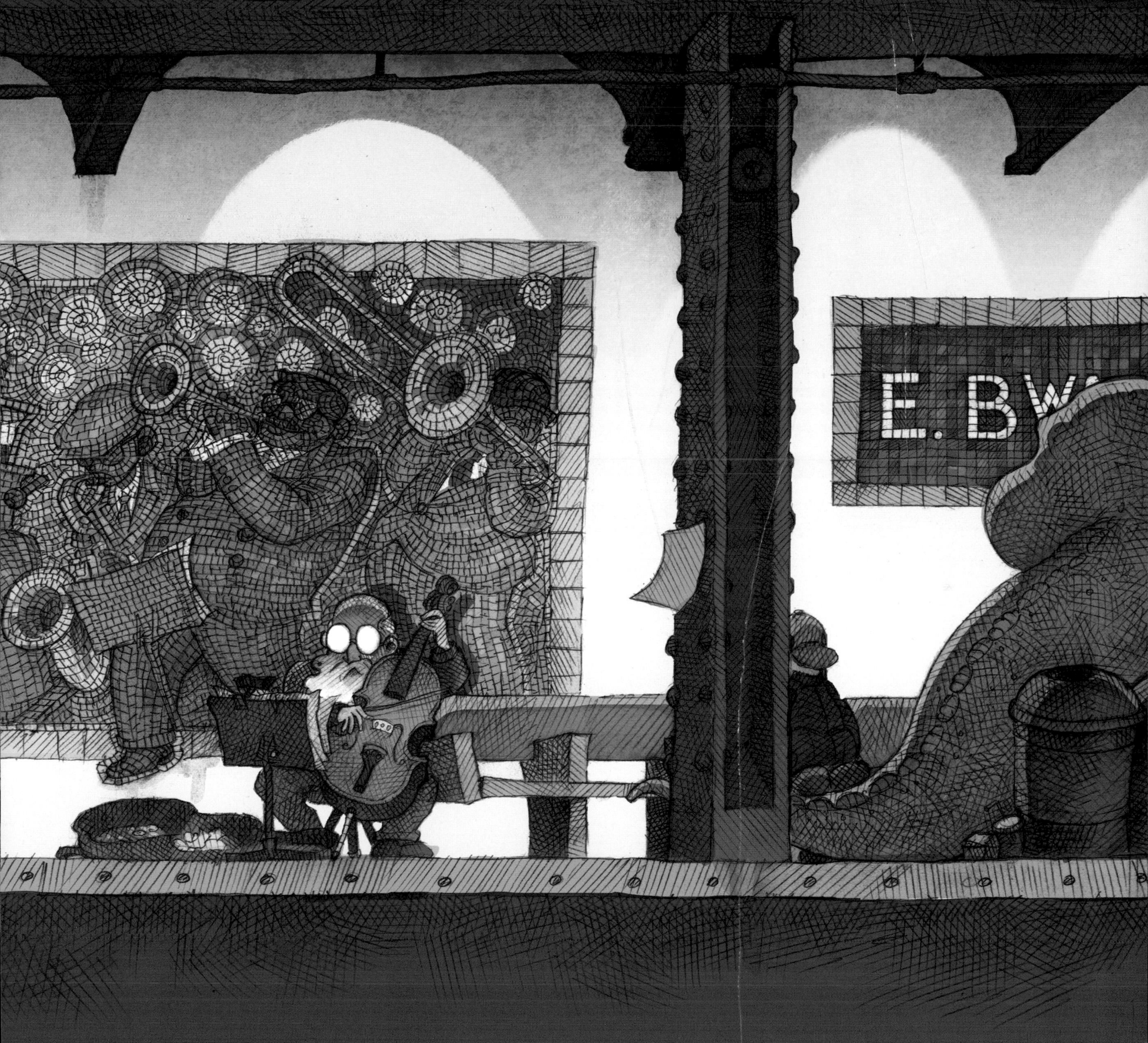
E. BW

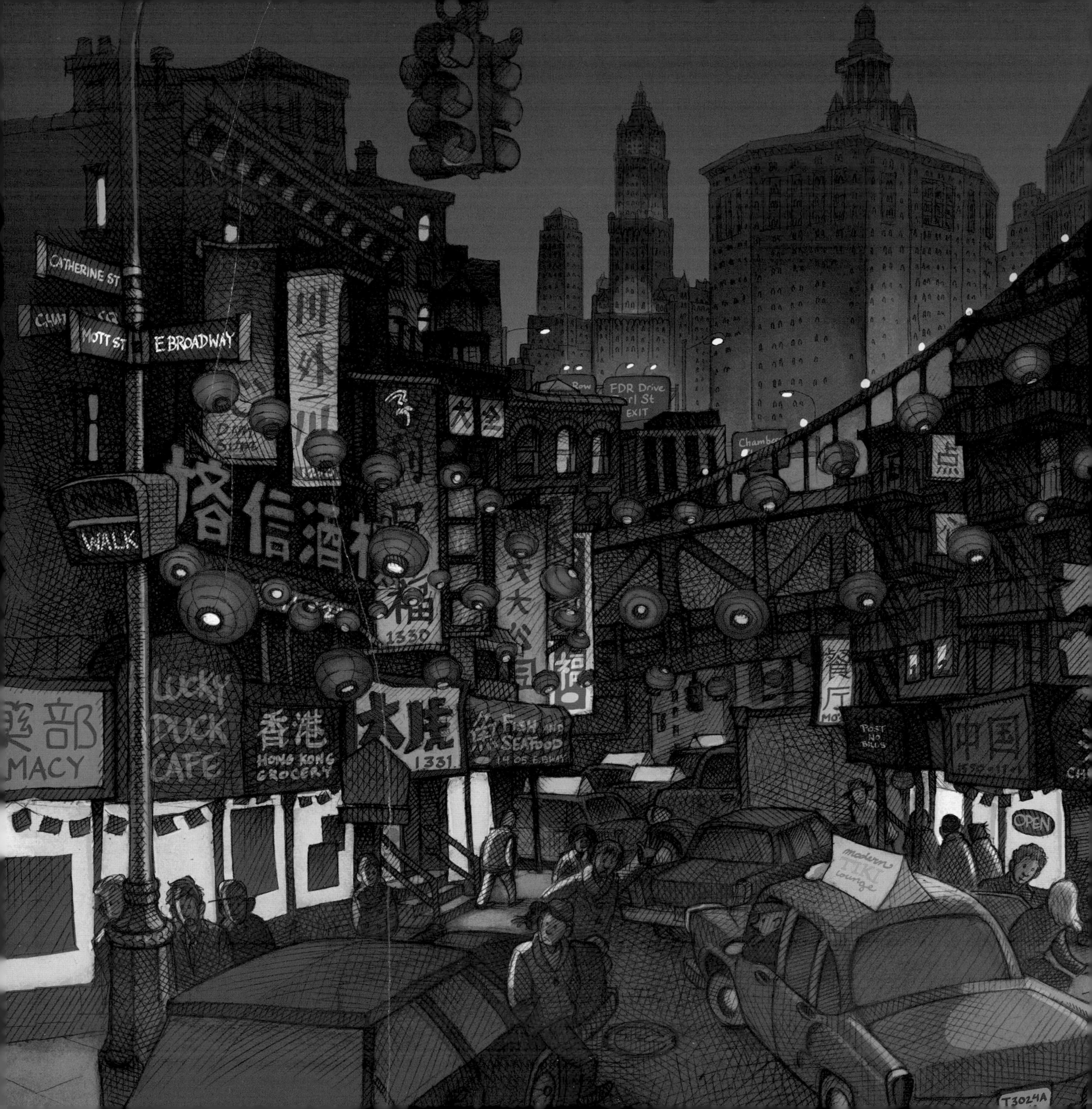
CATHERINE ST
MOTT ST
E BROADWAY
FDR Drive
EXIT
WALK
1330
LUCKY DUCK CAFE
MACY
香港
HONG KONG GROCERY
1331
FISH AND SEAFOOD
1405 E. BWAY
POST NO BILLS
OPEN
modern TIKI lounge
T3024A

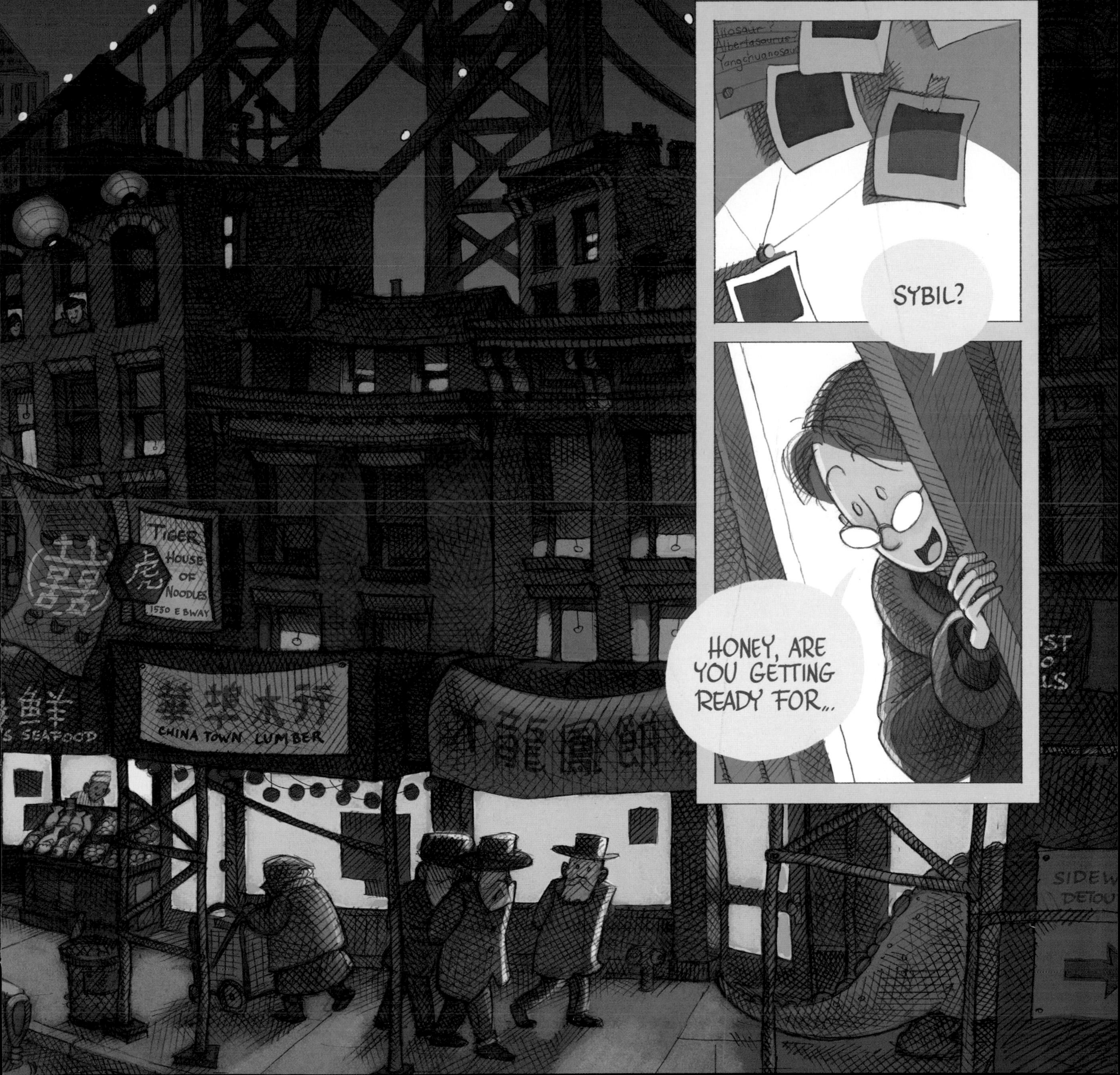

Allosaur?
Albertasaurus?
SYBIL?
HONEY, ARE YOU GETTING READY FOR...
TIGER HOUSE OF NOODLES
1550 E BWAY
CHINA TOWN LUMBER
SEAFOOD

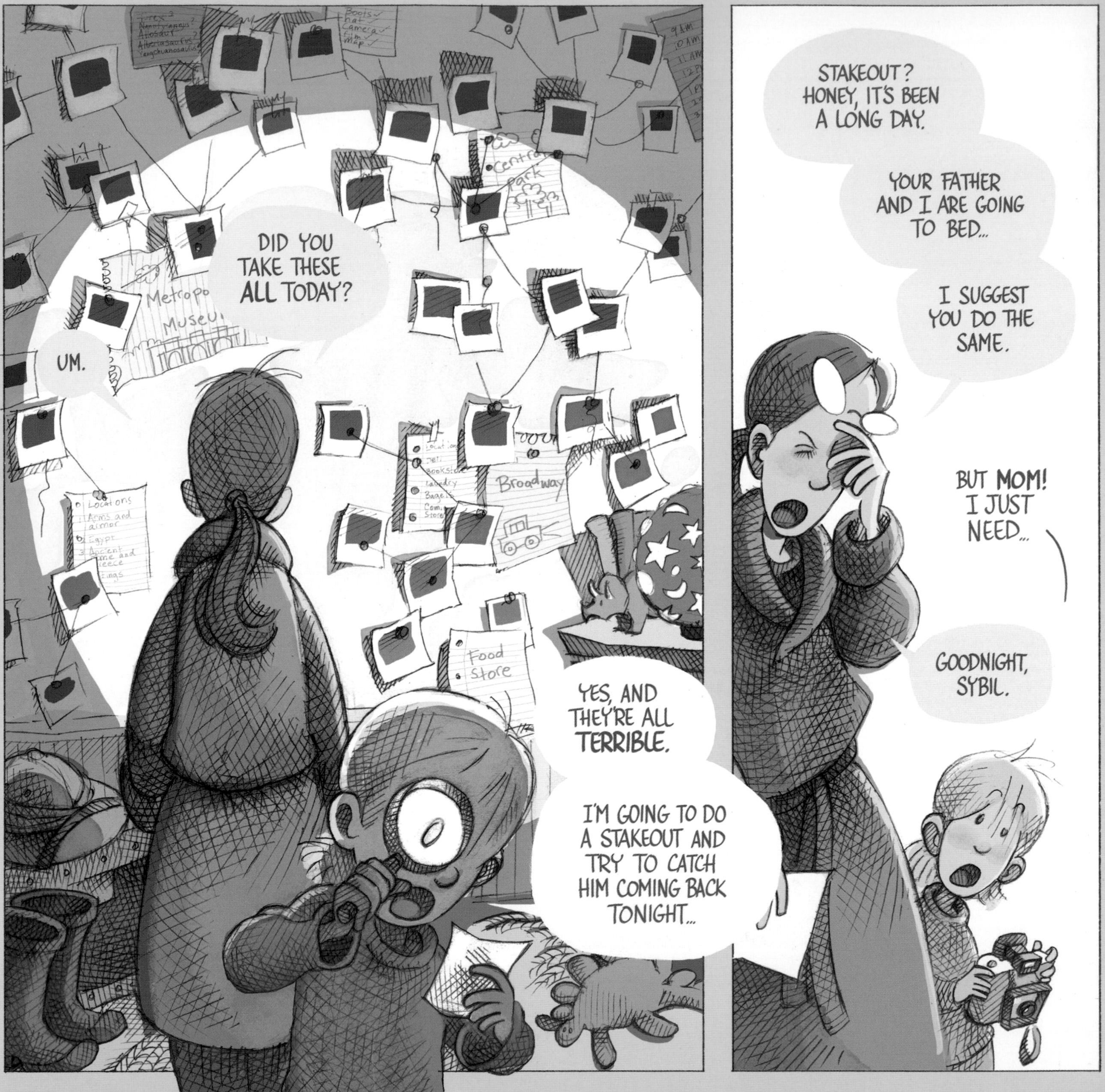

DID YOU TAKE THESE ALL TODAY?
UM.
YES, AND THEY'RE ALL TERRIBLE.
I'M GOING TO DO A STAKEOUT AND TRY TO CATCH HIM COMING BACK TONIGHT...
Broadway
Food Store
STAKEOUT? HONEY, IT'S BEEN A LONG DAY.
YOUR FATHER AND I ARE GOING TO BED...
I SUGGEST YOU DO THE SAME.
BUT MOM! I JUST NEED...
GOODNIGHT, SYBIL.

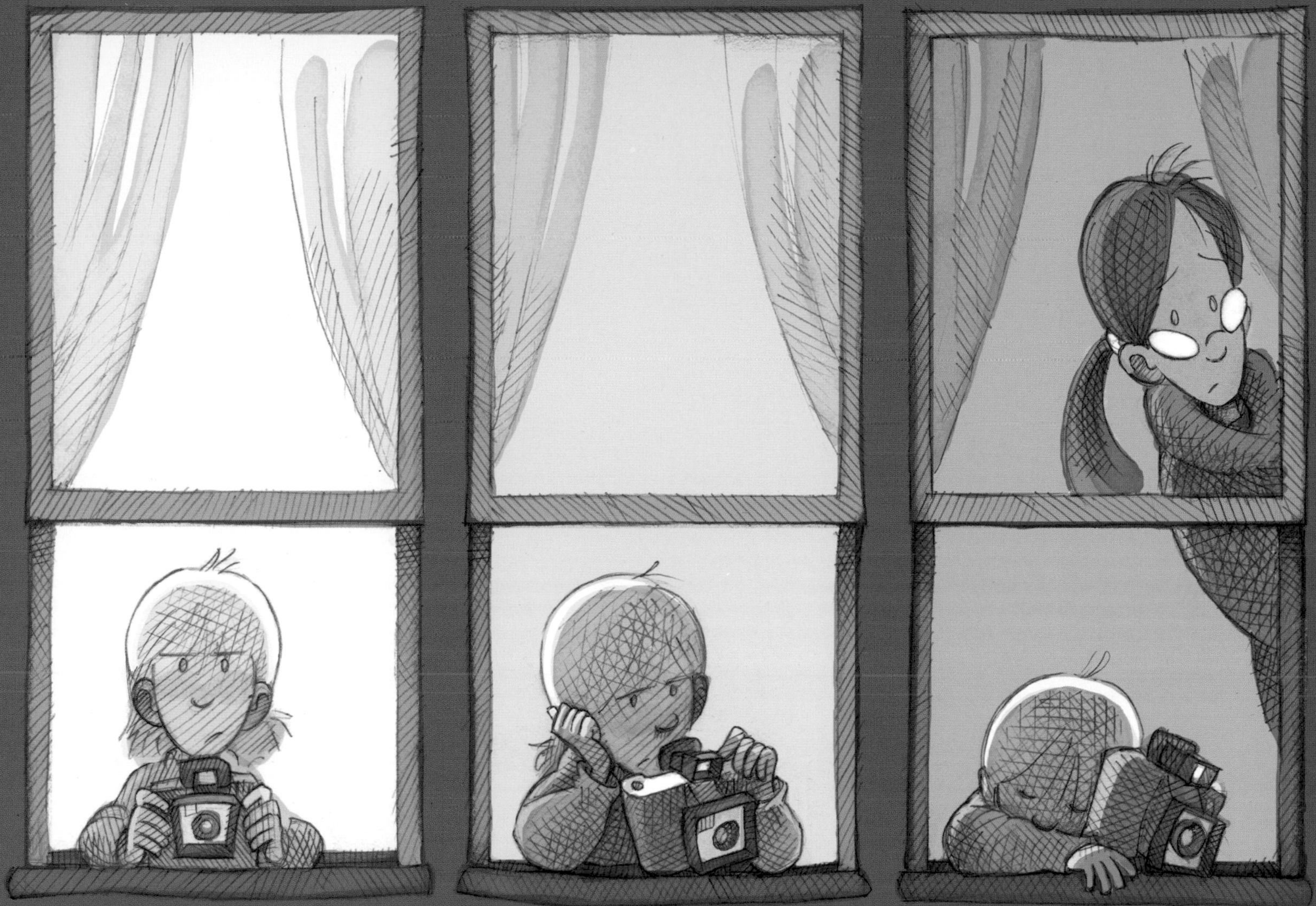

And when Bolivar returned home late at night...

...no one noticed that, either.

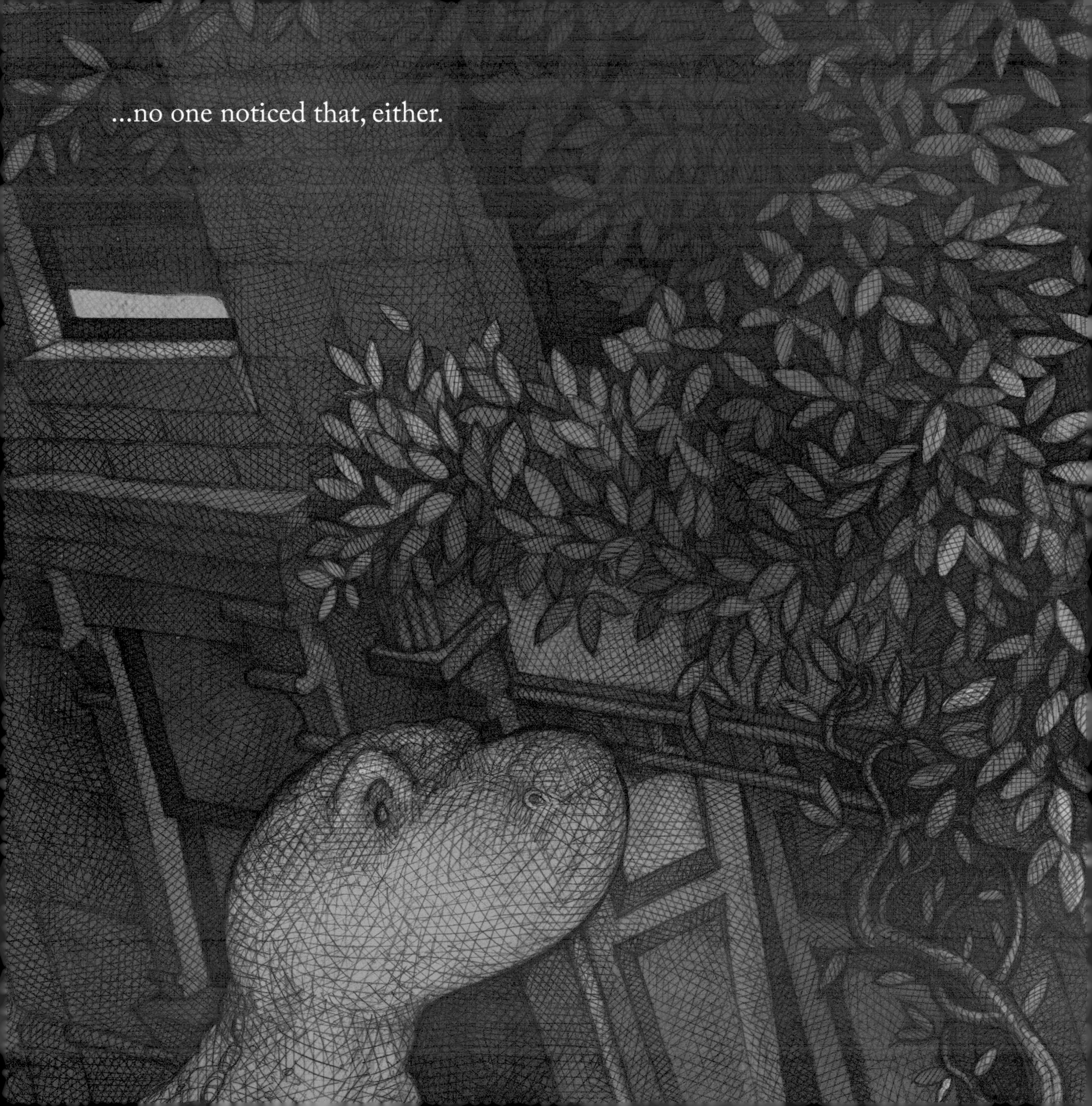

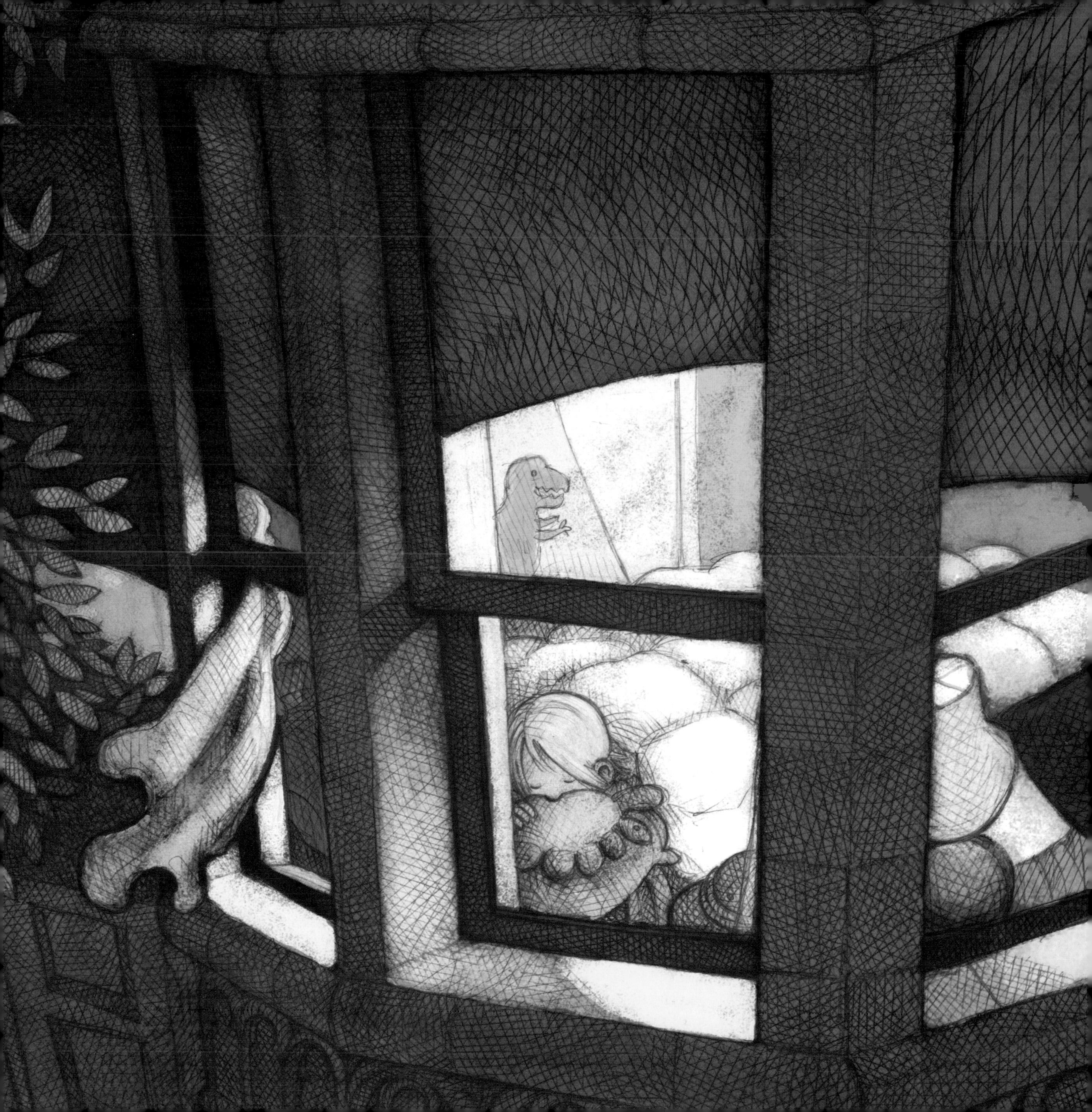

CHAPTER 3

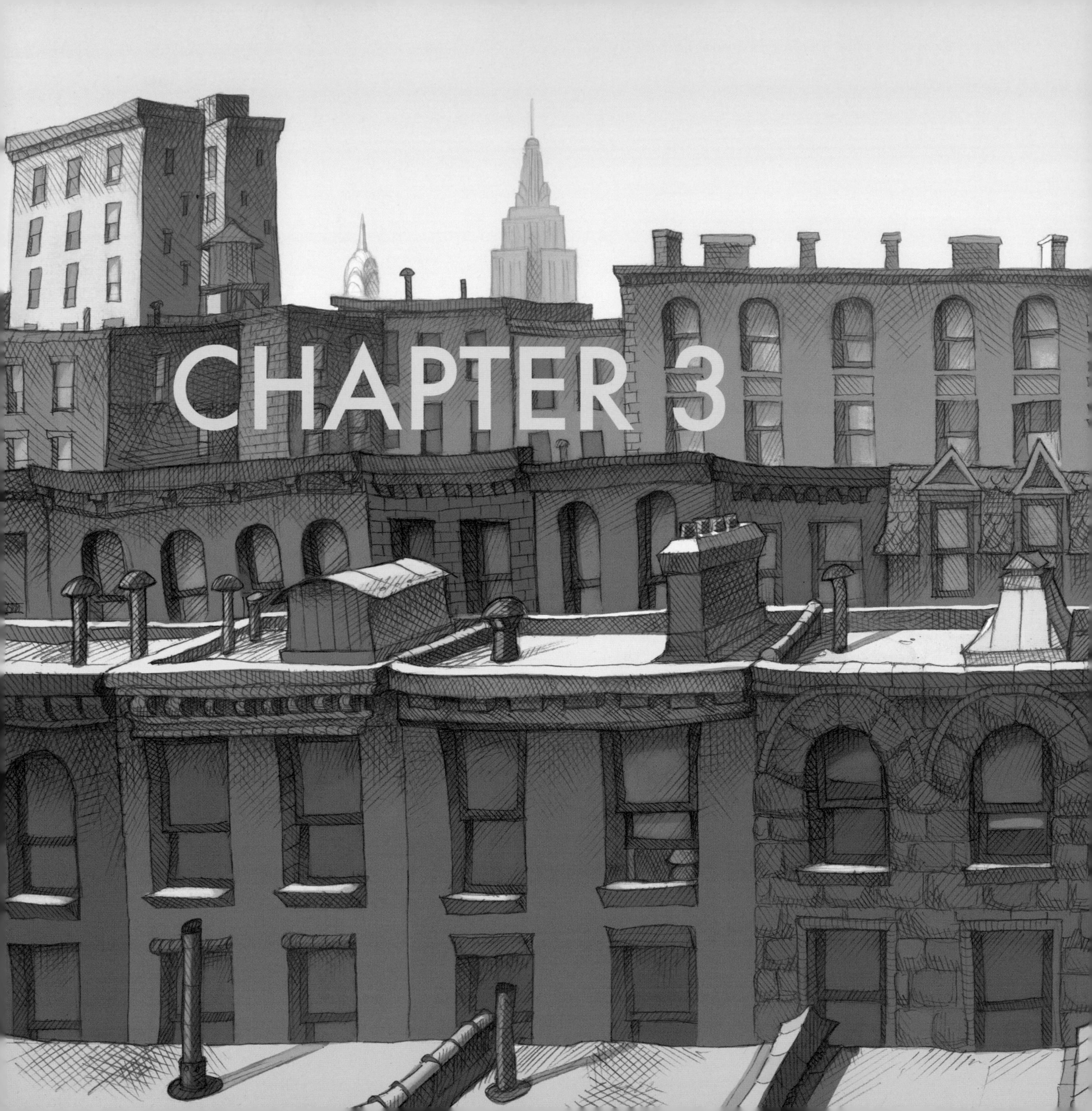

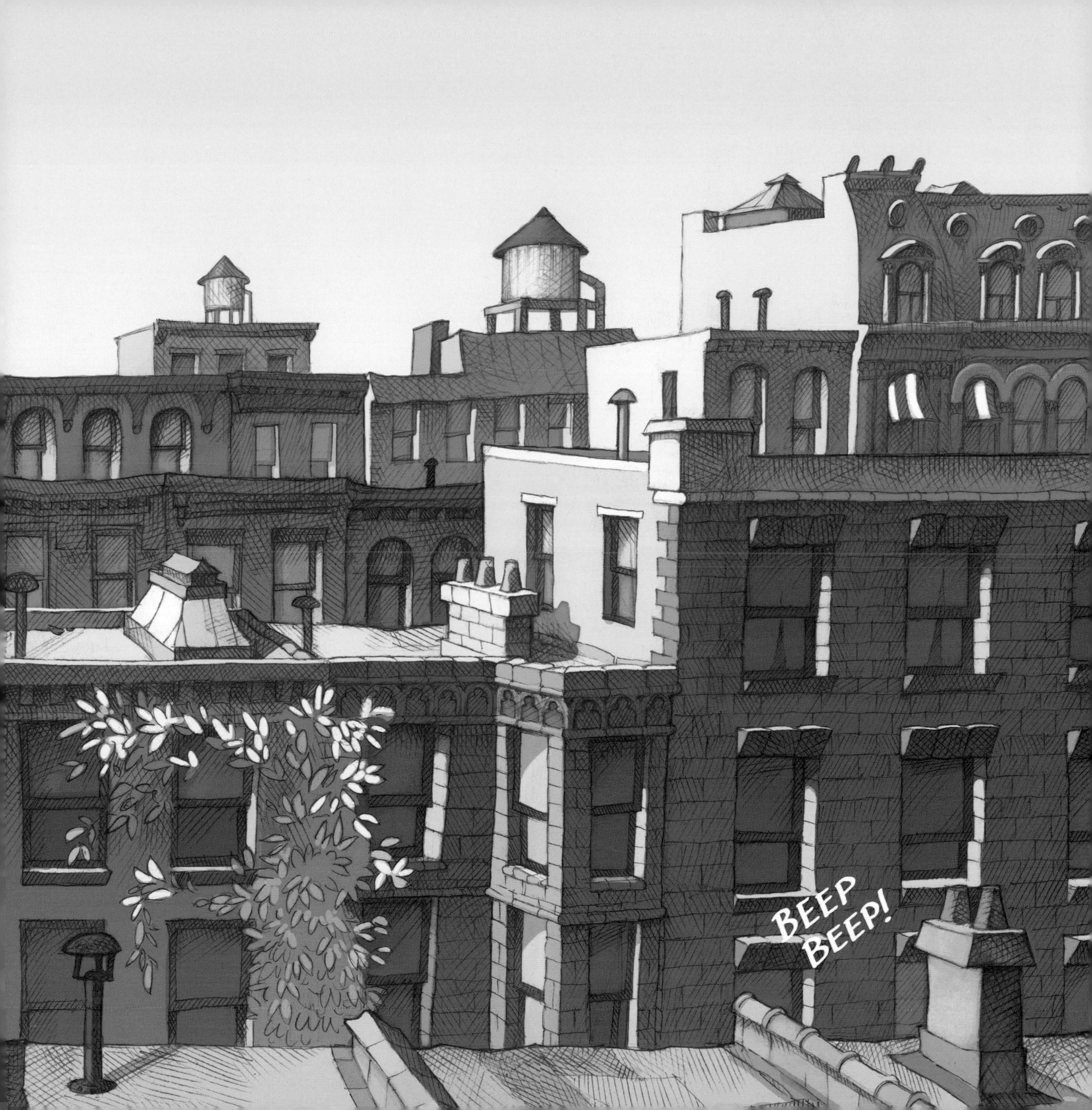
BEEP
BEEP!

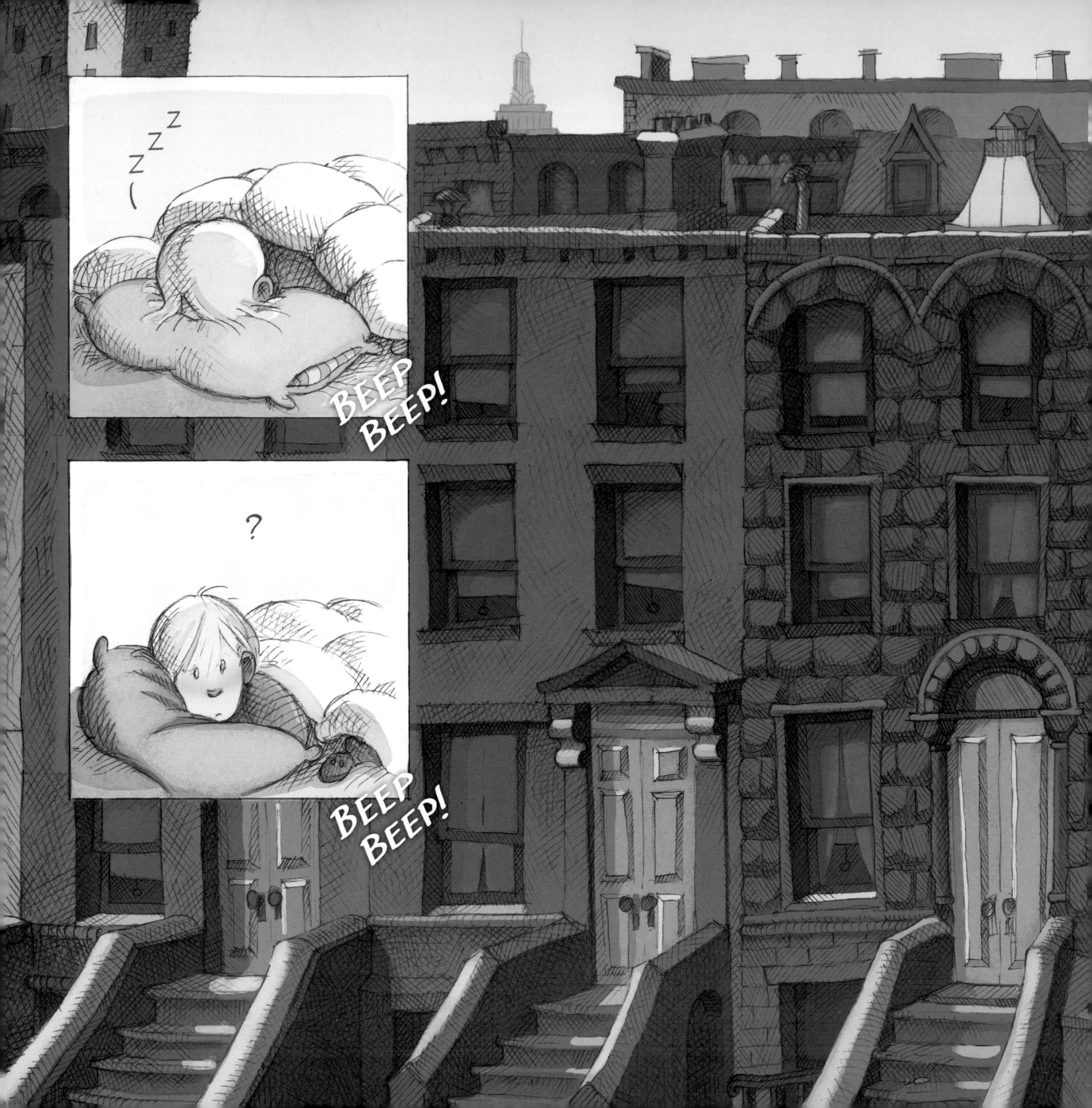
Z Z Z
BEEP BEEP!
?
BEEP BEEP!

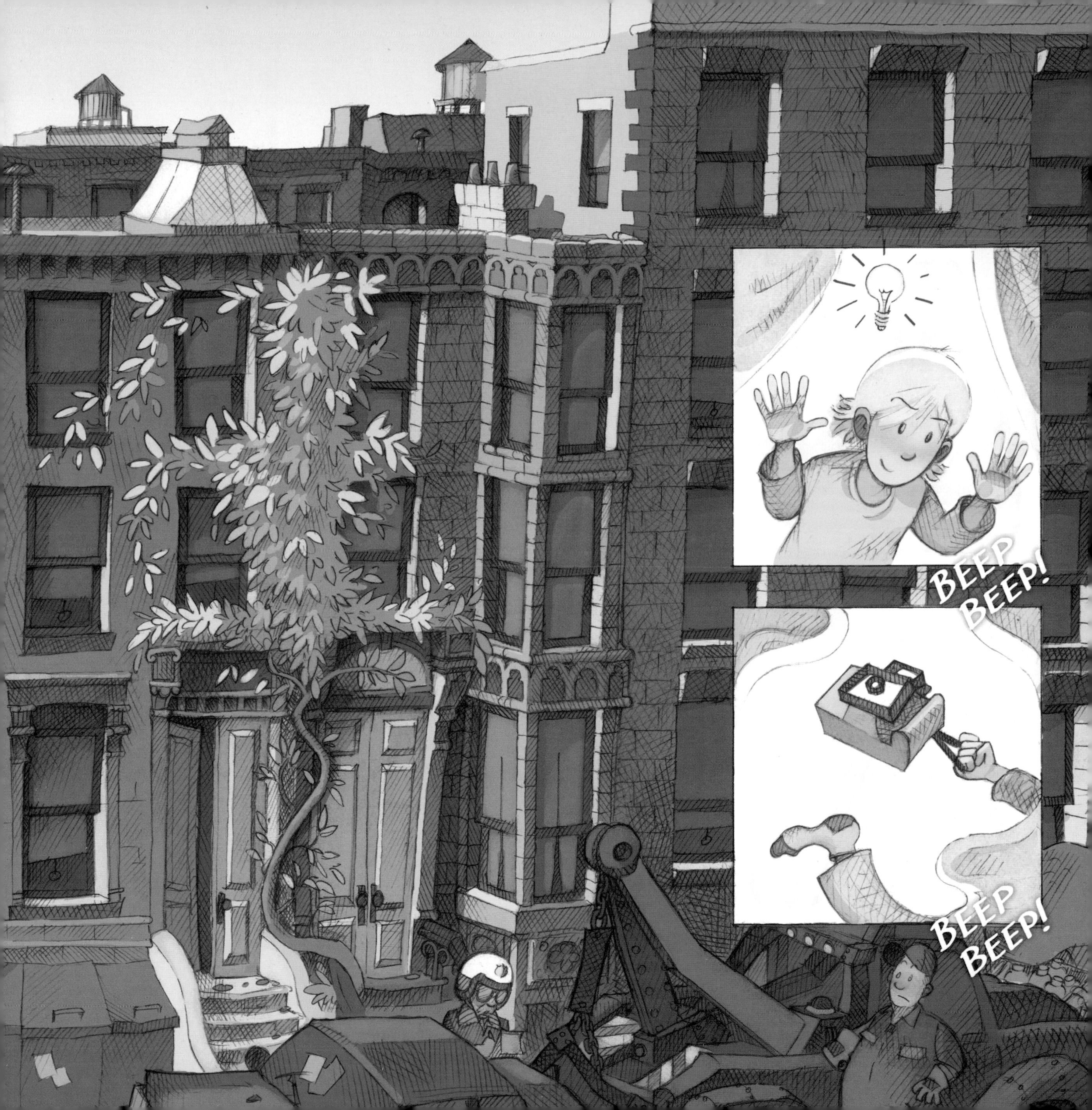
BEEP BEEP!
BEEP BEEP!

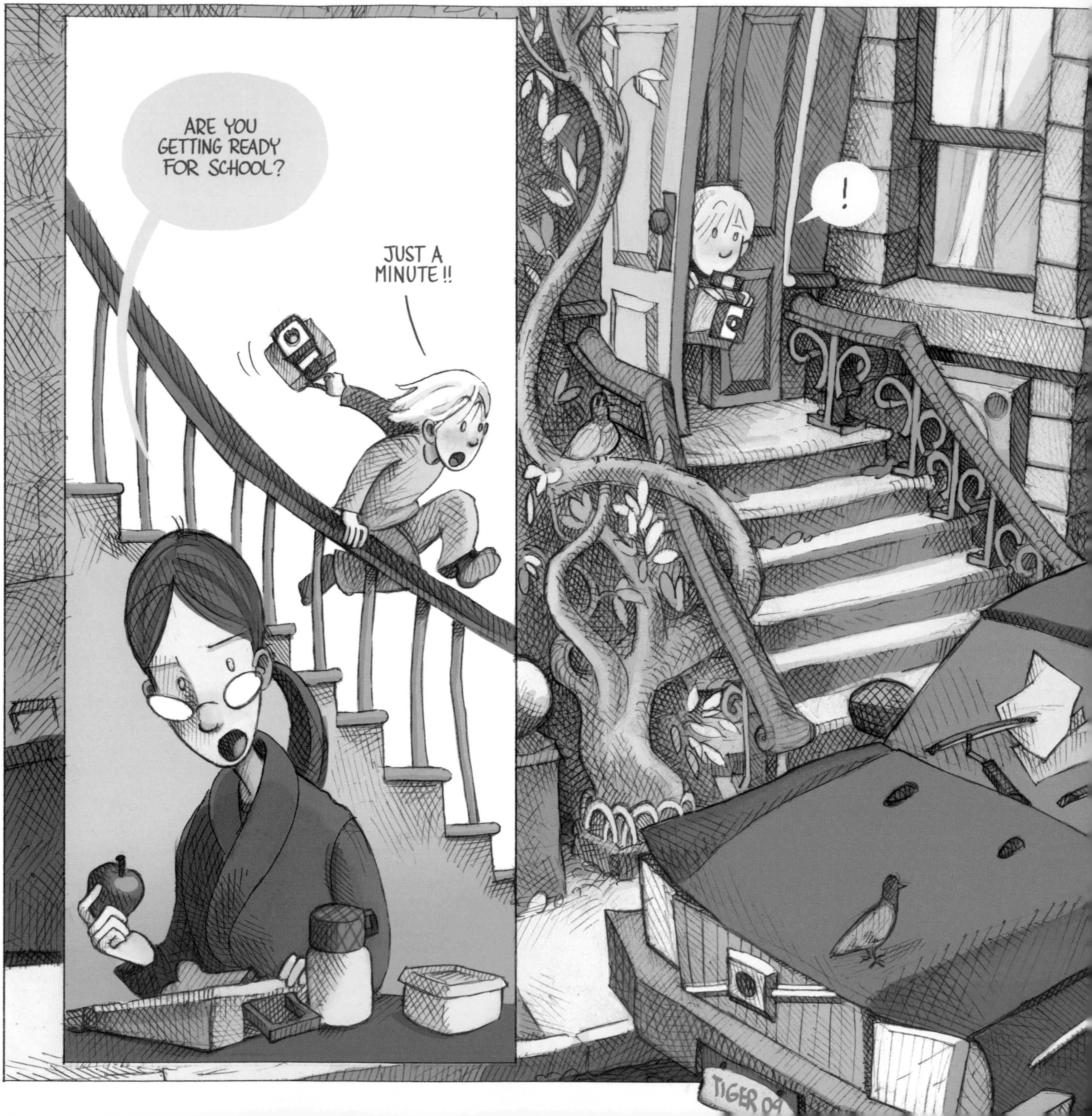
ARE YOU GETTING READY FOR SCHOOL?
JUST A MINUTE !!
!
TIGER 09

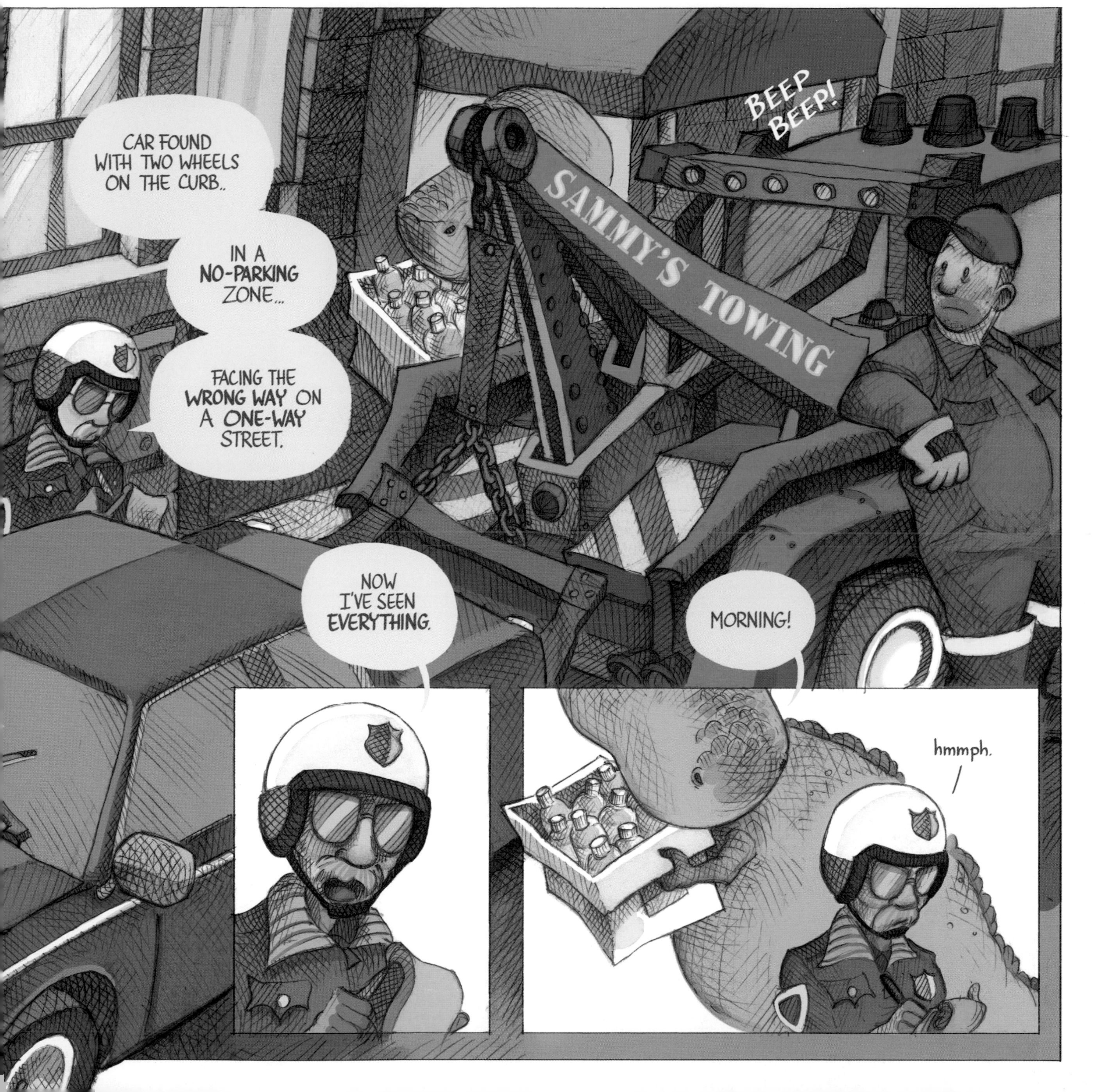
BEEP BEEP!
SAMMY'S TOWING
CAR FOUND WITH TWO WHEELS ON THE CURB..
IN A NO-PARKING ZONE...
FACING THE WRONG WAY ON A ONE-WAY STREET.
NOW I'VE SEEN EVERYTHING.
MORNING!
hmmph.

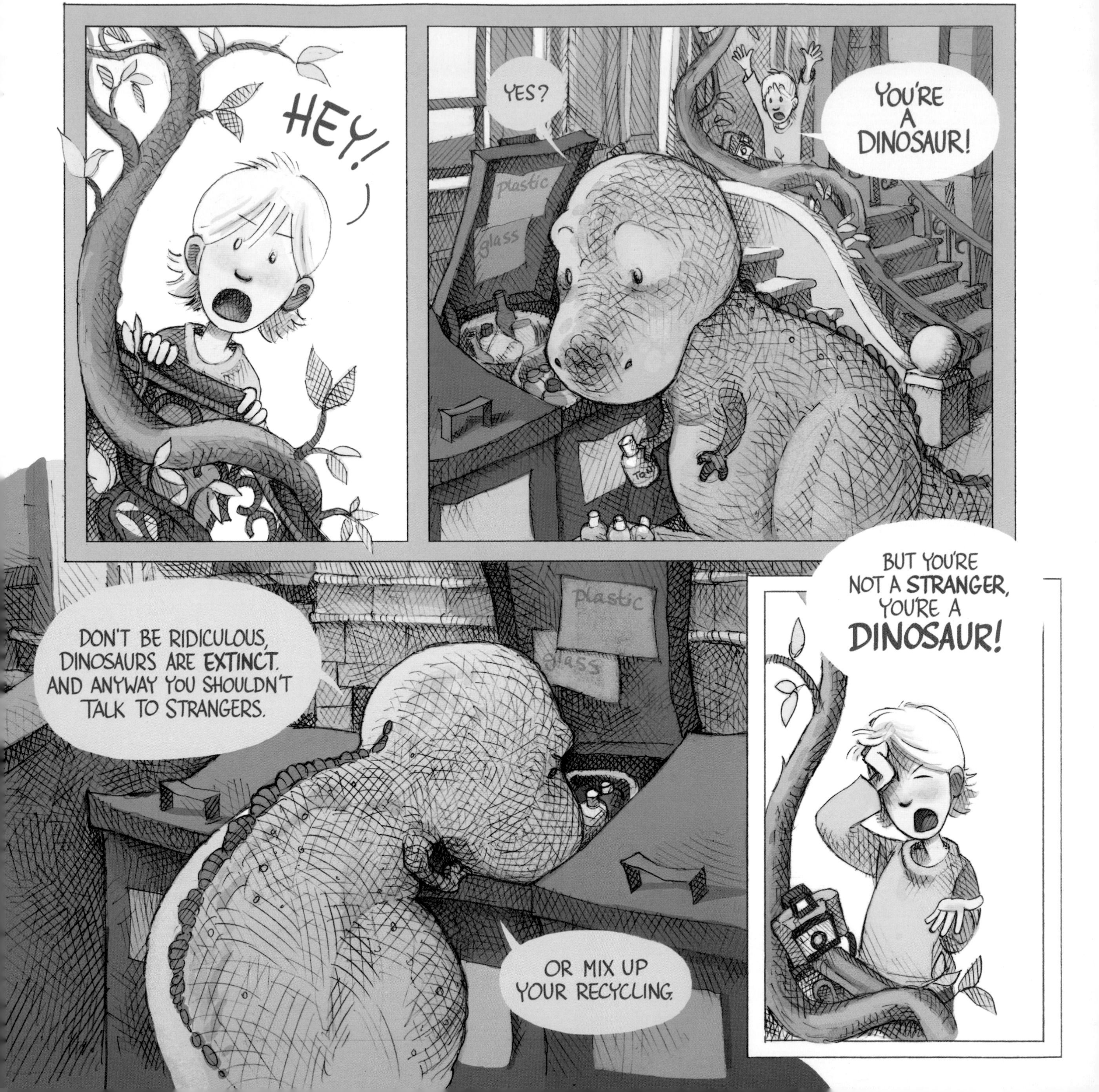
HEY!
YES?
YOU'RE A DINOSAUR!
plastic
glass
DON'T BE RIDICULOUS, DINOSAURS ARE **EXTINCT**. AND ANYWAY YOU SHOULDN'T TALK TO STRANGERS.
OR MIX UP YOUR RECYCLING.
BUT YOU'RE NOT A **STRANGER**, YOU'RE A **DINOSAUR!**

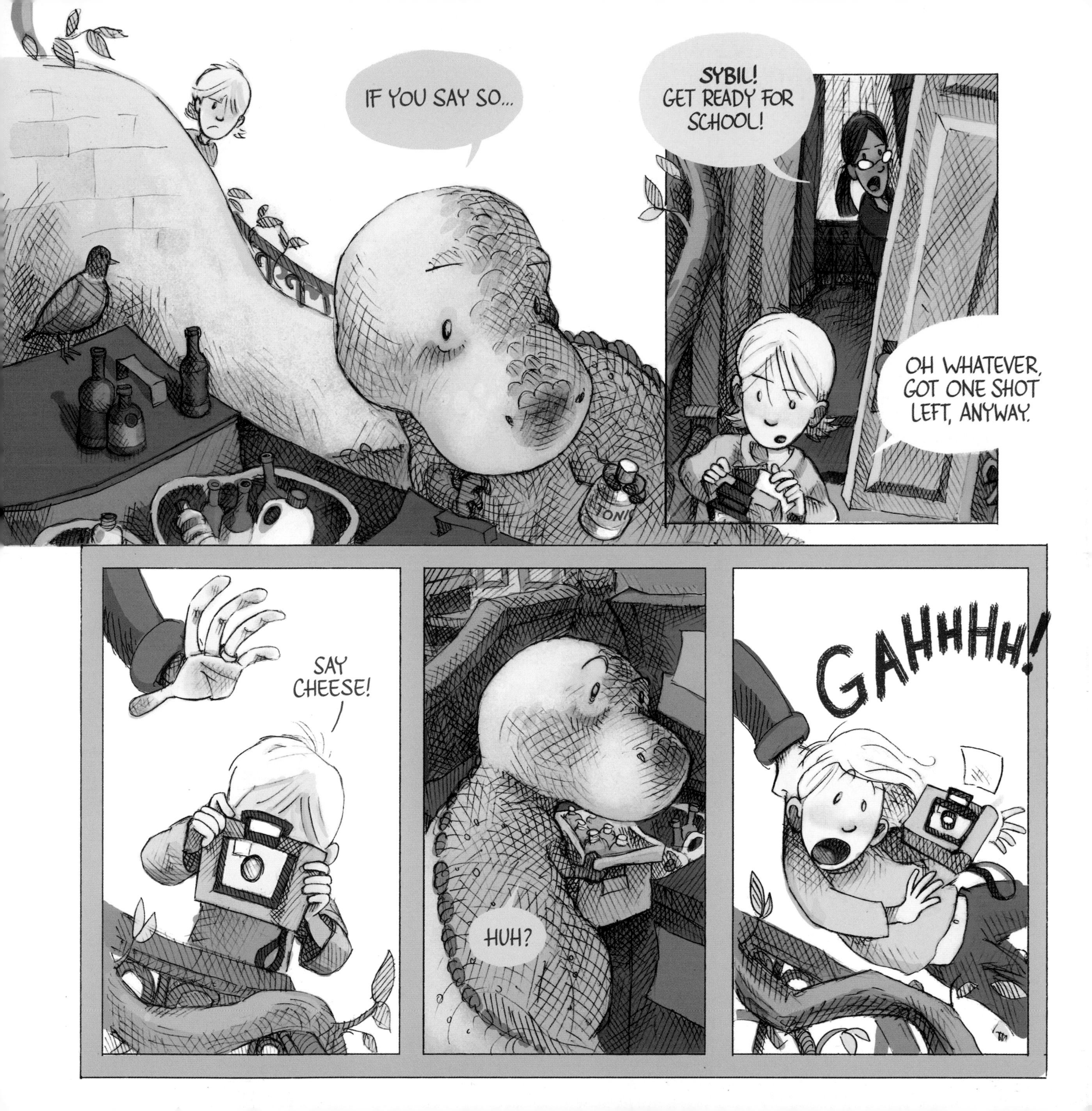
IF YOU SAY SO...
SYBIL! GET READY FOR SCHOOL!
OH WHATEVER, GOT ONE SHOT LEFT, ANYWAY.
TONIC
SAY CHEESE!
HUH?
GAHHHH!

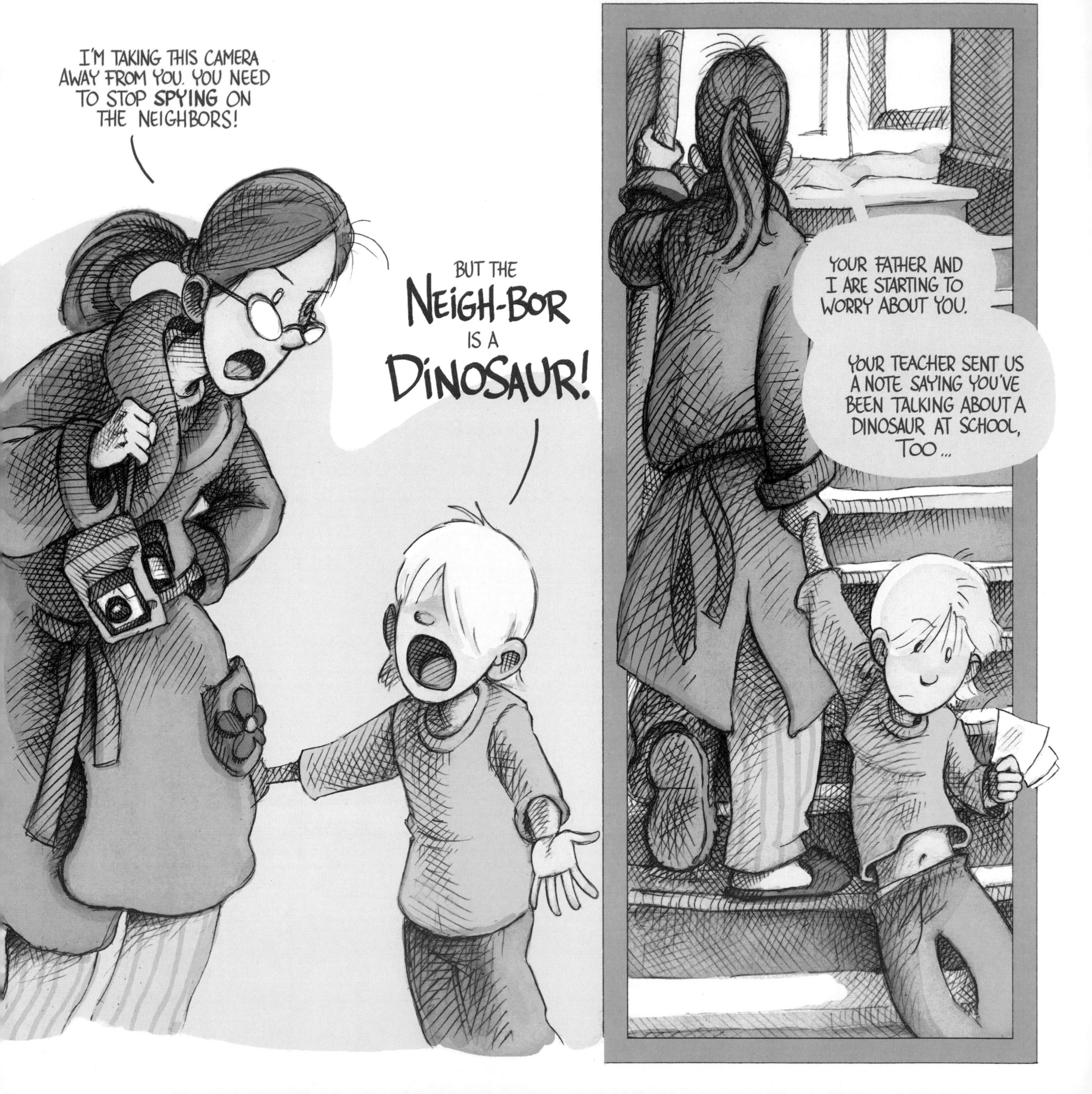
I'M TAKING THIS CAMERA AWAY FROM YOU. YOU NEED TO STOP **SPYING** ON THE NEIGHBORS!
BUT THE NEIGH-BOR IS A DINOSAUR!
YOUR FATHER AND I ARE STARTING TO WORRY ABOUT YOU.
YOUR TEACHER SENT US A NOTE SAYING YOU'VE BEEN TALKING ABOUT A DINOSAUR AT SCHOOL, TOO...

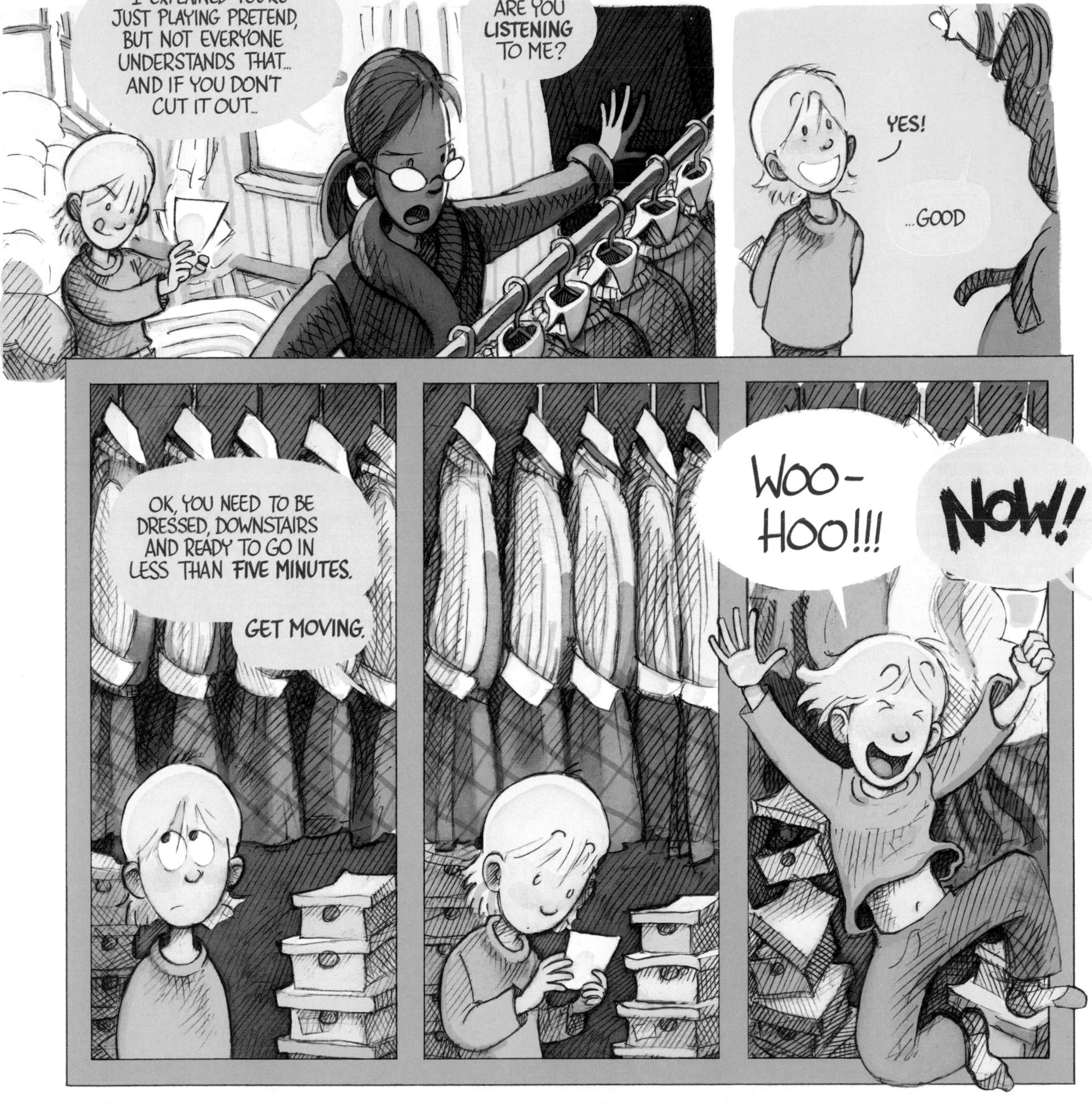
I EXPLAINED YOU'RE JUST PLAYING PRETEND, BUT NOT EVERYONE UNDERSTANDS THAT... AND IF YOU DON'T CUT IT OUT...
ARE YOU LISTENING TO ME?
YES!
...GOOD
OK, YOU NEED TO BE DRESSED, DOWNSTAIRS AND READY TO GO IN LESS THAN FIVE MINUTES.
GET MOVING.
WOO-HOO!!!
NOW!

One morning, Bolivar realized he was having an unusual day. First, he received a parking ticket.

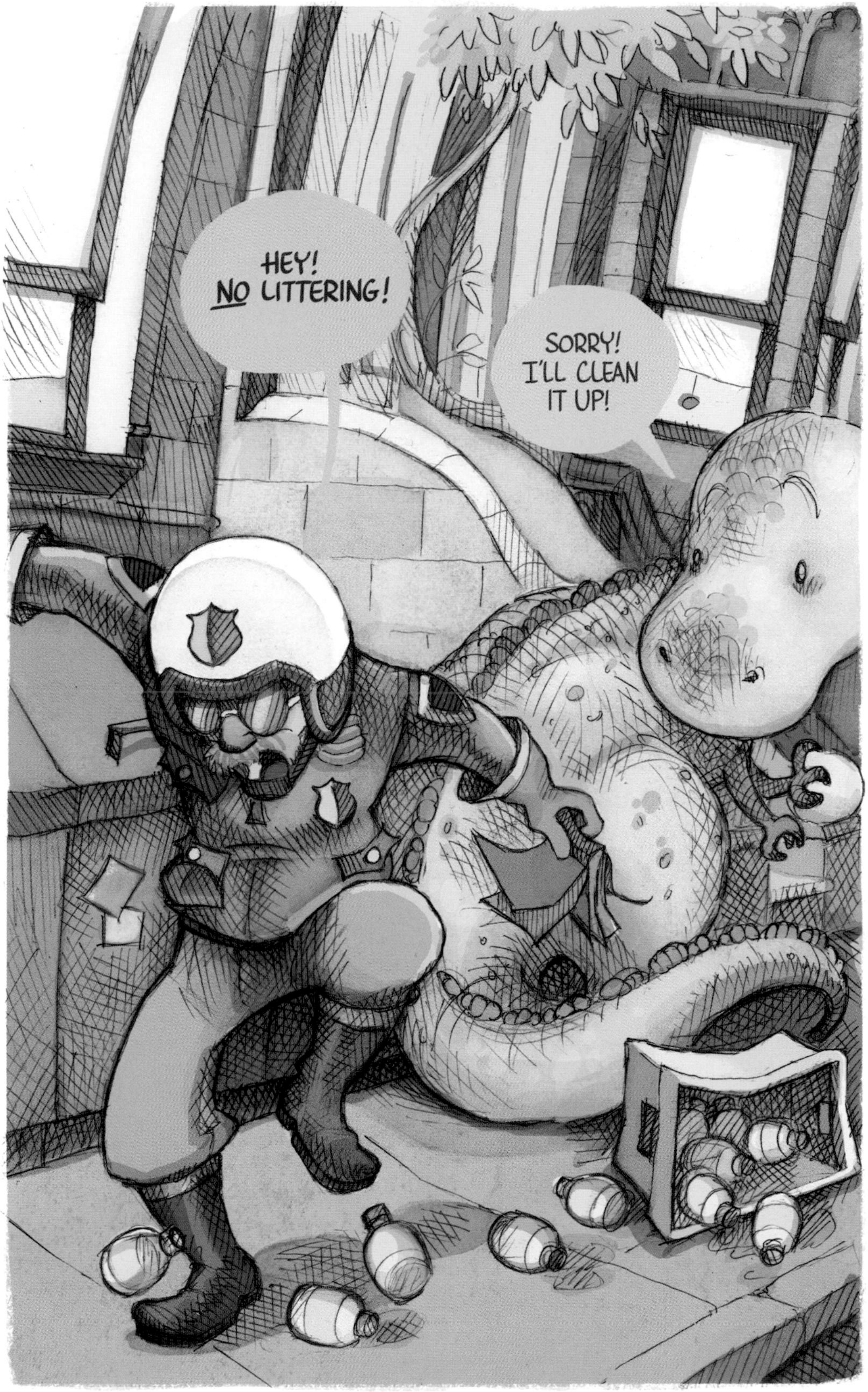
HEY! NO LITTERING!
SORRY! I'LL CLEAN IT UP!

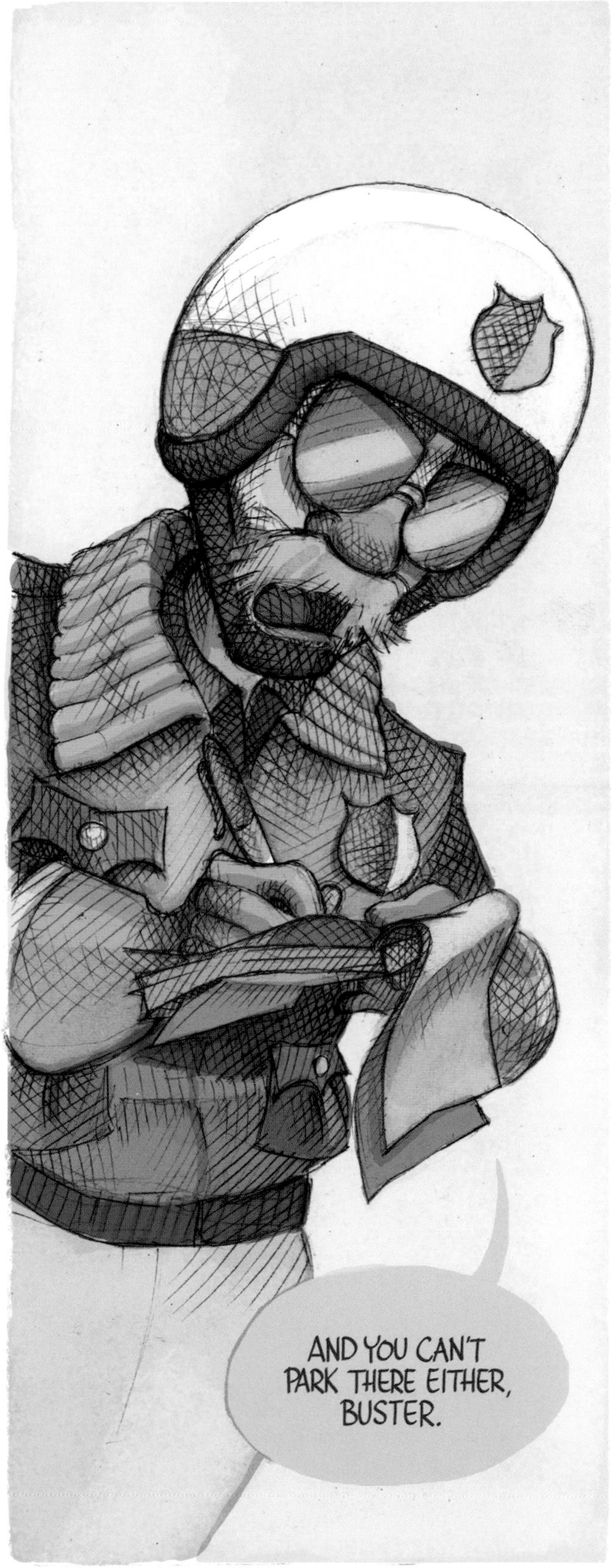
AND YOU CAN'T PARK THERE EITHER, BUSTER.

The police officer had been so busy ticketing cars, he didn't notice that Bolivar was not a car, but a dinosaur.

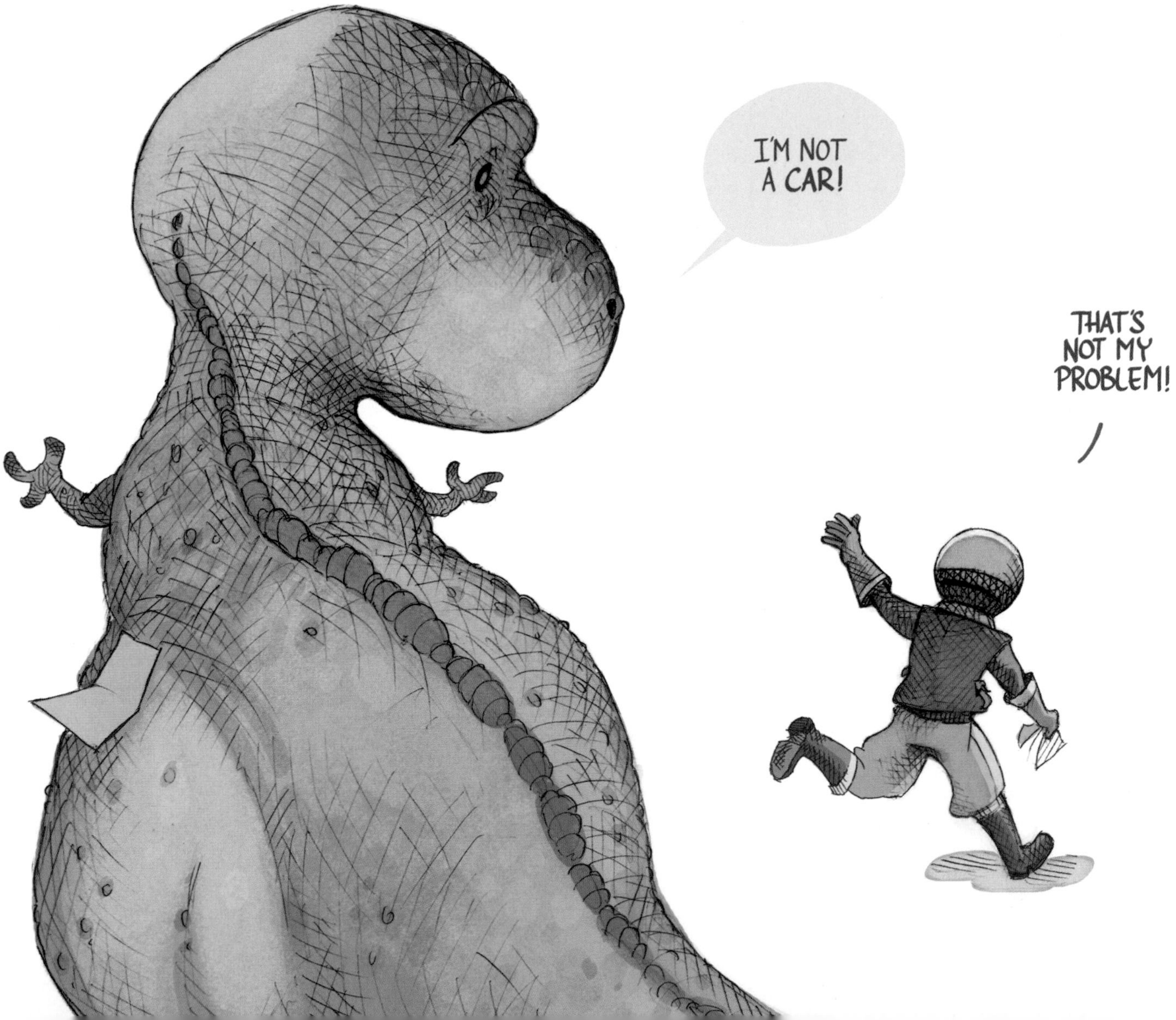
I'M NOT A CAR!
THAT'S NOT MY PROBLEM!

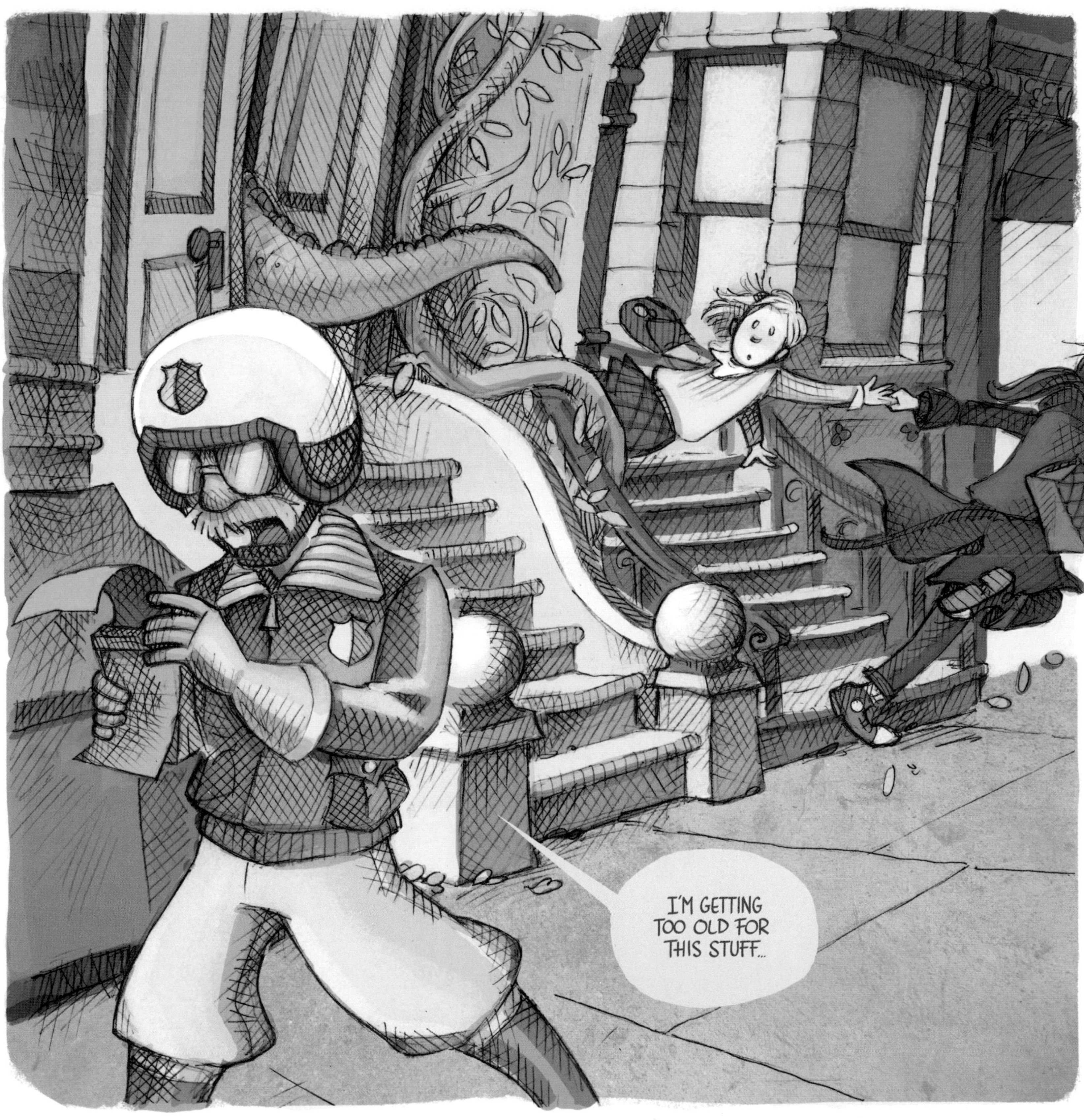
I'M GETTING TOO OLD FOR THIS STUFF...

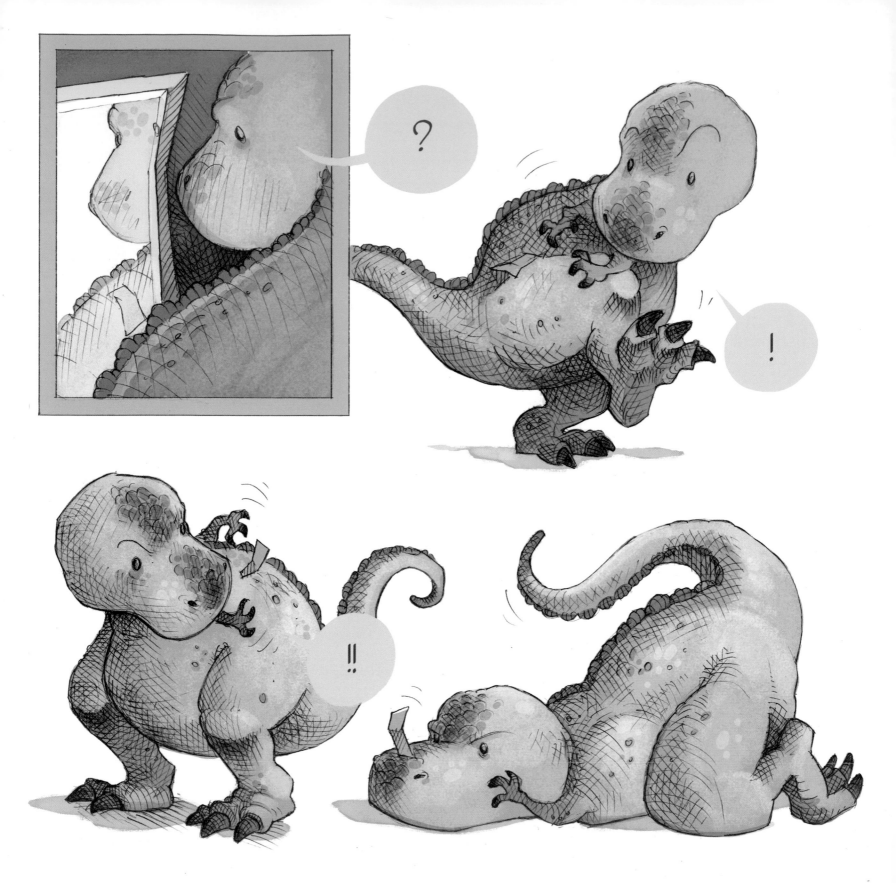

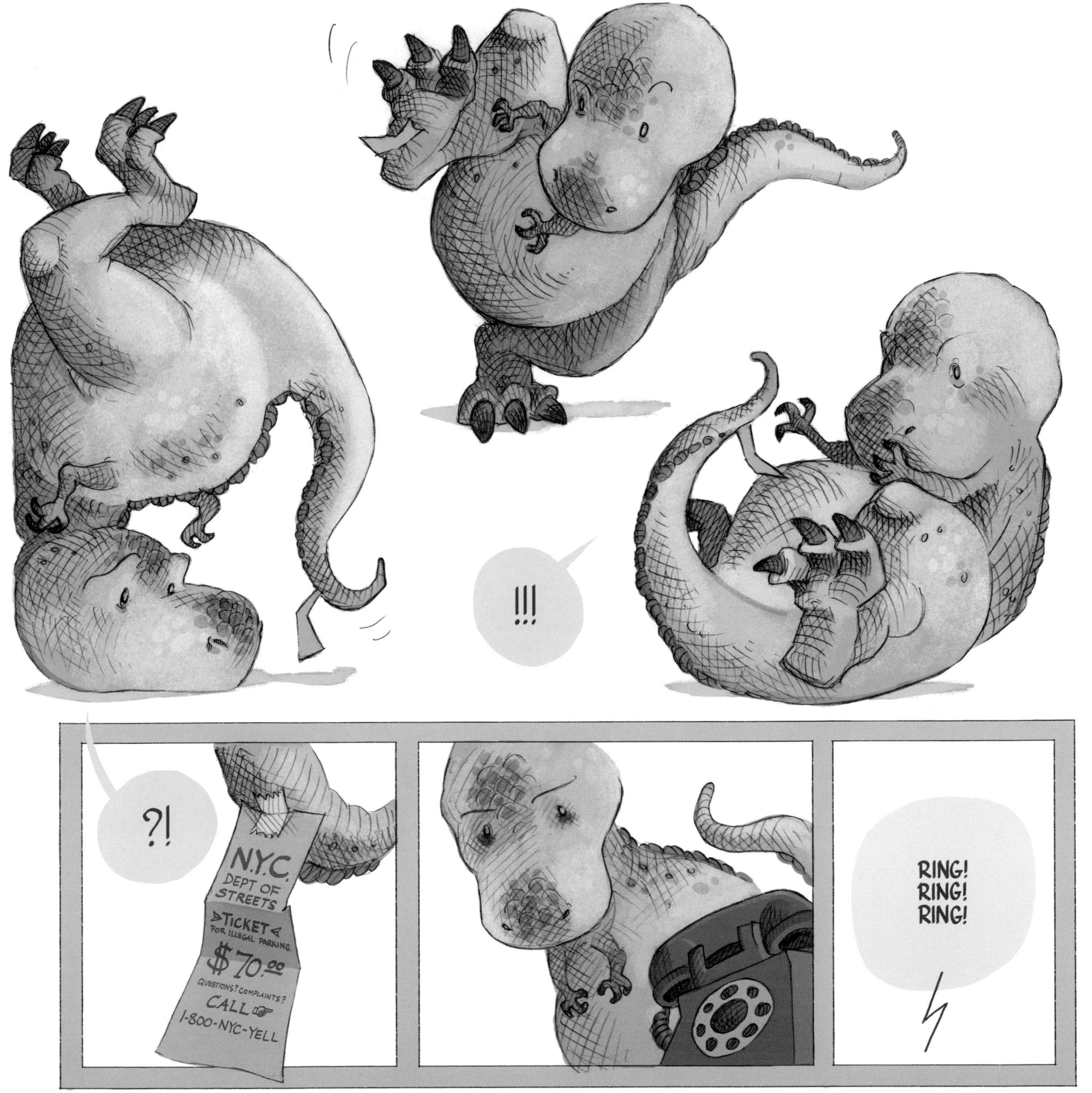
!!!
?!
N.Y.C. DEPT OF STREETS
TICKET FOR ILLEGAL PARKING
$70.00
QUESTIONS? COMPLAINTS? CALL 1-800-NYC-YELL
RING! RING! RING!

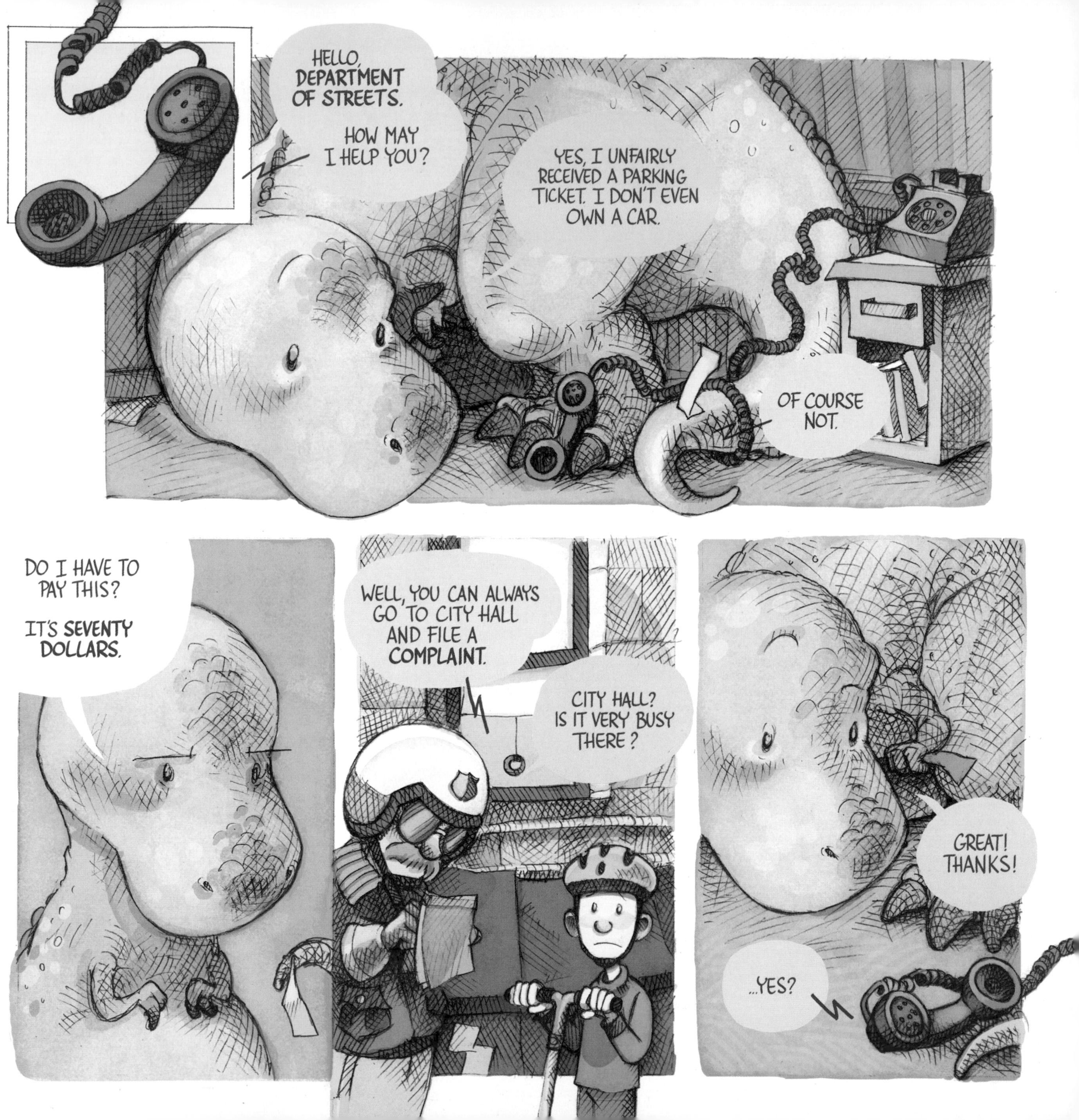
HELLO, DEPARTMENT OF STREETS.
HOW MAY I HELP YOU?
YES, I UNFAIRLY RECEIVED A PARKING TICKET. I DON'T EVEN OWN A CAR.
OF COURSE NOT.
DO I HAVE TO PAY THIS?
IT'S SEVENTY DOLLARS.
WELL, YOU CAN ALWAYS GO TO CITY HALL AND FILE A COMPLAINT.
CITY HALL? IS IT VERY BUSY THERE?
...YES?
GREAT! THANKS!

Bolivar considered himself a model citizen.
He had never broken the law.

He decided to go to City Hall and sort out the matter.

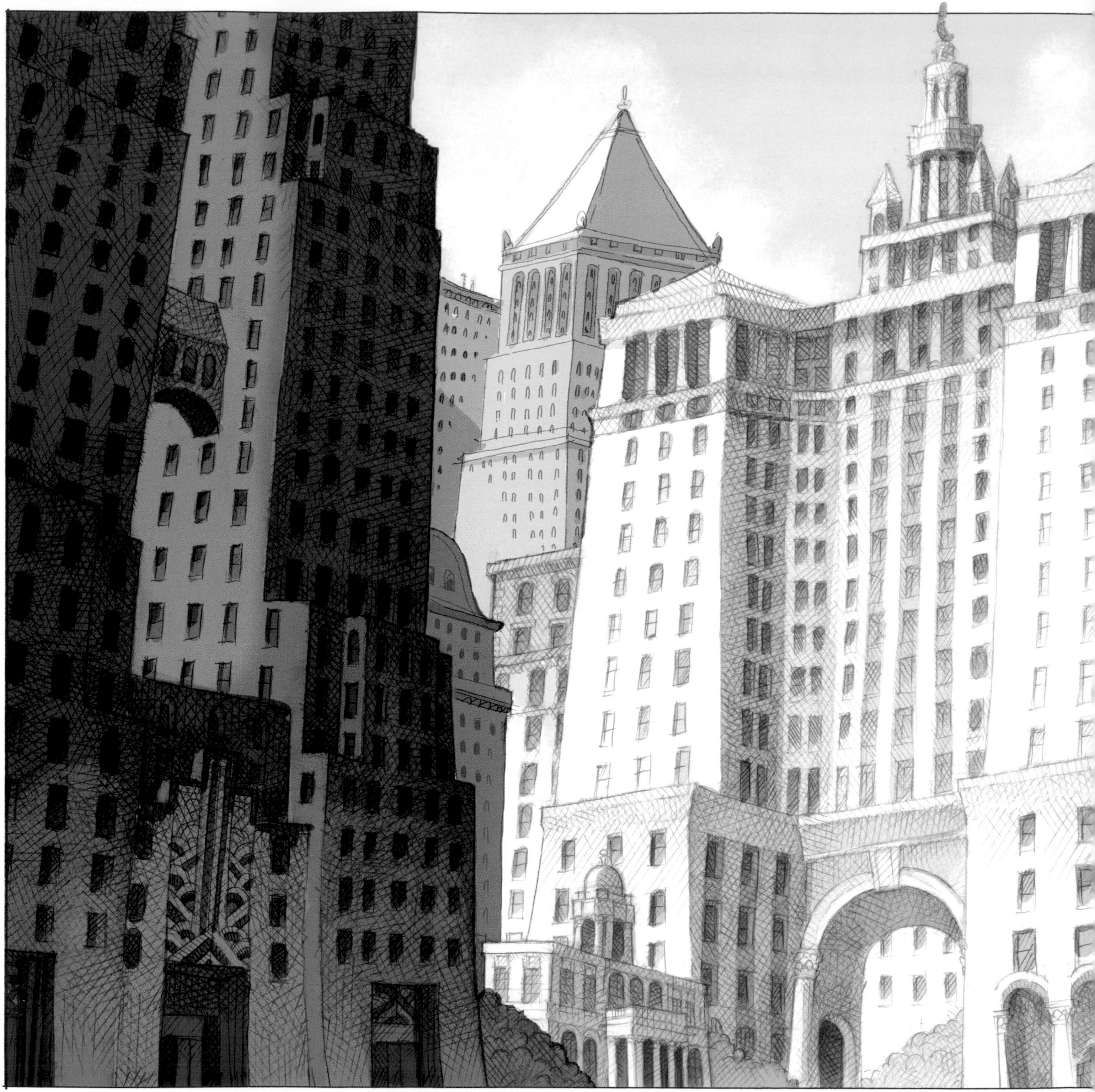

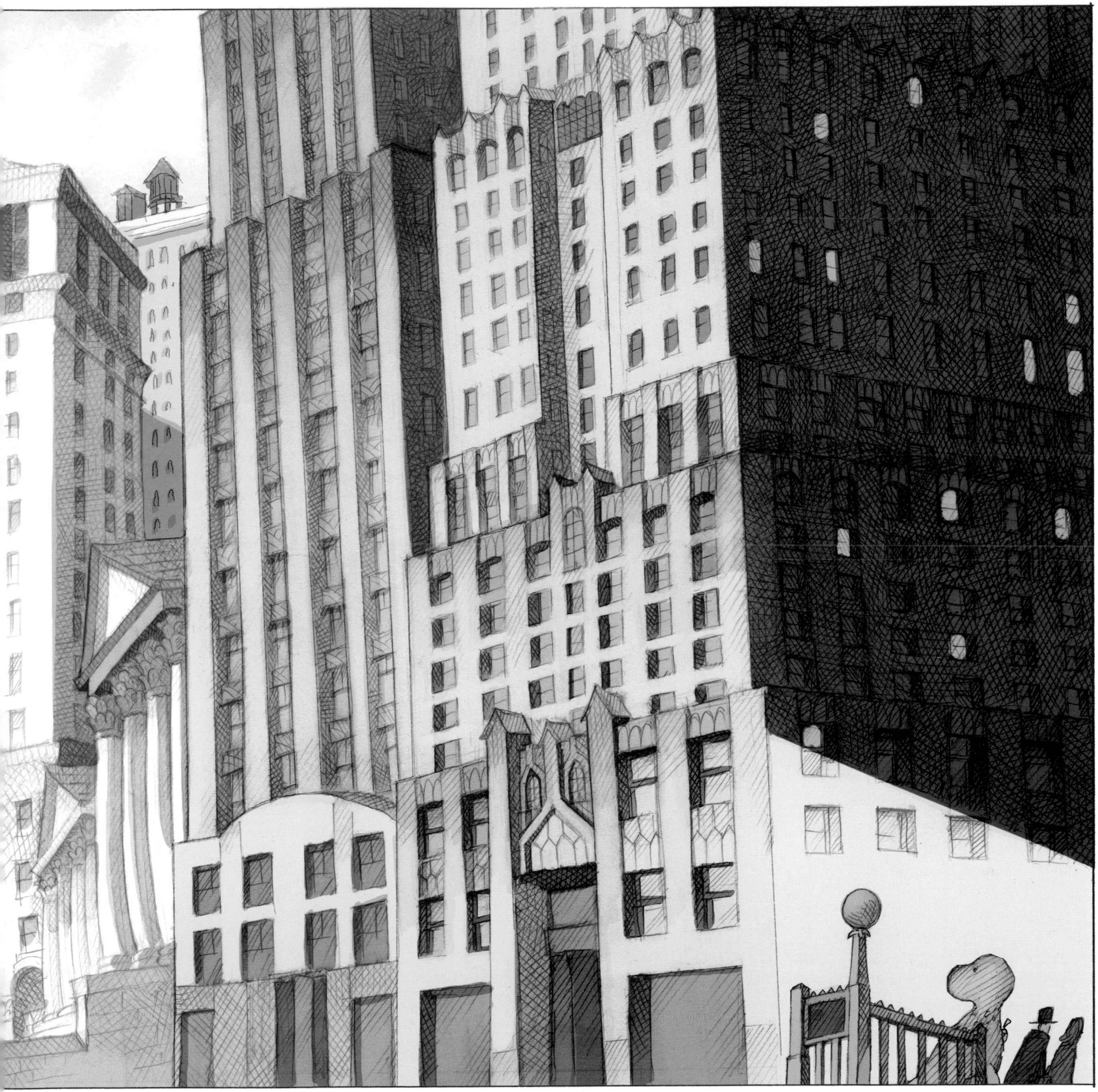

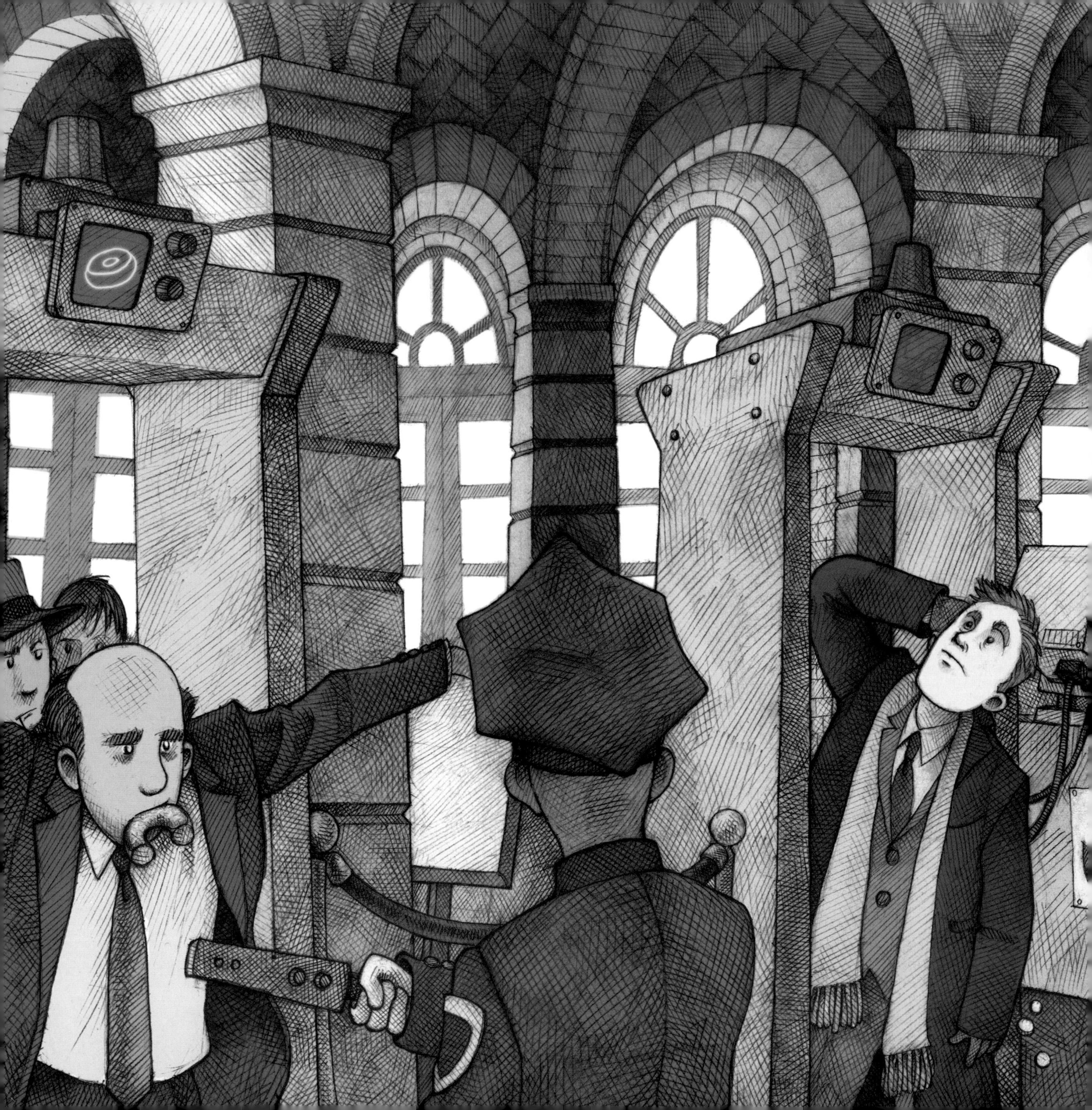

When Bolivar arrived at City Hall,
none of the guards tried to stop him.

They were too busy stopping people
to worry about stopping dinosaurs.

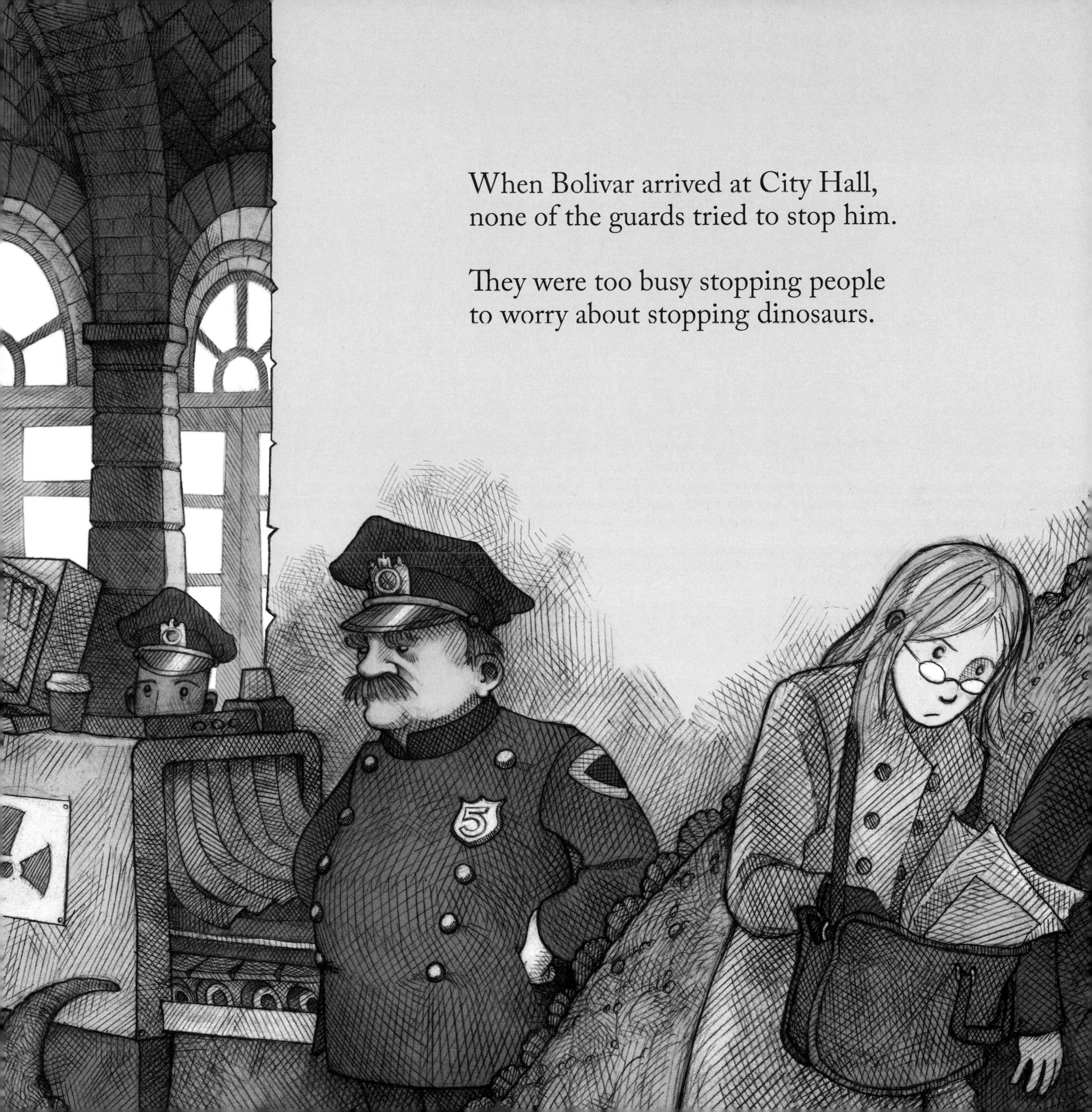
5

Like most dinosaurs, Bolivar had a terrible sense of direction.

He got lost in City Hall and stumbled into an important-looking room. It was the mayor's office!

At first, the mayor didn't realize there was a dinosaur in his office.

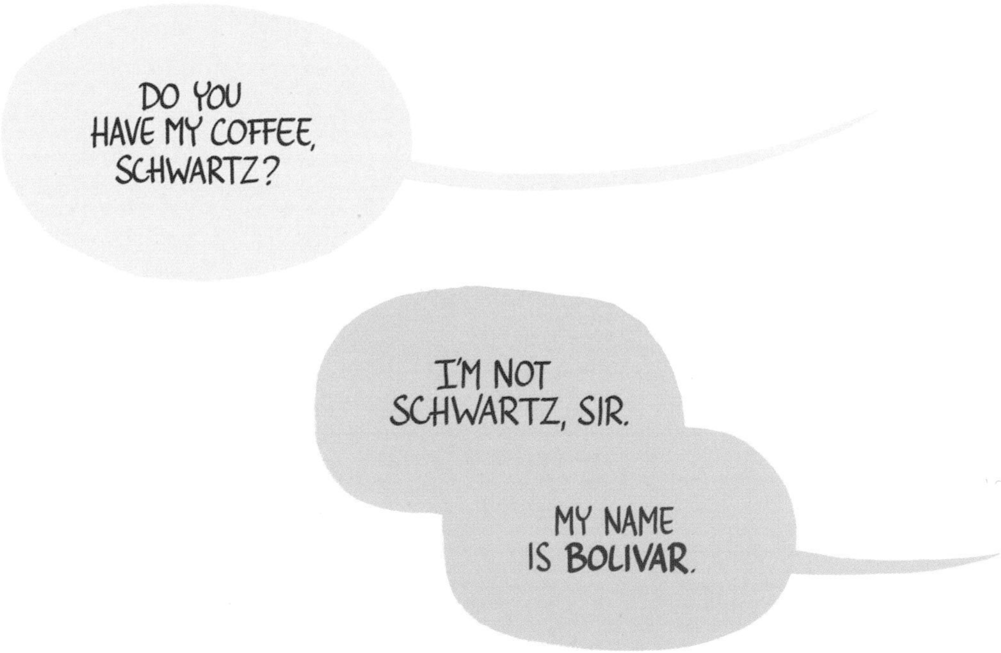
DO YOU HAVE MY COFFEE, SCHWARTZ?
I'M NOT SCHWARTZ, SIR.
MY NAME IS **BOLIVAR**.

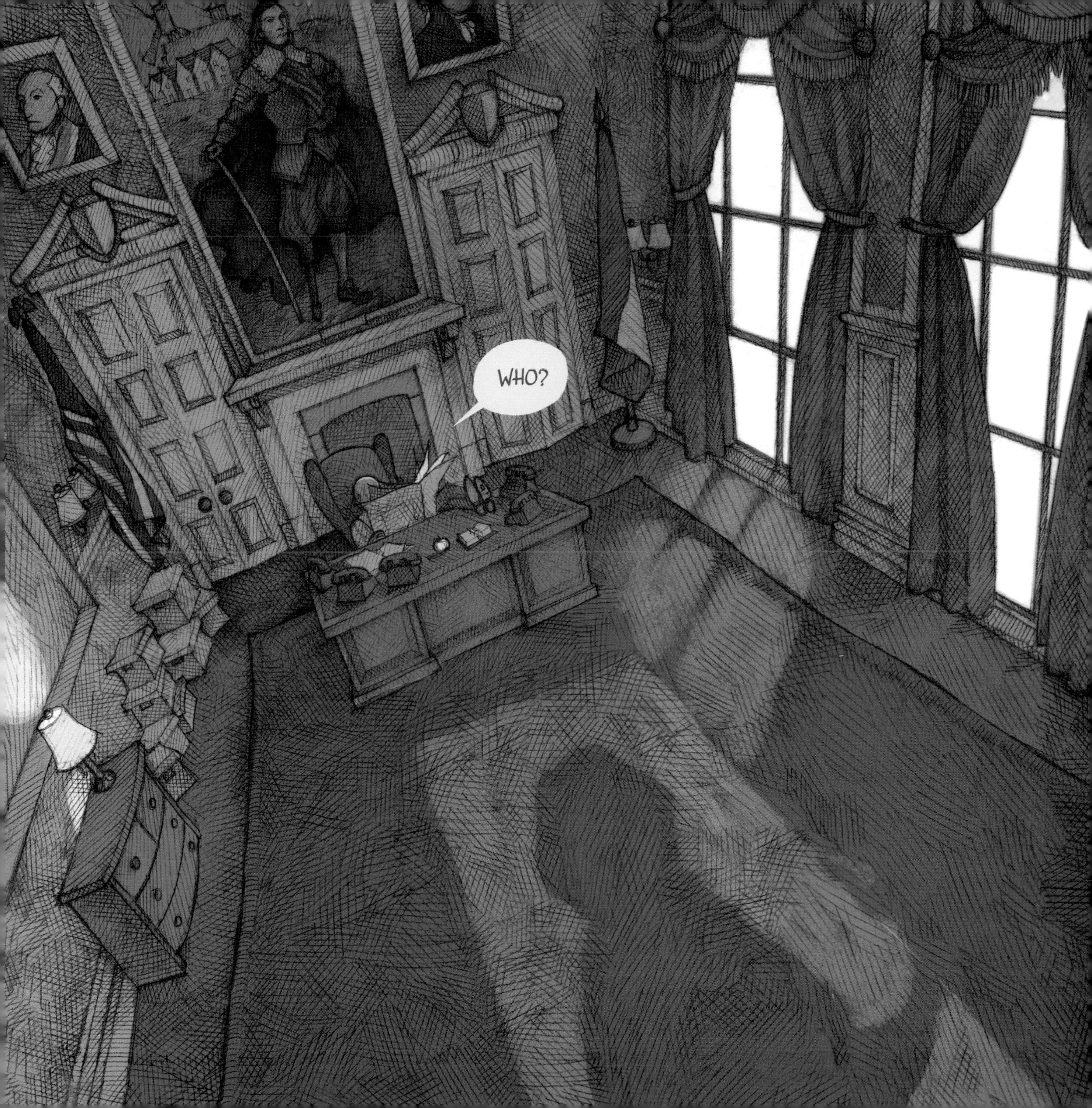
WHO?

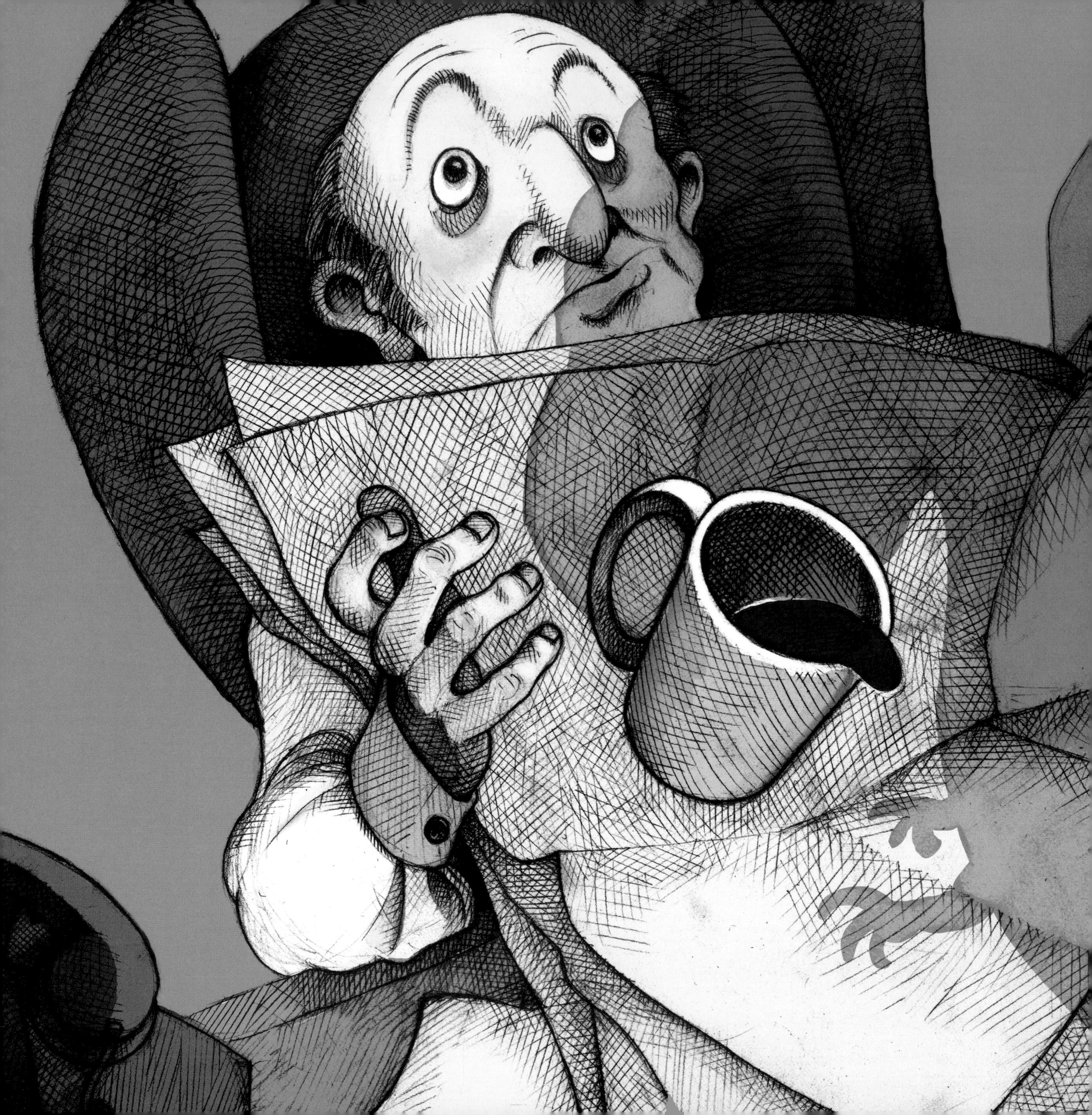

When the Mayor realized there *was* a dinosaur in his office, he was very surprised.

In fact, the Mayor was *so* very surprised...

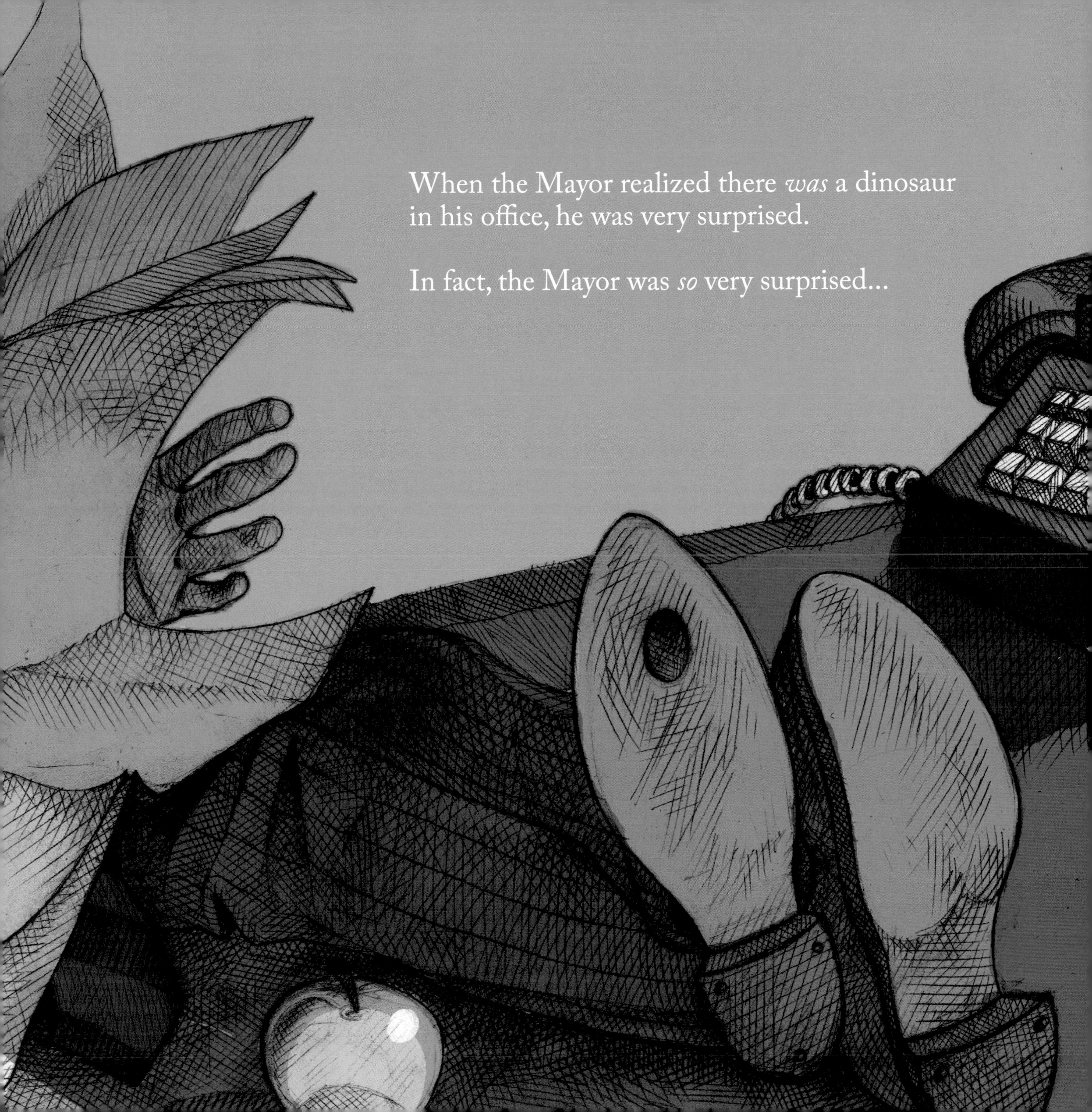

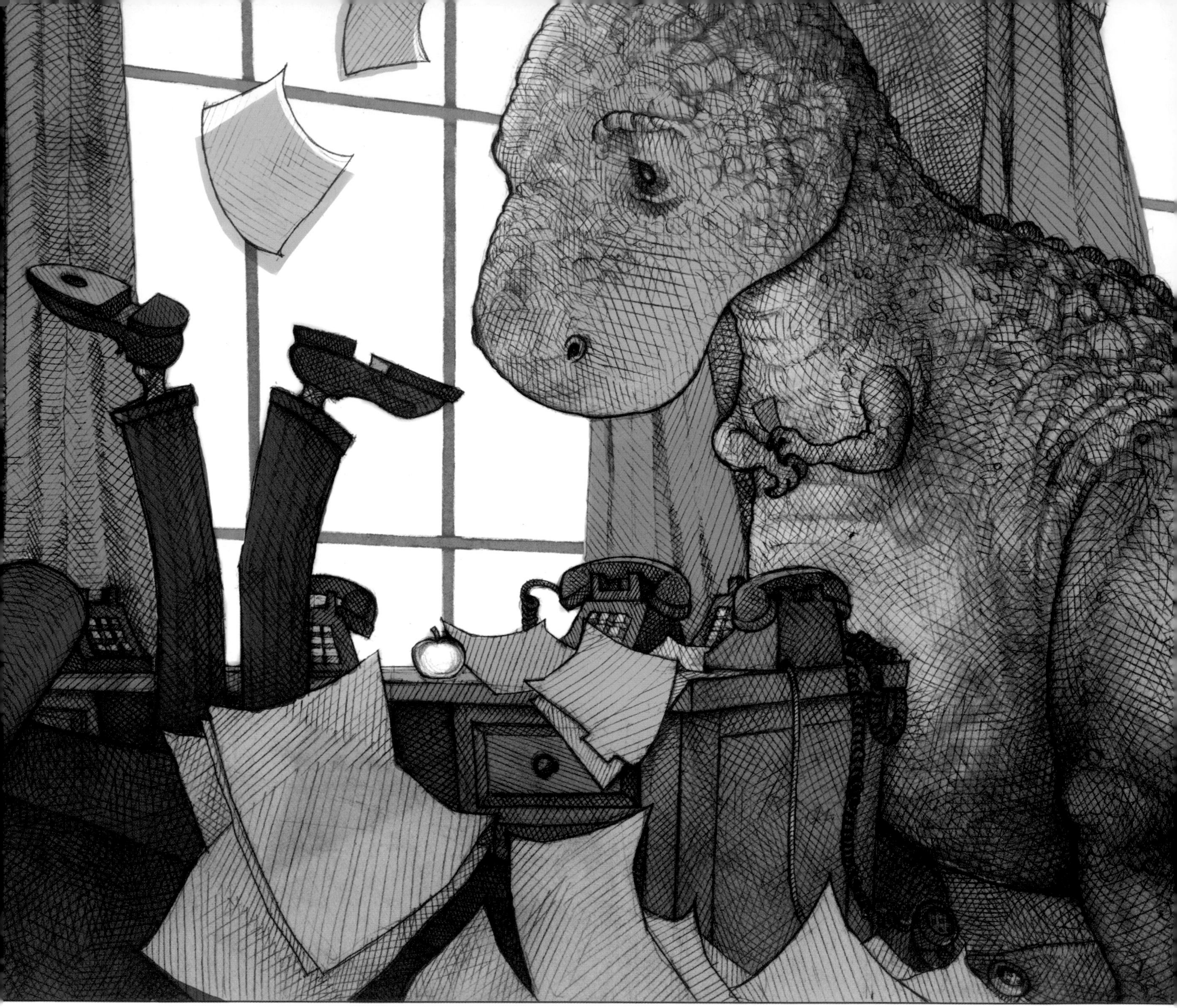

…he fainted. Bolivar didn't know what to do. He might not have parked illegally, but it was almost certainly illegal to make the mayor faint.

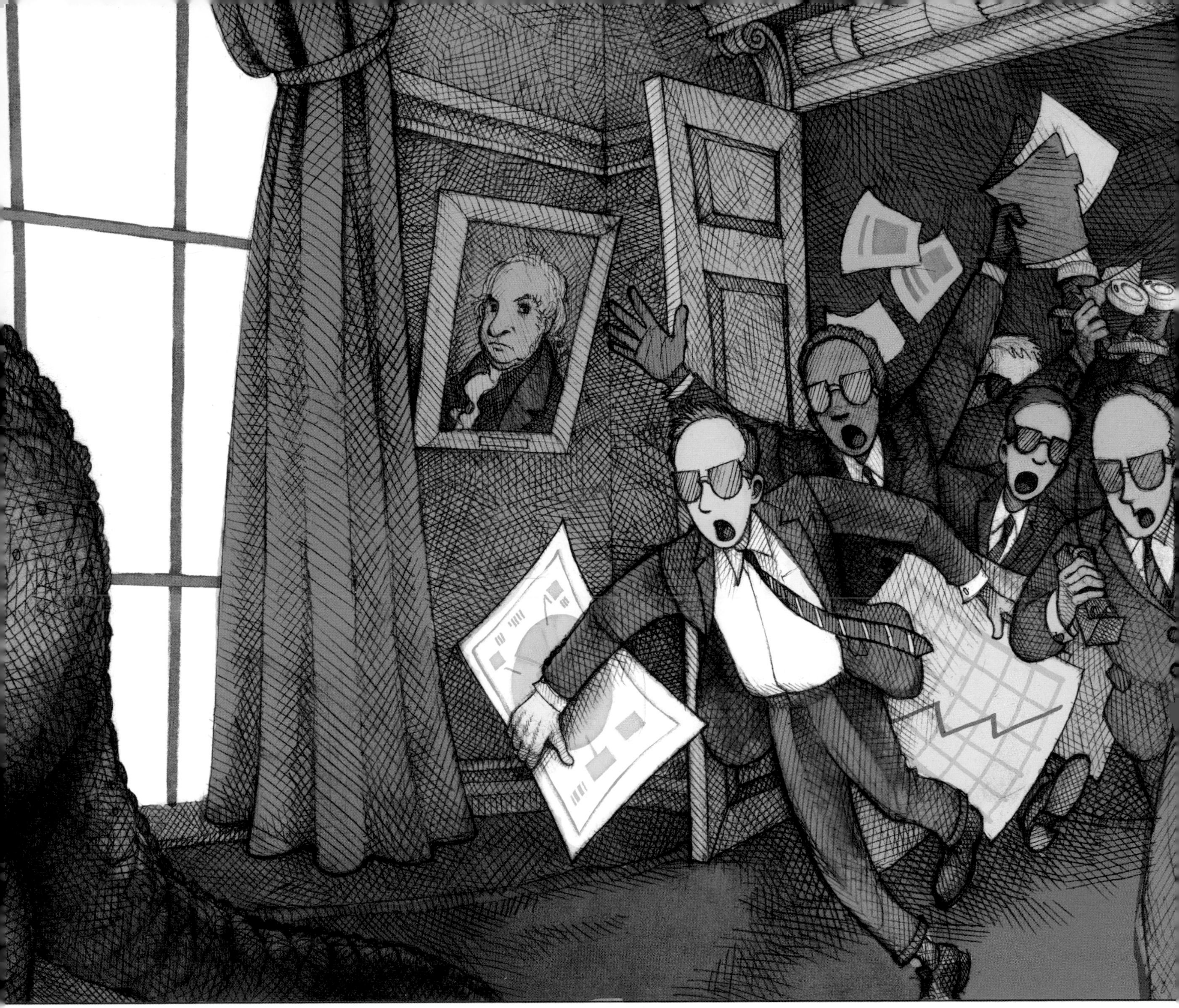

Suddenly, a group of men came charging into the office. Bolivar thought he'd be arrested for sure.

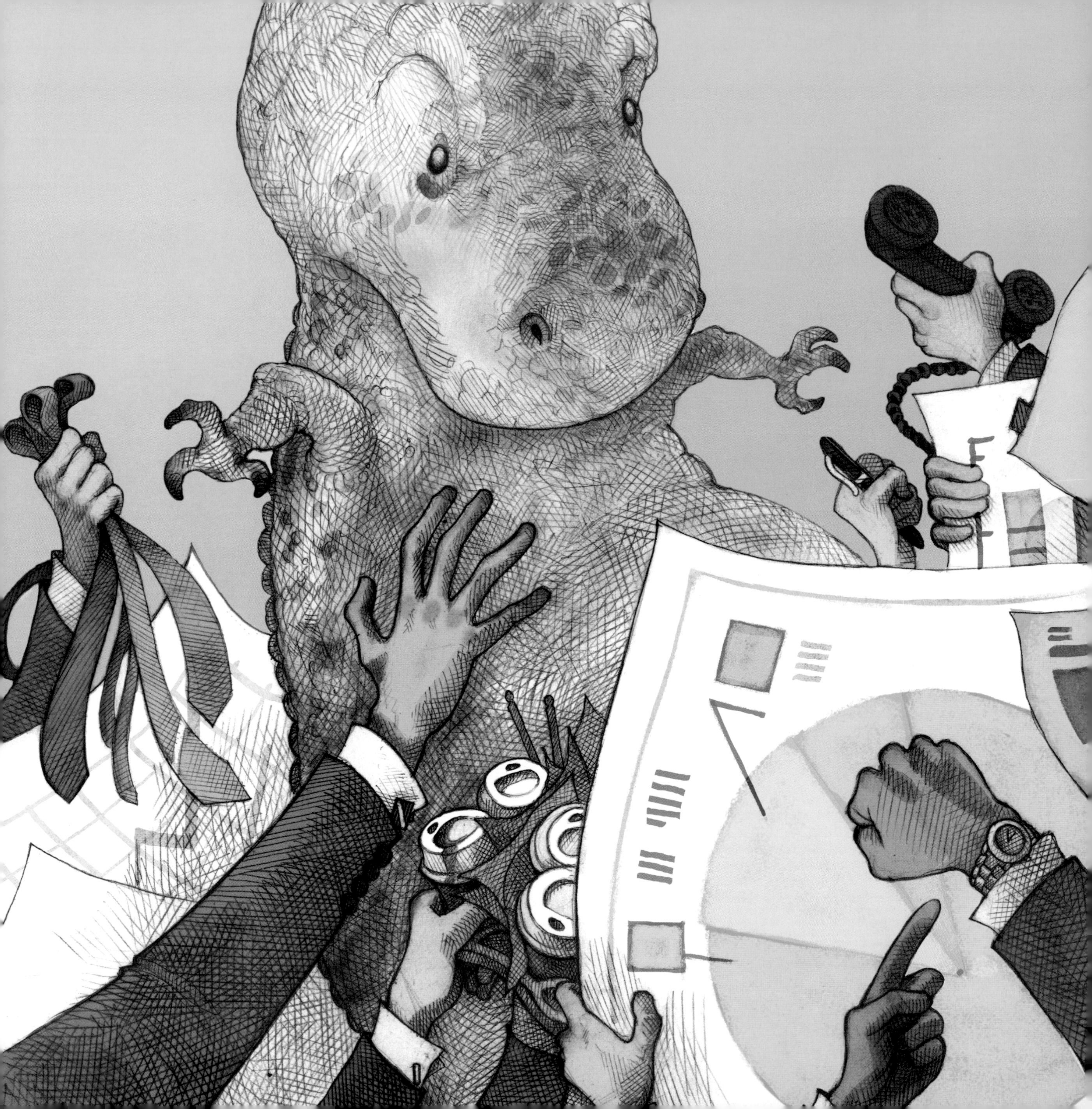

But he wasn't arrested.

The men were much too busy shouting to arrest a dinosaur.

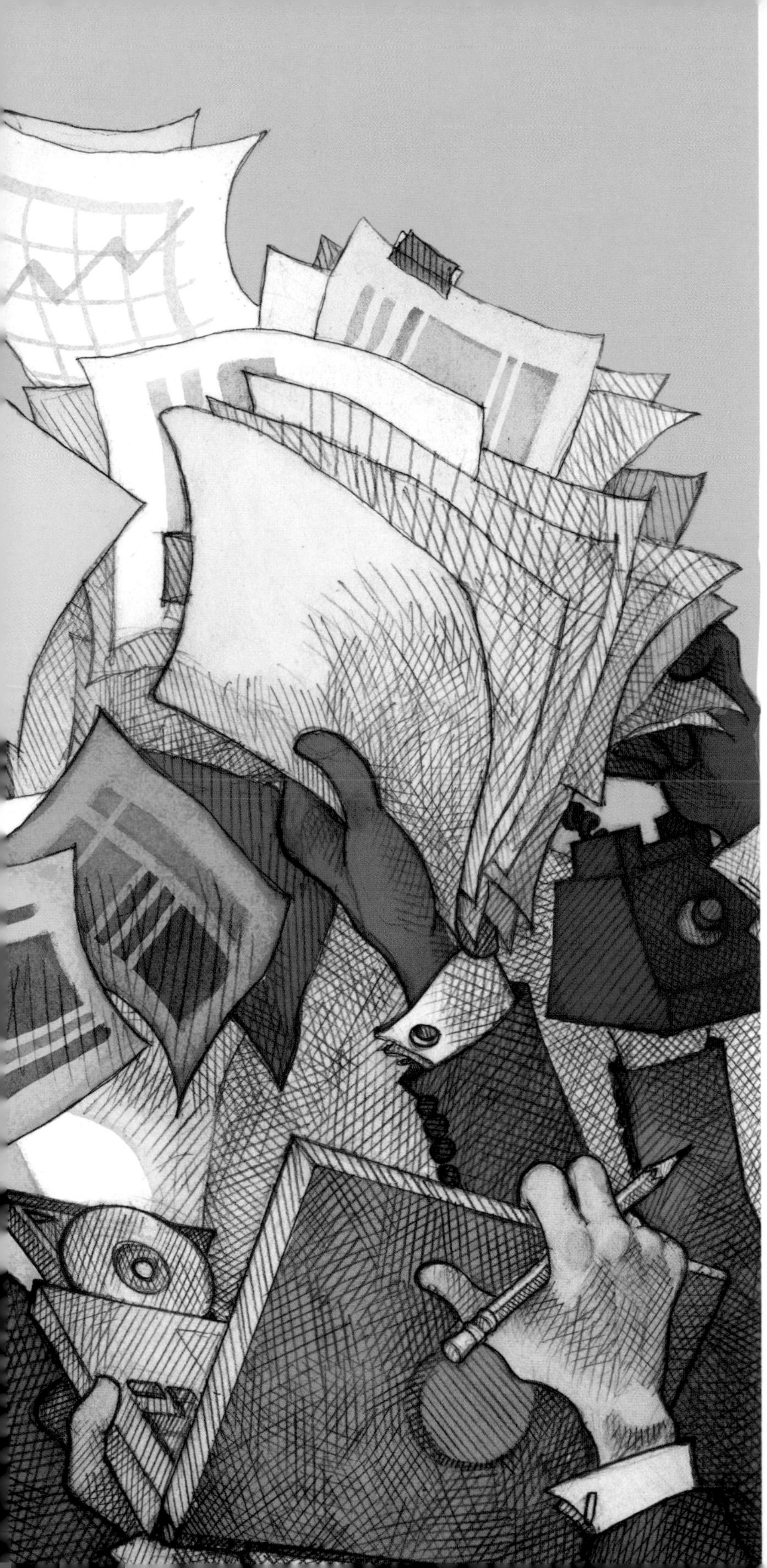
MR. MAYOR! MR. MAYOR!
YOU HAVE A PRESS CONFERENCE IN FIVE MINUTES, MR. MAYOR!
WE HAVE TO GO NOW!

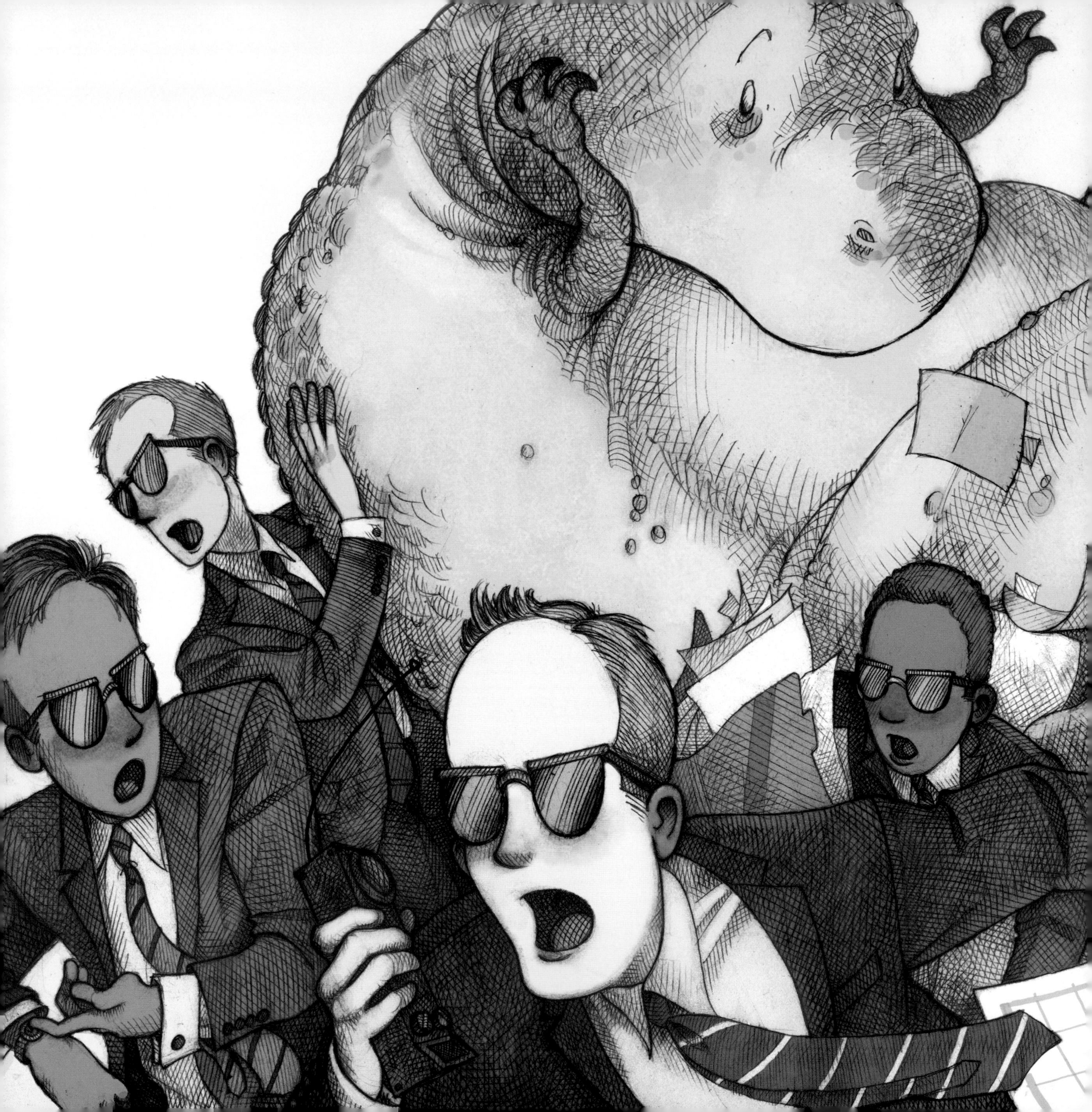

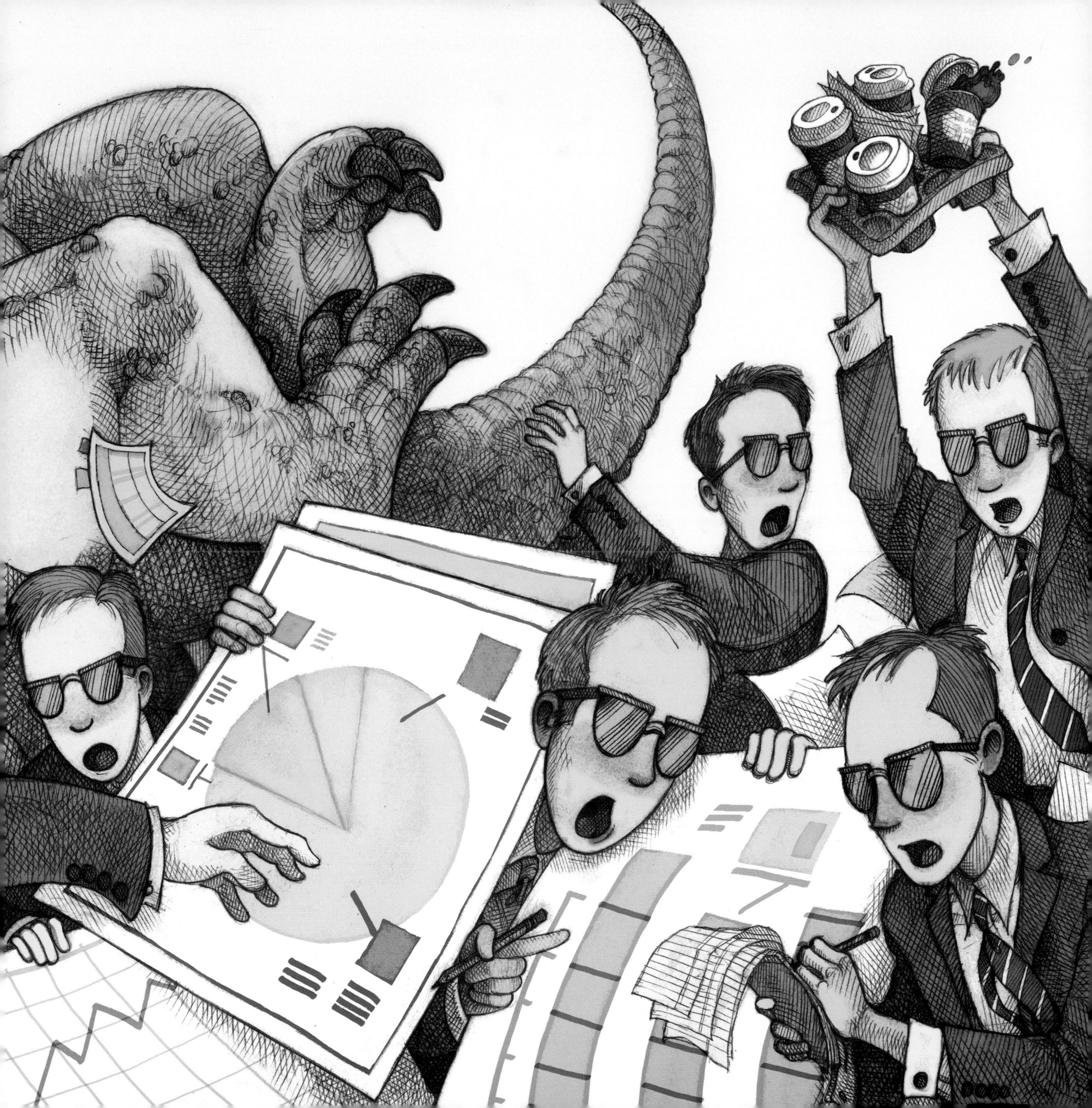

The men never noticed that Bolivar wasn't the mayor. The men didn't even notice that Bolivar was a dinosaur. They were much too busy getting him to the press conference on time.

When Bolivar reached the press conference, he was very nervous. He was so nervous, he forgot what the men told him to say.

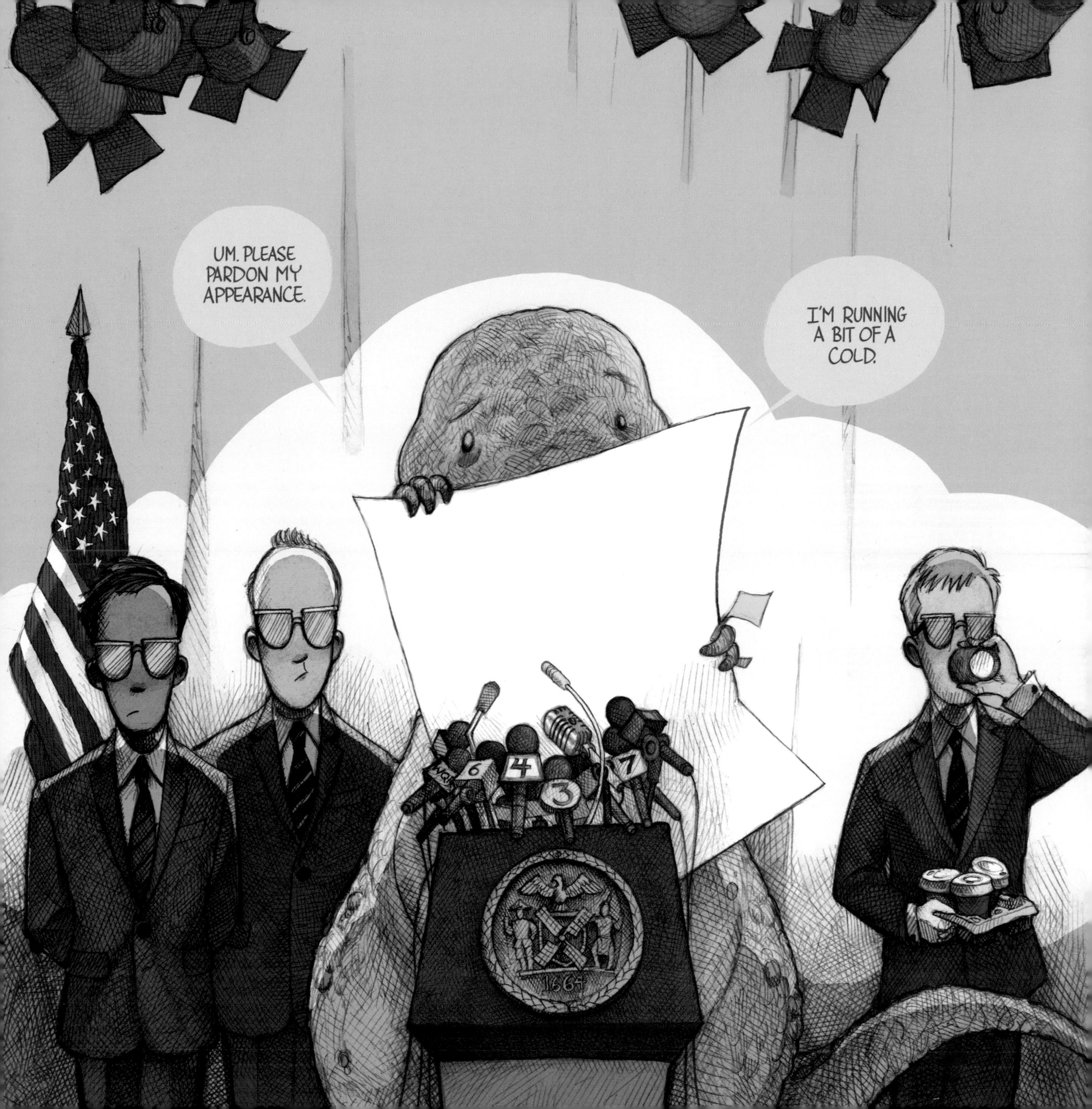
UM. PLEASE PARDON MY APPEARANCE.
I'M RUNNING A BIT OF A COLD.

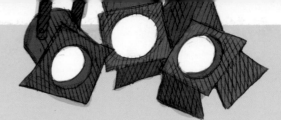

Bolivar shouldn't have worried.

Everyone was much too busy getting the scoop to realize that the mayor was a dinosaur.

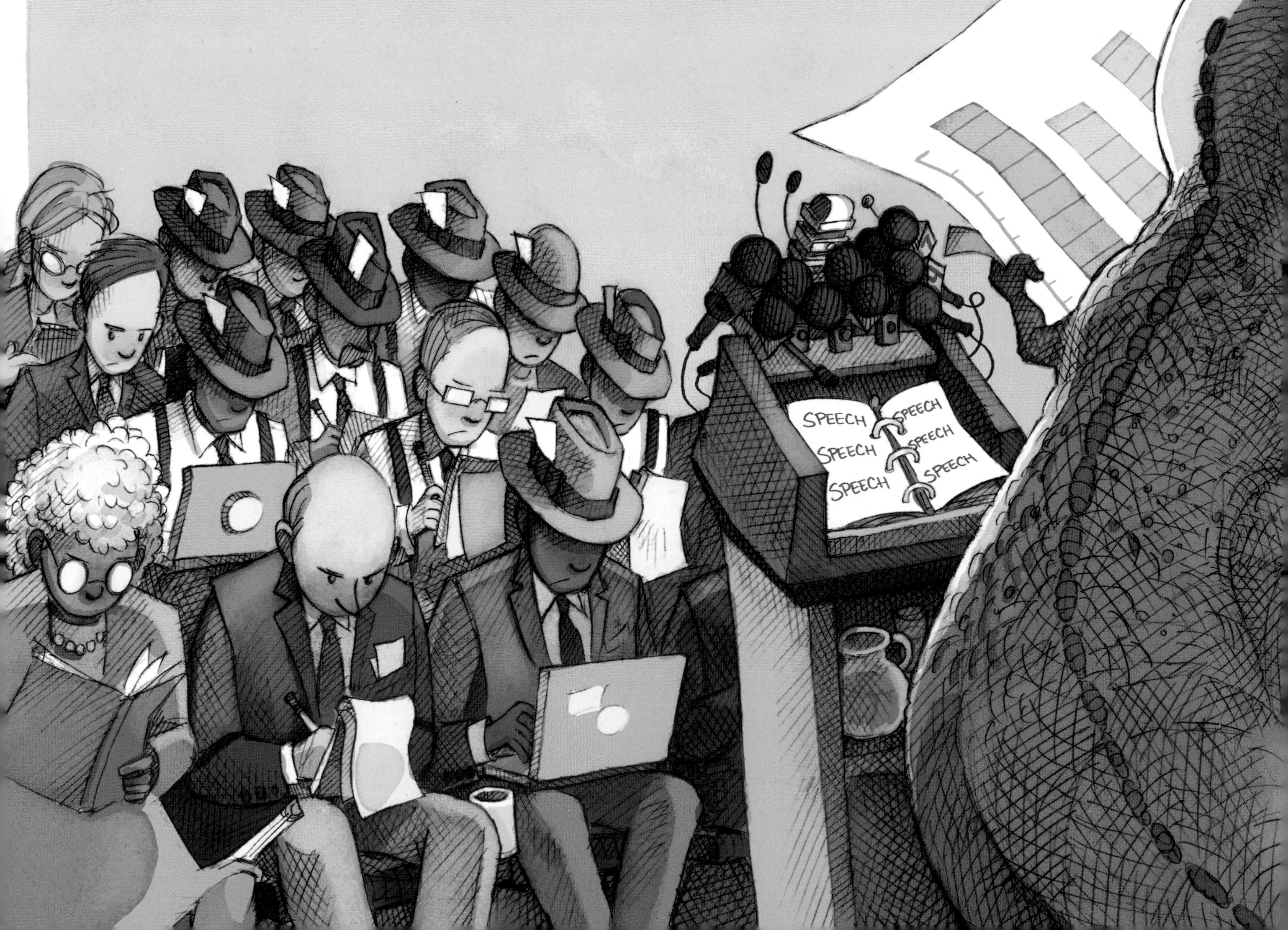
SPEECH
SPEECH
SPEECH
SPEECH
SPEECH
SPEECH

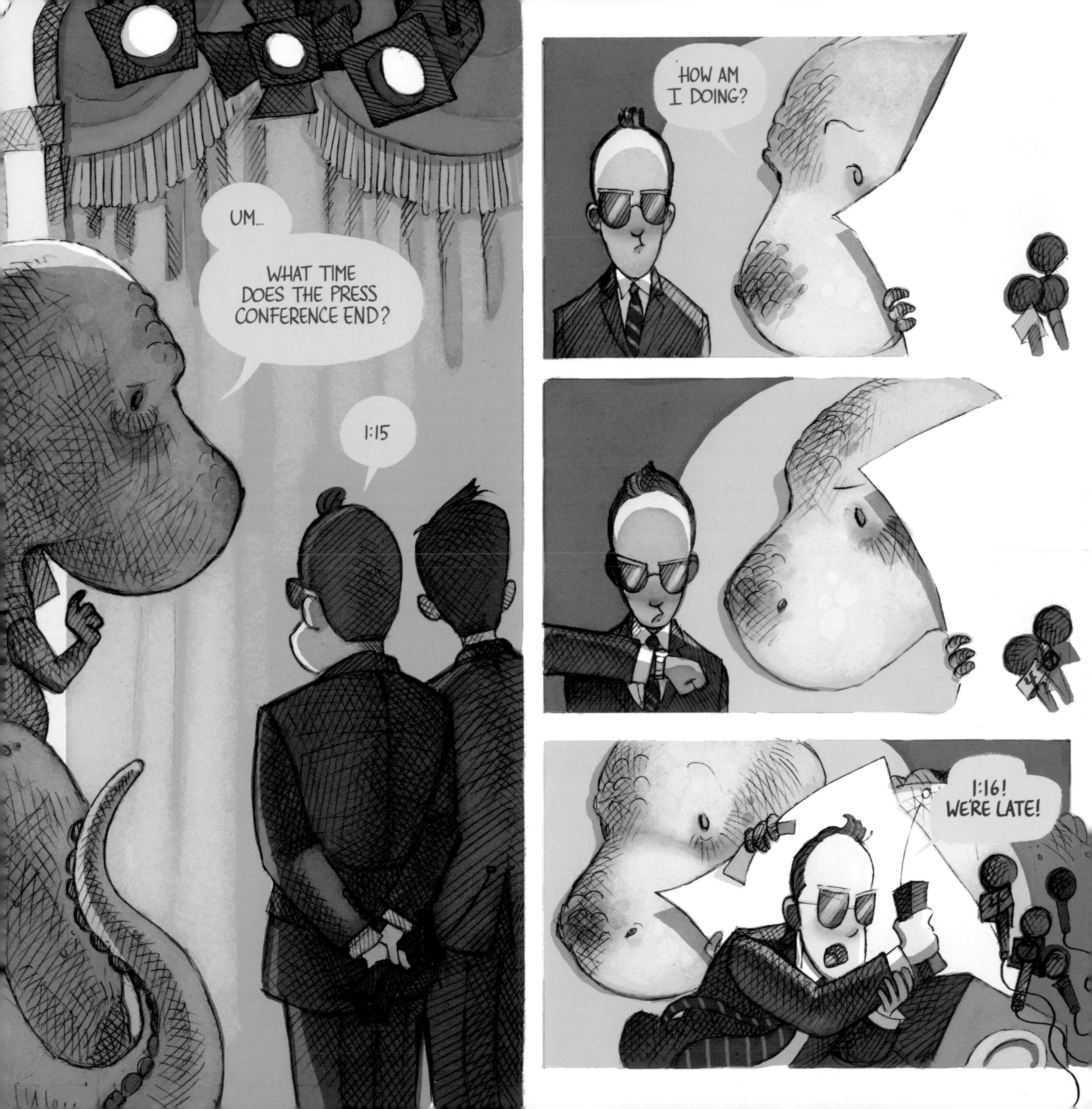
UM...
WHAT TIME DOES THE PRESS CONFERENCE END?
1:15
HOW AM I DOING?
1:16! WE'RE LATE!

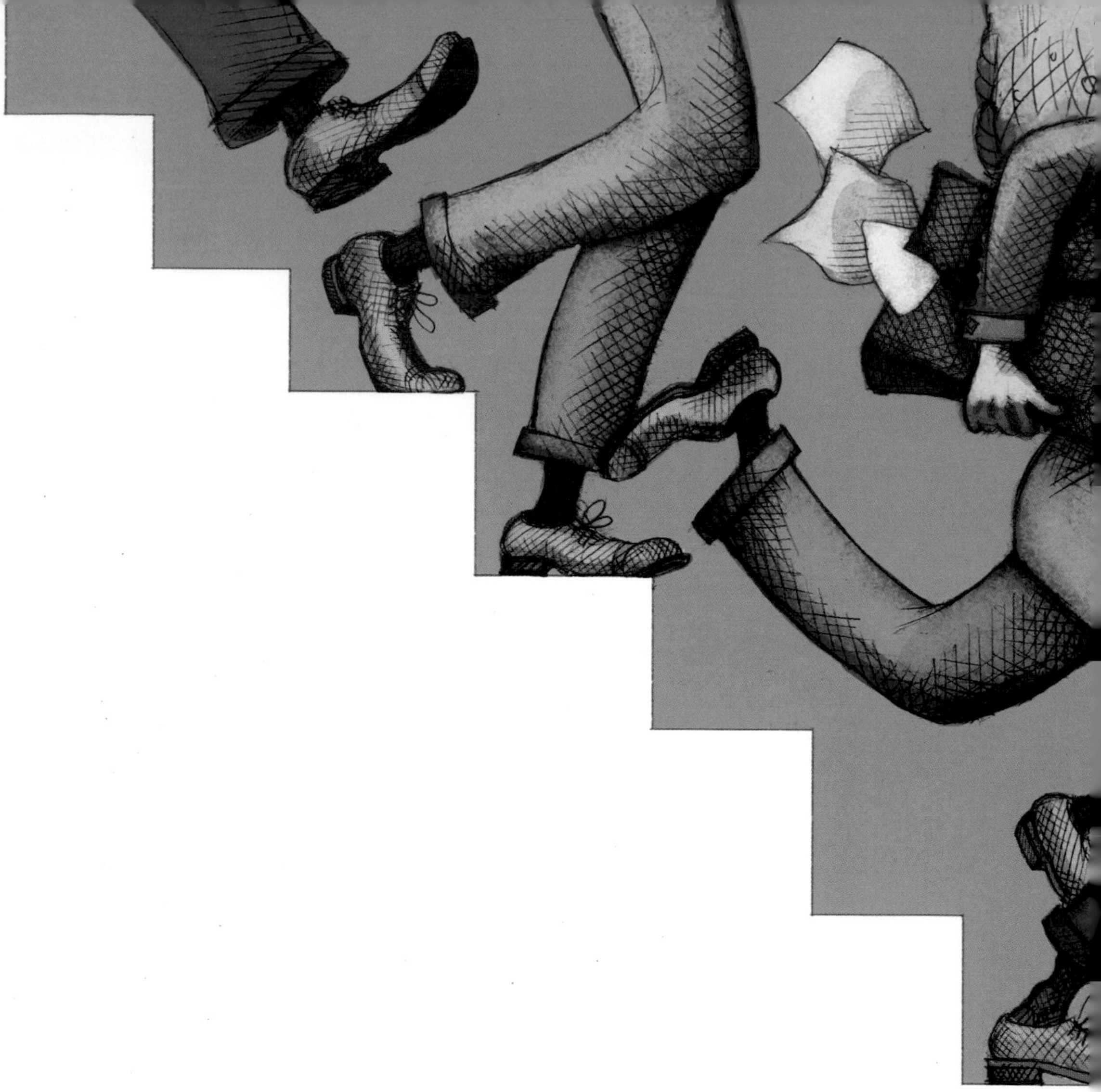

Bolivar never realized how busy the mayor was.

As soon as he was done in the press room, he was being taken somewhere else.

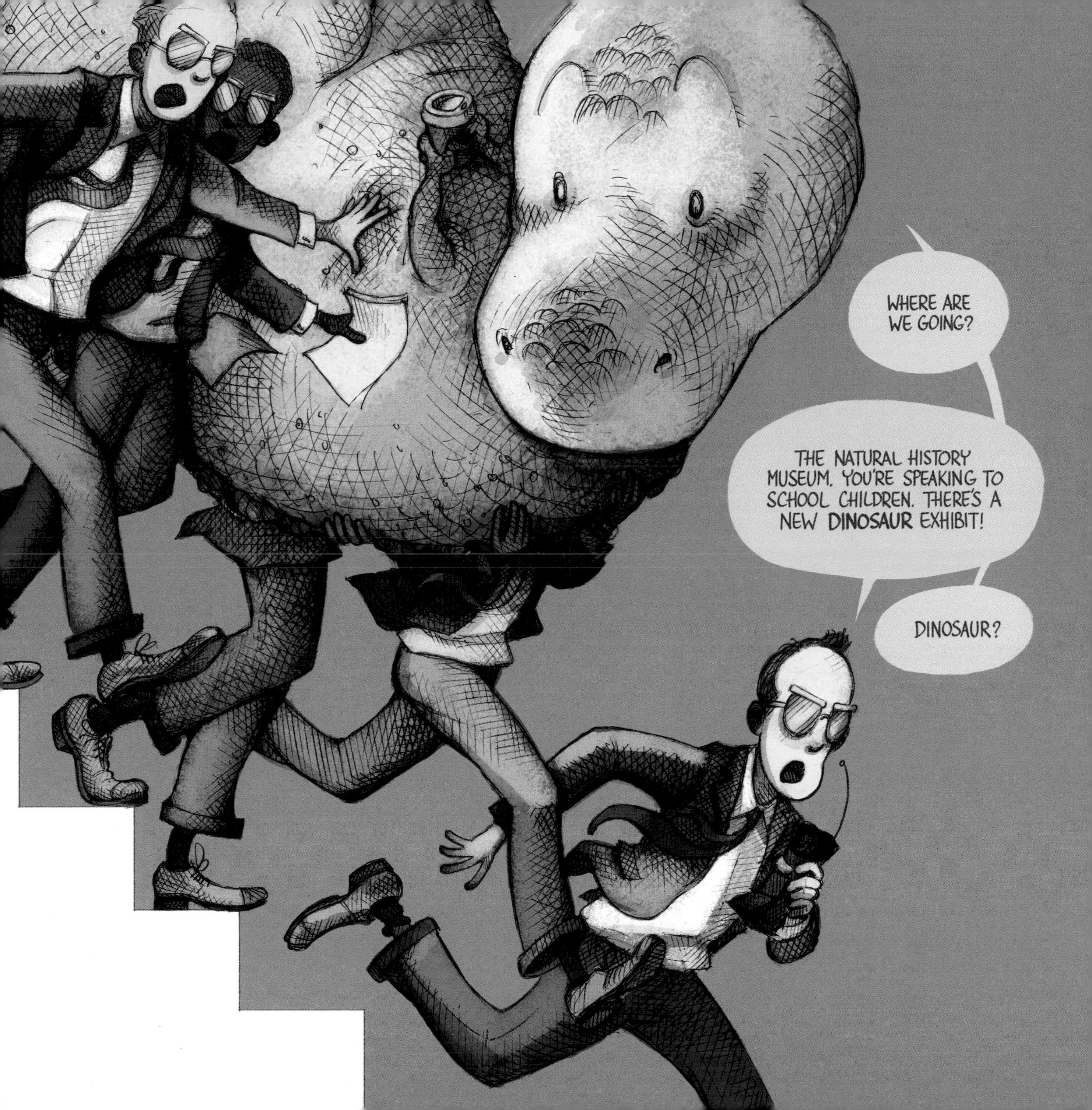
WHERE ARE WE GOING?
THE NATURAL HISTORY MUSEUM. YOU'RE SPEAKING TO SCHOOL CHILDREN. THERE'S A NEW **DINOSAUR** EXHIBIT!
DINOSAUR?

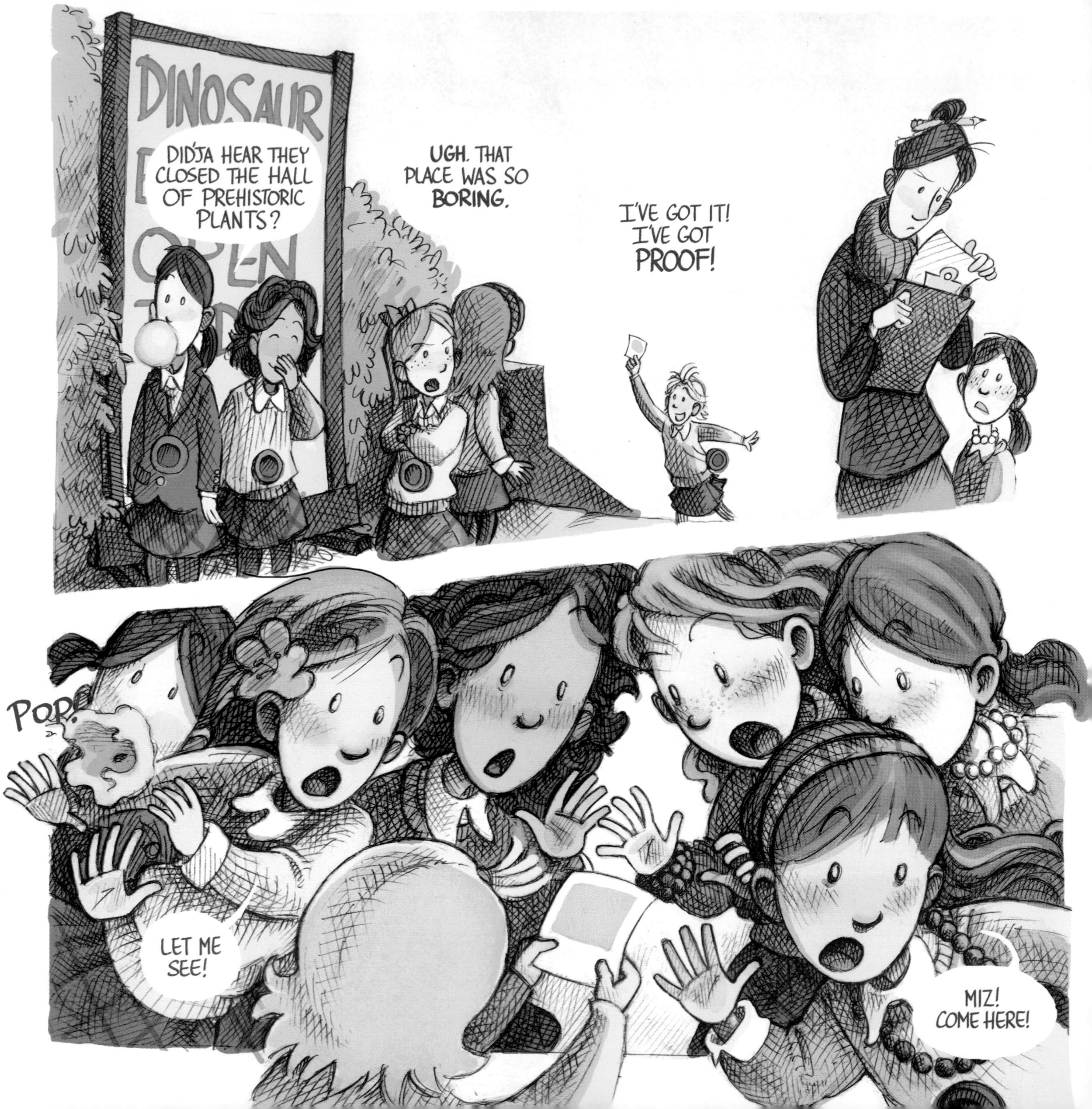
DINOSAUR
OPEN
DID'JA HEAR THEY CLOSED THE HALL OF PREHISTORIC PLANTS?
UGH. THAT PLACE WAS SO BORING.
I'VE GOT IT! I'VE GOT PROOF!
POP!
LET ME SEE!
MIZ! COME HERE!

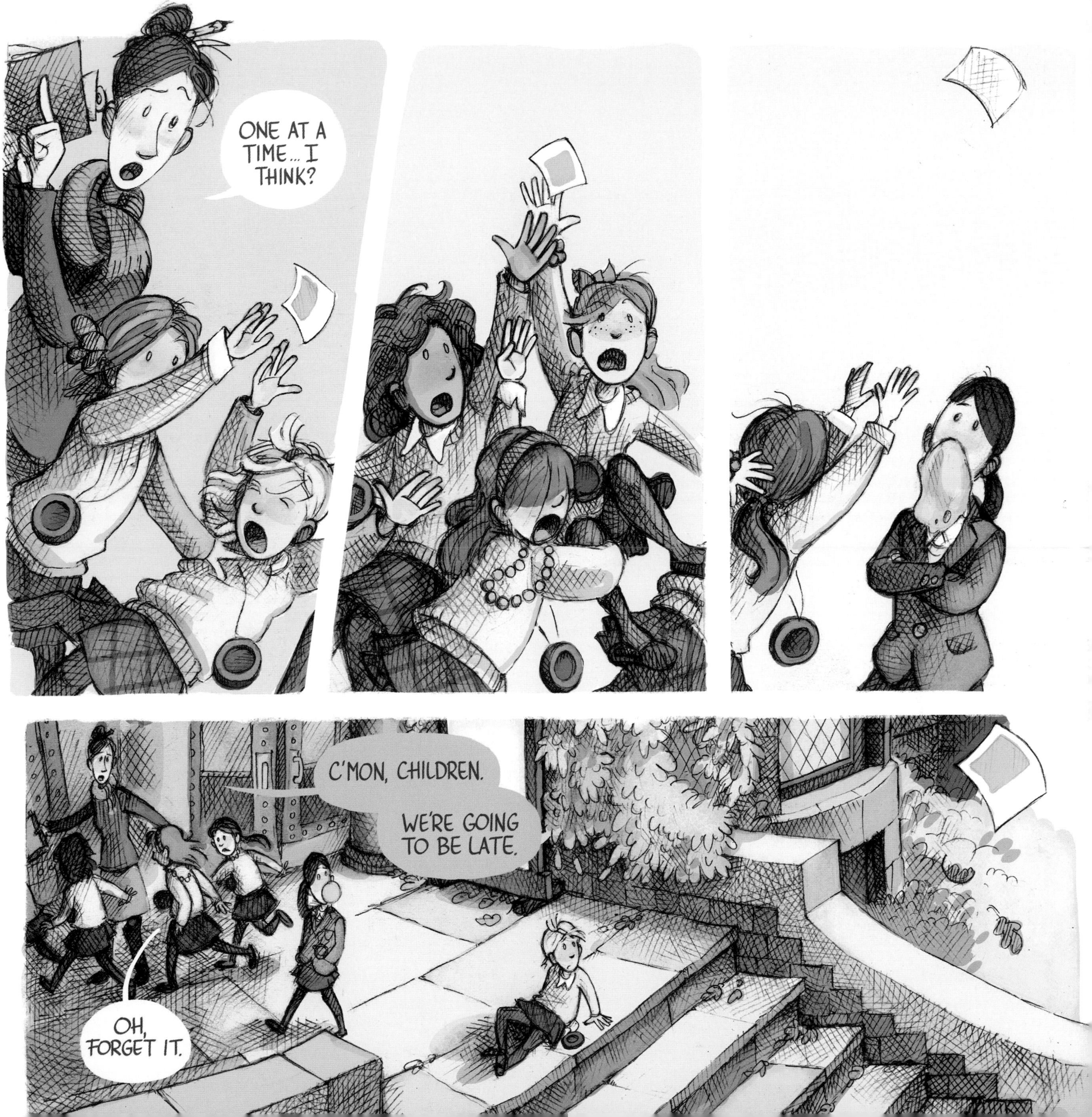
ONE AT A TIME... I THINK?
C'MON, CHILDREN.
WE'RE GOING TO BE LATE.
OH, FORGET IT.

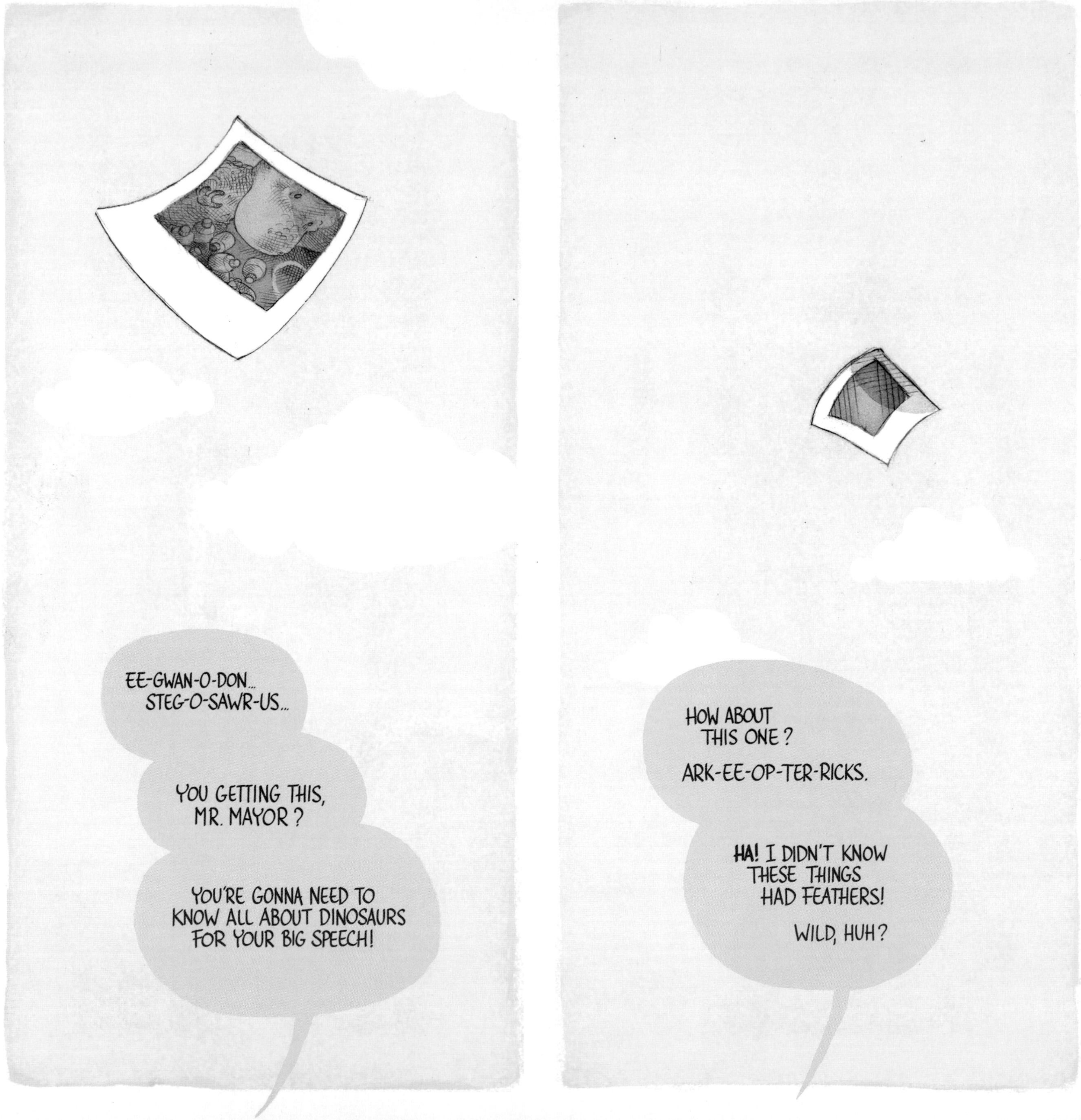
EE-GWAN-O-DON... STEG-O-SAWR-US...
YOU GETTING THIS, MR. MAYOR?
YOU'RE GONNA NEED TO KNOW ALL ABOUT DINOSAURS FOR YOUR BIG SPEECH!
HOW ABOUT THIS ONE?
ARK-EE-OP-TER-RICKS.
HA! I DIDN'T KNOW THESE THINGS HAD FEATHERS!
WILD, HUH?

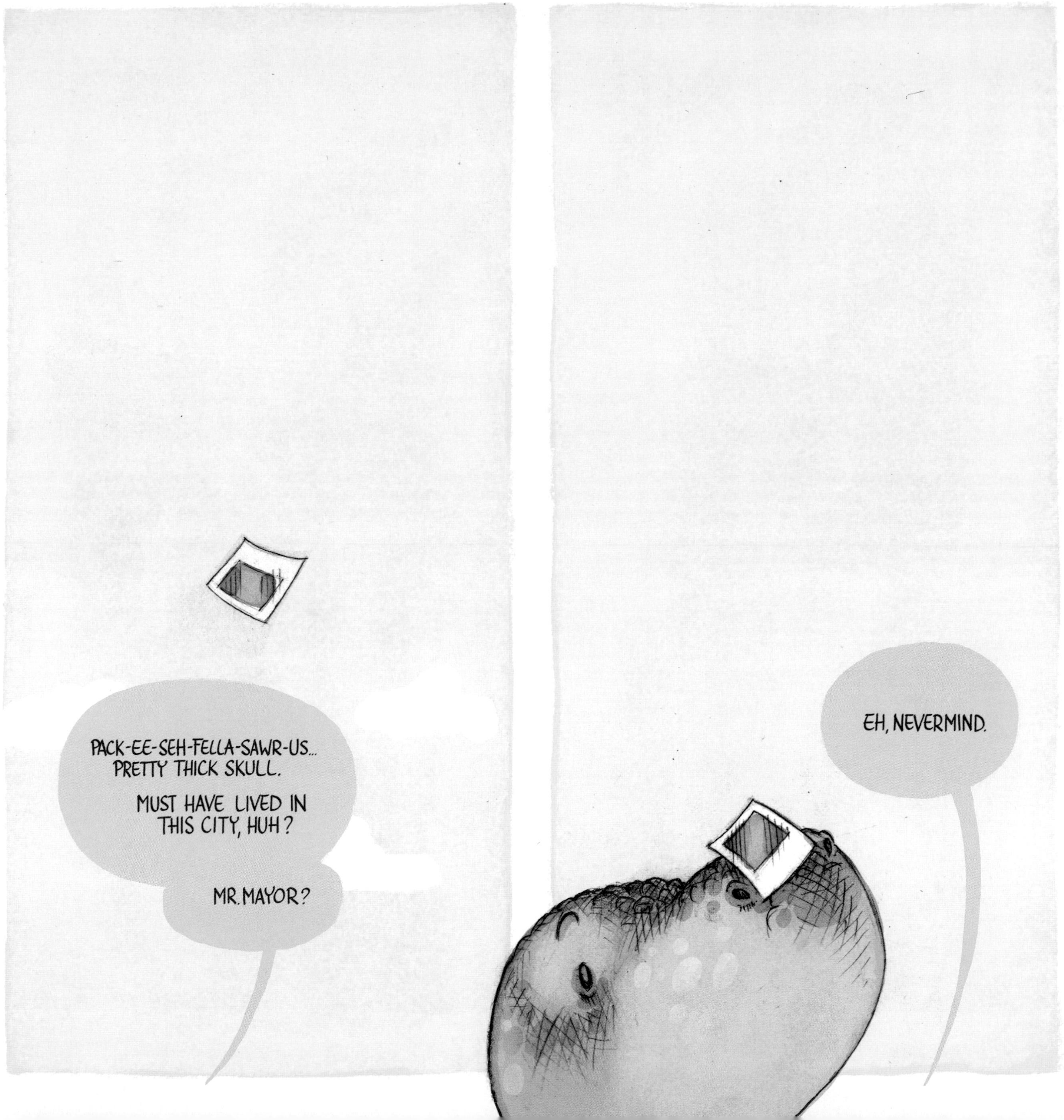
PACK-EE-SEH-FELLA-SAWR-US... PRETTY THICK SKULL.
MUST HAVE LIVED IN THIS CITY, HUH?
MR. MAYOR?
EH, NEVERMIND.

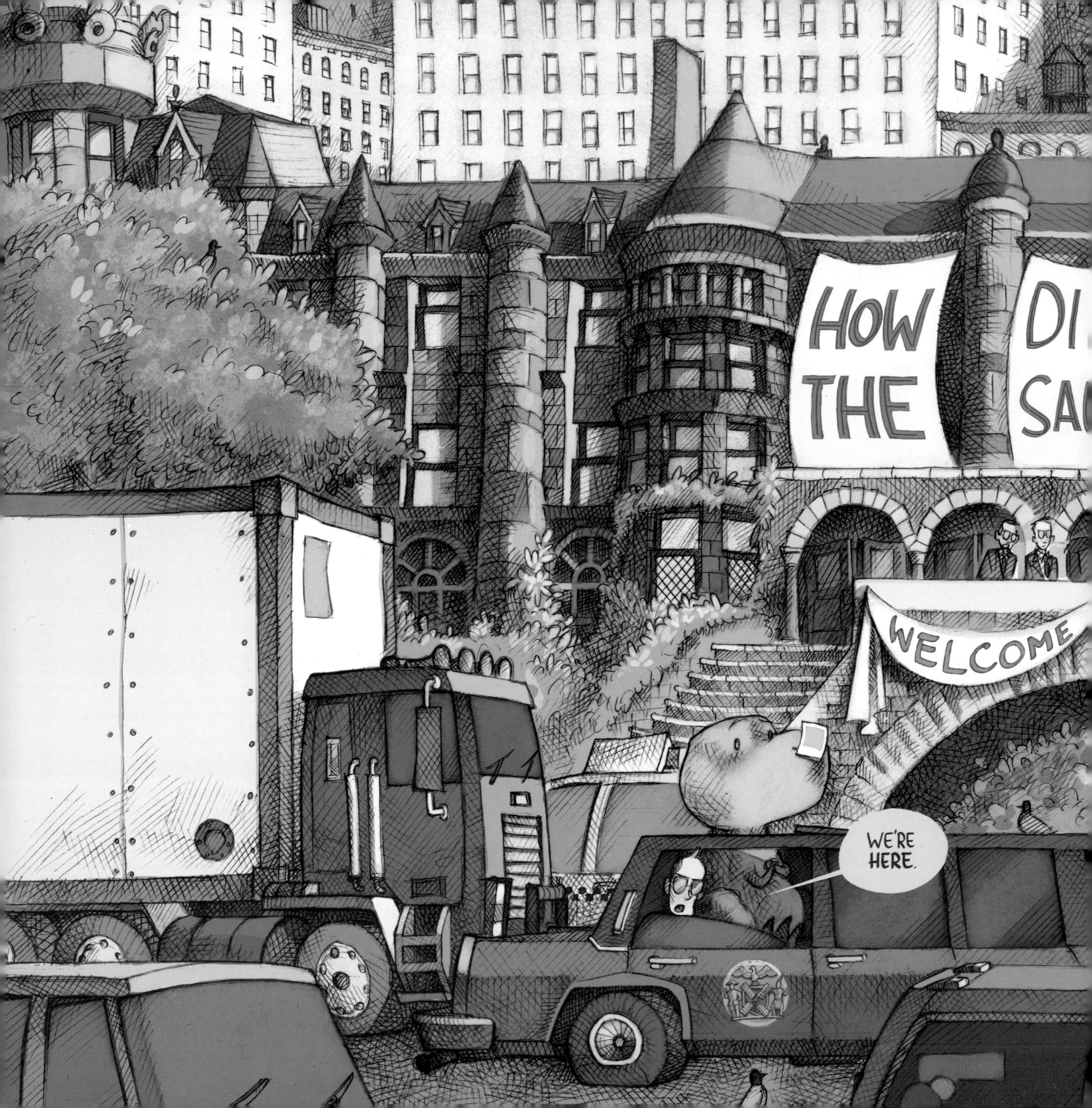
HOW THE
DI SA
WELCOME
WE'RE HERE.

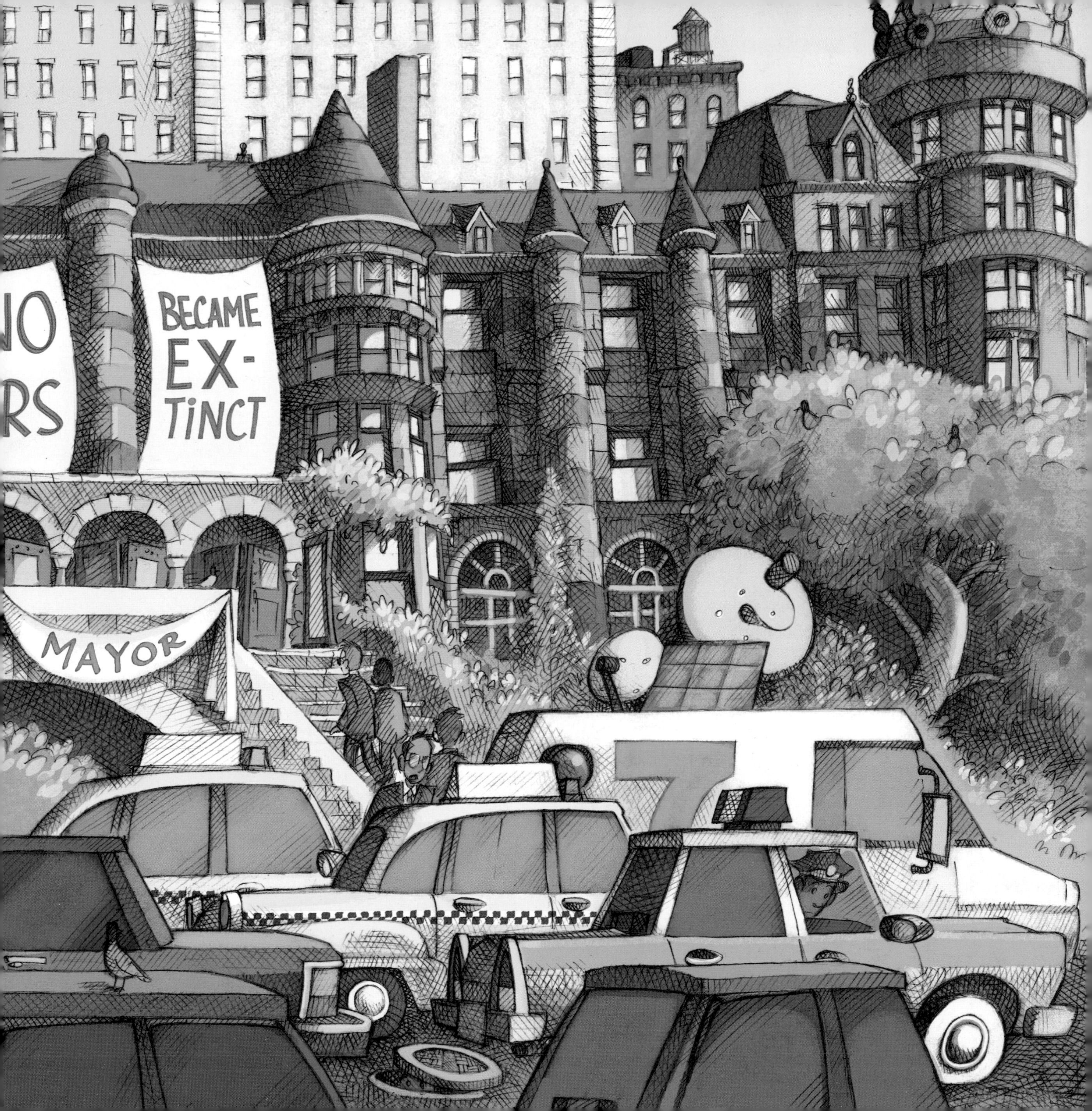
NO
RS
BECAME
EX-
TiNCT
MAYOR

CHAPTER 4

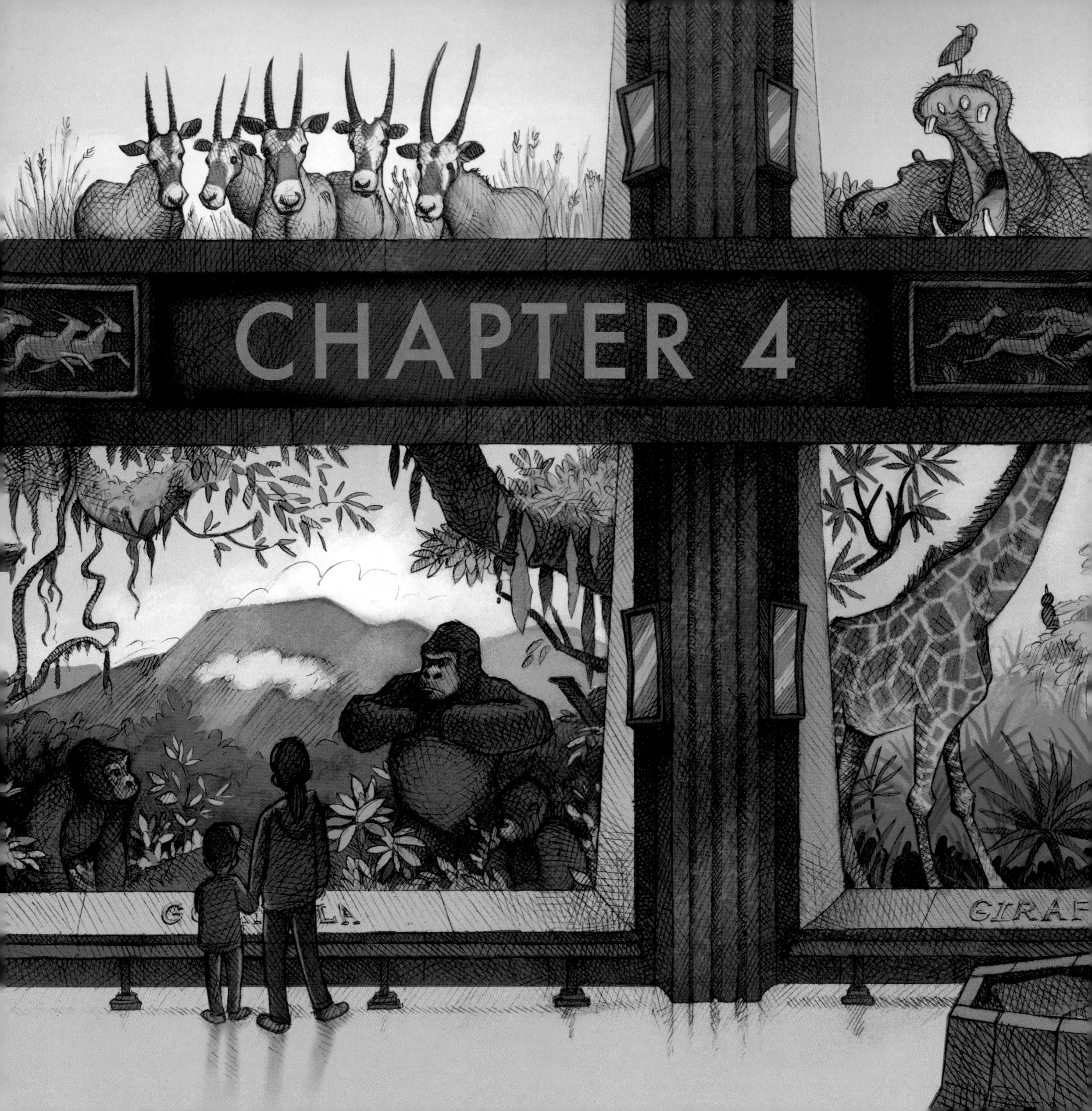
GIRAF

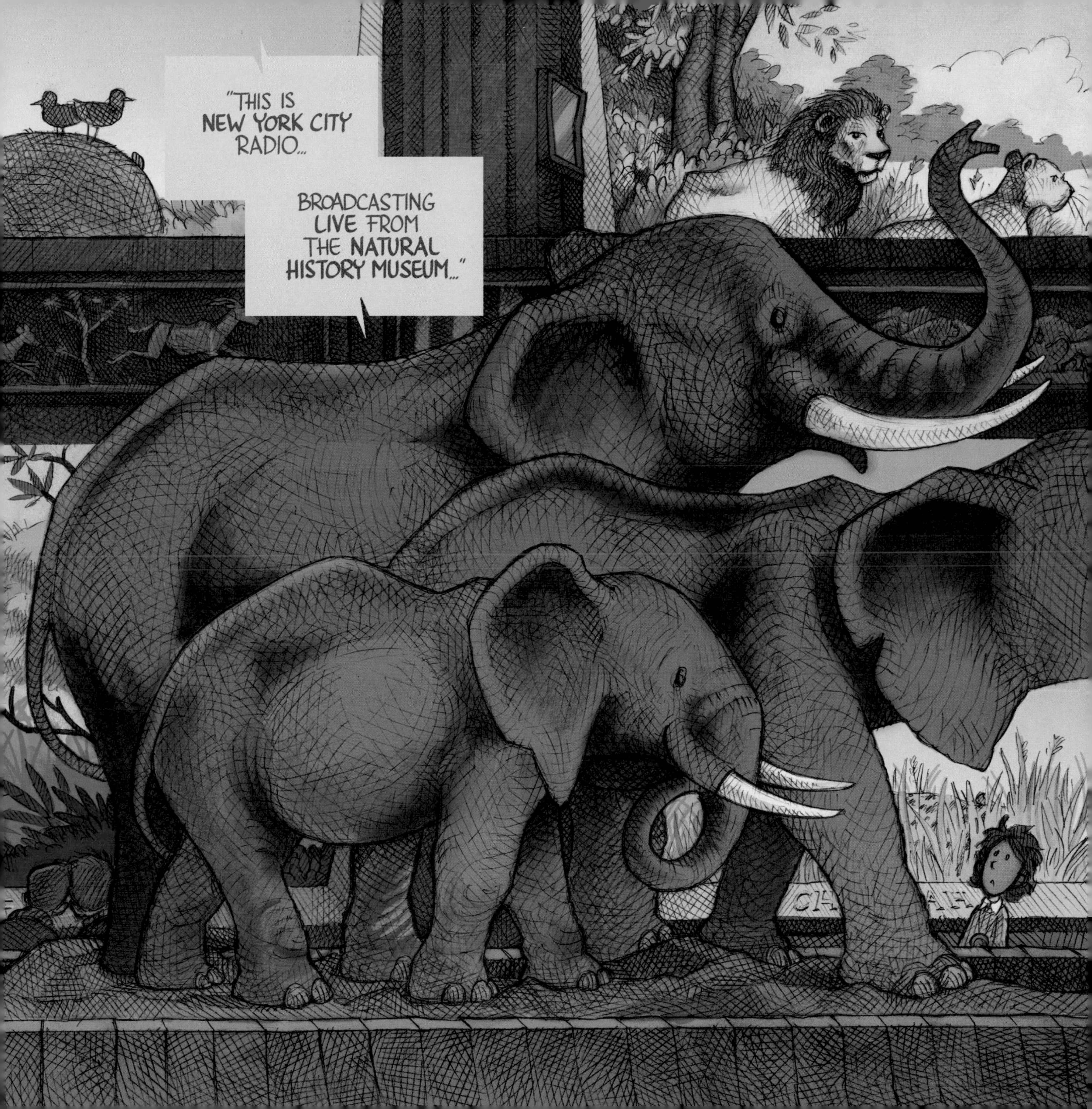
"THIS IS NEW YORK CITY RADIO...
BROADCASTING LIVE FROM THE NATURAL HISTORY MUSEUM..."

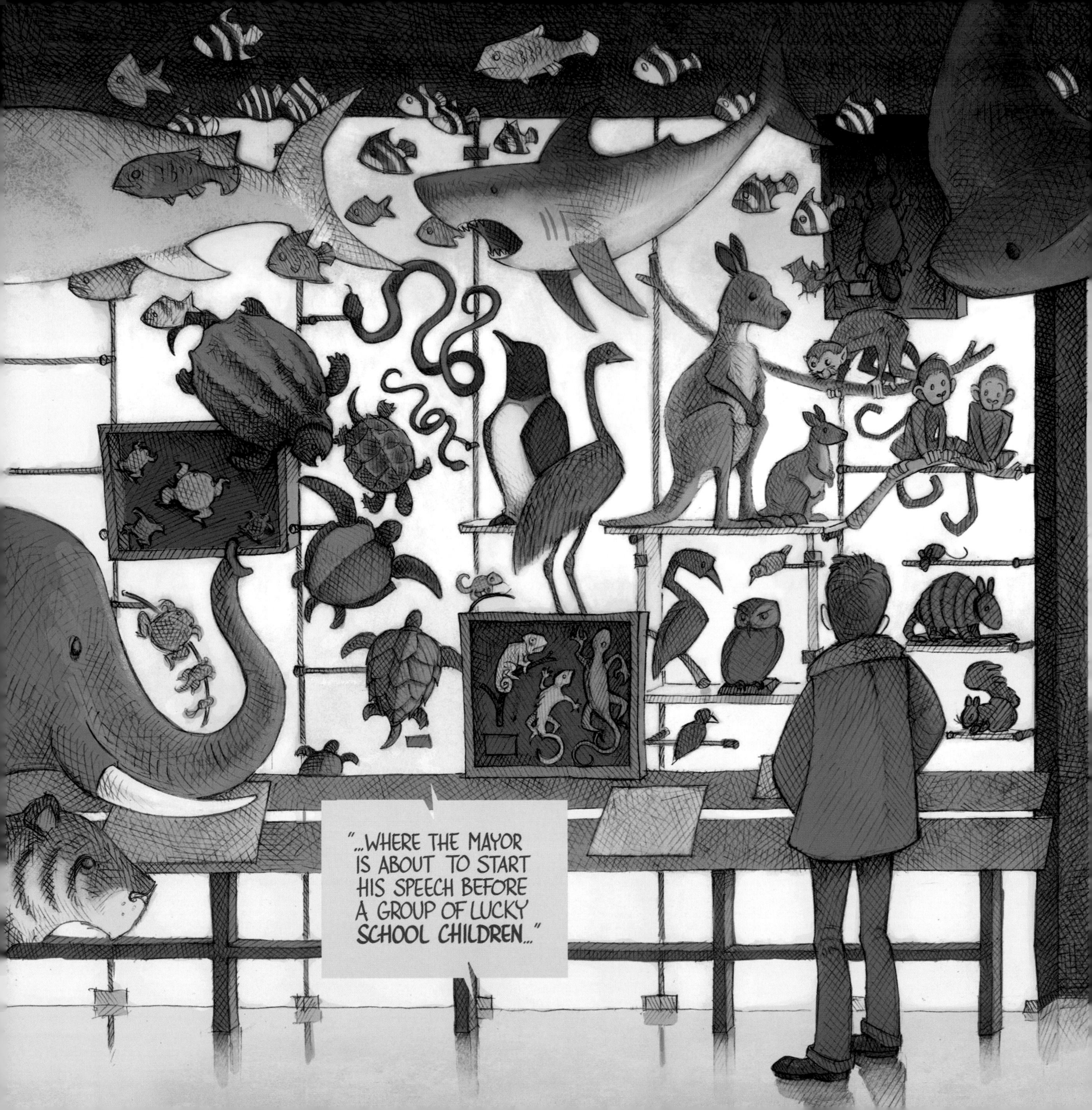
"...WHERE THE MAYOR IS ABOUT TO START HIS SPEECH BEFORE A GROUP OF LUCKY SCHOOL CHILDREN..."

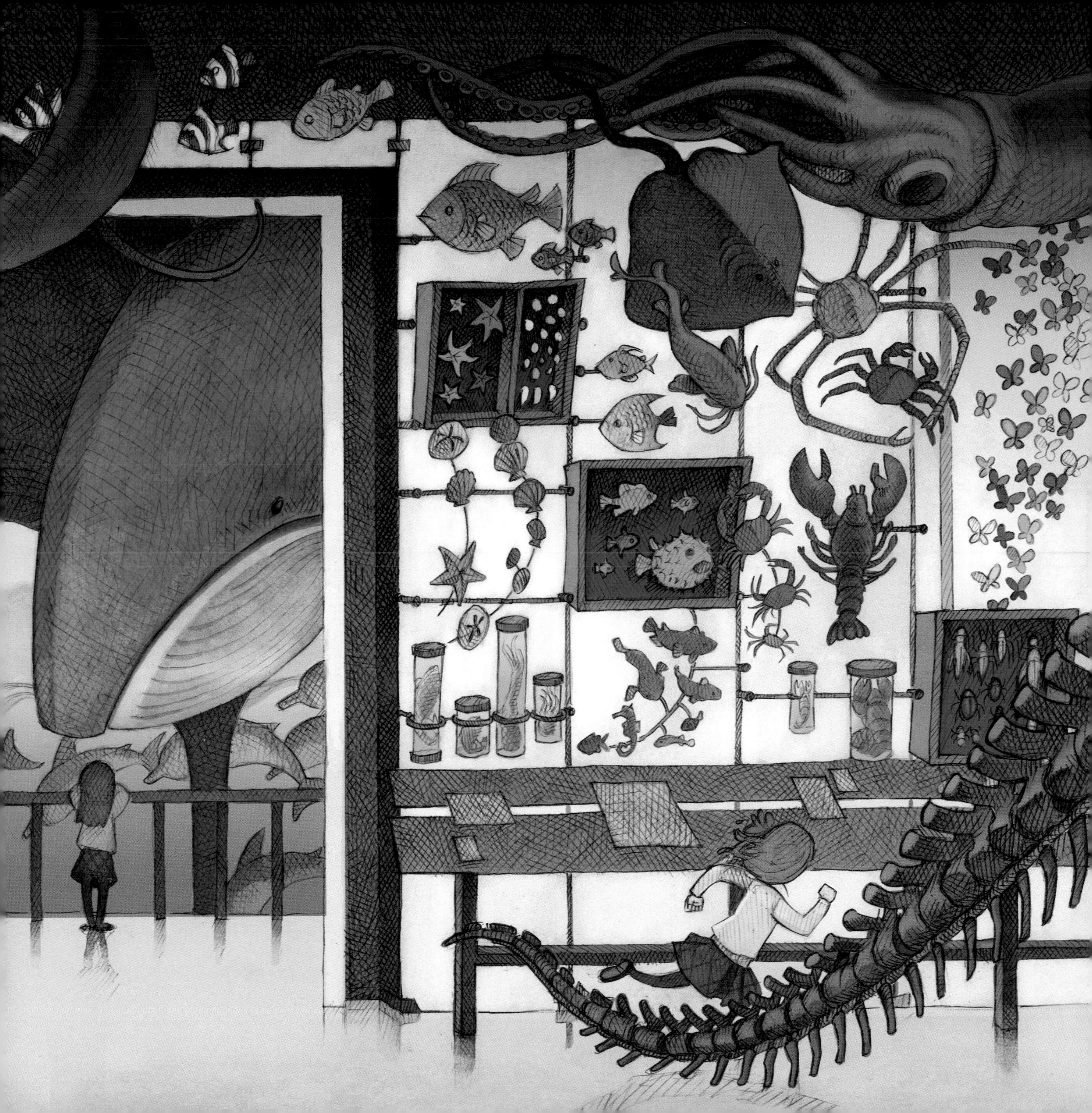

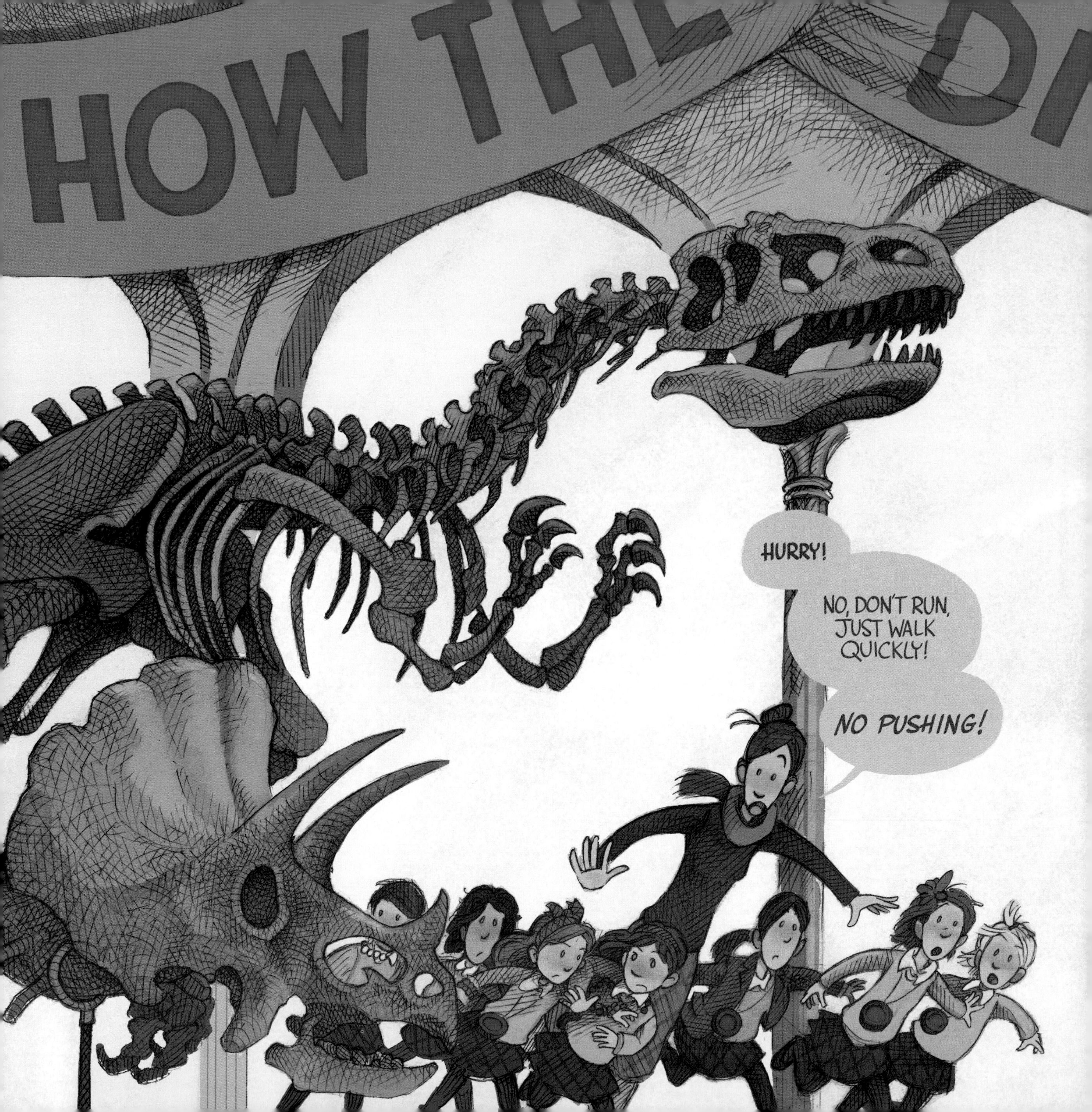
HURRY!
NO, DON'T RUN, JUST WALK QUICKLY!
NO PUSHING!

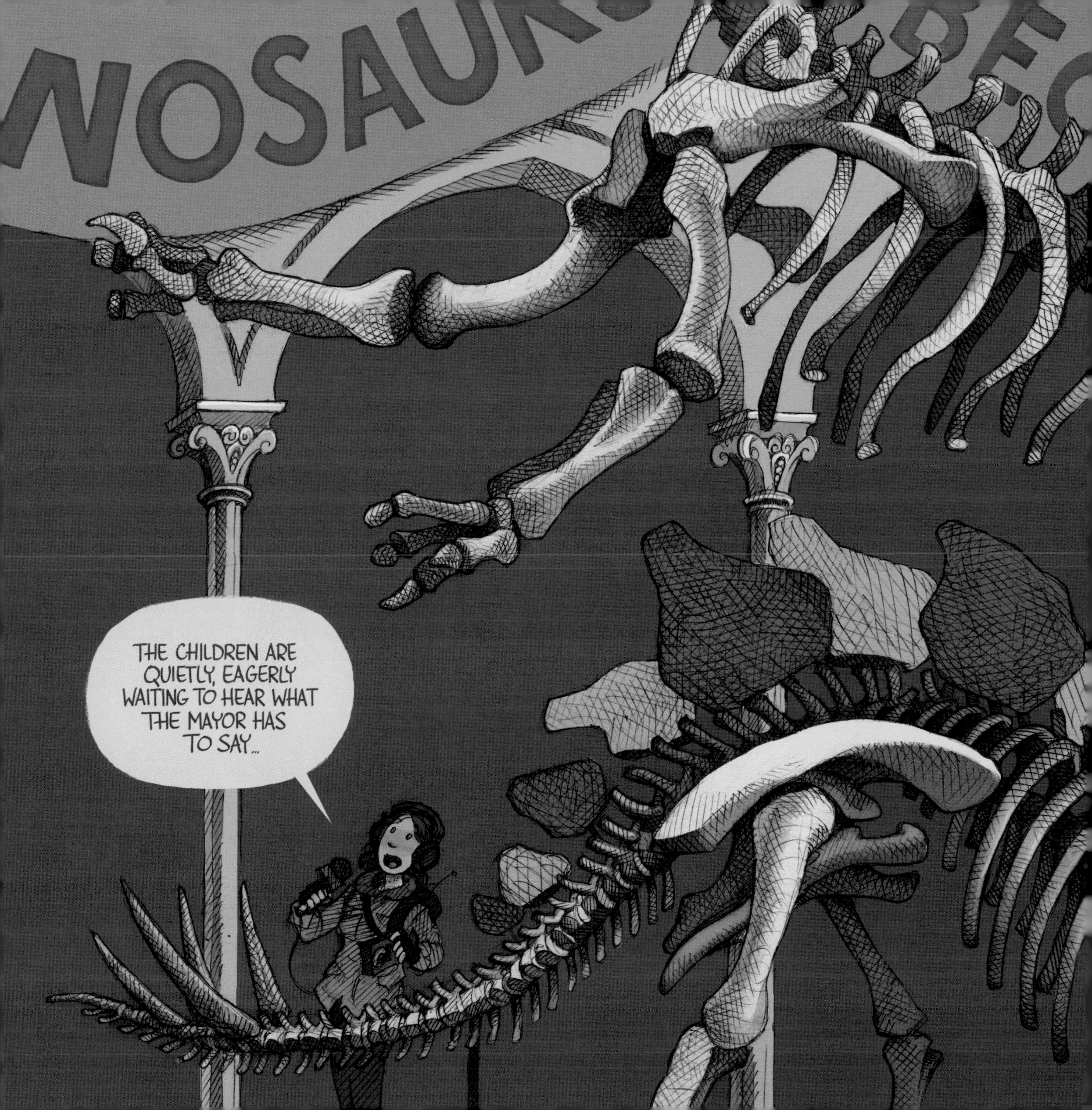
NOSAUR
BEC
THE CHILDREN ARE QUIETLY, EAGERLY WAITING TO HEAR WHAT THE MAYOR HAS TO SAY...

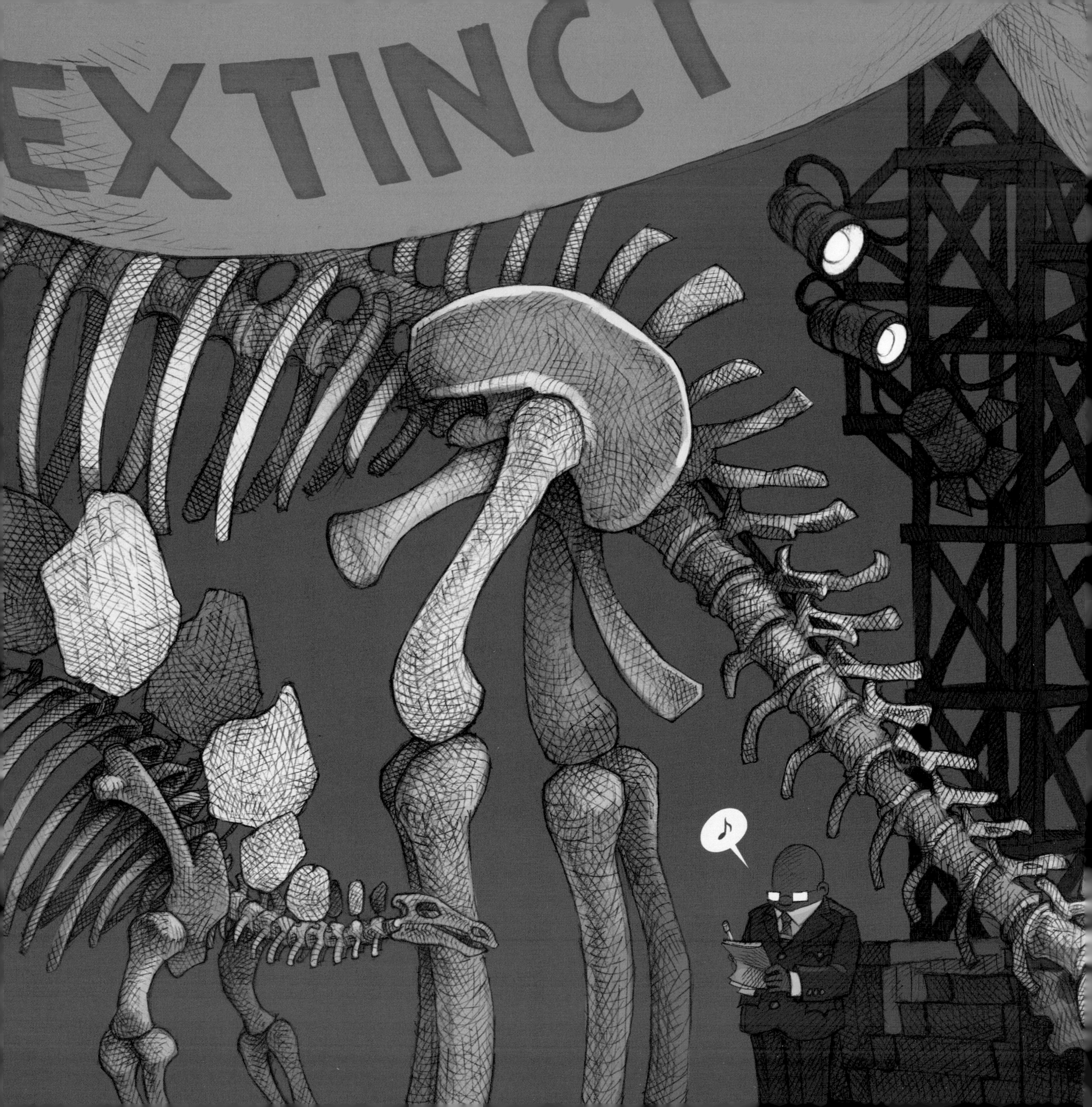
EXTINCT
♪

When Bolivar arrived at the Natural History Museum, he was still concerned that someone would notice he wasn't really the mayor.

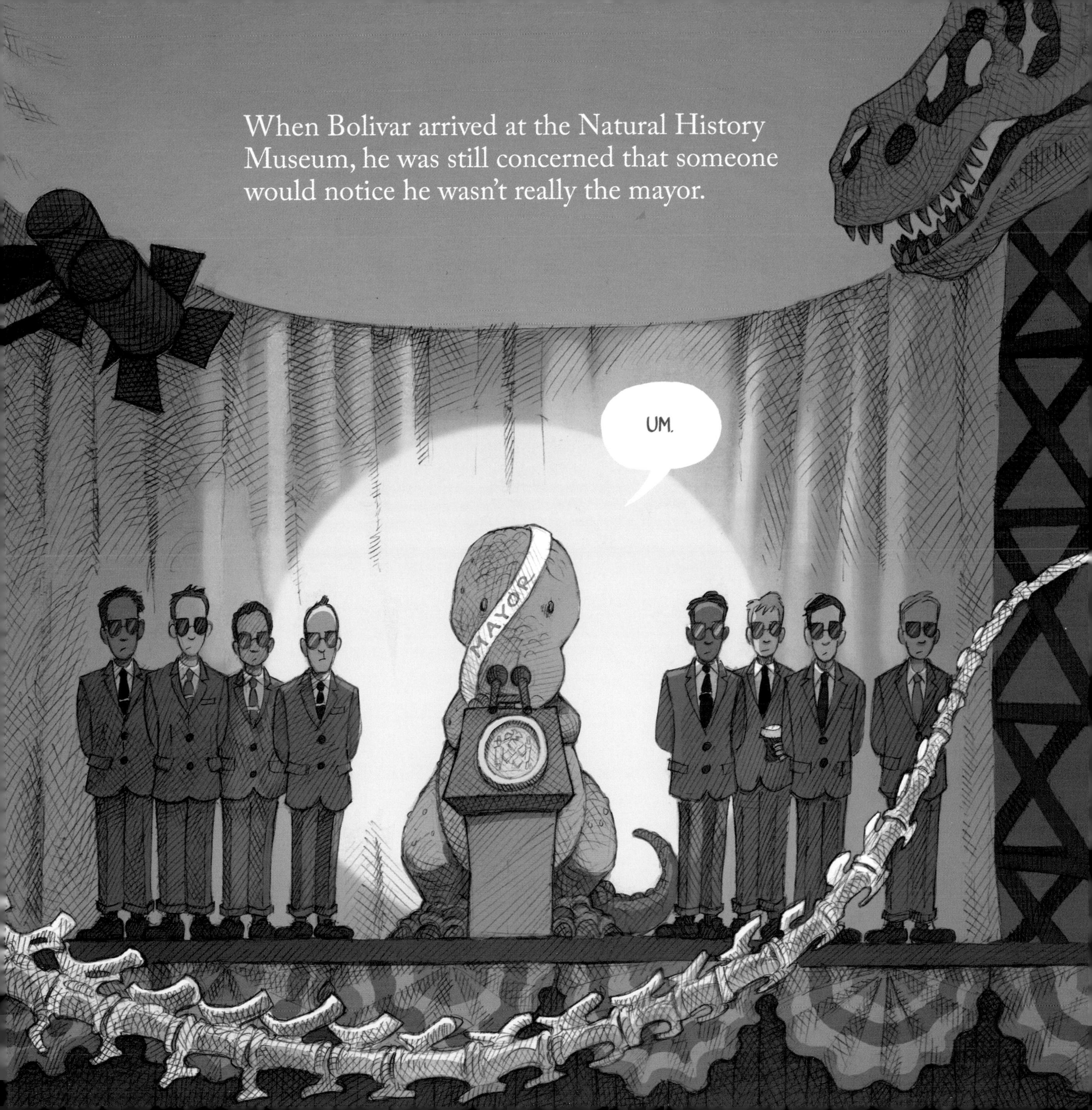
UM.
MAYOR

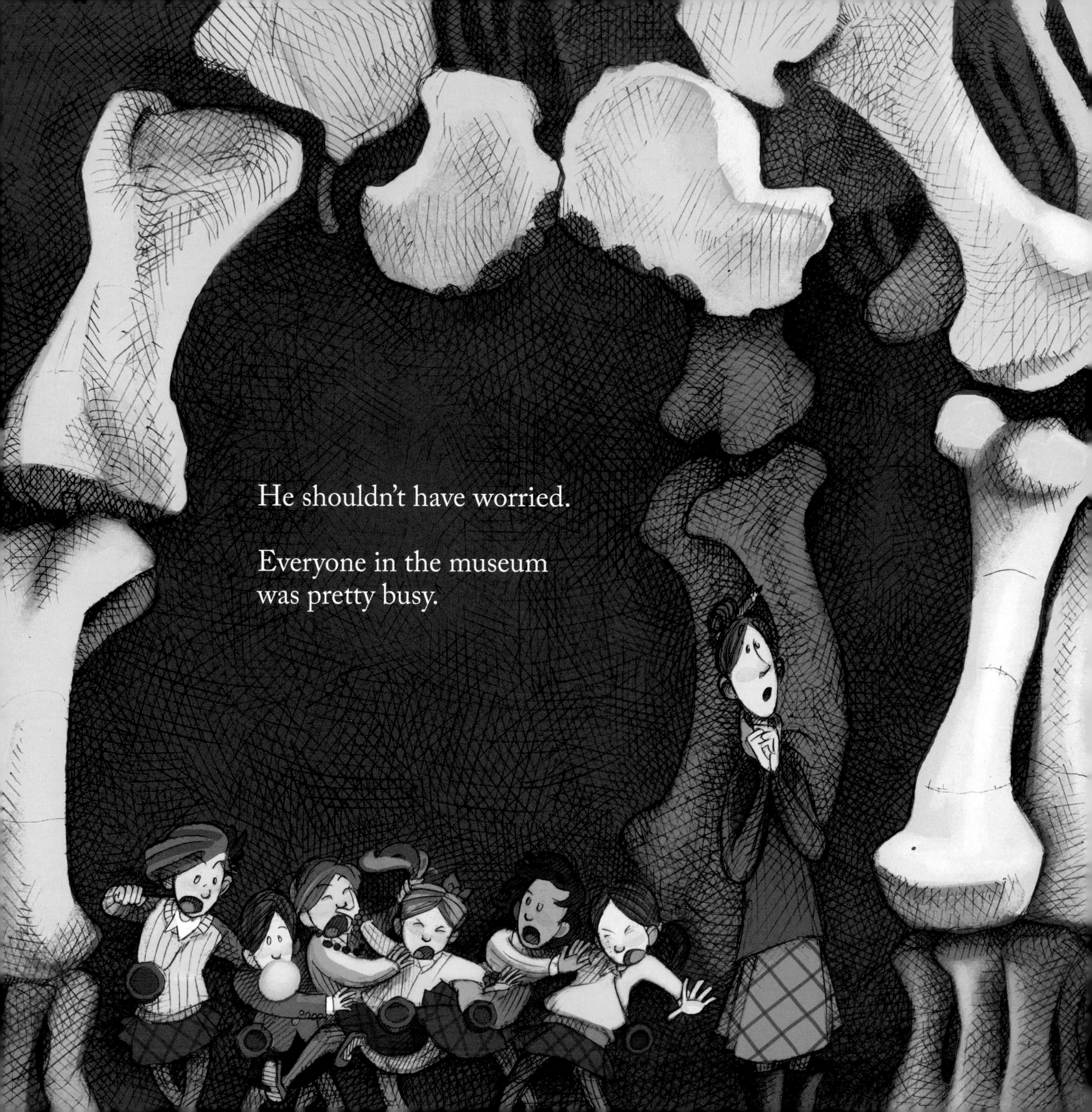
He shouldn't have worried.

Everyone in the museum was pretty busy.

Except one person.

When she looked at the mayor, she realized that he wasn't the mayor at all.

He was a dinosaur.

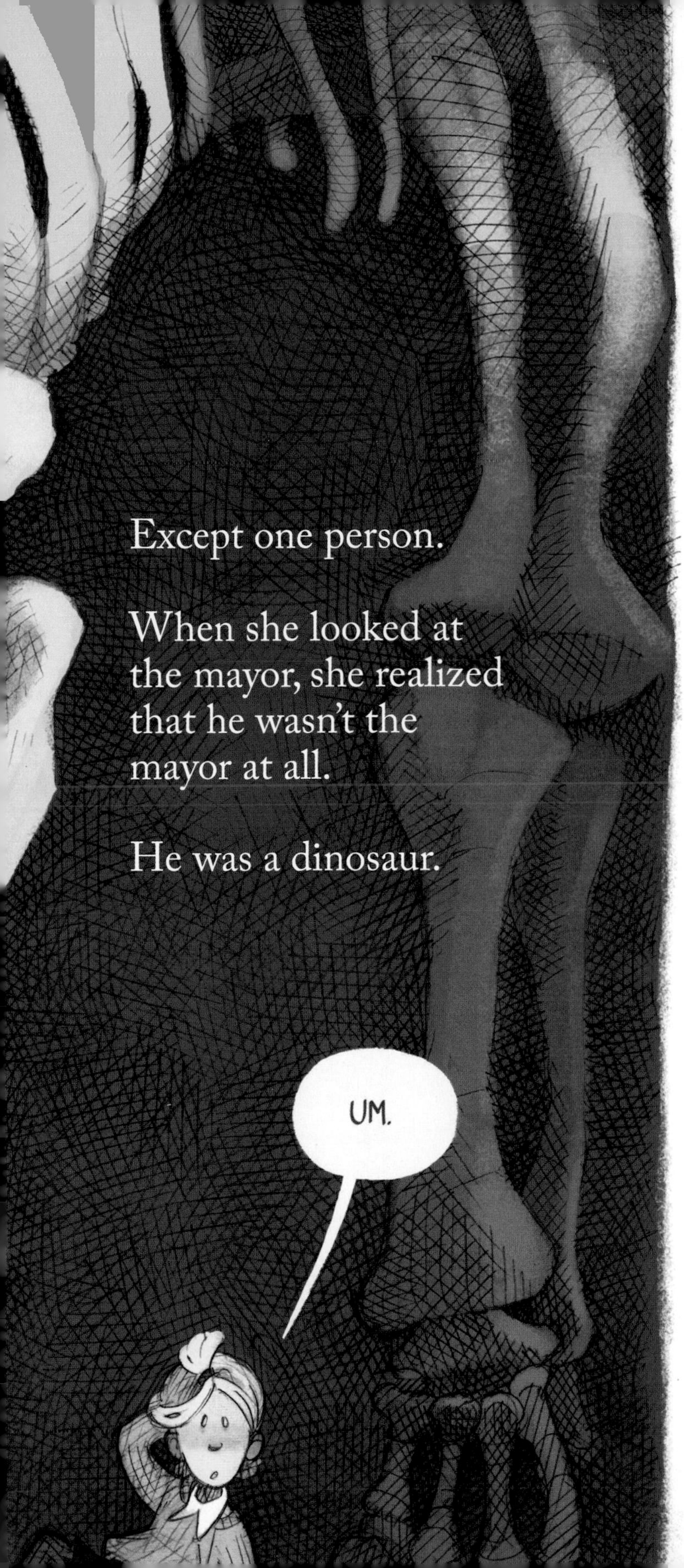
UM.

She decided to tell her teacher.

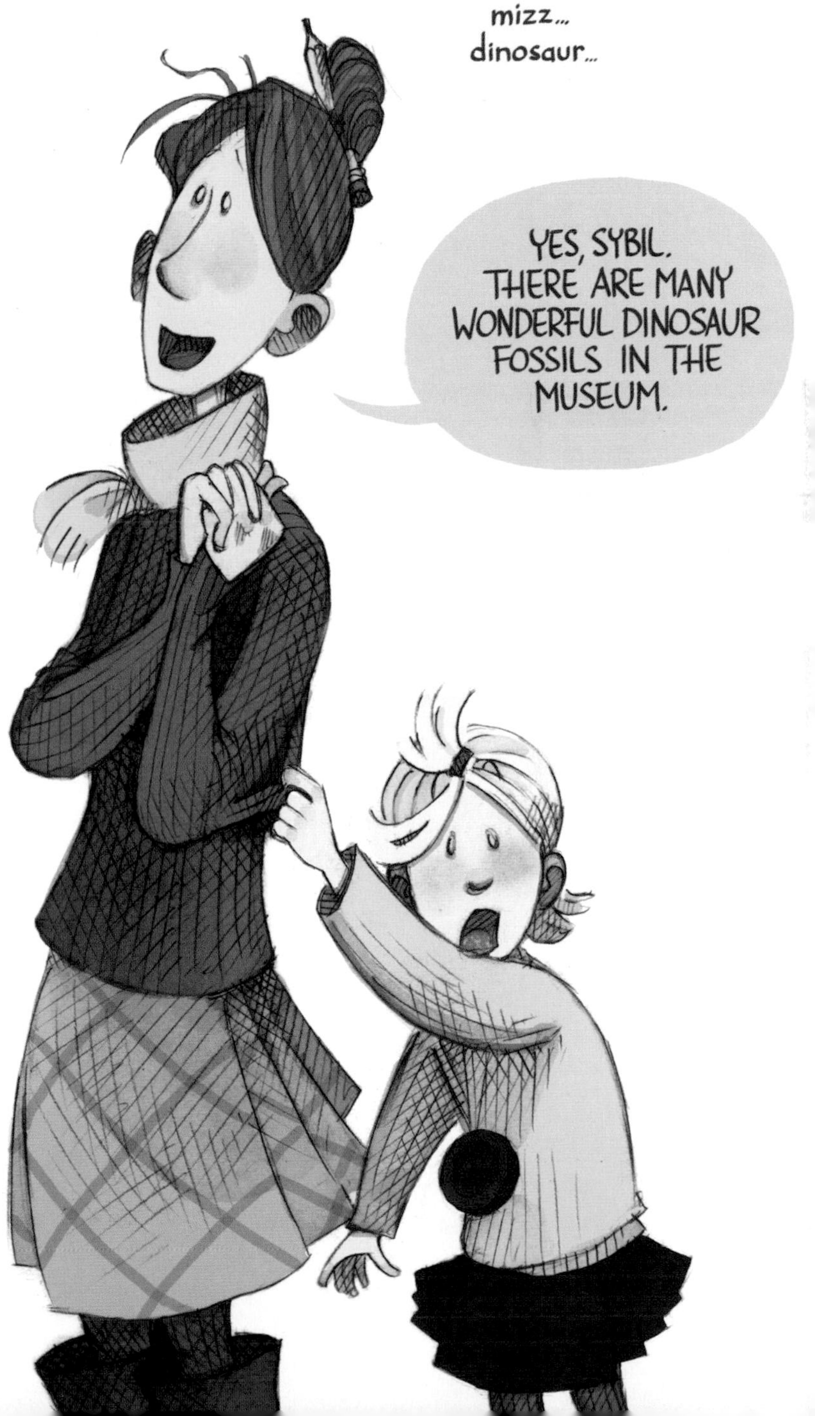
mizz...
dinosaur...
YES, SYBIL. THERE ARE MANY WONDERFUL DINOSAUR FOSSILS IN THE MUSEUM.

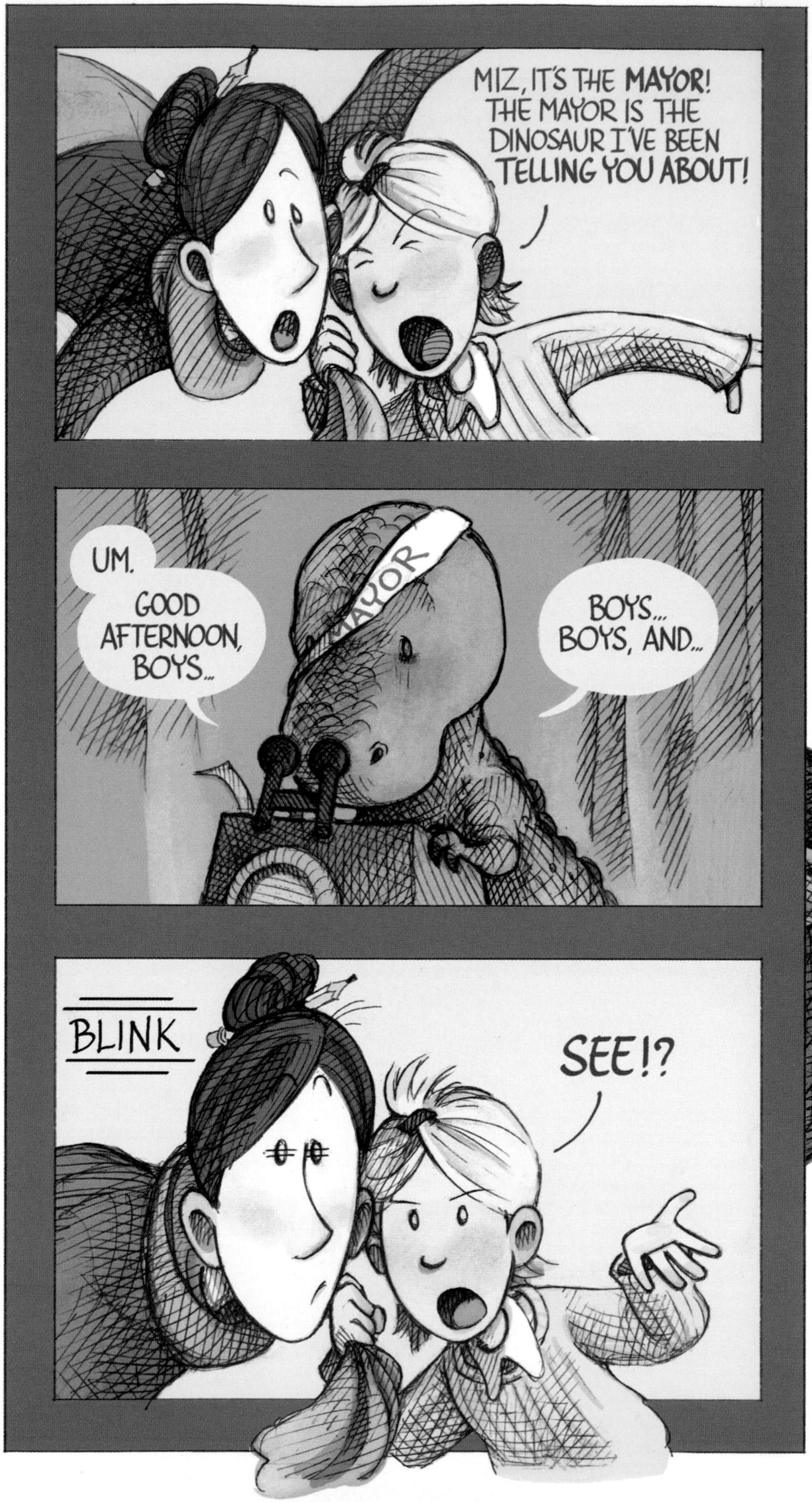
MIZ, IT'S THE **MAYOR**! THE MAYOR IS THE DINOSAUR I'VE BEEN **TELLING YOU ABOUT**!
UM.
GOOD AFTERNOON, BOYS...
MAYOR
BOYS... BOYS, AND...
BLINK
SEE!?

The teacher didn't want anyone to panic, so she found a museum guard.

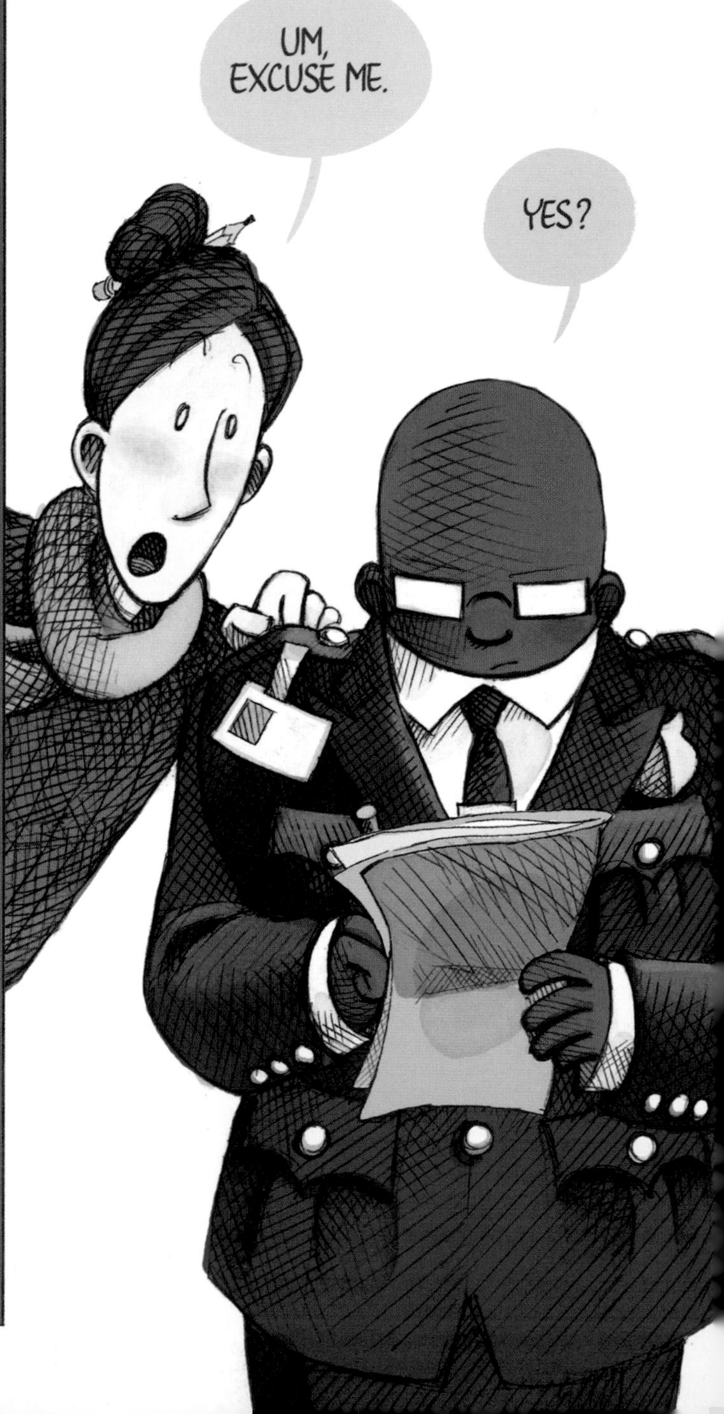
UM, EXCUSE ME.
YES?

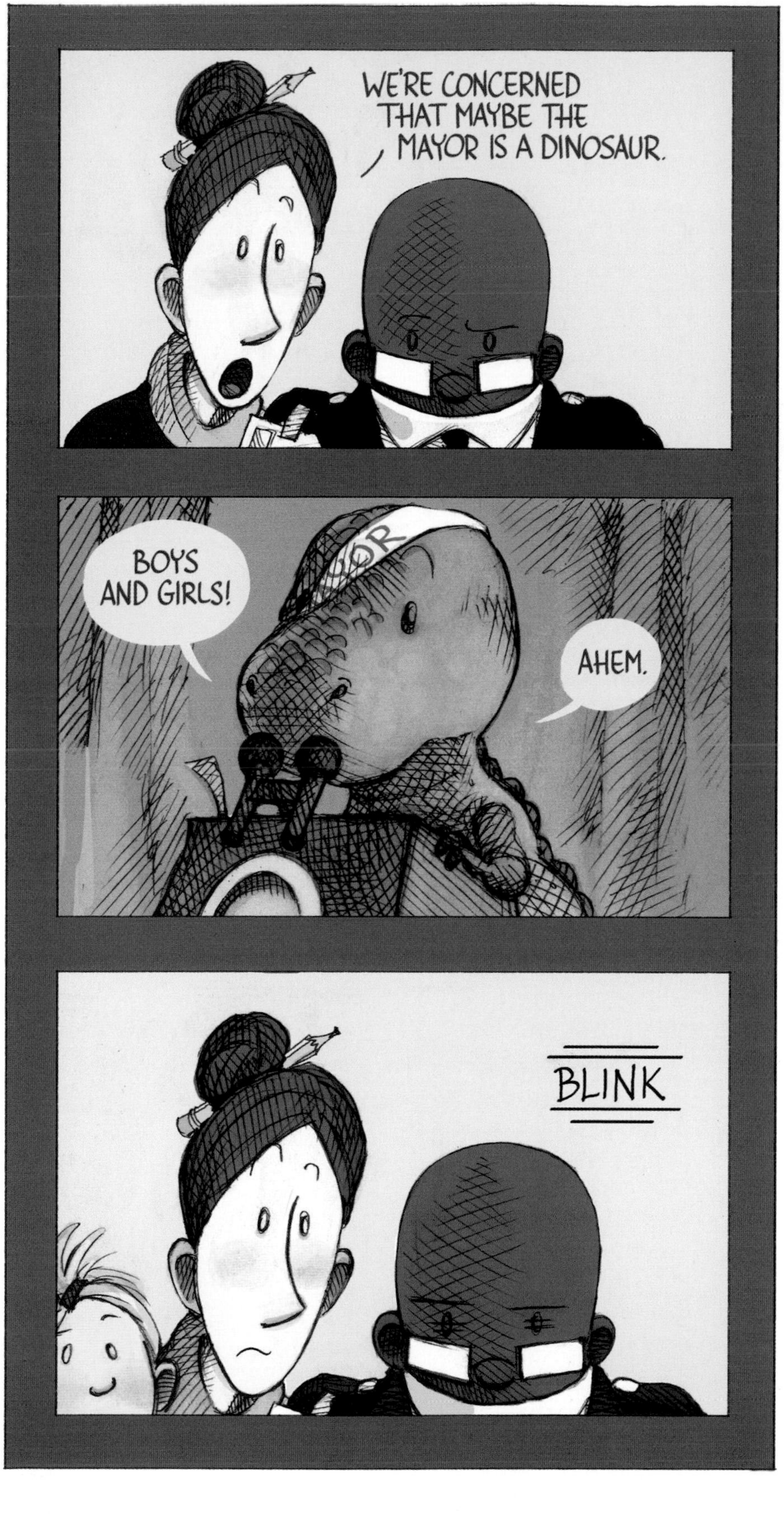
WE'RE CONCERNED THAT MAYBE THE MAYOR IS A DINOSAUR.
BOYS AND GIRLS!
AHEM.
BLINK

He had to squint a bit, but he decided the mayor was a dinosaur, too.

...maybe.

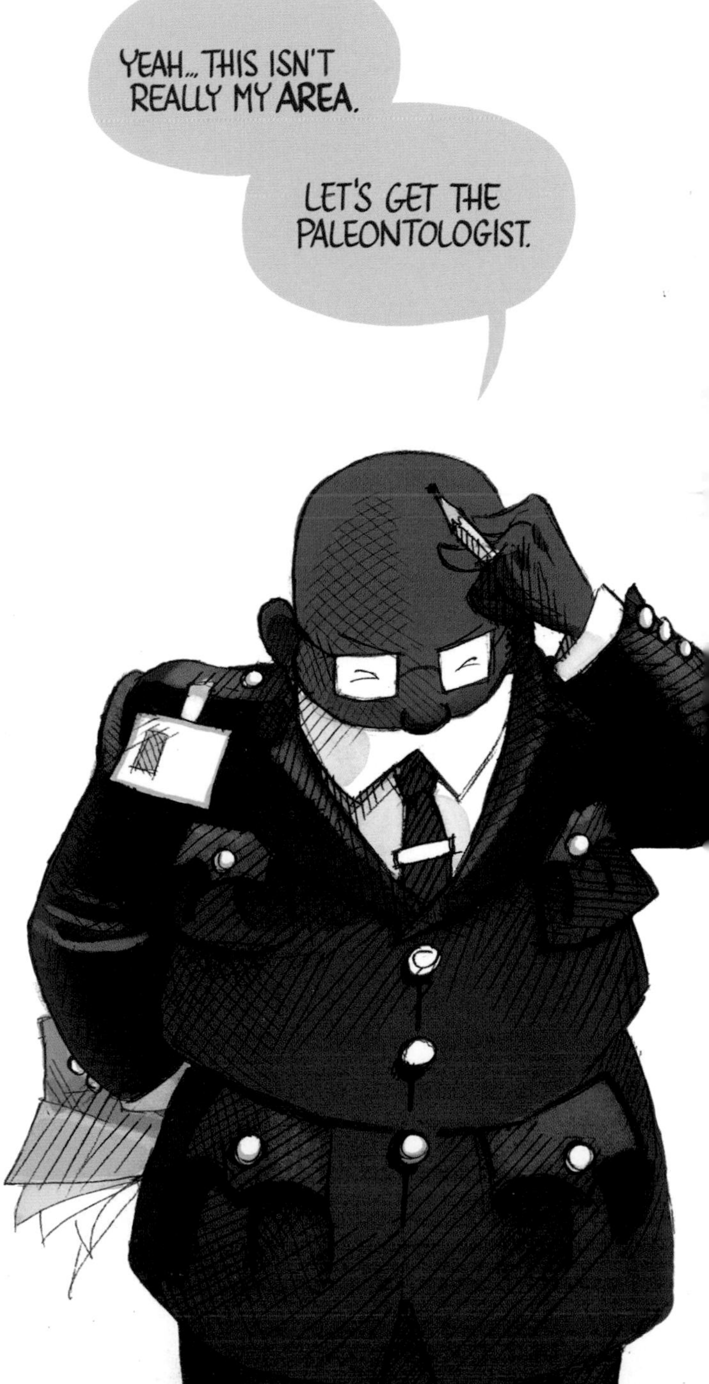
YEAH... THIS ISN'T REALLY MY **AREA**.
LET'S GET THE PALEONTOLOGIST.

Now the paleontologist was a leader in his field.

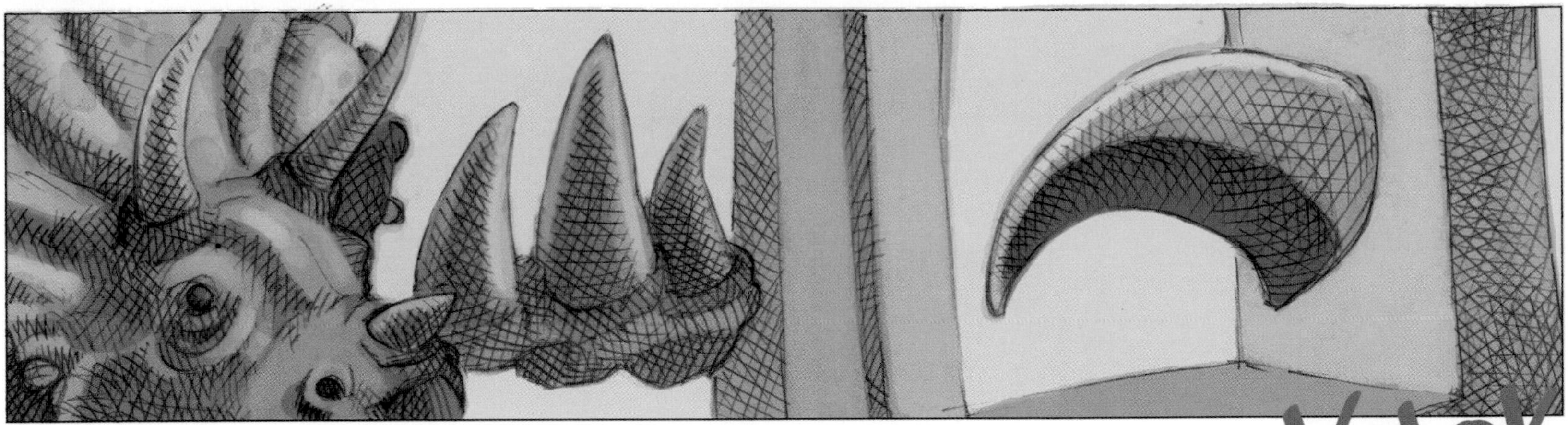
KNOK!

He knew a lot about dinosaurs.

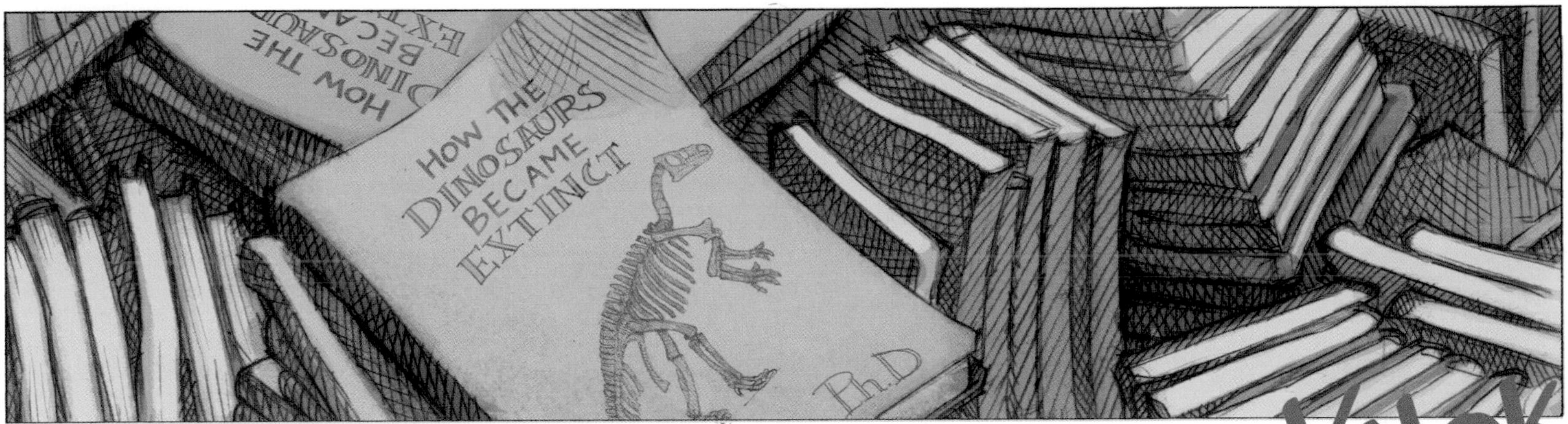
HOW THE DINOSAURS BECAME EXTINCT
Ph.D
KNOK!

He had written a book about dinosaurs.

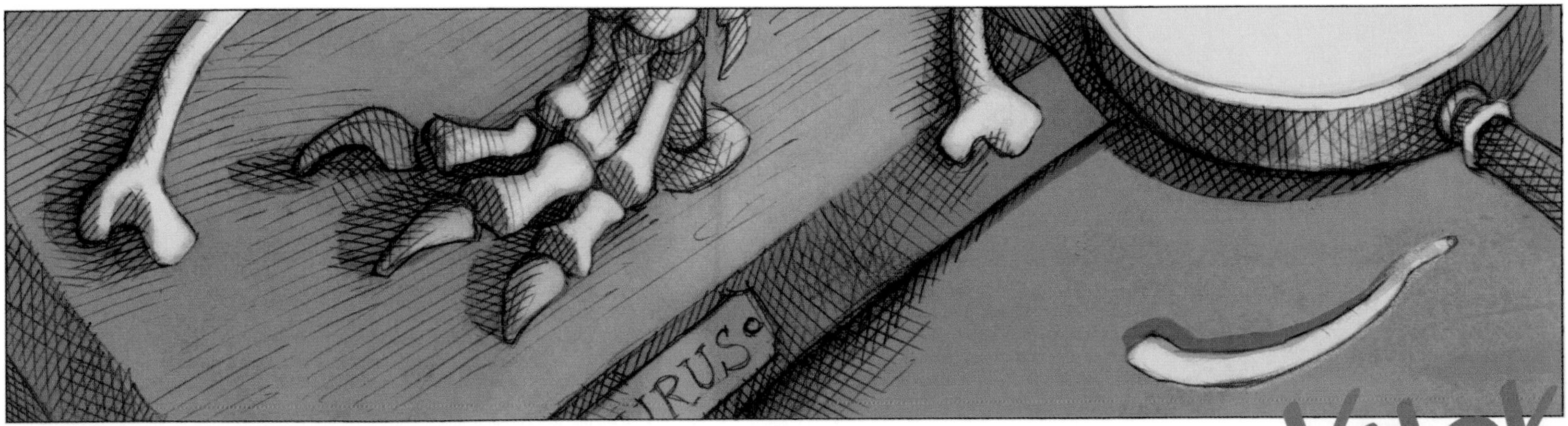
KNOK!

He had even discovered a dinosaur.

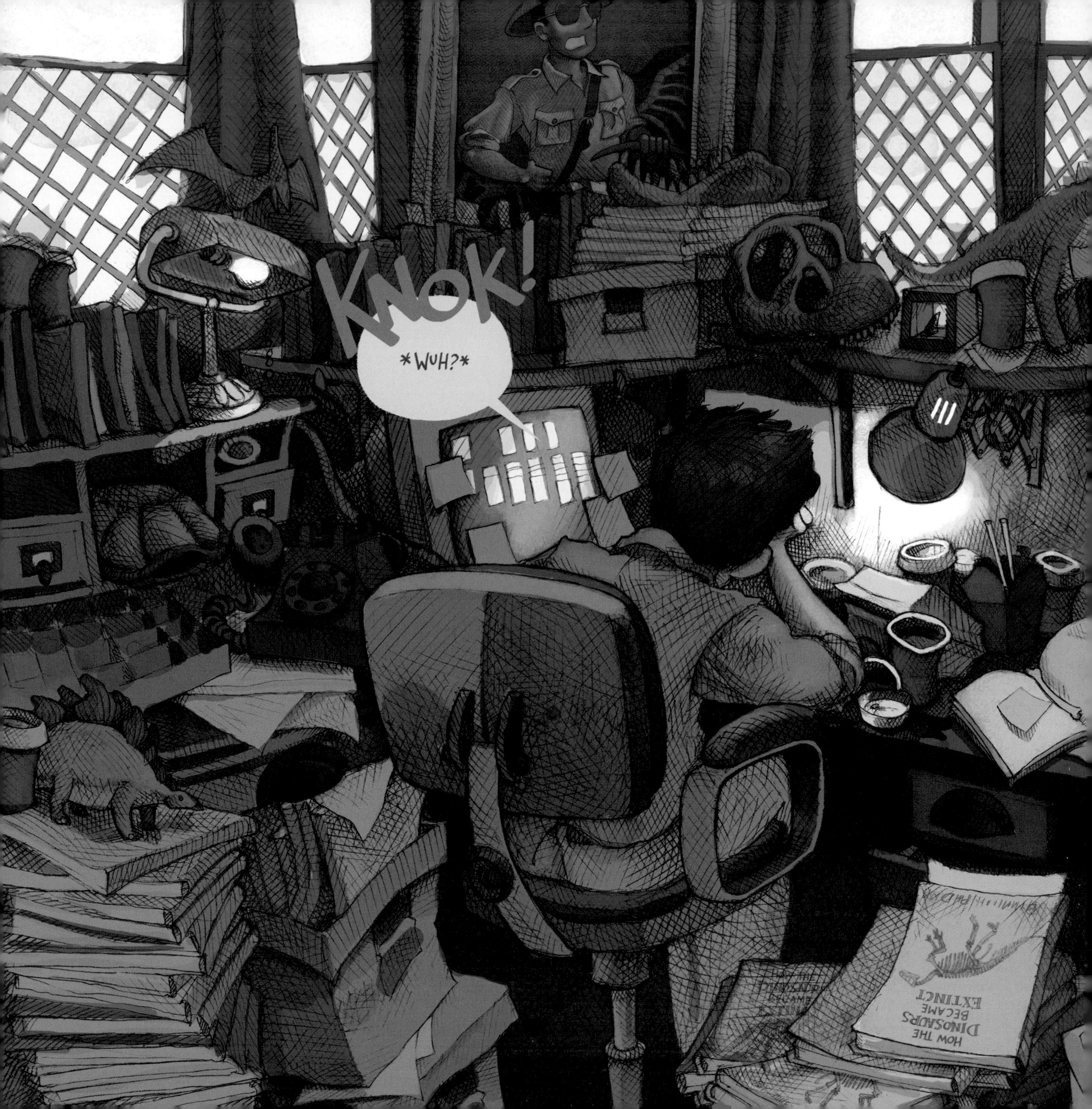
KNOK!
WUH?
HOW THE DINOSAURS BECAME EXTINCT

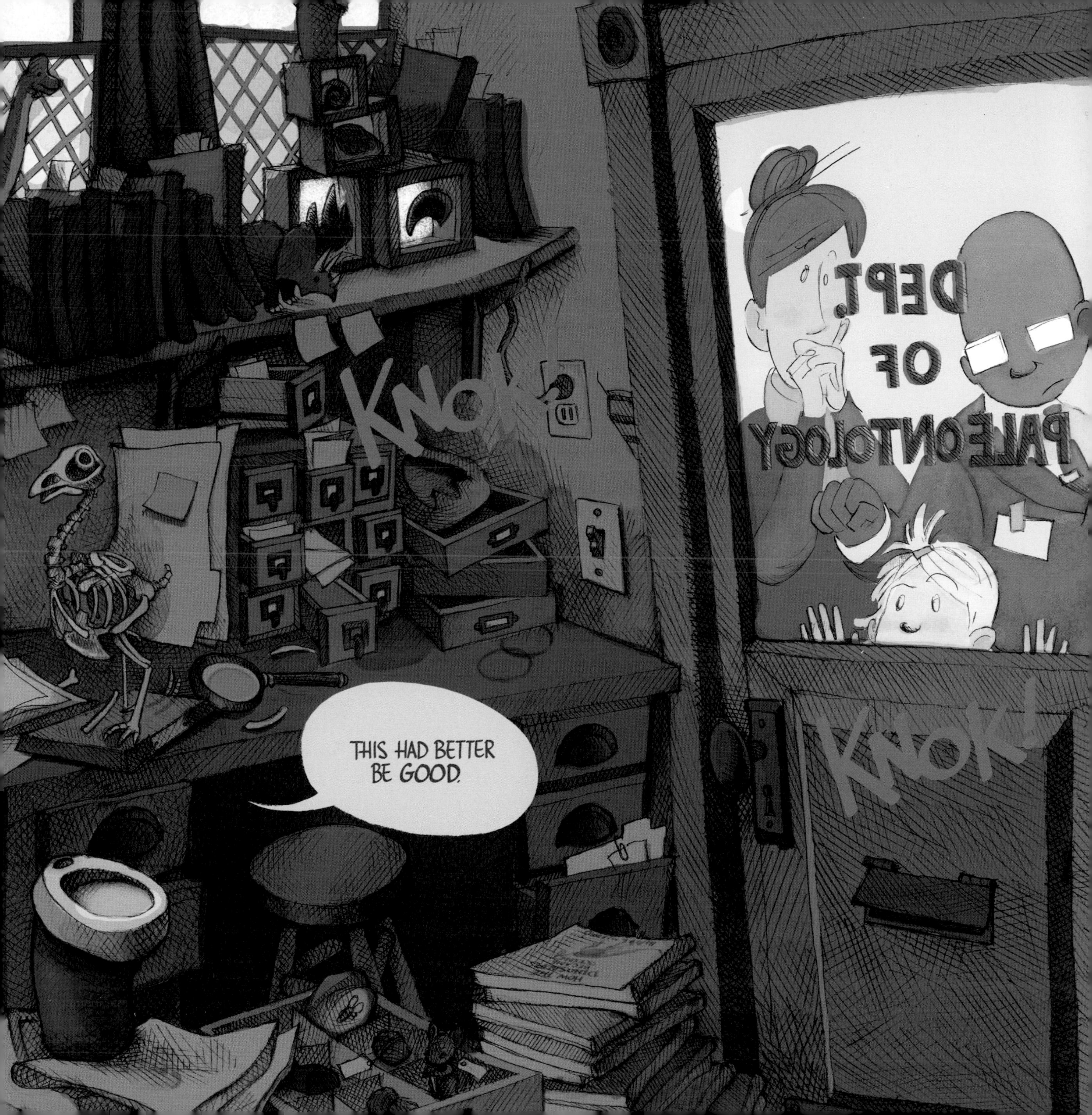
KNOK!
DEPT. OF PALEONTOLOGY
KNOK!
THIS HAD BETTER BE GOOD.

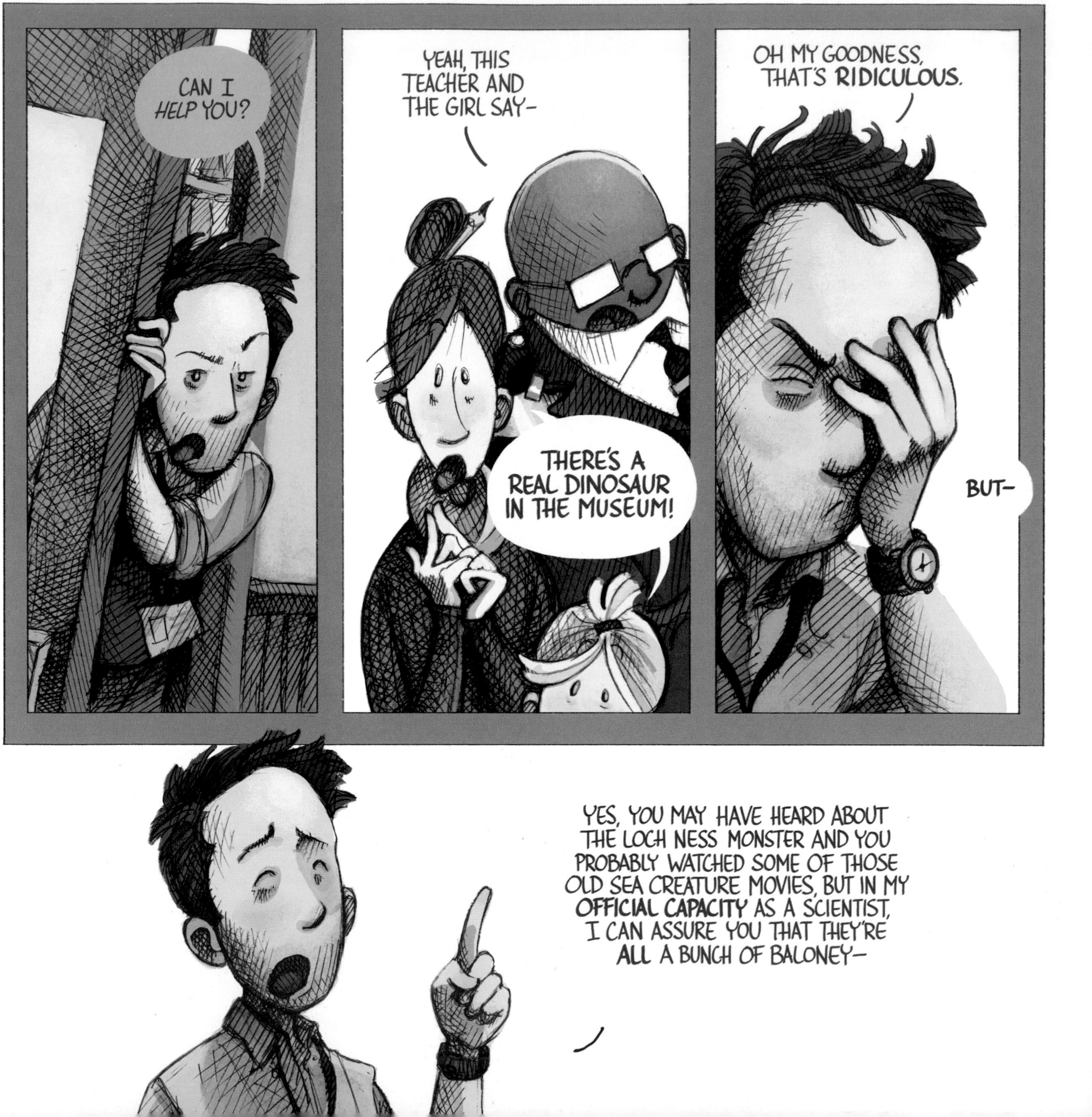
CAN I HELP YOU?
YEAH, THIS TEACHER AND THE GIRL SAY-
THERE'S A REAL DINOSAUR IN THE MUSEUM!
OH MY GOODNESS, THAT'S RIDICULOUS.
BUT-
YES, YOU MAY HAVE HEARD ABOUT THE LOCH NESS MONSTER AND YOU PROBABLY WATCHED SOME OF THOSE OLD SEA CREATURE MOVIES, BUT IN MY OFFICIAL CAPACITY AS A SCIENTIST, I CAN ASSURE YOU THAT THEY'RE ALL A BUNCH OF BALONEY-

Or so the paleontologist thought.

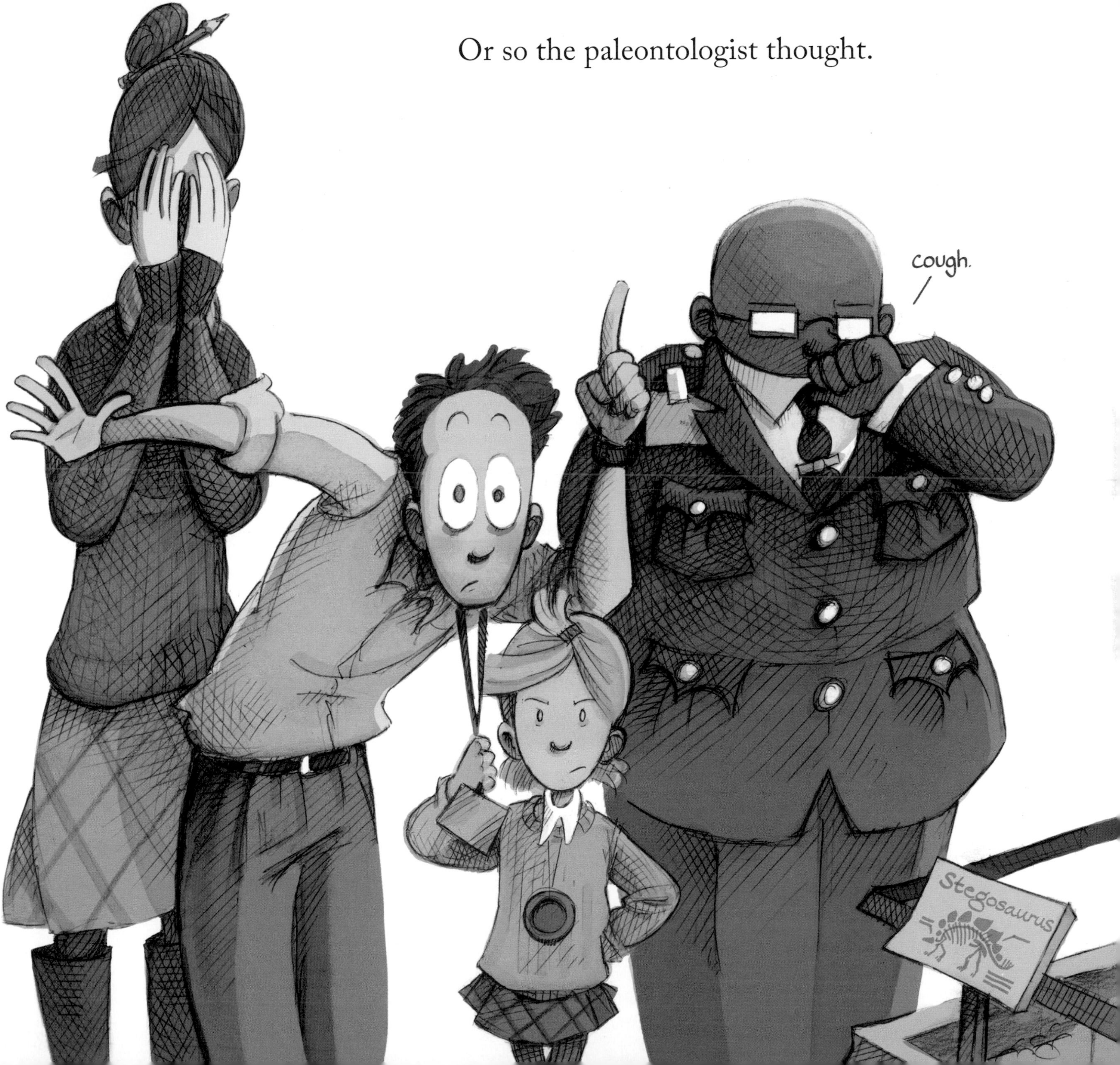
cough.
Stegosaurus

Bolivar really enjoyed being the mayor. He had never had an audience before. He decided to tell one of his favorite jokes.

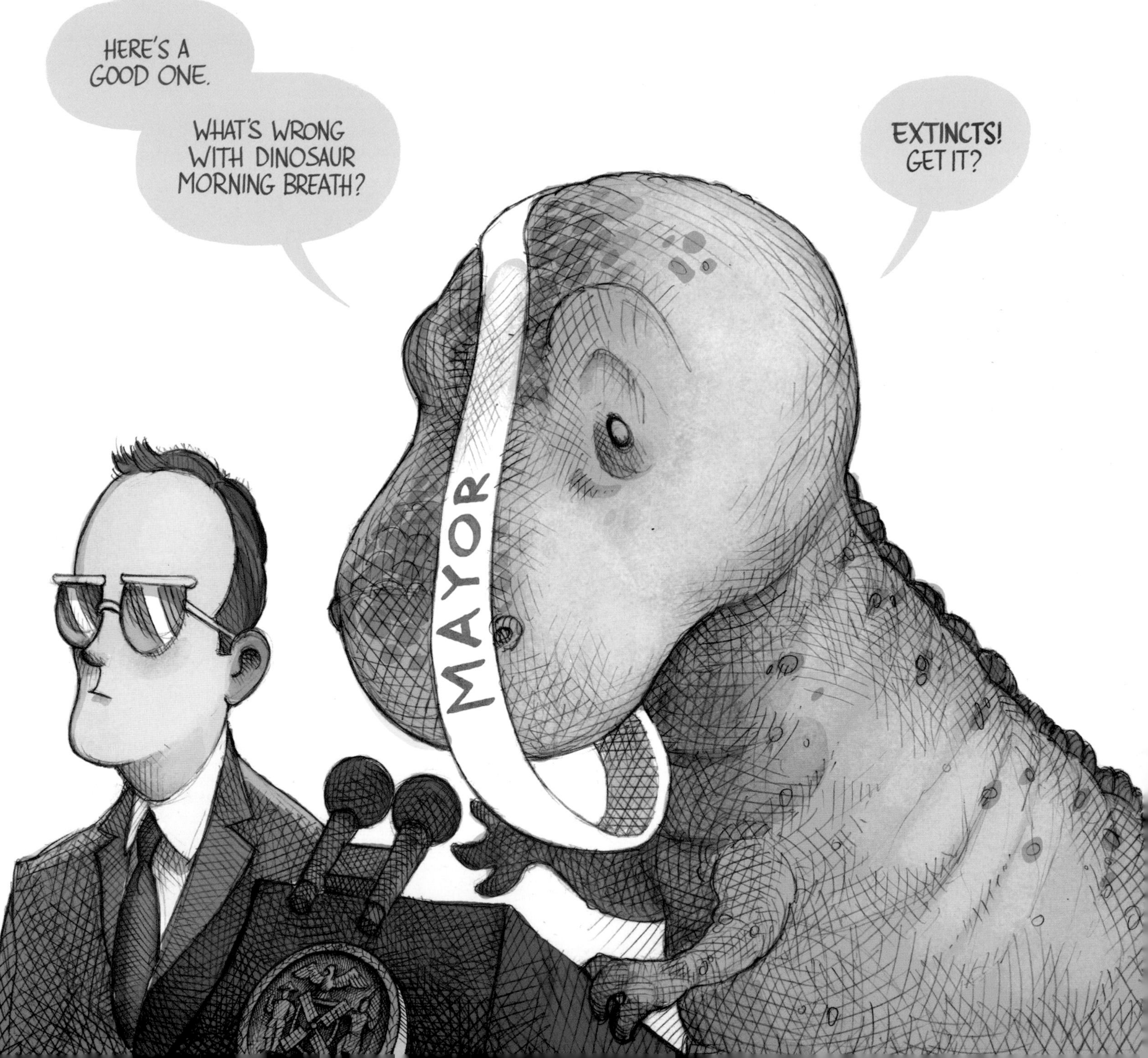
HERE'S A GOOD ONE.
WHAT'S WRONG WITH DINOSAUR MORNING BREATH?
EXTINCTS! GET IT?
MAYOR

That's when someone shouted...

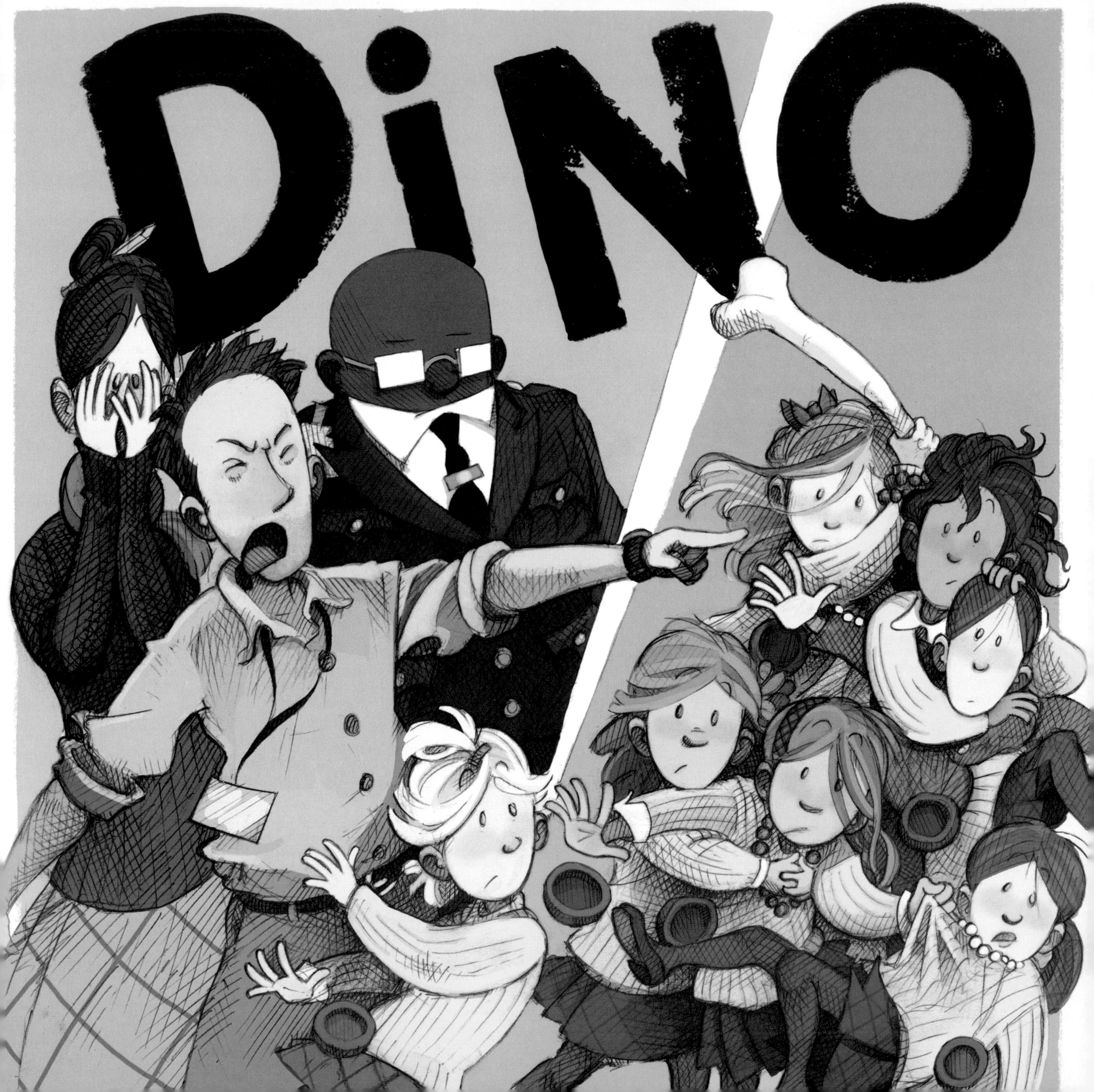
DiNO

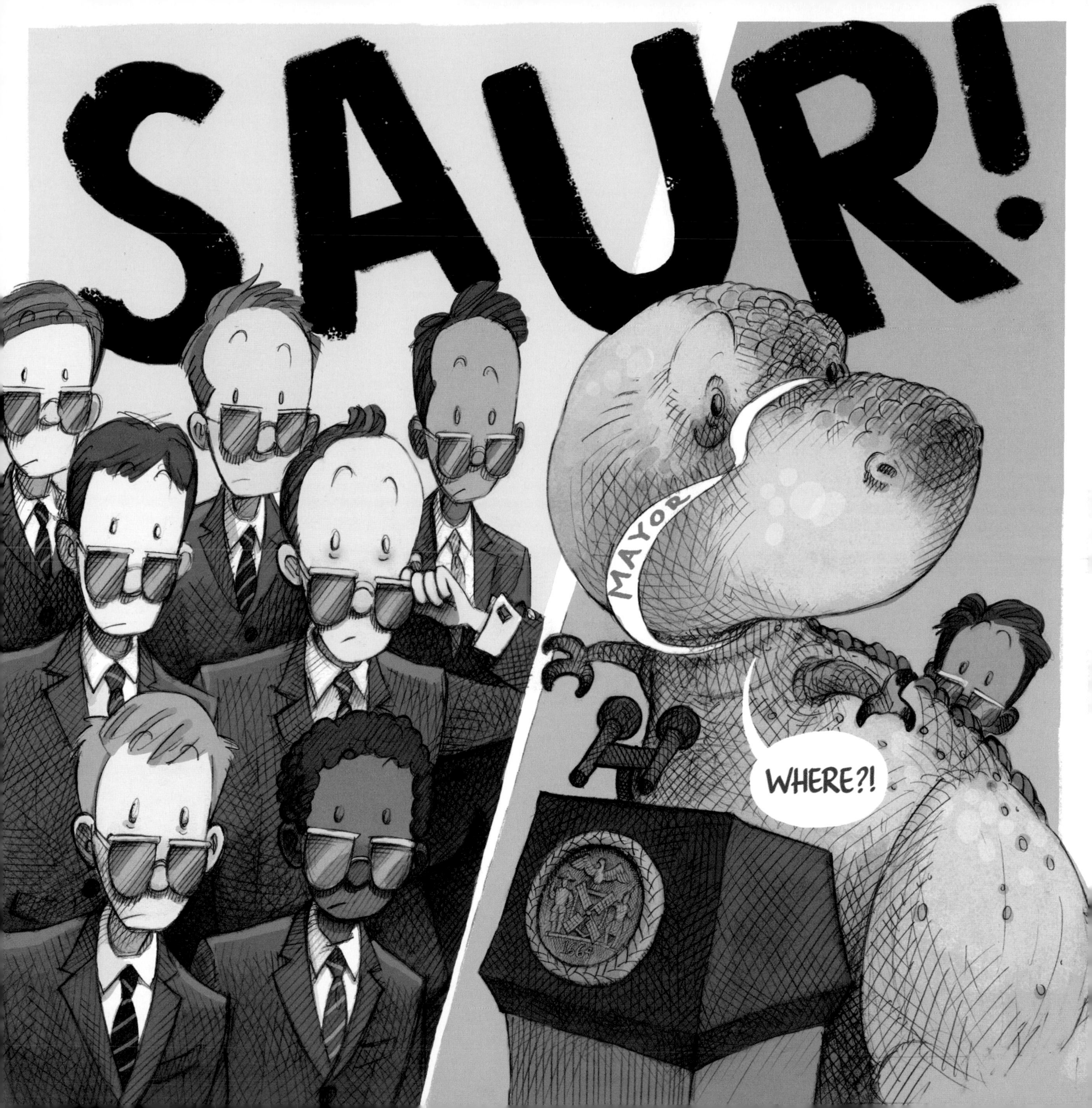
SAUR!
MAYOR
WHERE?!

Bolivar was so busy being the mayor, he completely forgot that he was a dinosaur.

That's why he decided to run.

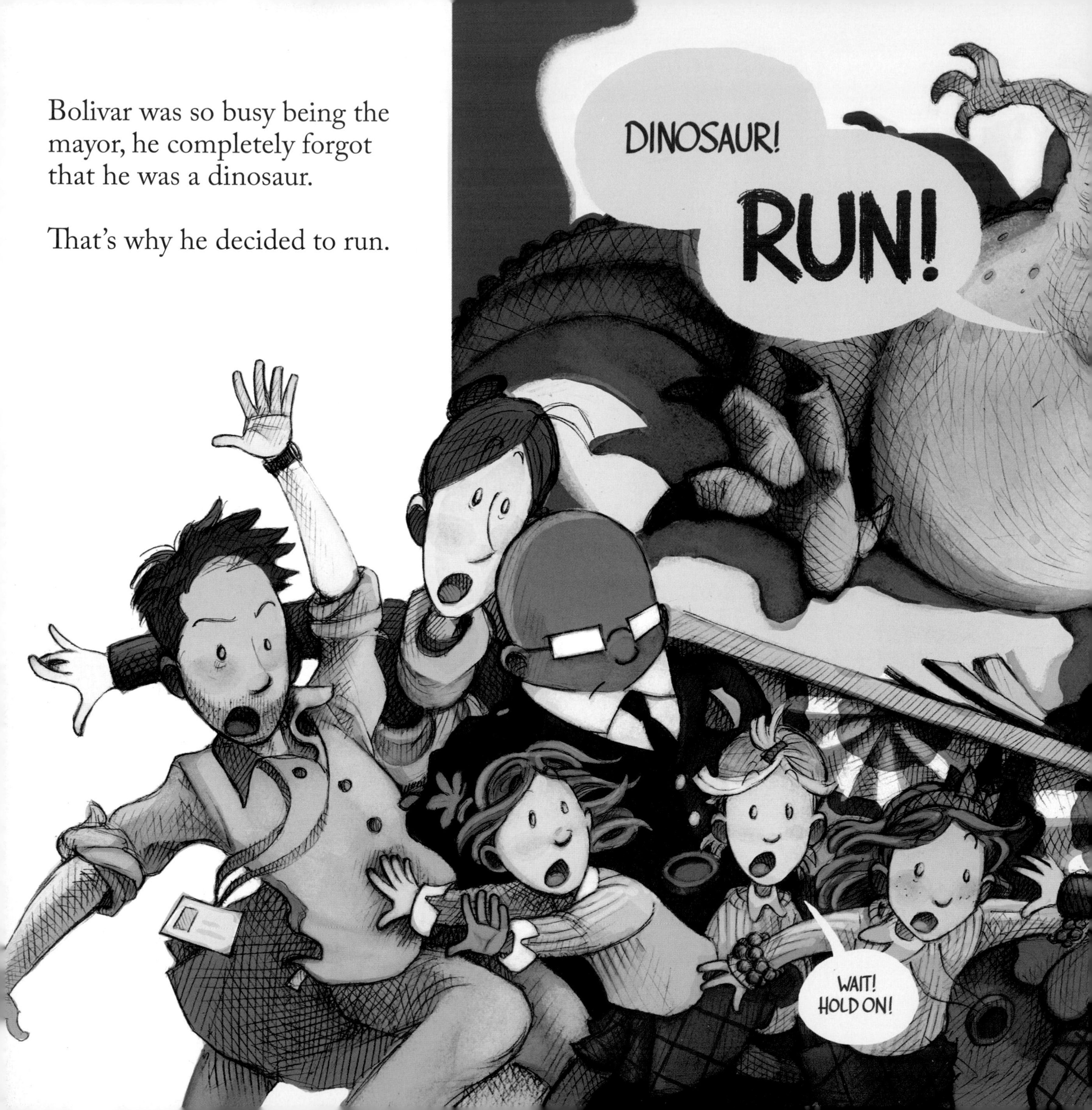
DINOSAUR!
RUN!
WAIT! HOLD ON!

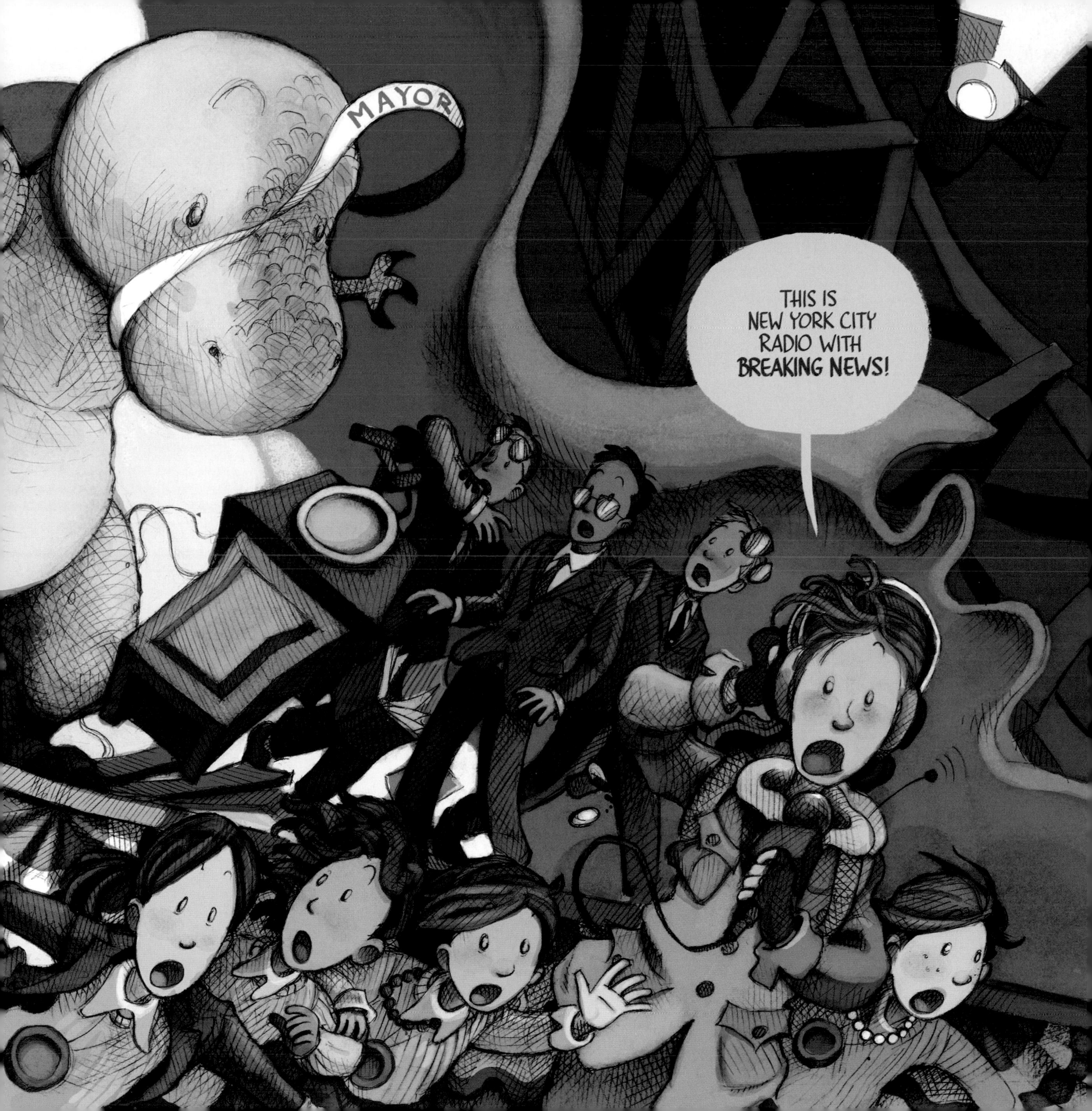
MAYOR
THIS IS NEW YORK CITY RADIO WITH BREAKING NEWS!

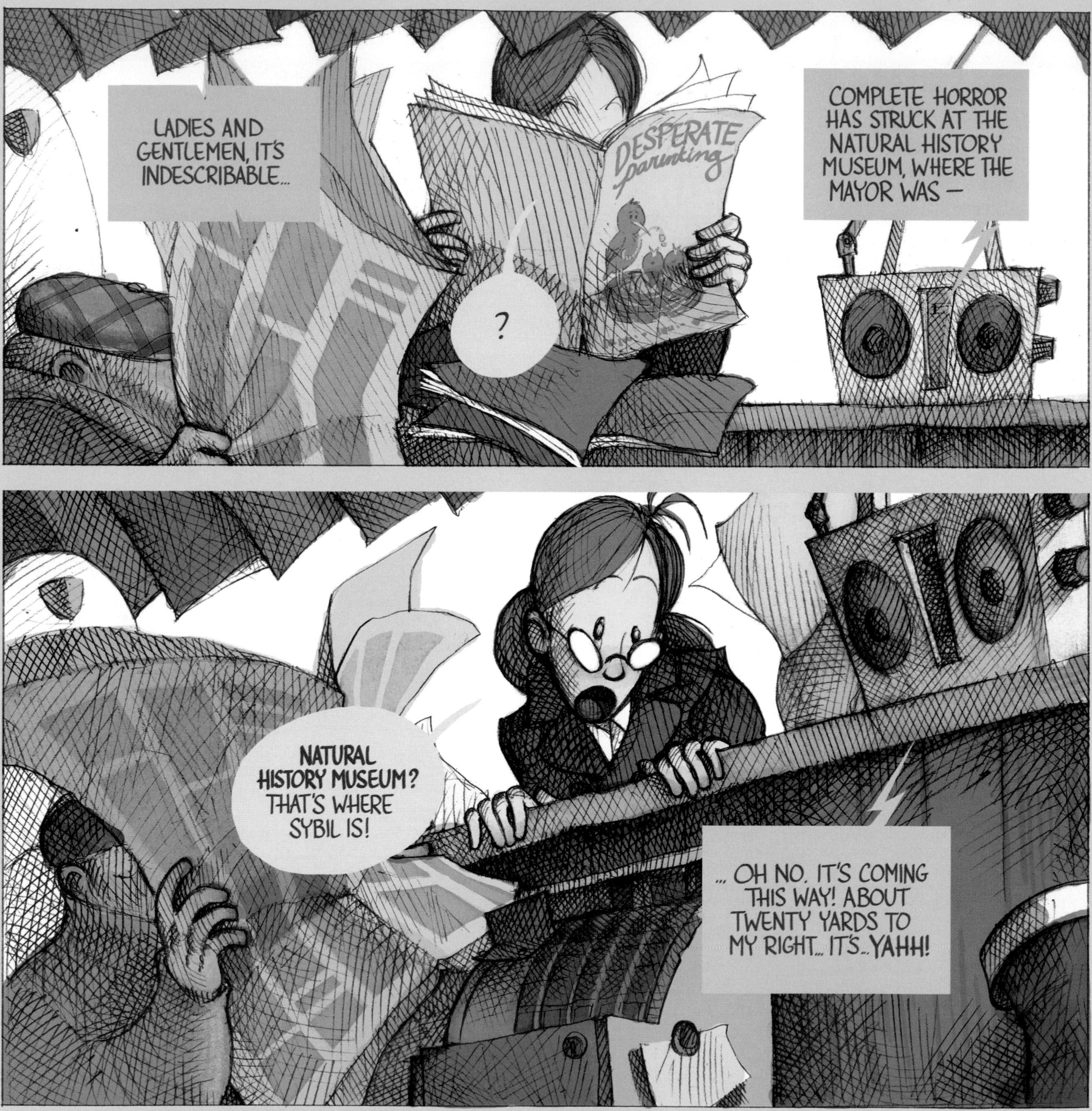
LADIES AND GENTLEMEN, IT'S INDESCRIBABLE...
DESPERATE parenting
?
COMPLETE HORROR HAS STRUCK AT THE NATURAL HISTORY MUSEUM, WHERE THE MAYOR WAS —
NATURAL HISTORY MUSEUM? THAT'S WHERE SYBIL IS!
... OH NO. IT'S COMING THIS WAY! ABOUT TWENTY YARDS TO MY RIGHT... IT'S... YAHH!

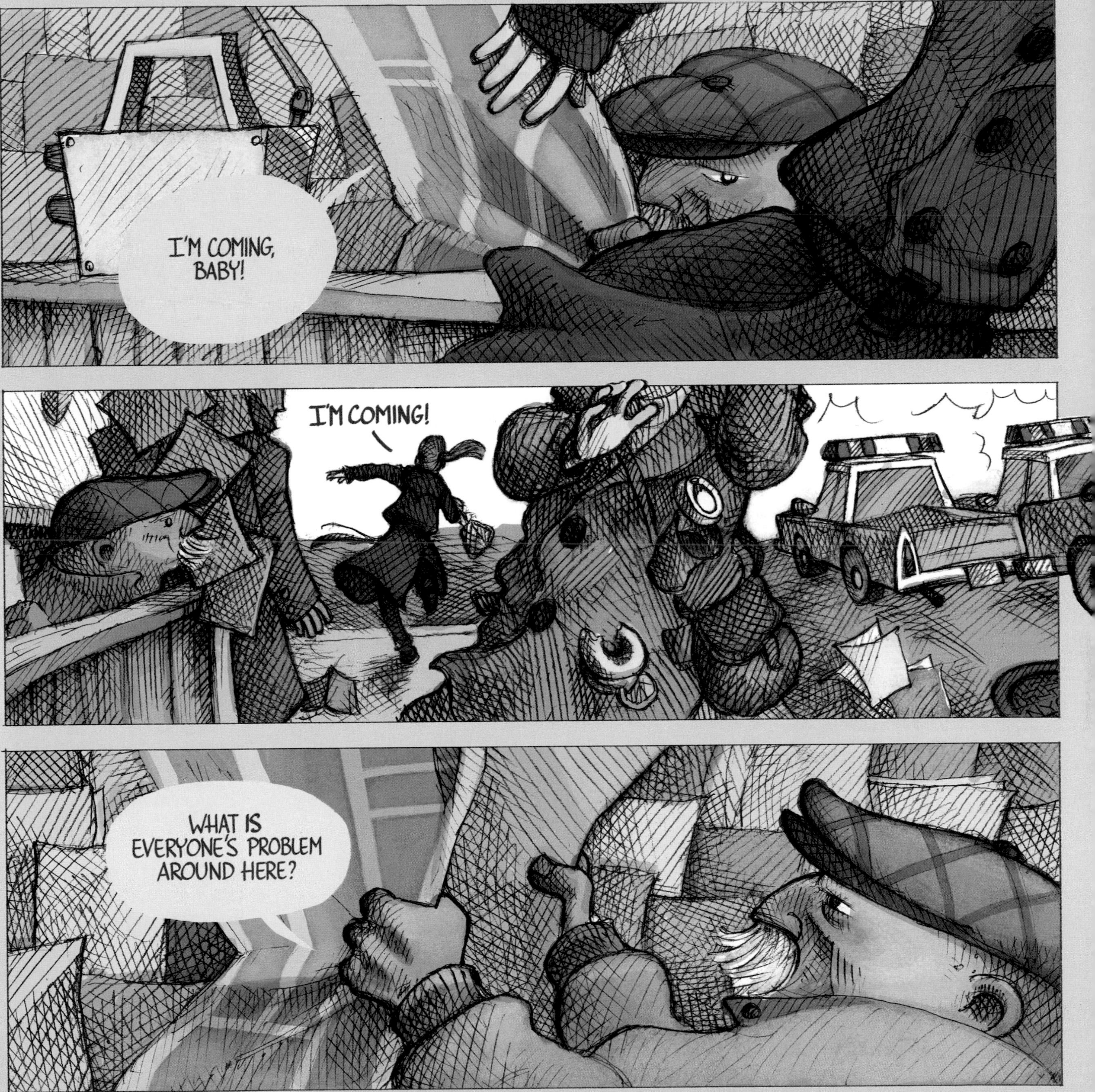
I'M COMING, BABY!
I'M COMING!
WHAT IS EVERYONE'S PROBLEM AROUND HERE?

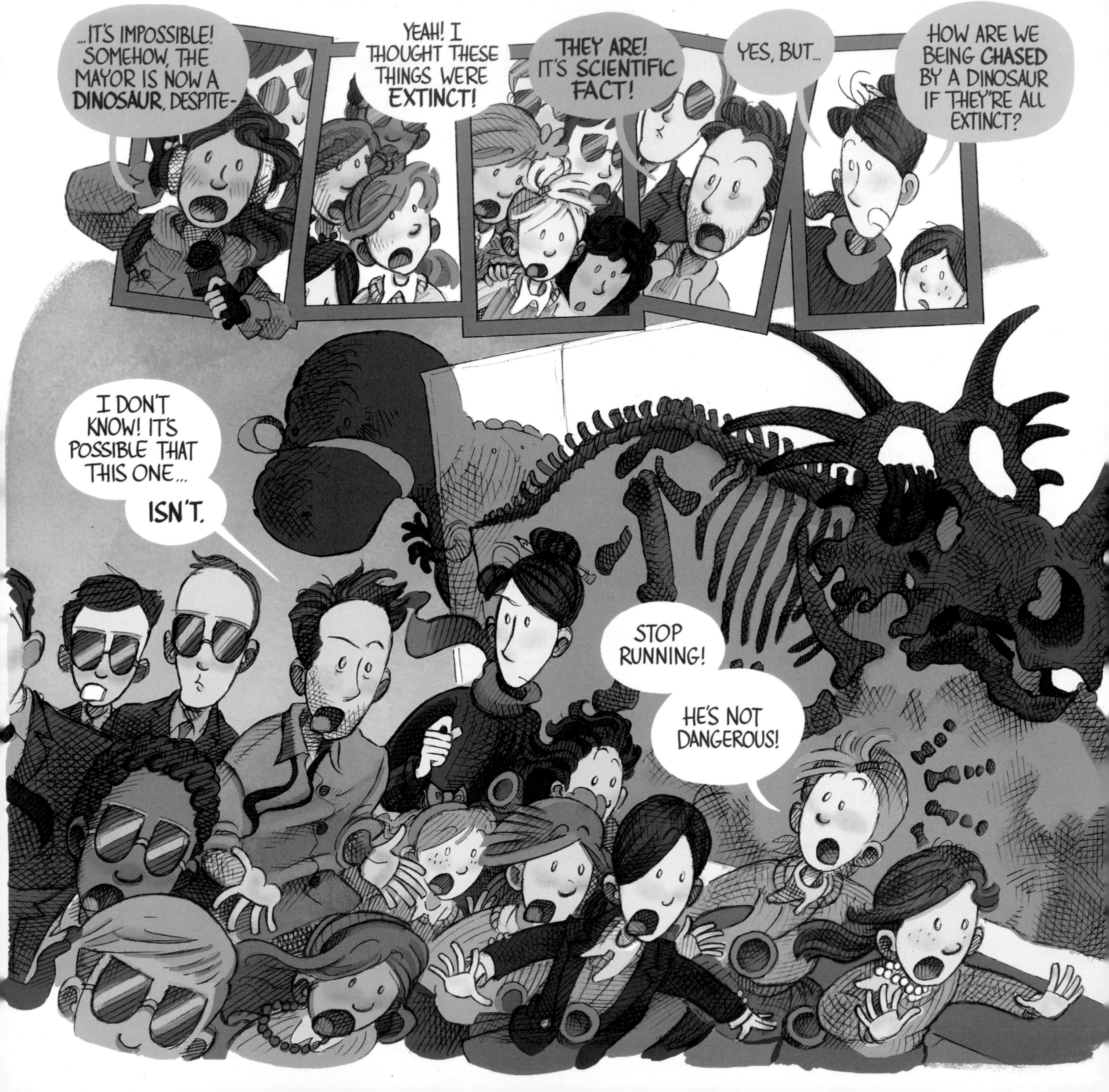
...IT'S IMPOSSIBLE! SOMEHOW, THE MAYOR IS NOW A DINOSAUR, DESPITE-
YEAH! I THOUGHT THESE THINGS WERE EXTINCT!
THEY ARE! IT'S SCIENTIFIC FACT!
YES, BUT...
HOW ARE WE BEING CHASED BY A DINOSAUR IF THEY'RE ALL EXTINCT?
I DON'T KNOW! IT'S POSSIBLE THAT THIS ONE...
ISN'T.
STOP RUNNING!
HE'S NOT DANGEROUS!

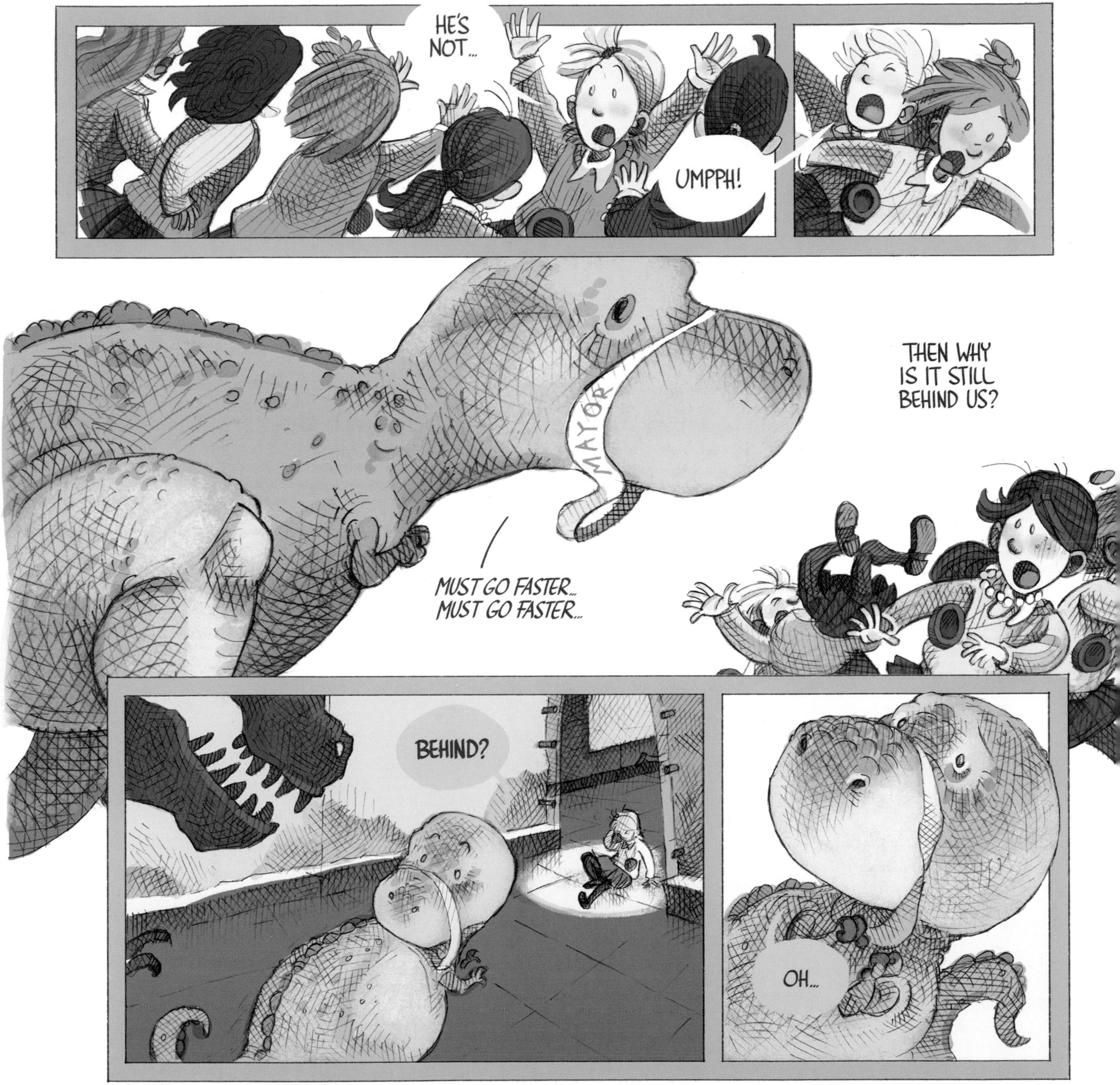
HE'S NOT...
UMPPH!
MAYOR
THEN WHY IS IT STILL BEHIND US?
MUST GO FASTER... MUST GO FASTER...
BEHIND?
OH...

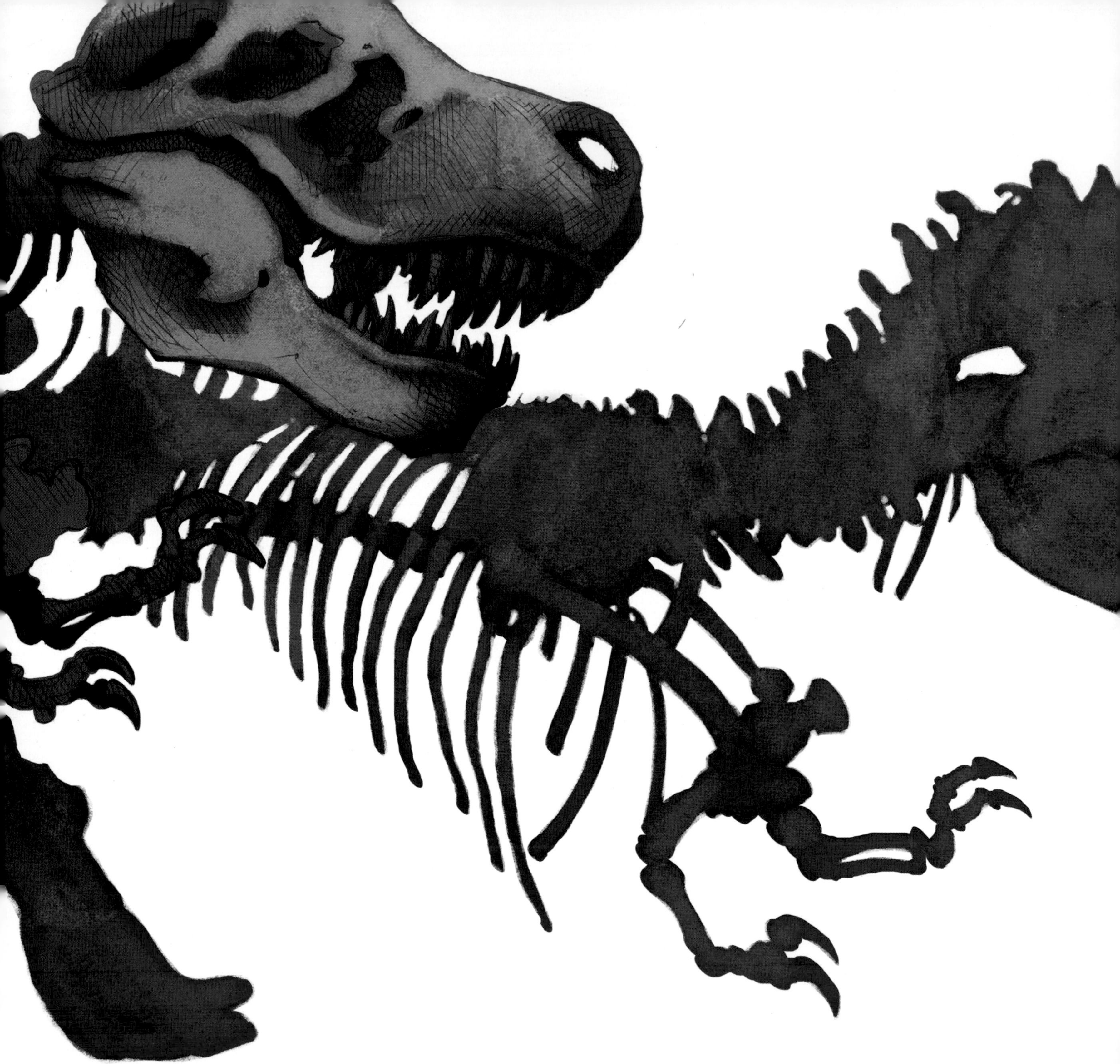

When Bolivar looked over his shoulder,
he finally realized the truth.

He was the dinosaur, and everyone
was running from *him*.

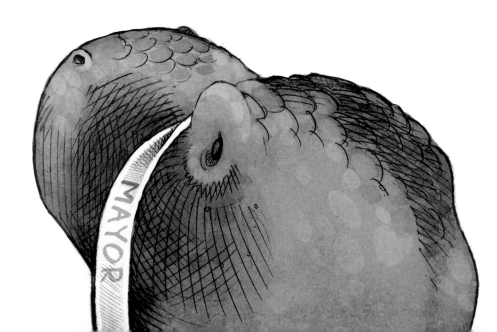

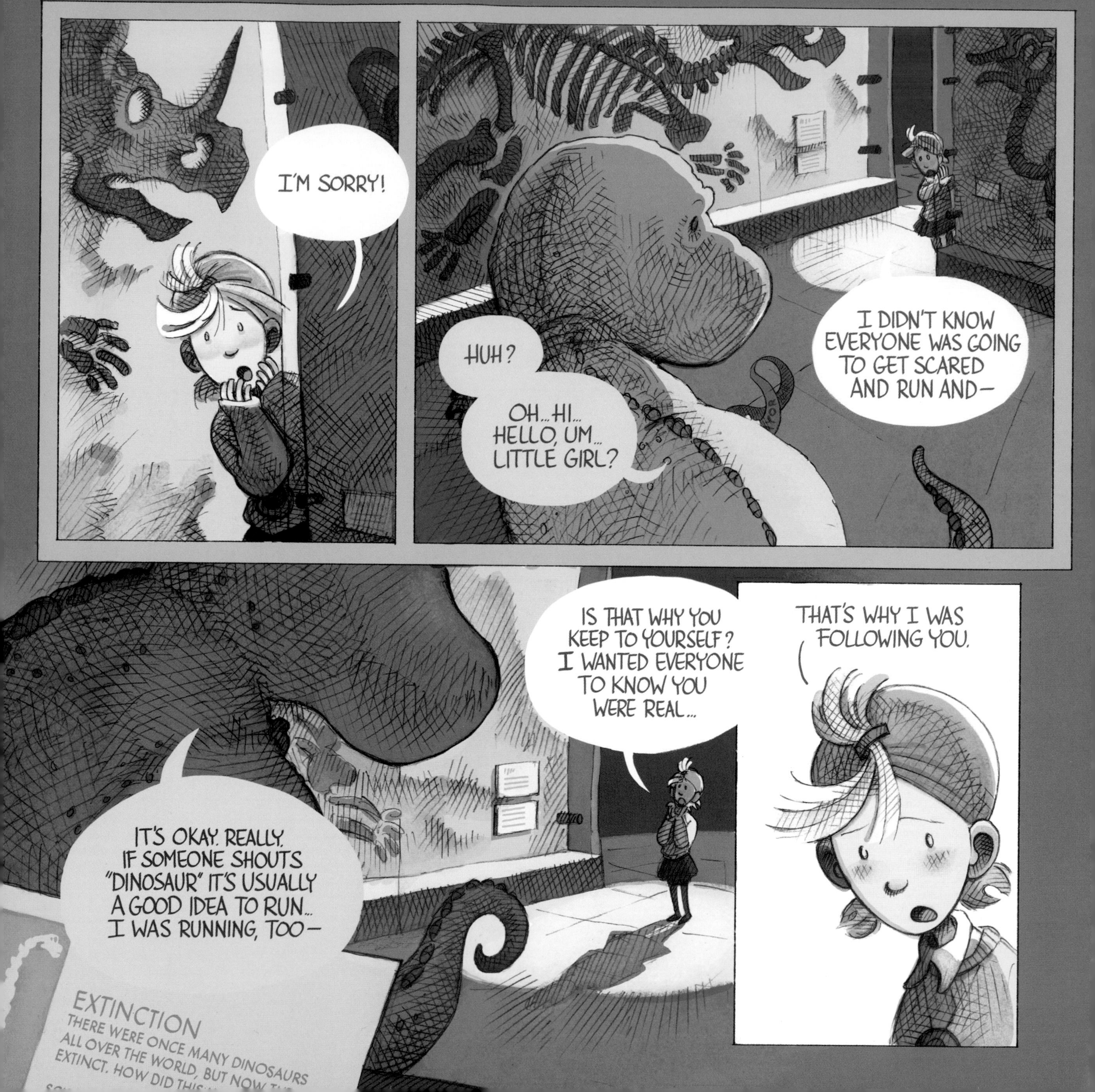
I'M SORRY!
HUH?
OH... HI... HELLO, UM... LITTLE GIRL?
I DIDN'T KNOW EVERYONE WAS GOING TO GET SCARED AND RUN AND—
IT'S OKAY. REALLY. IF SOMEONE SHOUTS "DINOSAUR" IT'S USUALLY A GOOD IDEA TO RUN... I WAS RUNNING, TOO—
IS THAT WHY YOU KEEP TO YOURSELF? I WANTED EVERYONE TO KNOW YOU WERE REAL...
THAT'S WHY I WAS FOLLOWING YOU.
EXTINCTION
THERE WERE ONCE MANY DINOSAURS
ALL OVER THE WORLD, BUT NOW
EXTINCT. HOW DID THIS

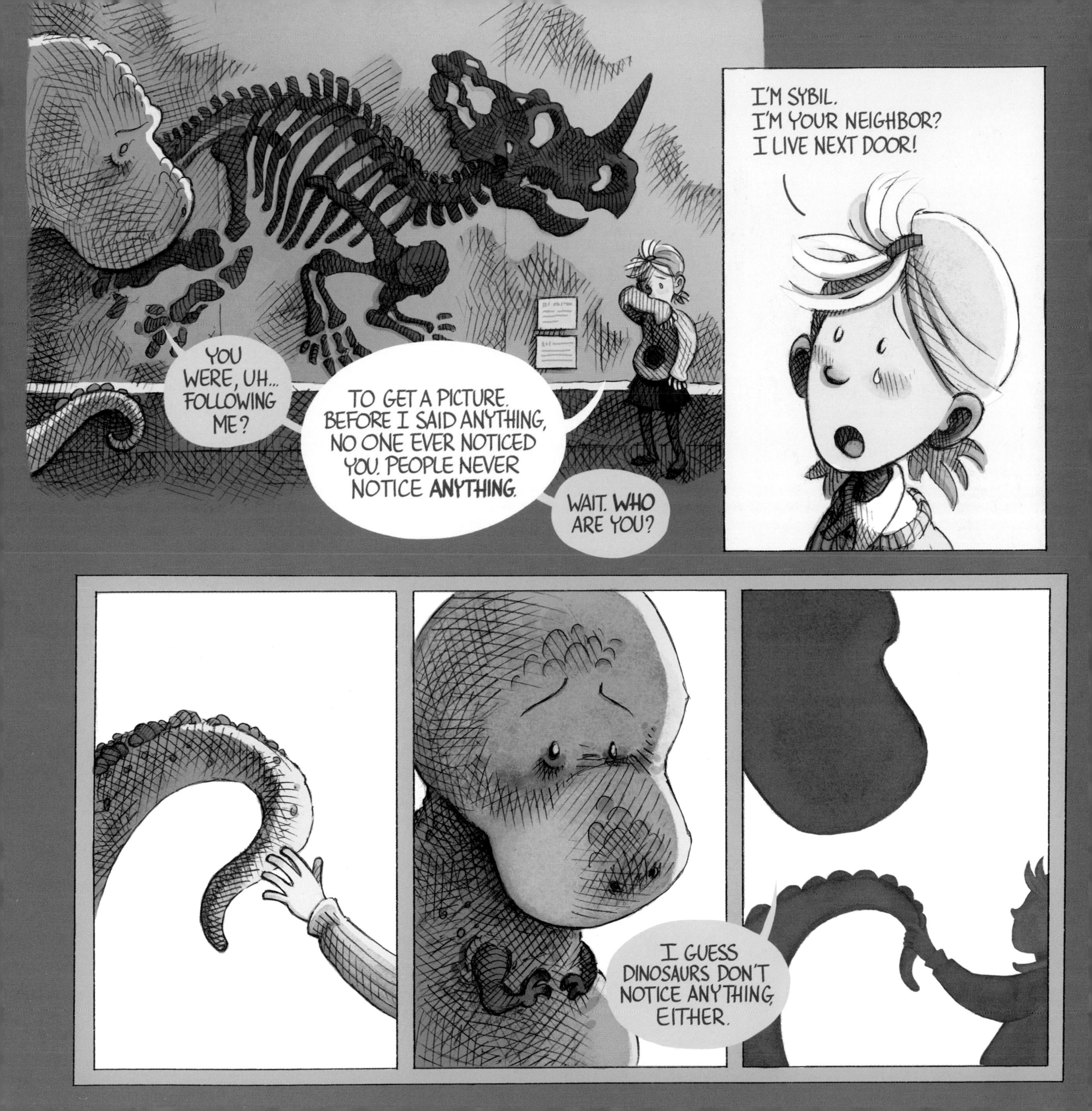
YOU WERE, UH... FOLLOWING ME?
TO GET A PICTURE. BEFORE I SAID ANYTHING, NO ONE EVER NOTICED YOU. PEOPLE NEVER NOTICE **ANYTHING**.
WAIT. **WHO** ARE YOU?
I'M SYBIL. I'M YOUR NEIGHBOR? I LIVE NEXT DOOR!
I GUESS DINOSAURS DON'T NOTICE ANYTHING, EITHER.

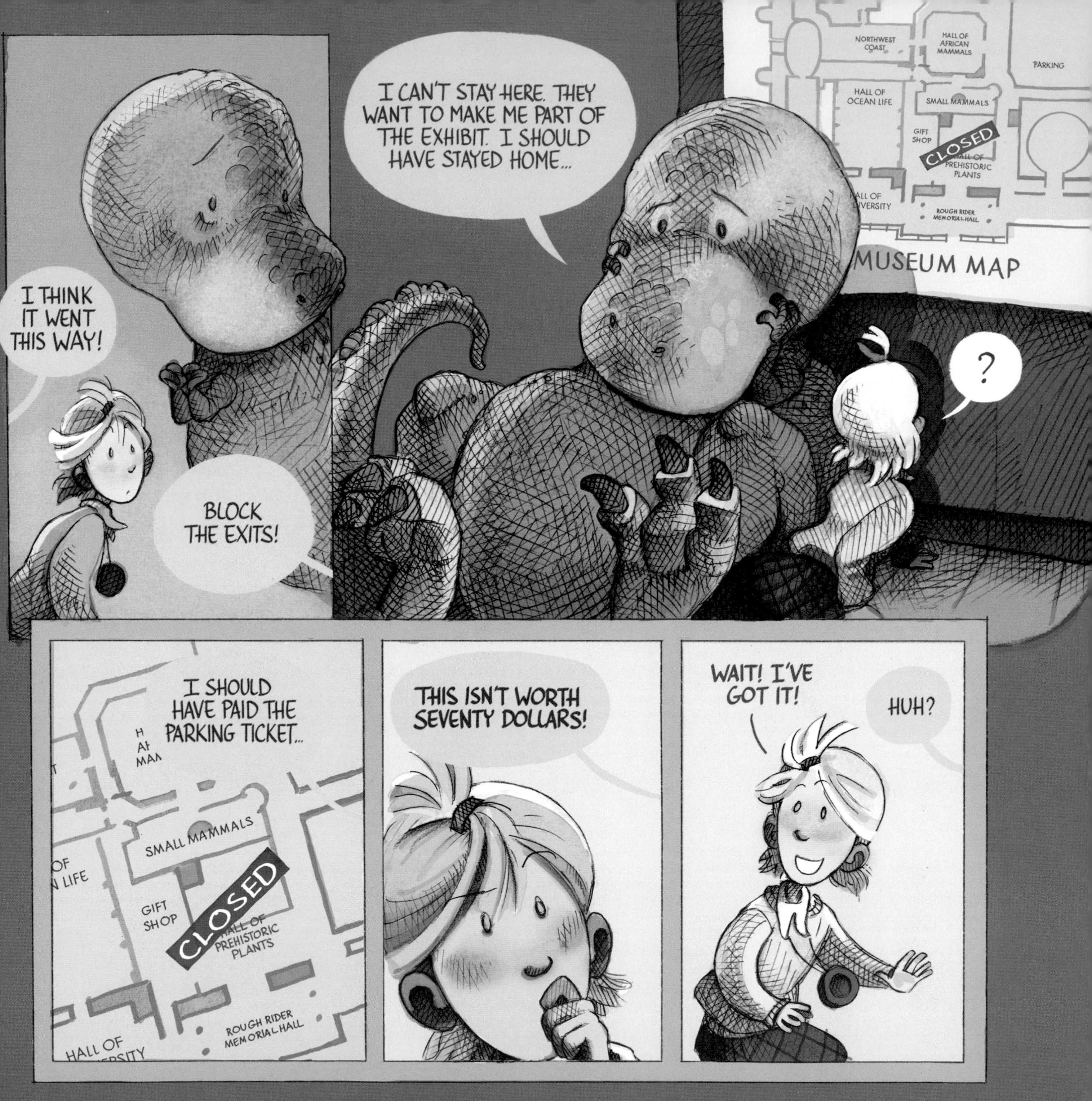
I THINK IT WENT THIS WAY!
BLOCK THE EXITS!
I CAN'T STAY HERE. THEY WANT TO MAKE ME PART OF THE EXHIBIT. I SHOULD HAVE STAYED HOME...
NORTHWEST COAST
HALL OF AFRICAN MAMMALS
PARKING
HALL OF OCEAN LIFE
SMALL MAMMALS
GIFT SHOP
CLOSED
HALL OF PREHISTORIC PLANTS
ROUGH RIDER MEMORIAL HALL
MUSEUM MAP
?
I SHOULD HAVE PAID THE PARKING TICKET...
SMALL MAMMALS
GIFT SHOP
CLOSED
HALL OF PREHISTORIC PLANTS
ROUGH RIDER MEMORIAL HALL
THIS ISN'T WORTH SEVENTY DOLLARS!
WAIT! I'VE GOT IT!
HUH?

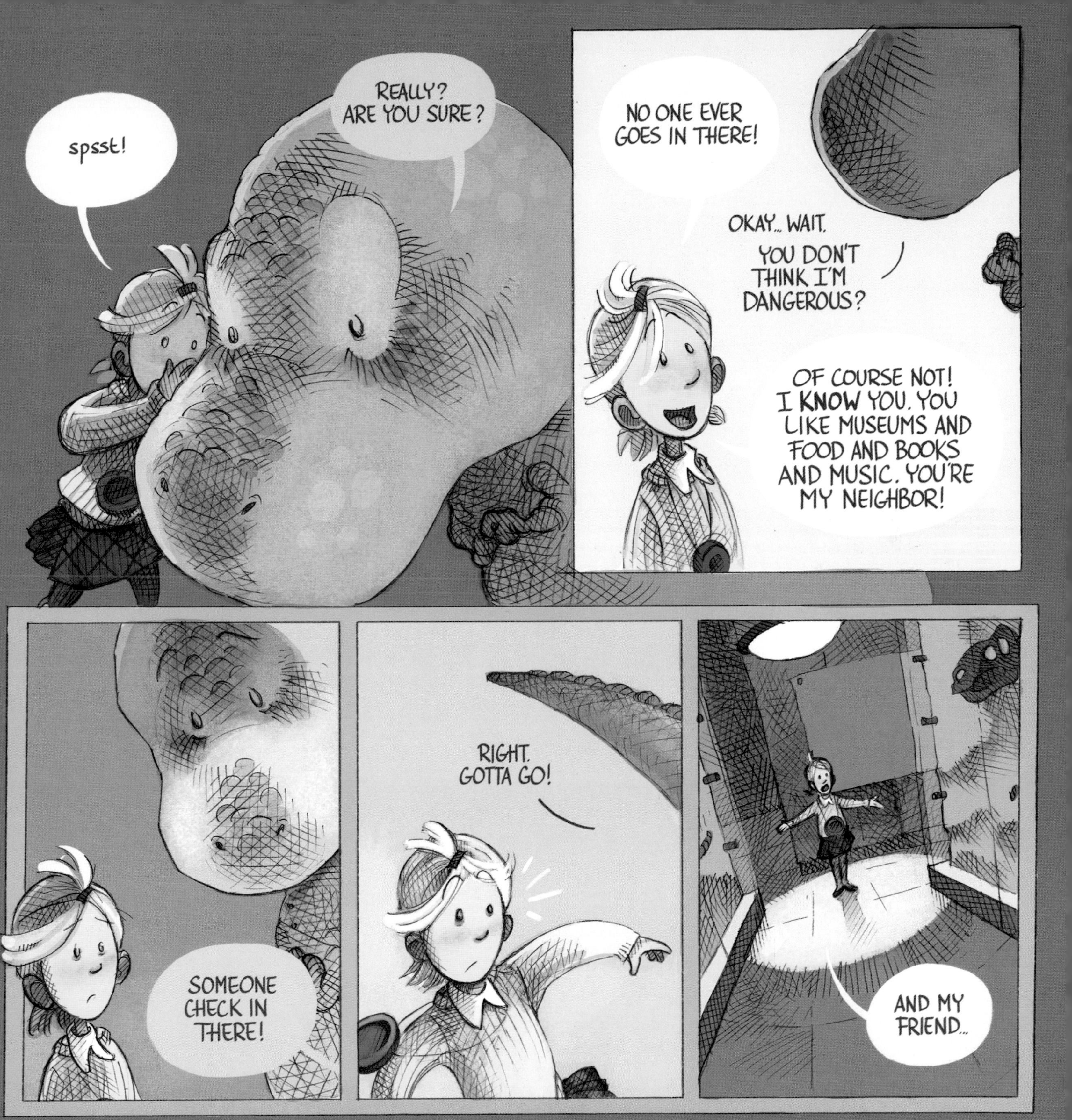
spsst!
REALLY? ARE YOU SURE?
NO ONE EVER GOES IN THERE!
OKAY... WAIT.
YOU DON'T THINK I'M DANGEROUS?
OF COURSE NOT! I **KNOW** YOU. YOU LIKE MUSEUMS AND FOOD AND BOOKS AND MUSIC. YOU'RE MY NEIGHBOR!
SOMEONE CHECK IN THERE!
RIGHT. GOTTA GO!
AND MY FRIEND...

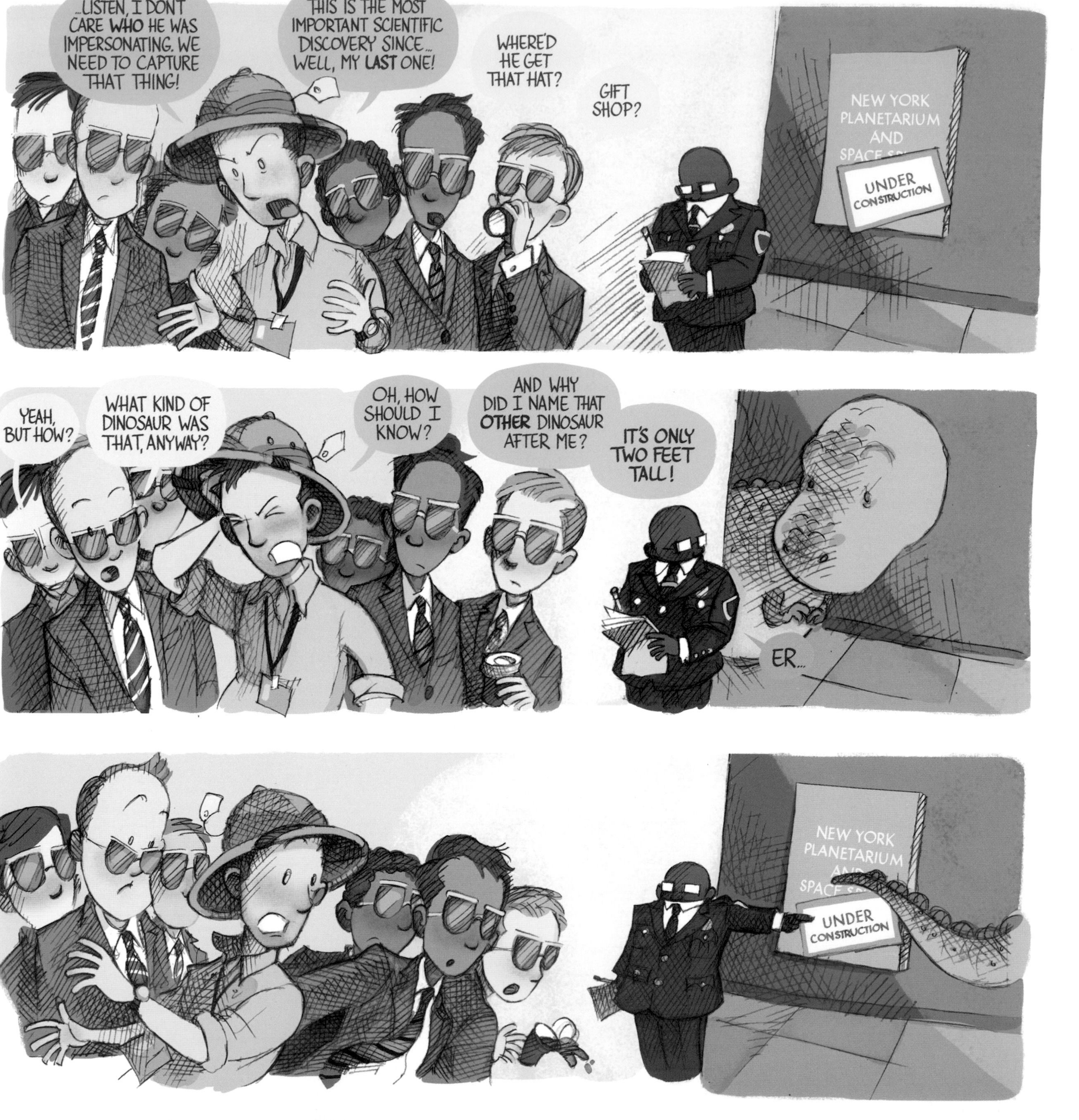

...LISTEN, I DON'T CARE **WHO** HE WAS IMPERSONATING. WE NEED TO CAPTURE THAT THING!
THIS IS THE MOST IMPORTANT SCIENTIFIC DISCOVERY SINCE... WELL, MY **LAST** ONE!
WHERE'D HE GET THAT HAT?
GIFT SHOP?
NEW YORK PLANETARIUM AND
UNDER CONSTRUCTION
YEAH, BUT HOW?
WHAT KIND OF DINOSAUR WAS THAT, ANYWAY?
OH, HOW SHOULD I KNOW?
AND WHY DID I NAME THAT **OTHER** DINOSAUR AFTER ME?
IT'S ONLY TWO FEET TALL!
ER...
NEW YORK PLANETARIUM
UNDER CONSTRUCTION

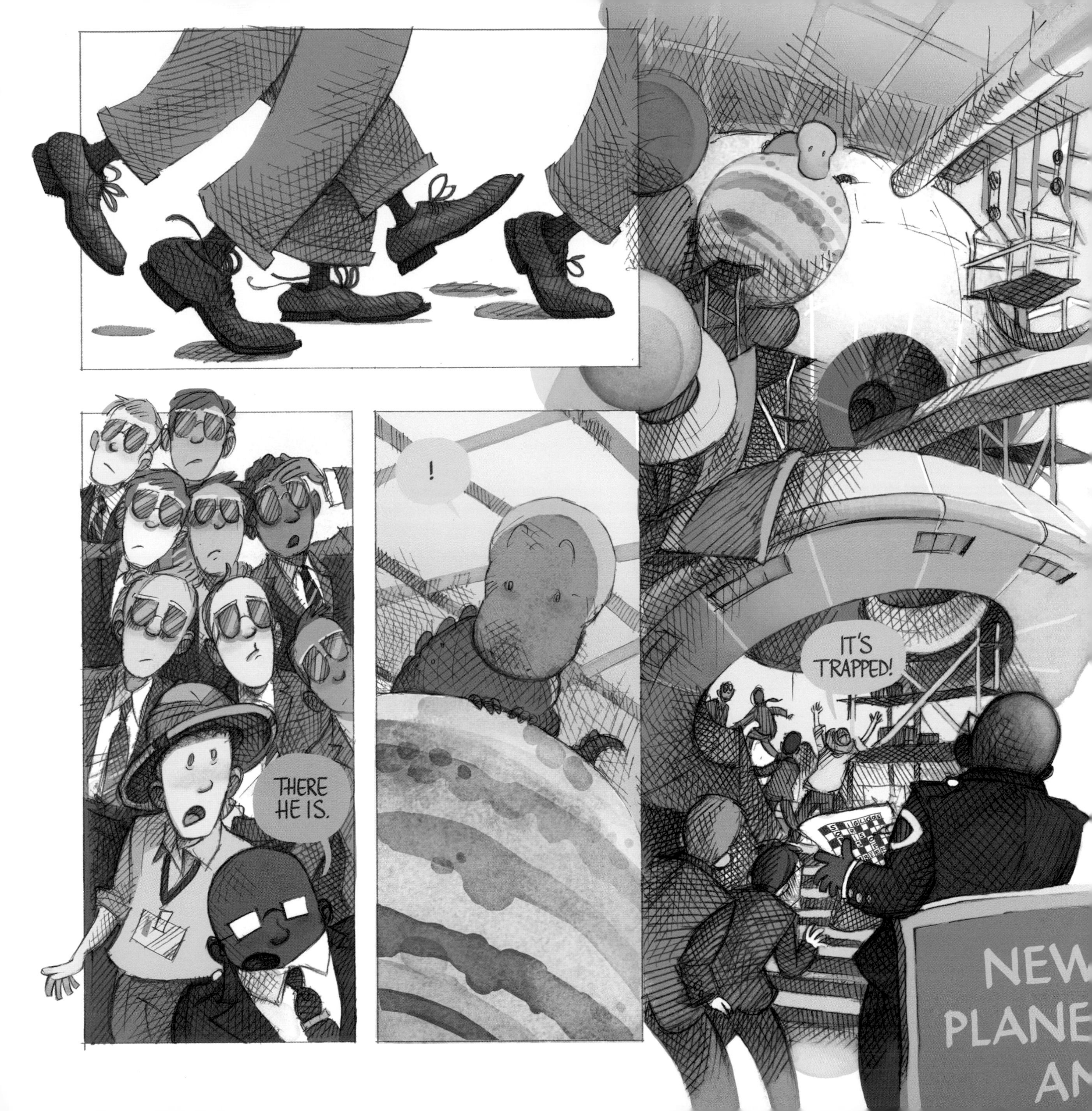
THERE HE IS.
!
IT'S TRAPPED!
NEW
PLANE
AN

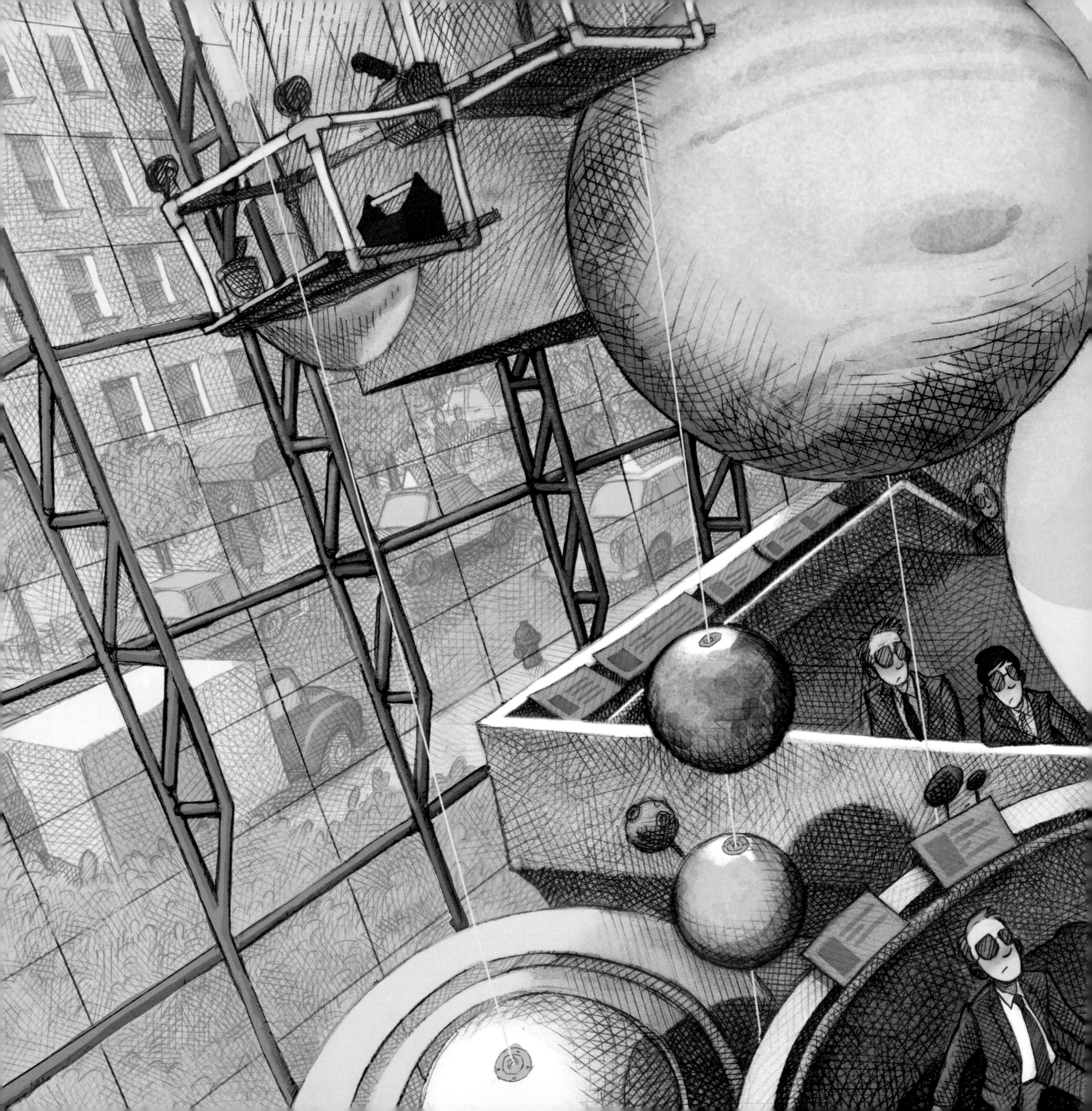

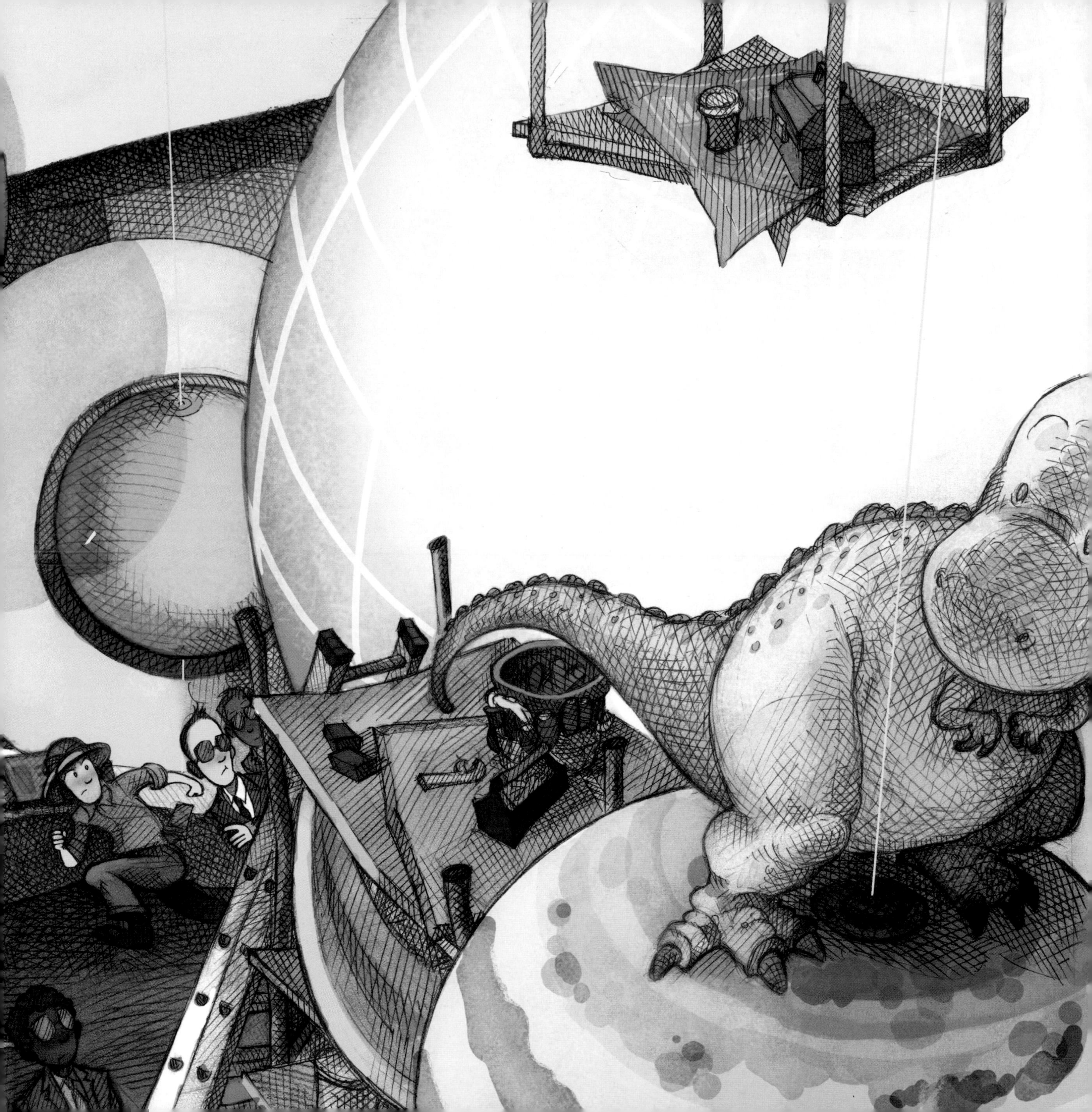

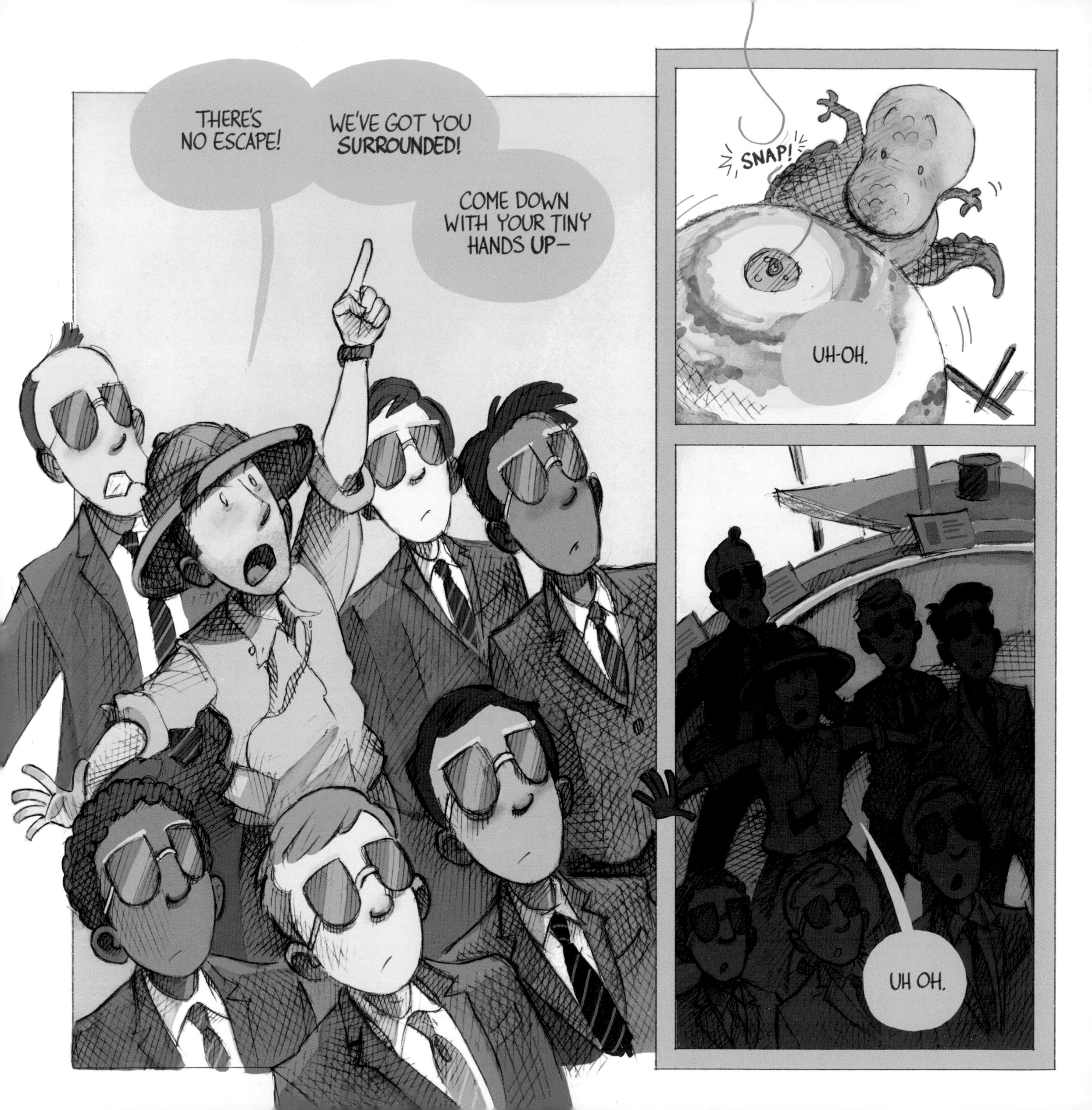
THERE'S NO ESCAPE!
WE'VE GOT YOU SURROUNDED!
COME DOWN WITH YOUR TINY HANDS UP—
SNAP!
UH-OH.
UH OH.

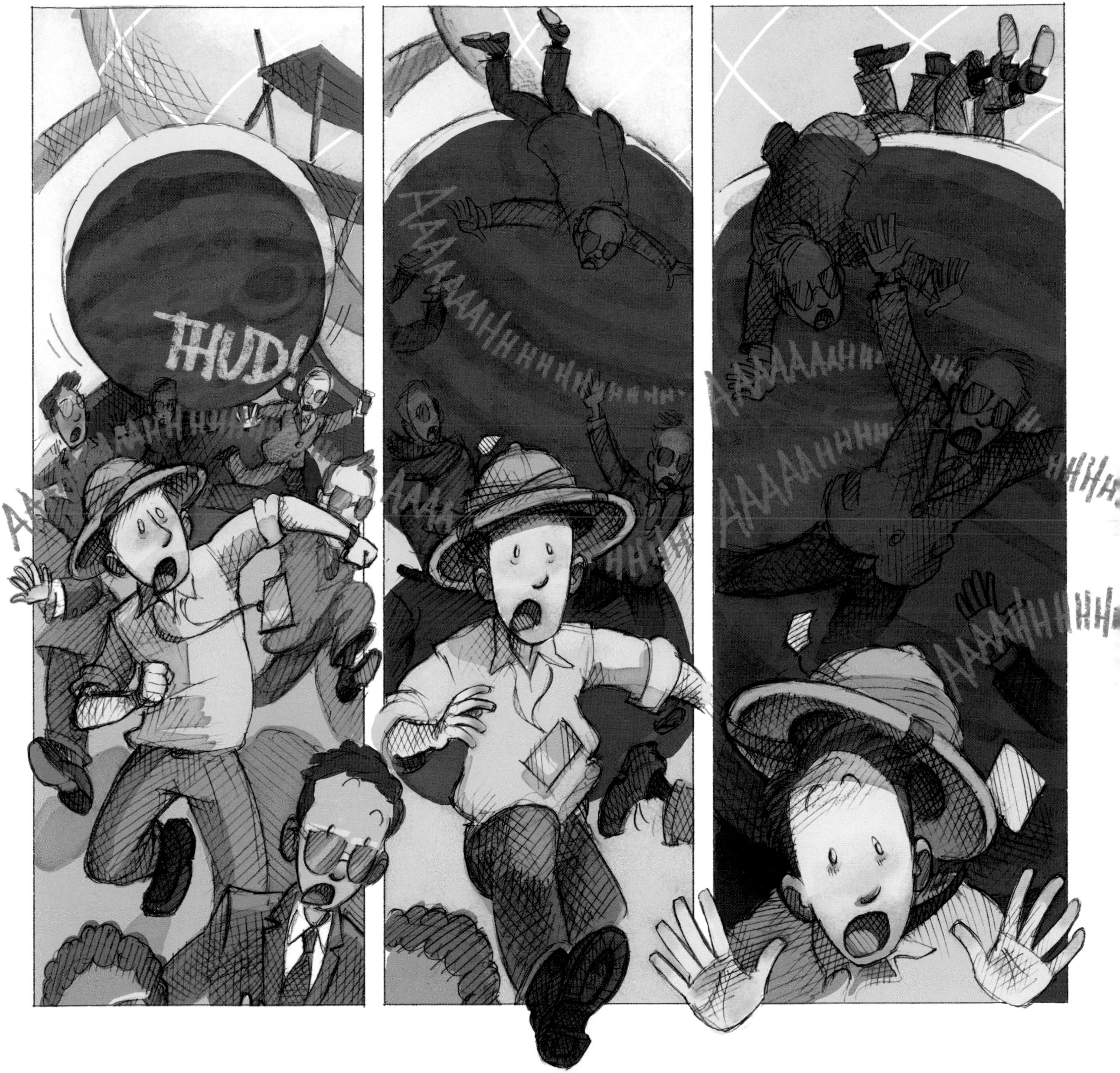
THUD!

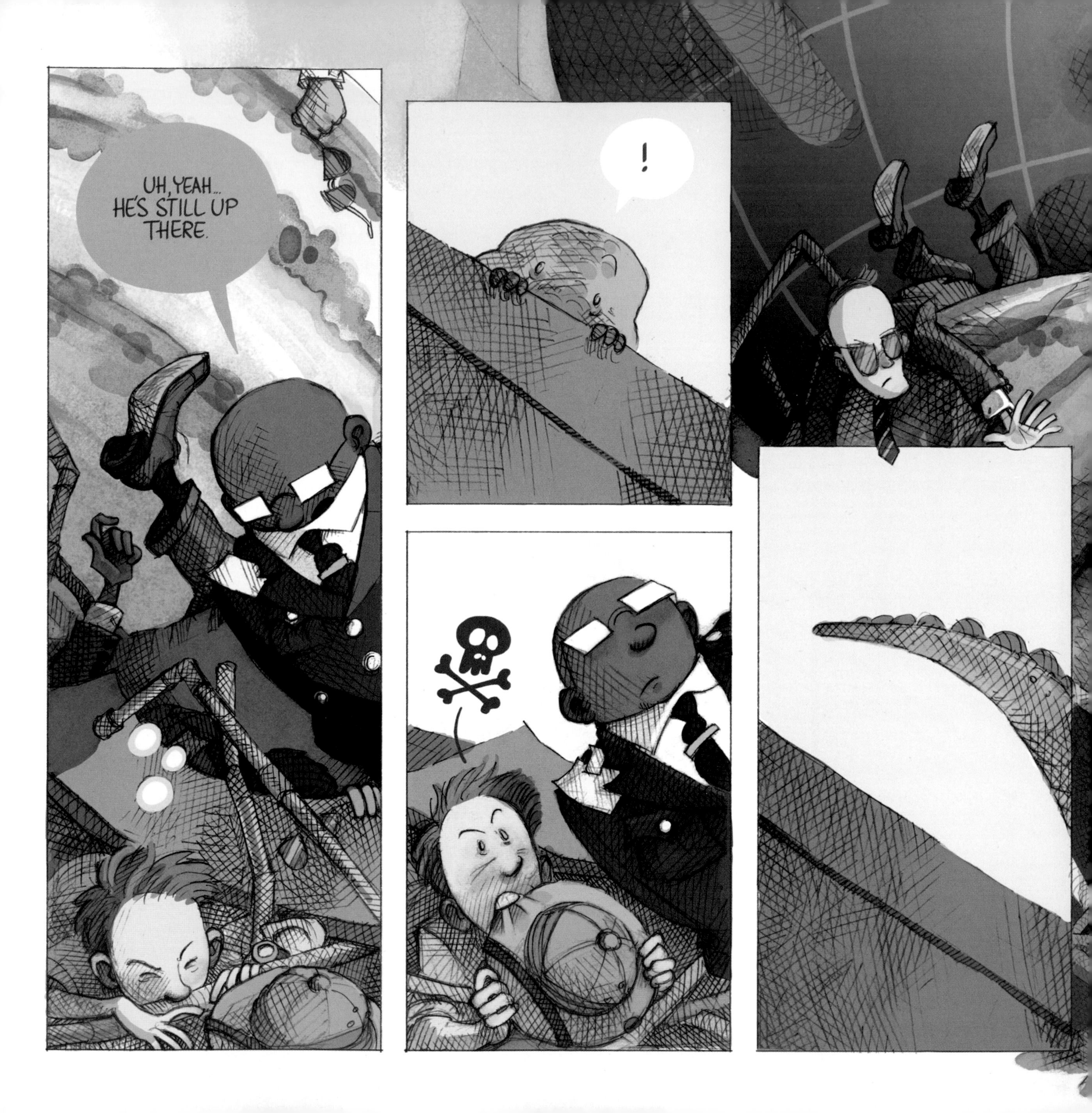
UH, YEAH... HE'S STILL UP THERE.
!

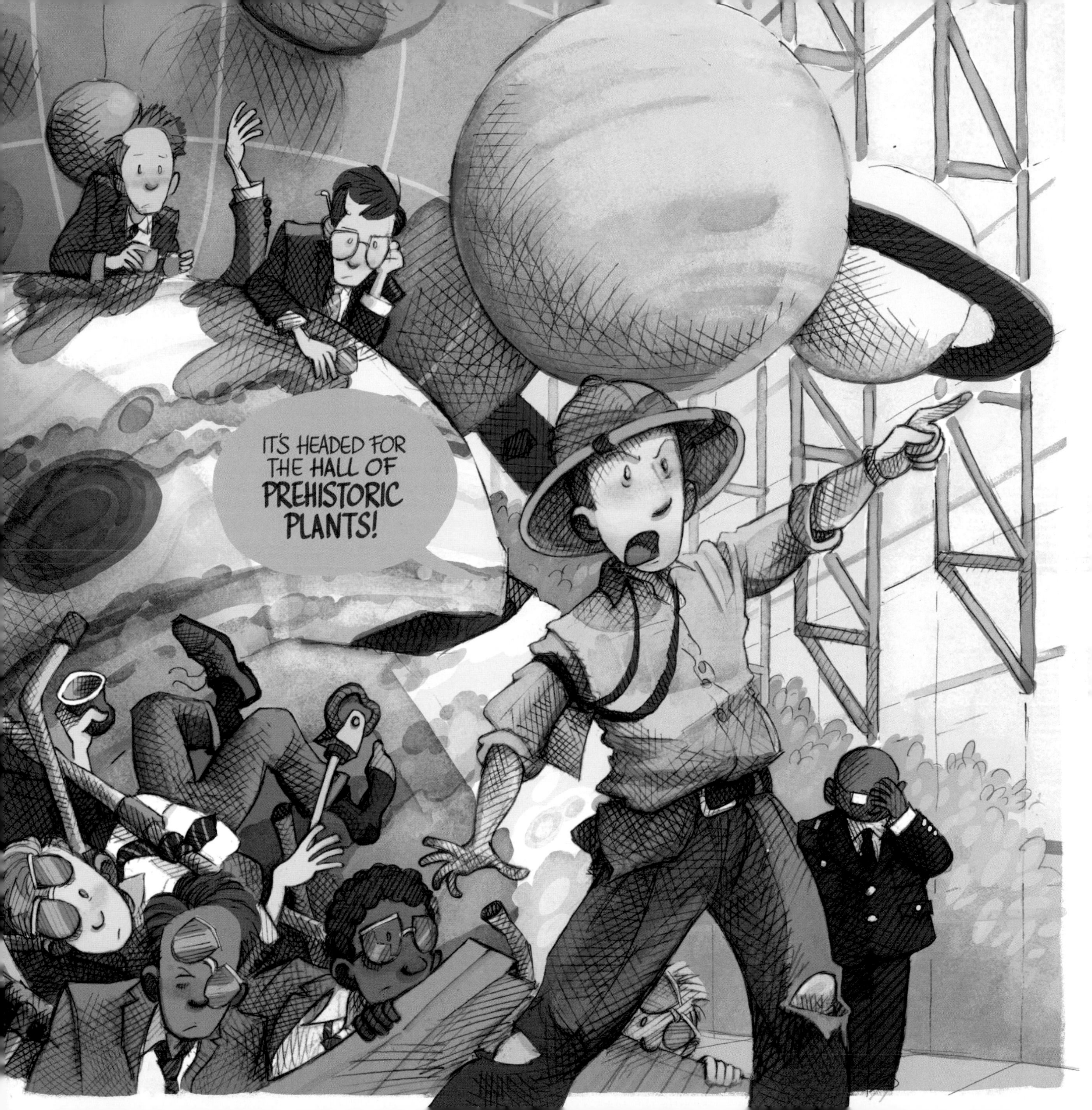
IT'S HEADED FOR THE HALL OF PREHISTORIC PLANTS!

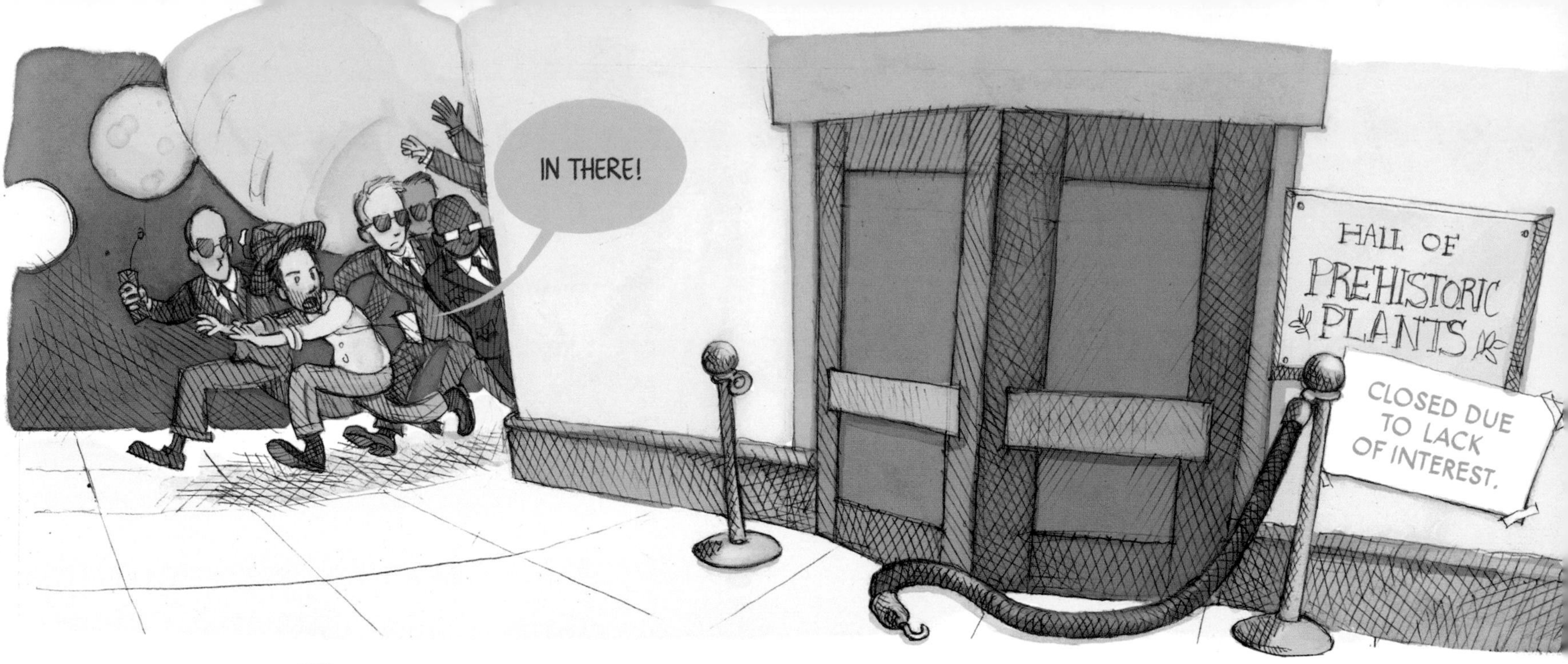
IN THERE!
HALL OF PREHISTORIC PLANTS
CLOSED DUE TO LACK OF INTEREST.

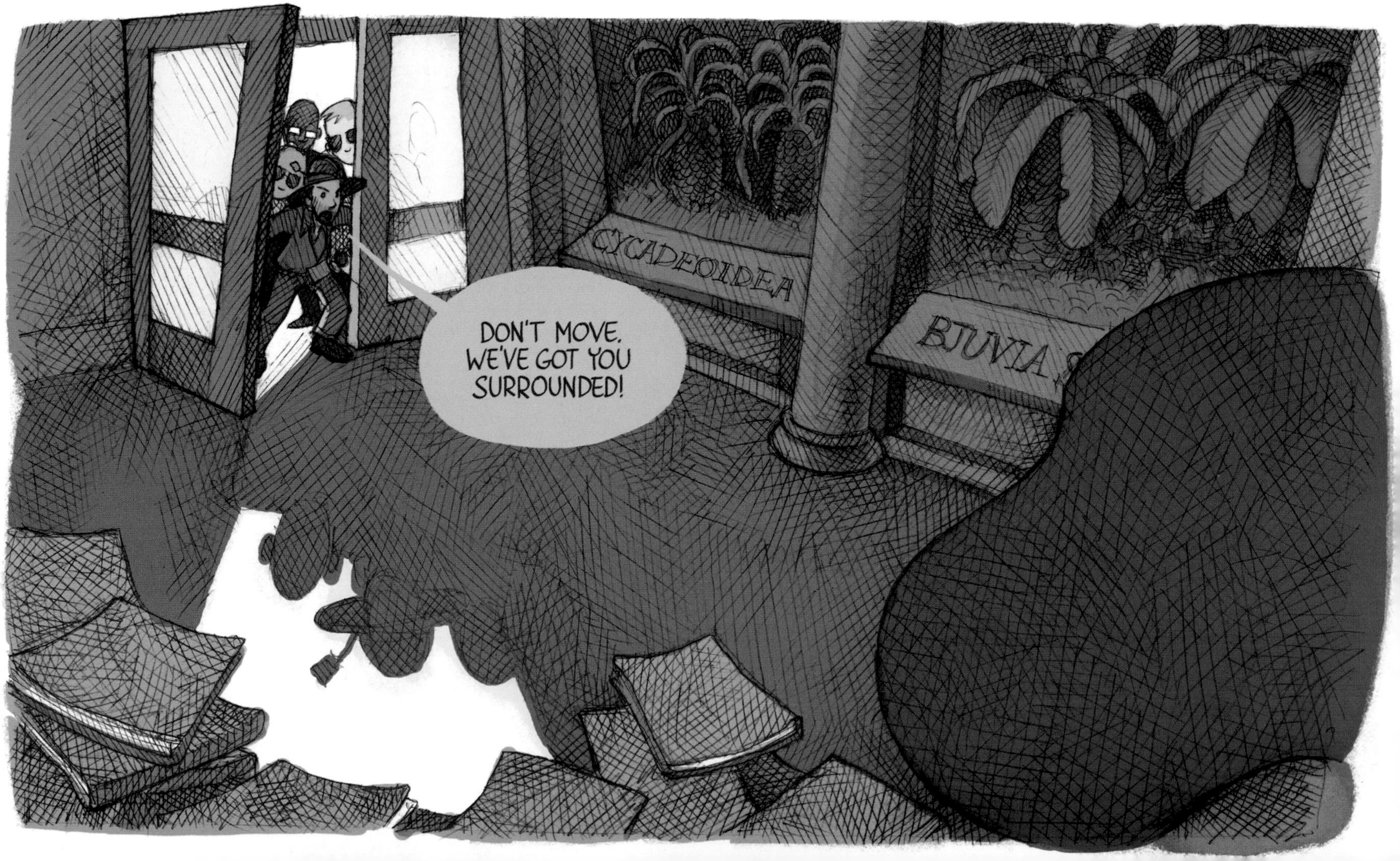
CYCADEOIDEA
BJUVIA
DON'T MOVE. WE'VE GOT YOU SURROUNDED!

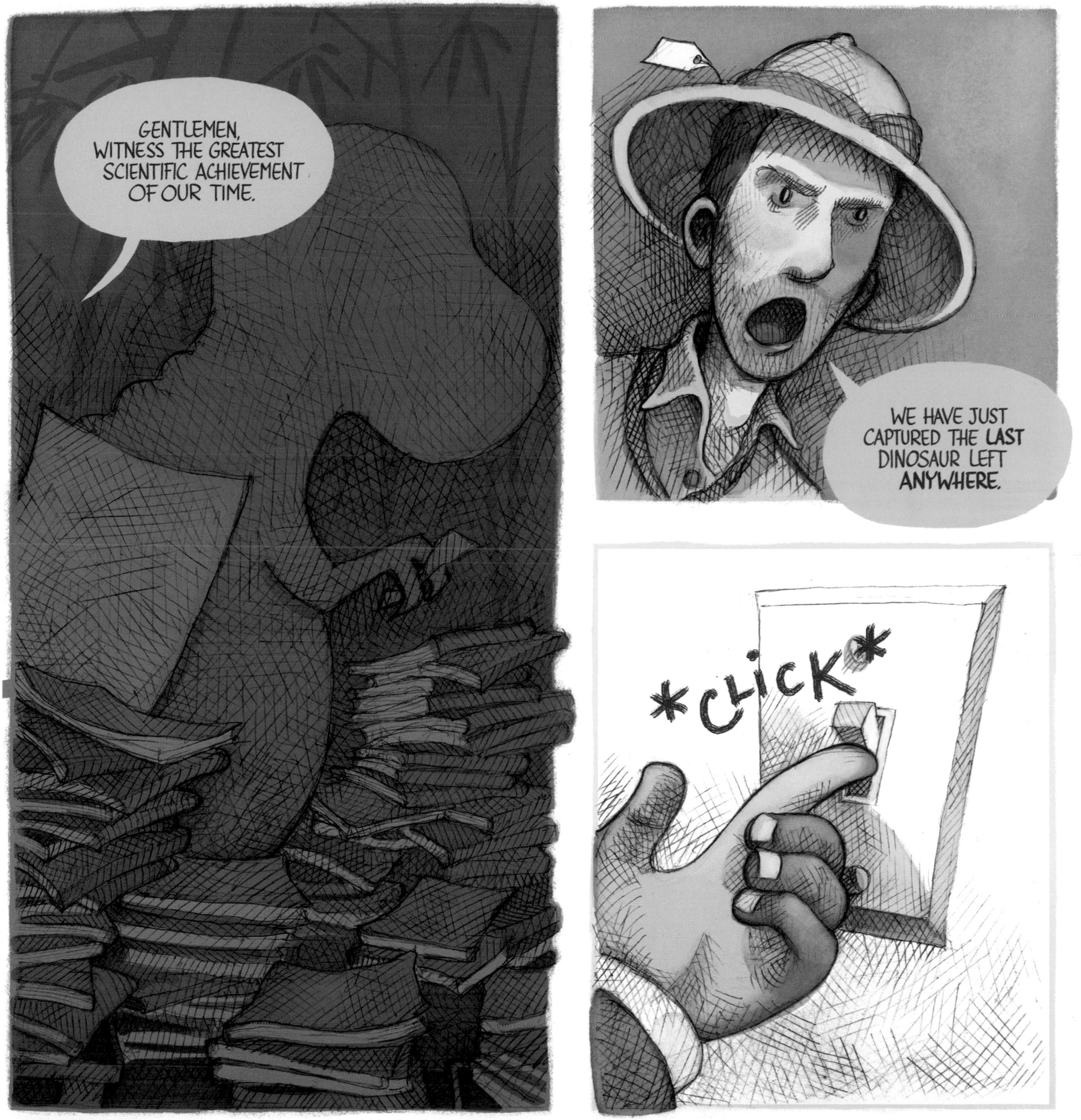
GENTLEMEN, WITNESS THE GREATEST SCIENTIFIC ACHIEVEMENT OF OUR TIME.
WE HAVE JUST CAPTURED THE **LAST** DINOSAUR LEFT **ANYWHERE.**
CLICK

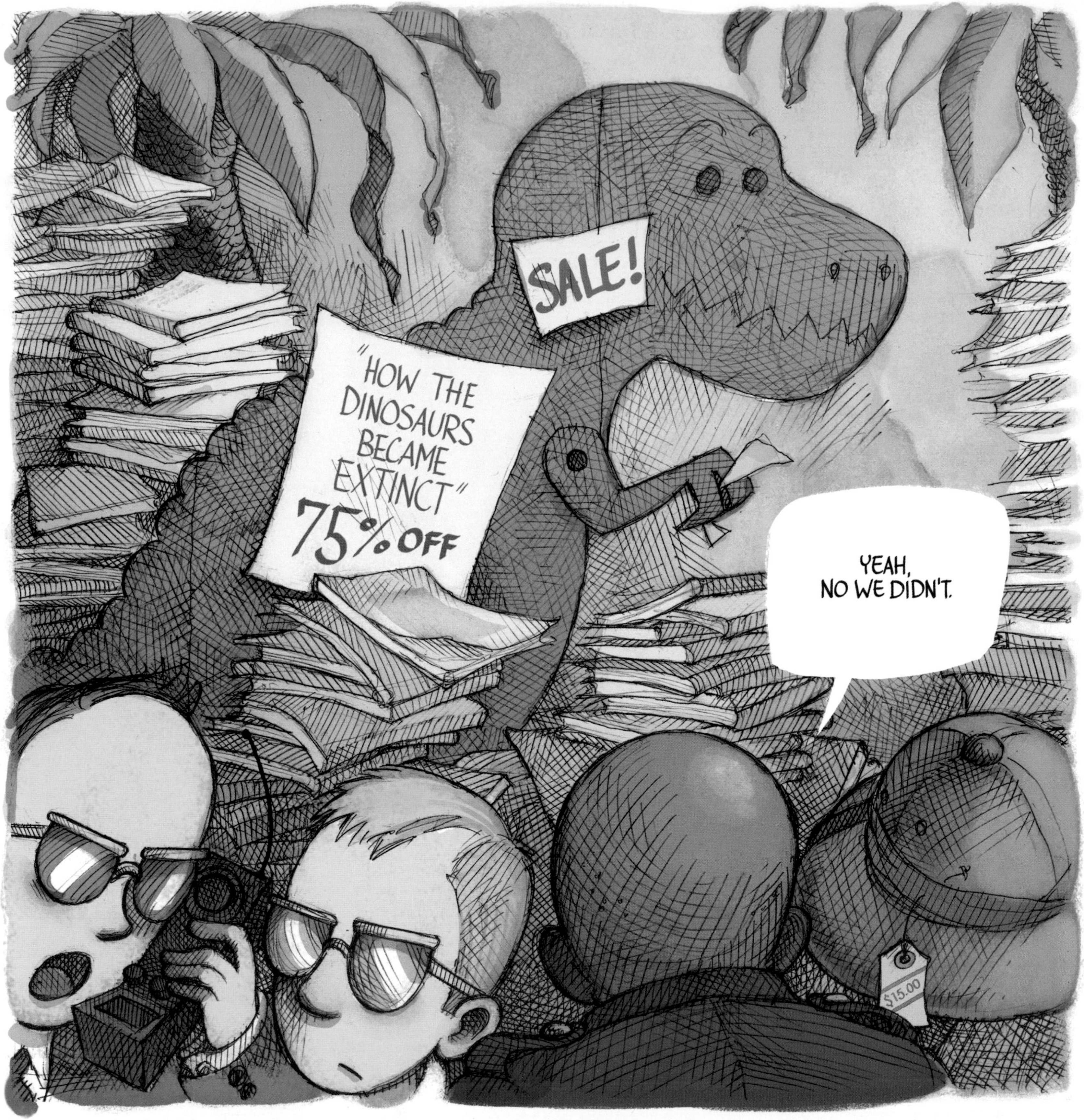
SALE!
"HOW THE DINOSAURS BECAME EXTINCT"
75% OFF
YEAH, NO WE DIDN'T.
$15.00

After Bolivar escaped, he still had to be careful.

Everyone would have heard there was a real
dinosaur at the Natural History Museum.

And everyone in the city would be outside, looking for him.

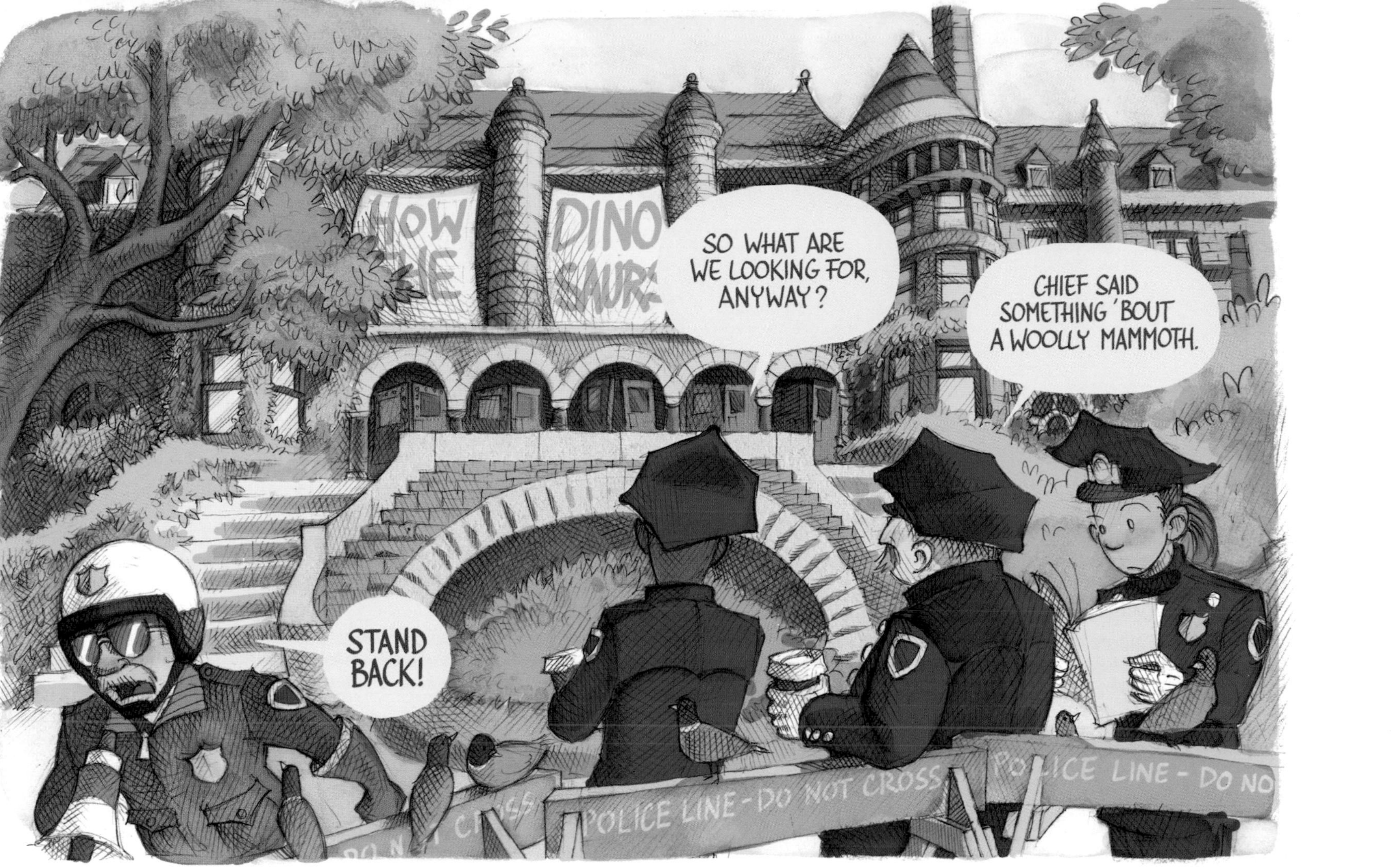
SO WHAT ARE WE LOOKING FOR, ANYWAY?
CHIEF SAID SOMETHING 'BOUT A WOOLLY MAMMOTH.
STAND BACK!
POLICE LINE-DO NOT CROSS

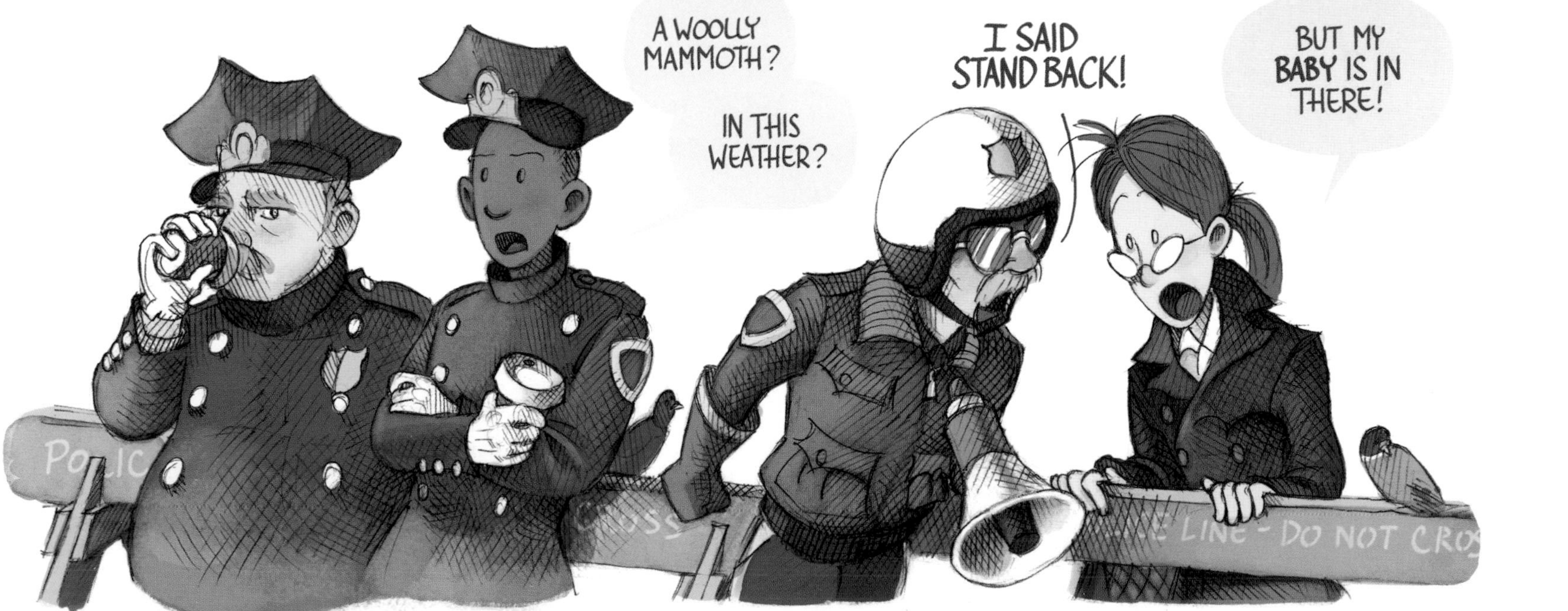
A WOOLLY MAMMOTH?
IN THIS WEATHER?
I SAID STAND BACK!
BUT MY **BABY** IS IN THERE!
LINE - DO NOT CRO

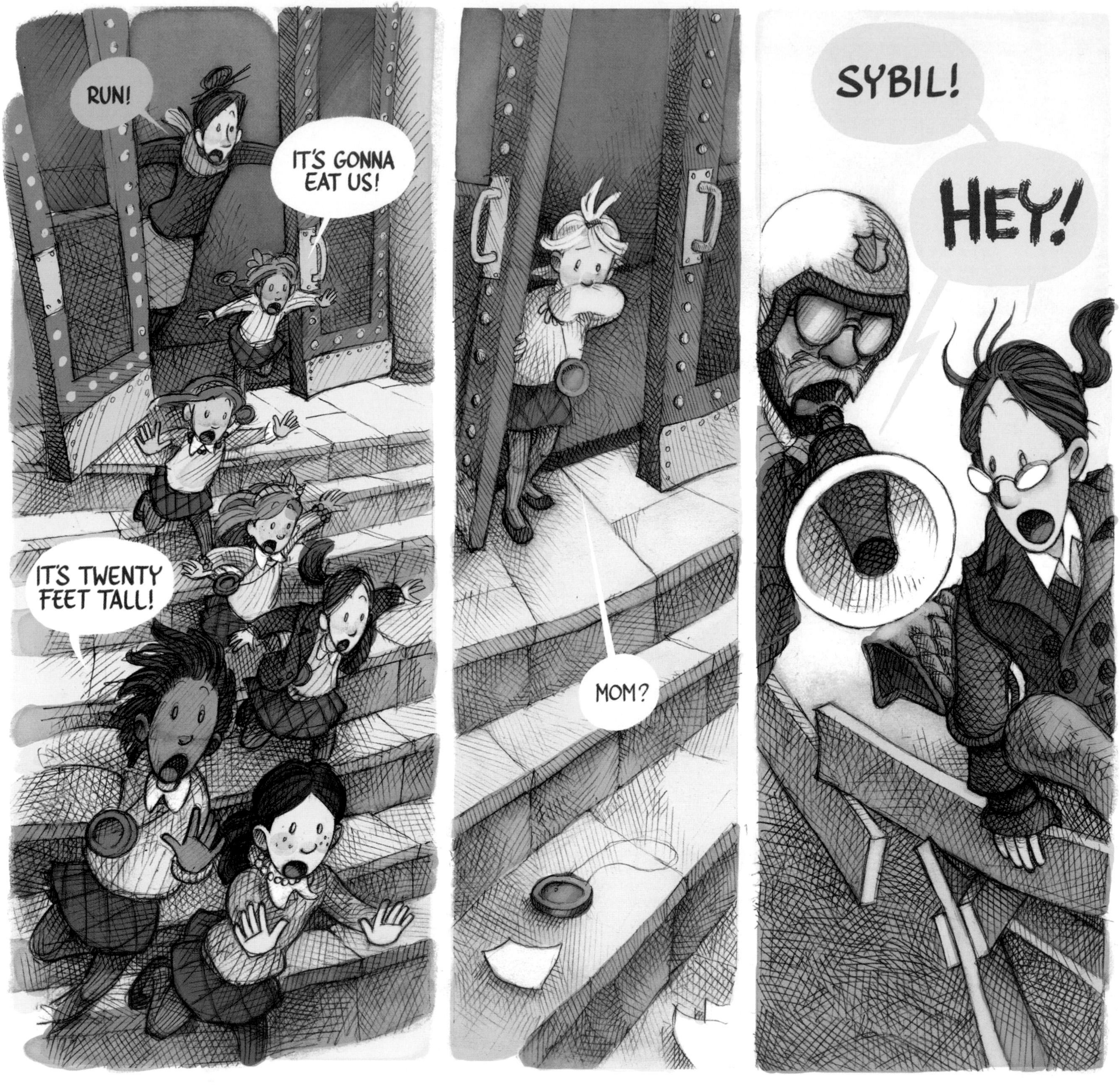
RUN!
IT'S GONNA EAT US!
IT'S TWENTY FEET TALL!
MOM?
SYBIL!
HEY!

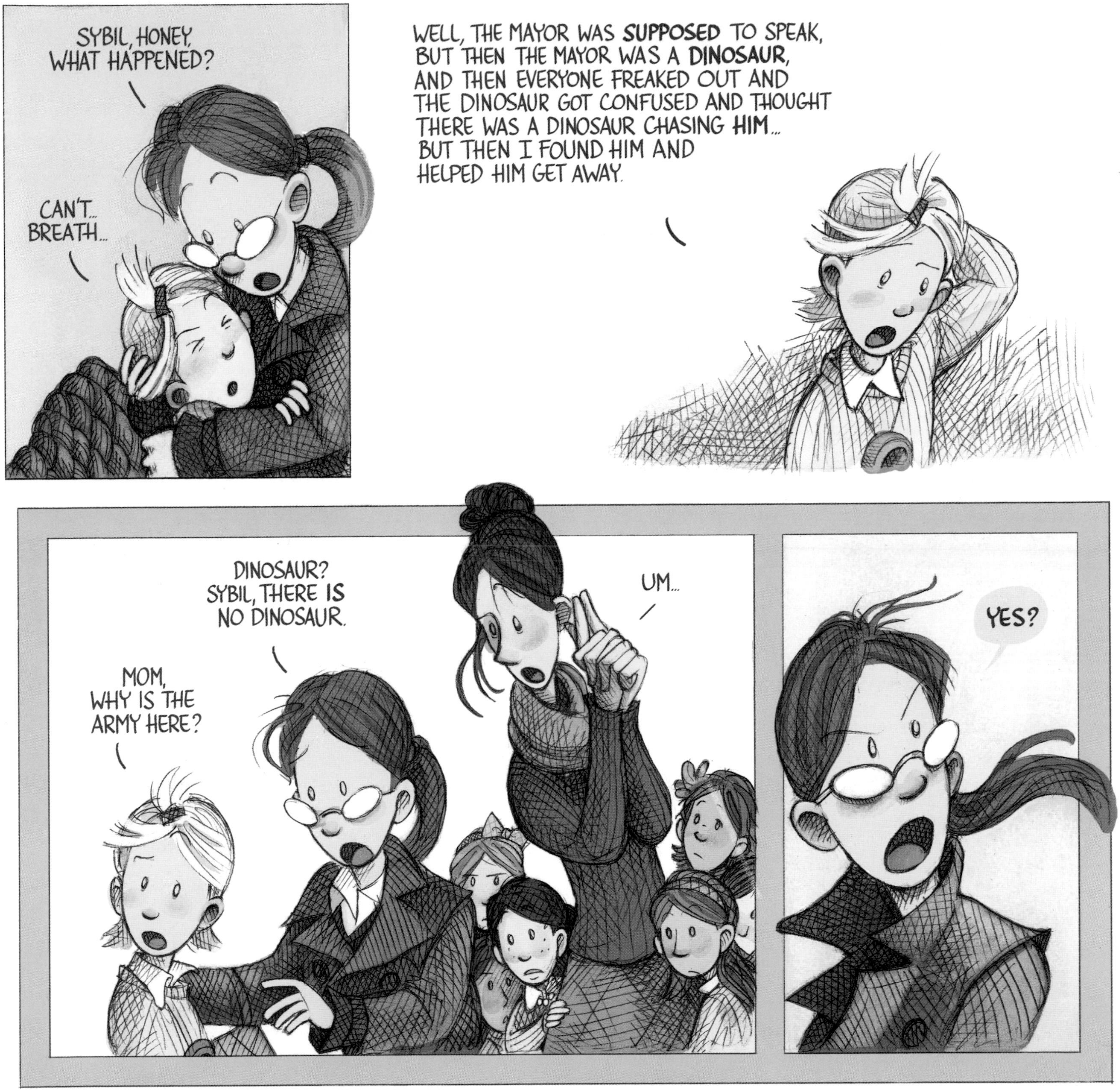
SYBIL, HONEY, WHAT HAPPENED?
CAN'T... BREATH...
WELL, THE MAYOR WAS **SUPPOSED** TO SPEAK, BUT THEN THE MAYOR WAS A **DINOSAUR**, AND THEN EVERYONE FREAKED OUT AND THE DINOSAUR GOT CONFUSED AND THOUGHT THERE WAS A DINOSAUR CHASING **HIM**... BUT THEN I FOUND HIM AND HELPED HIM GET AWAY.
MOM, WHY IS THE ARMY HERE?
DINOSAUR? SYBIL, THERE **IS** NO DINOSAUR.
UM...
YES?

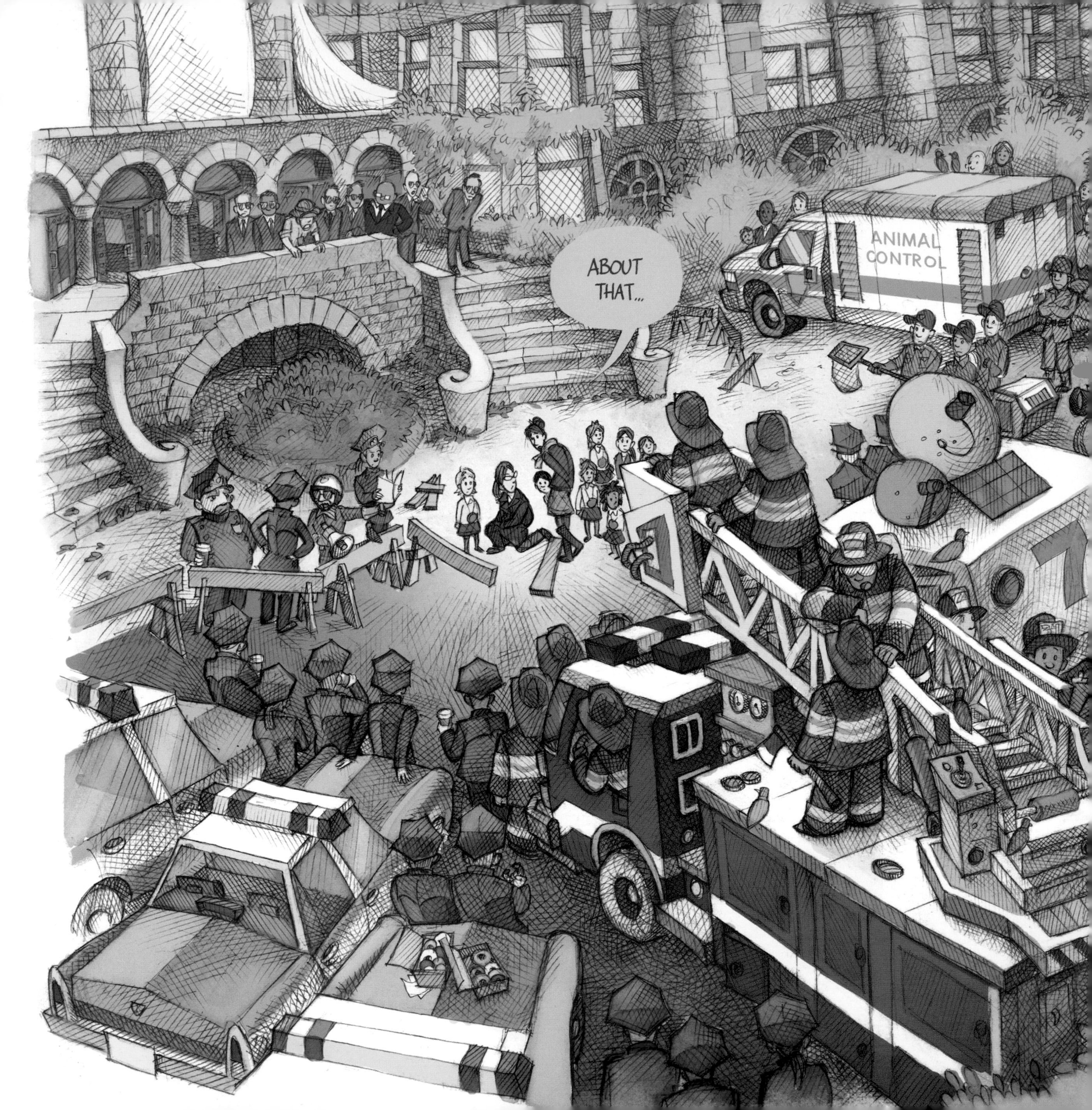
ANIMAL CONTROL
ABOUT THAT...

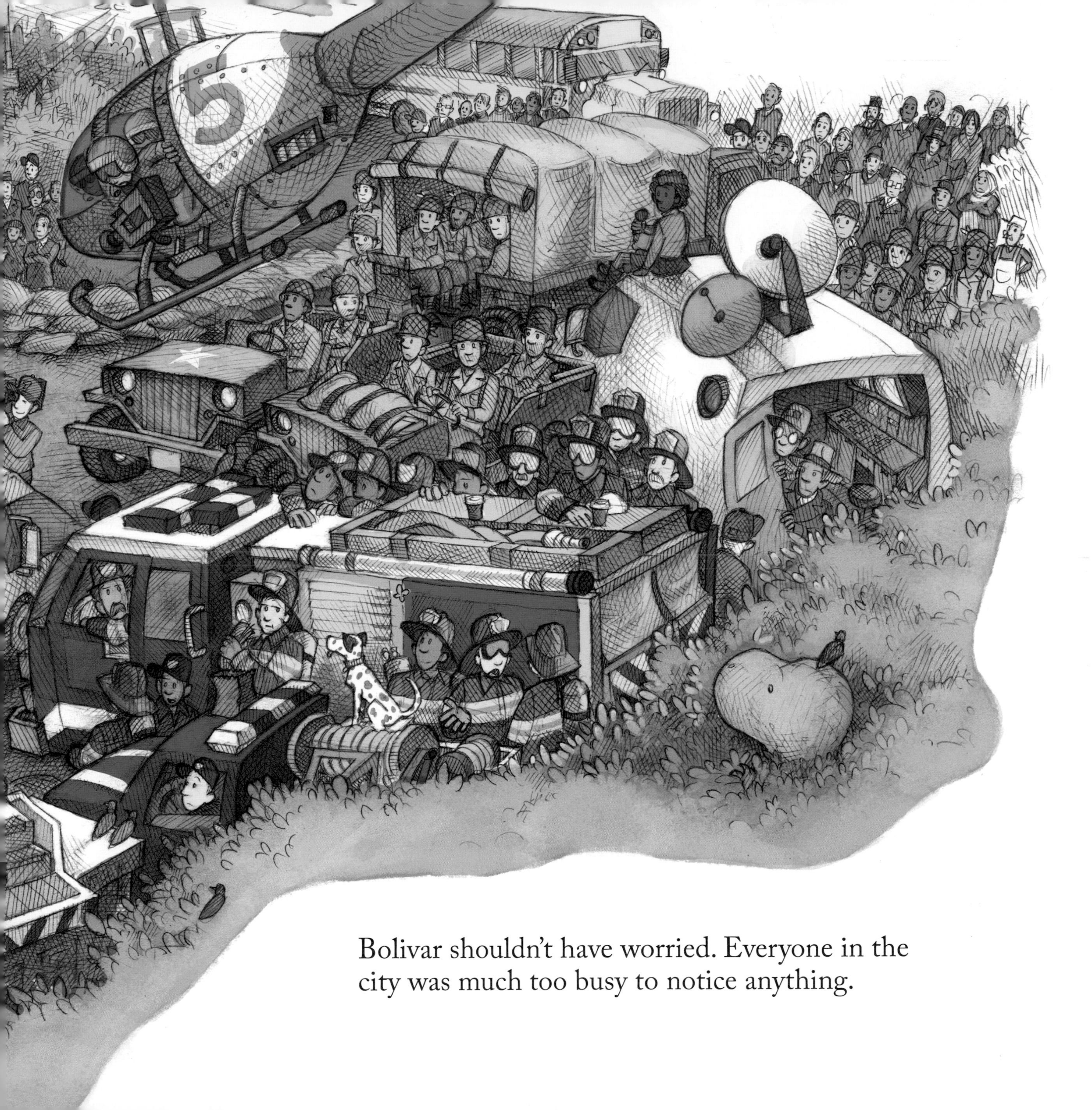

Bolivar shouldn't have worried. Everyone in the city was much too busy to notice anything.

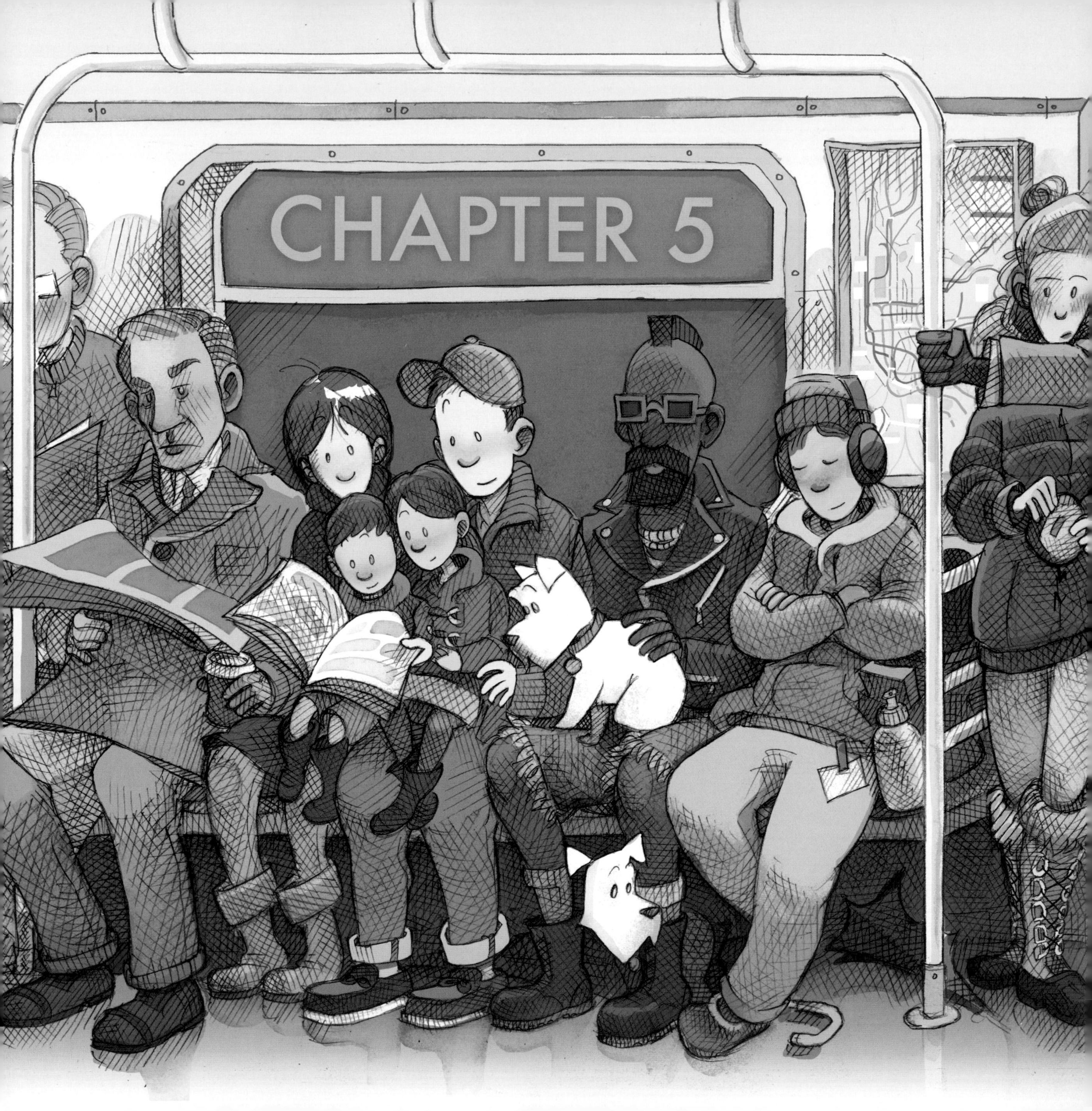
CHAPTER 5

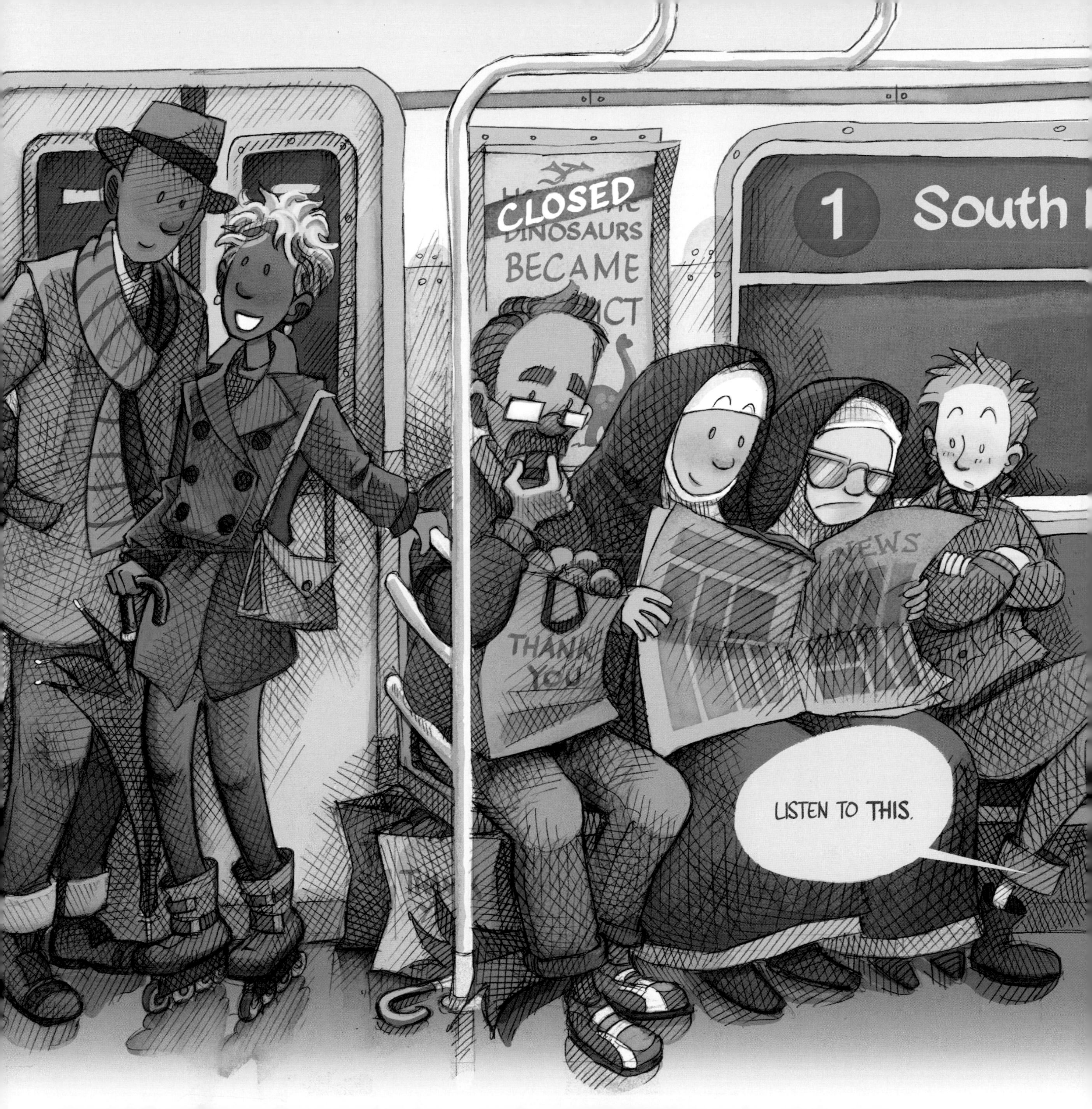
CLOSED
DINOSAURS
BECAME
1 South
THANK YOU
LISTEN TO THIS.

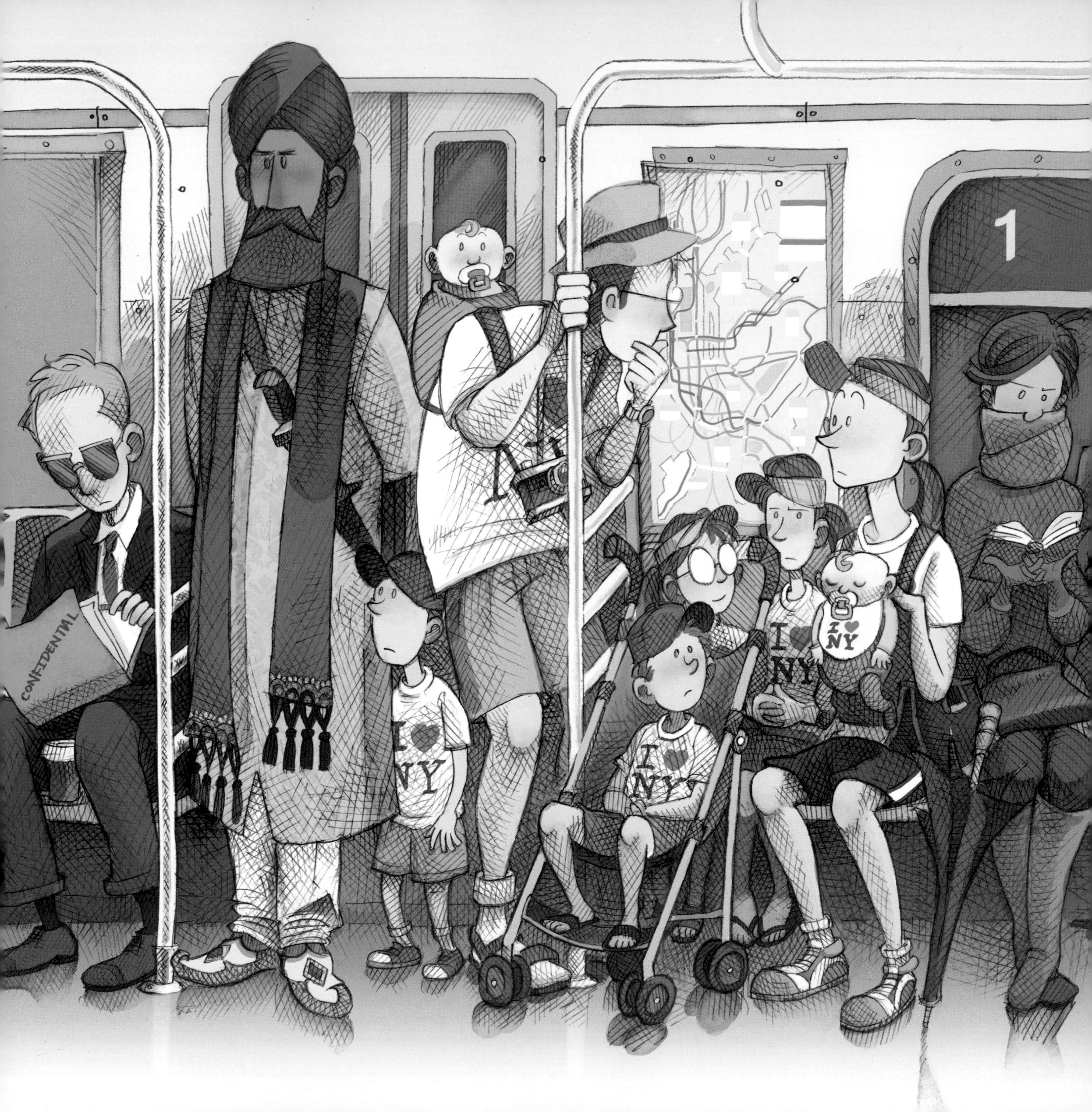
1
CONFIDENTIAL
I ♥ NY
I ♥ NY
I ♥ NY
I ♥ NY

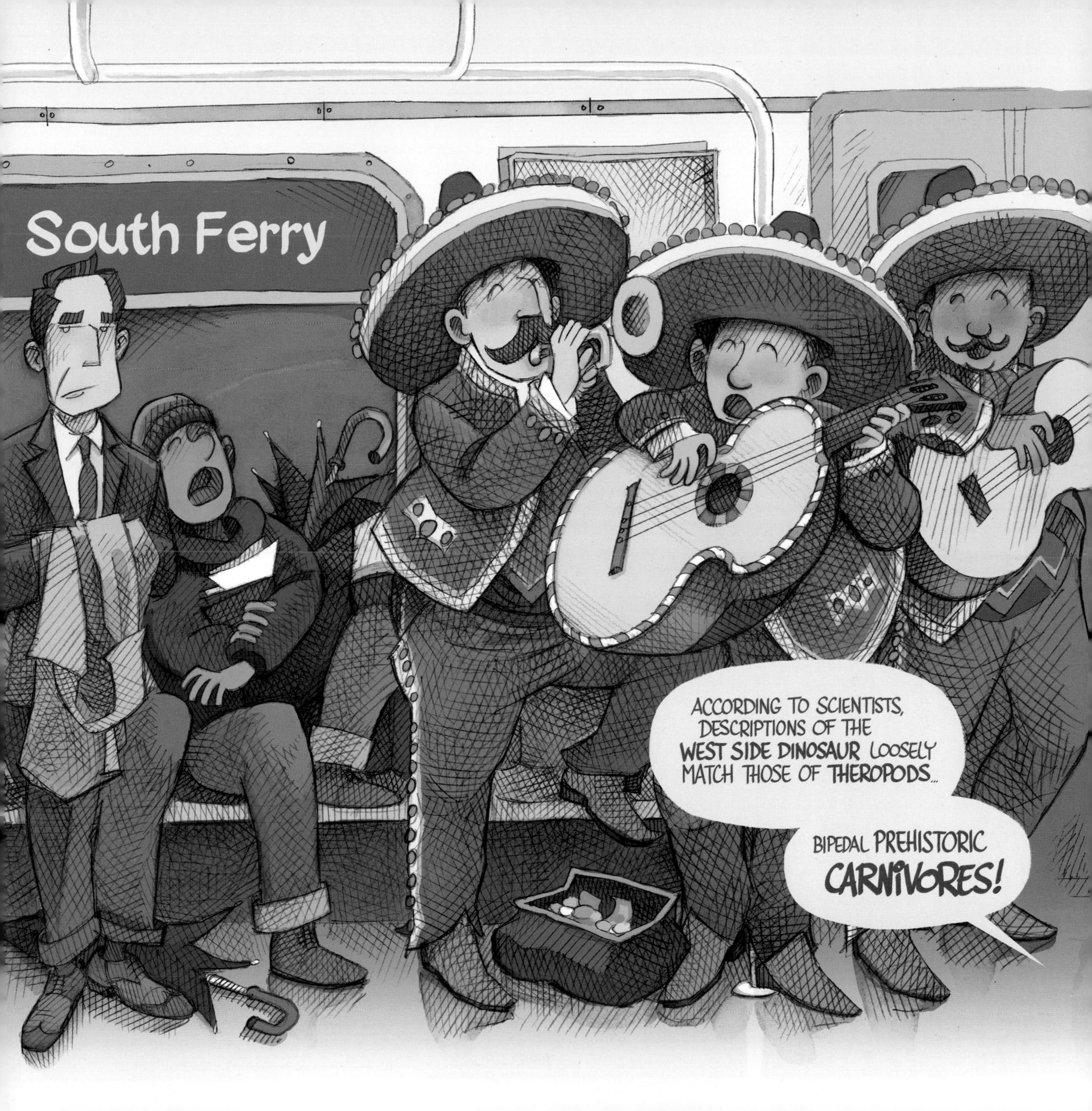
South Ferry
ACCORDING TO SCIENTISTS, DESCRIPTIONS OF THE WEST SIDE DINOSAUR LOOSELY MATCH THOSE OF THEROPODS...
BIPEDAL PREHISTORIC CARNIVORES!

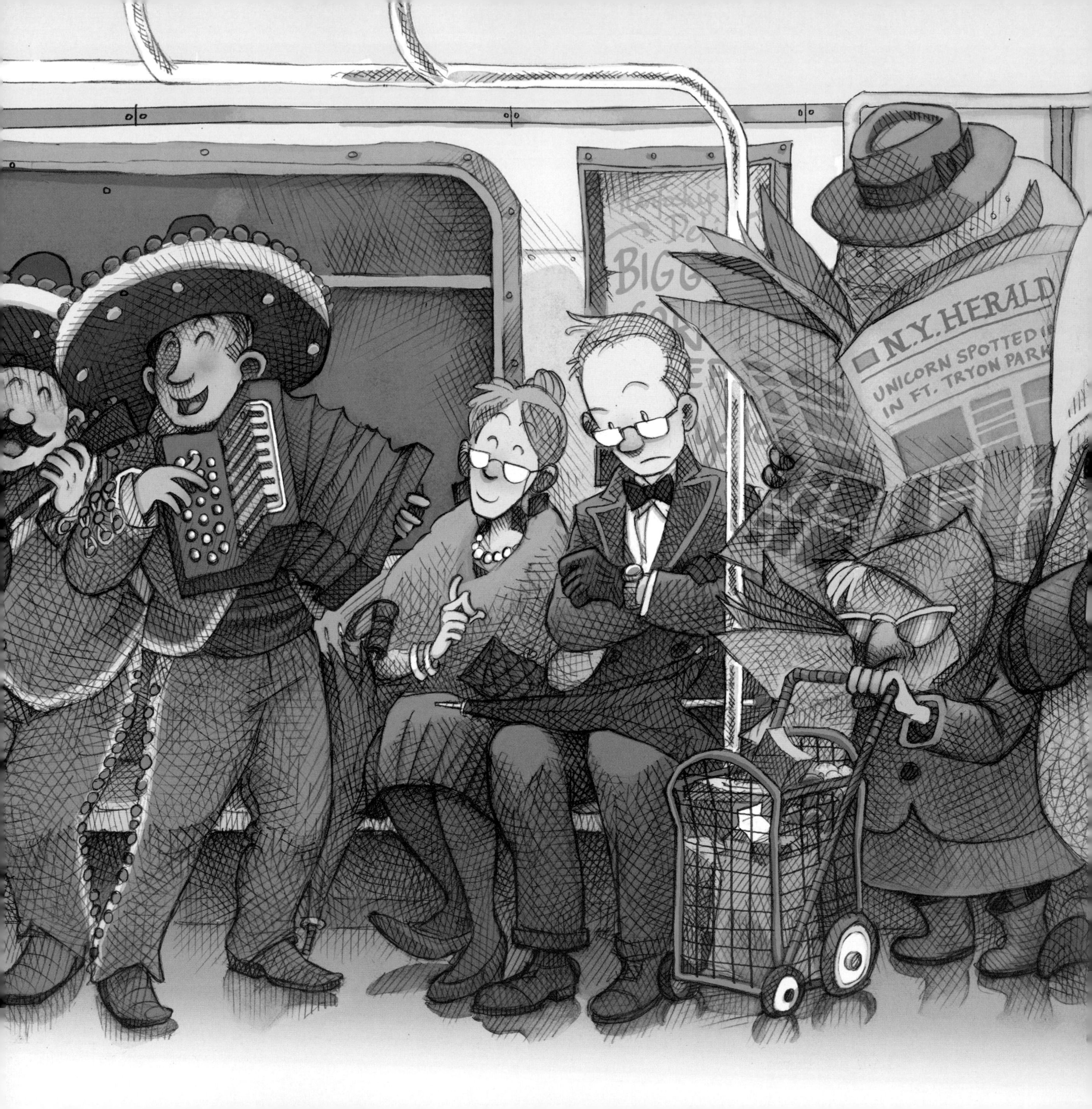
N.Y. HERALD
UNICORN SPOTTED IN
IN FT. TRYON PARK

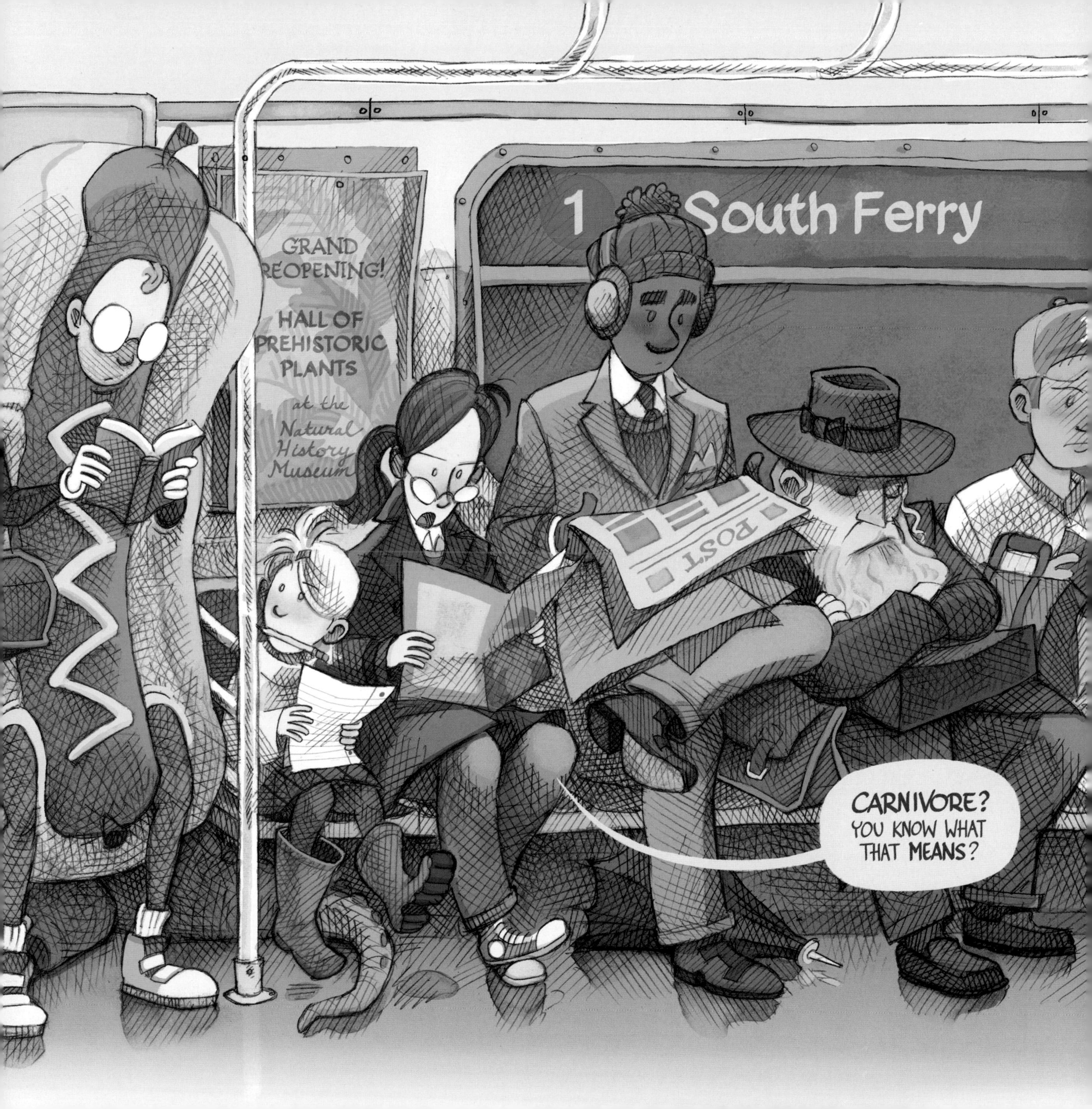
1 South Ferry
GRAND REOPENING!
HALL OF PREHISTORIC PLANTS
at the Natural History Museum
POST
CARNIVORE? YOU KNOW WHAT THAT MEANS?

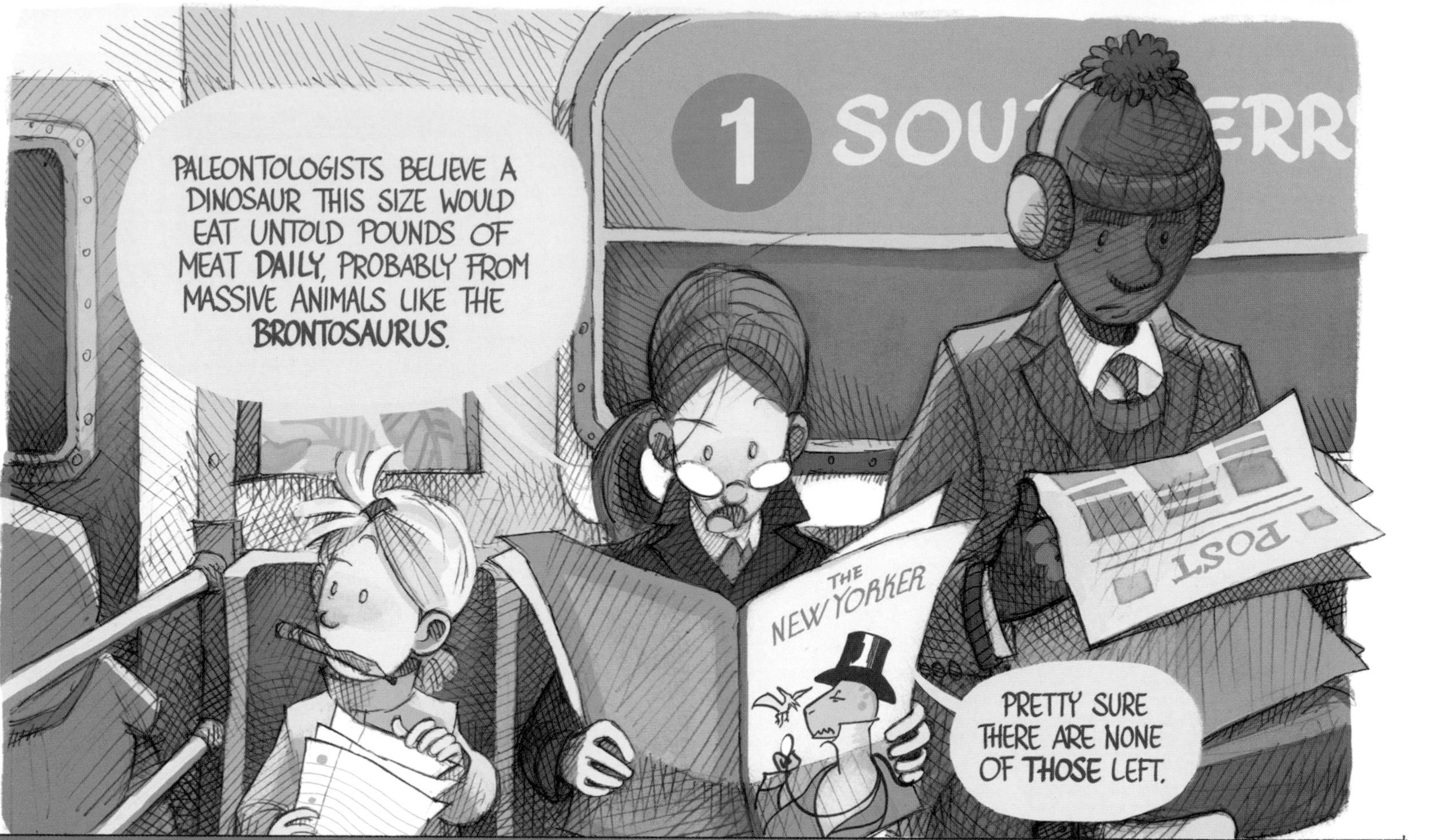
PALEONTOLOGISTS BELIEVE A DINOSAUR THIS SIZE WOULD EAT UNTOLD POUNDS OF MEAT **DAILY**, PROBABLY FROM MASSIVE ANIMALS LIKE THE **BRONTOSAURUS**.
THE NEW YORKER
POST
PRETTY SURE THERE ARE NONE OF **THOSE** LEFT.

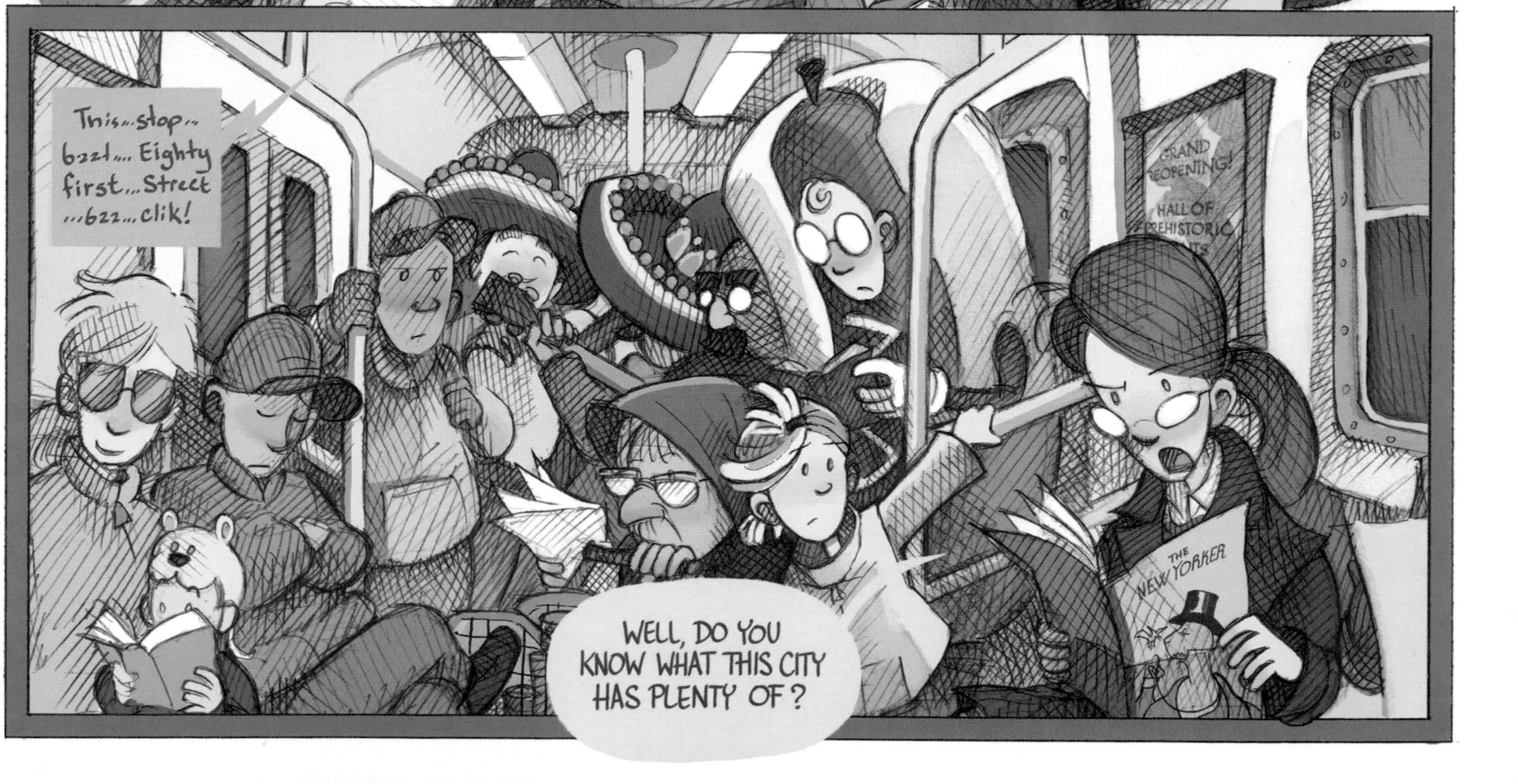
This... stop... bzzt... Eighty first... Street ...bzz... clik!
WELL, DO YOU KNOW WHAT THIS CITY HAS PLENTY OF?
THE NEW YORKER

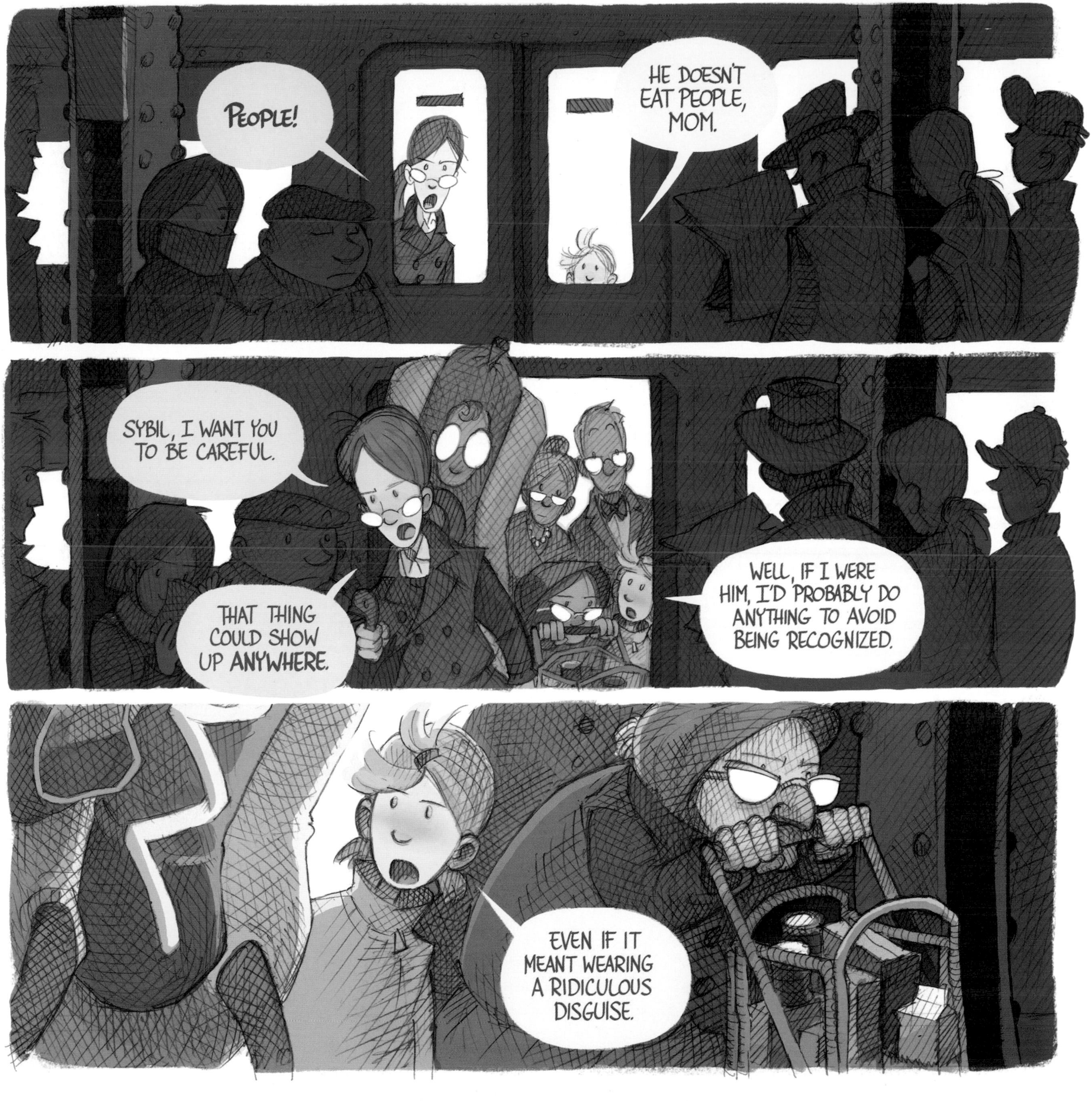
PEOPLE!
HE DOESN'T EAT PEOPLE, MOM.
SYBIL, I WANT YOU TO BE CAREFUL.
THAT THING COULD SHOW UP ANYWHERE.
WELL, IF I WERE HIM, I'D PROBABLY DO ANYTHING TO AVOID BEING RECOGNIZED.
EVEN IF IT MEANT WEARING A RIDICULOUS DISGUISE.

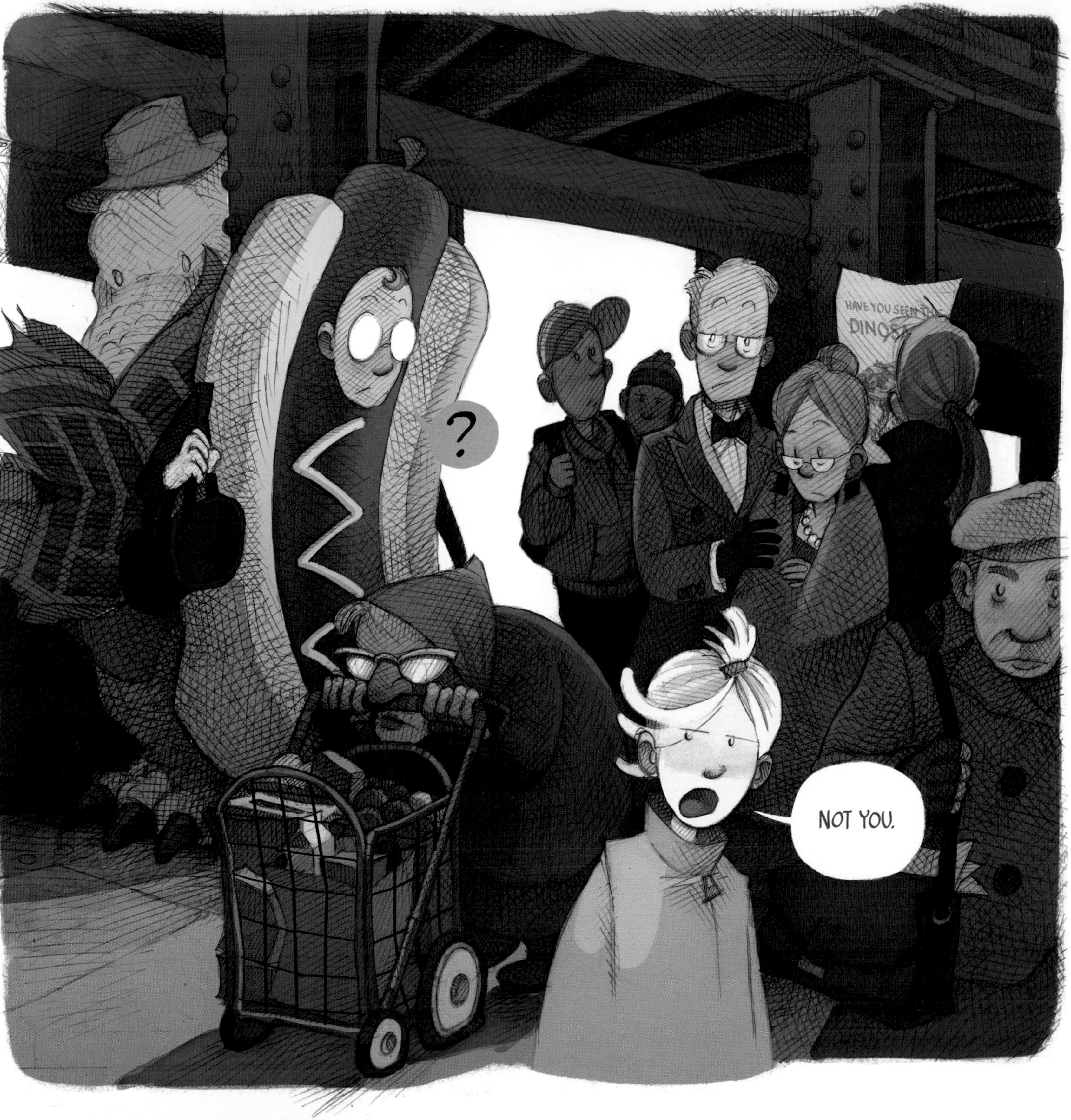
?
NOT YOU.

Bolivar was a dinosaur. He was the last dinosaur left anywhere.

Like any dinosaur, Bolivar didn't like attention.
And that's why he had a problem.

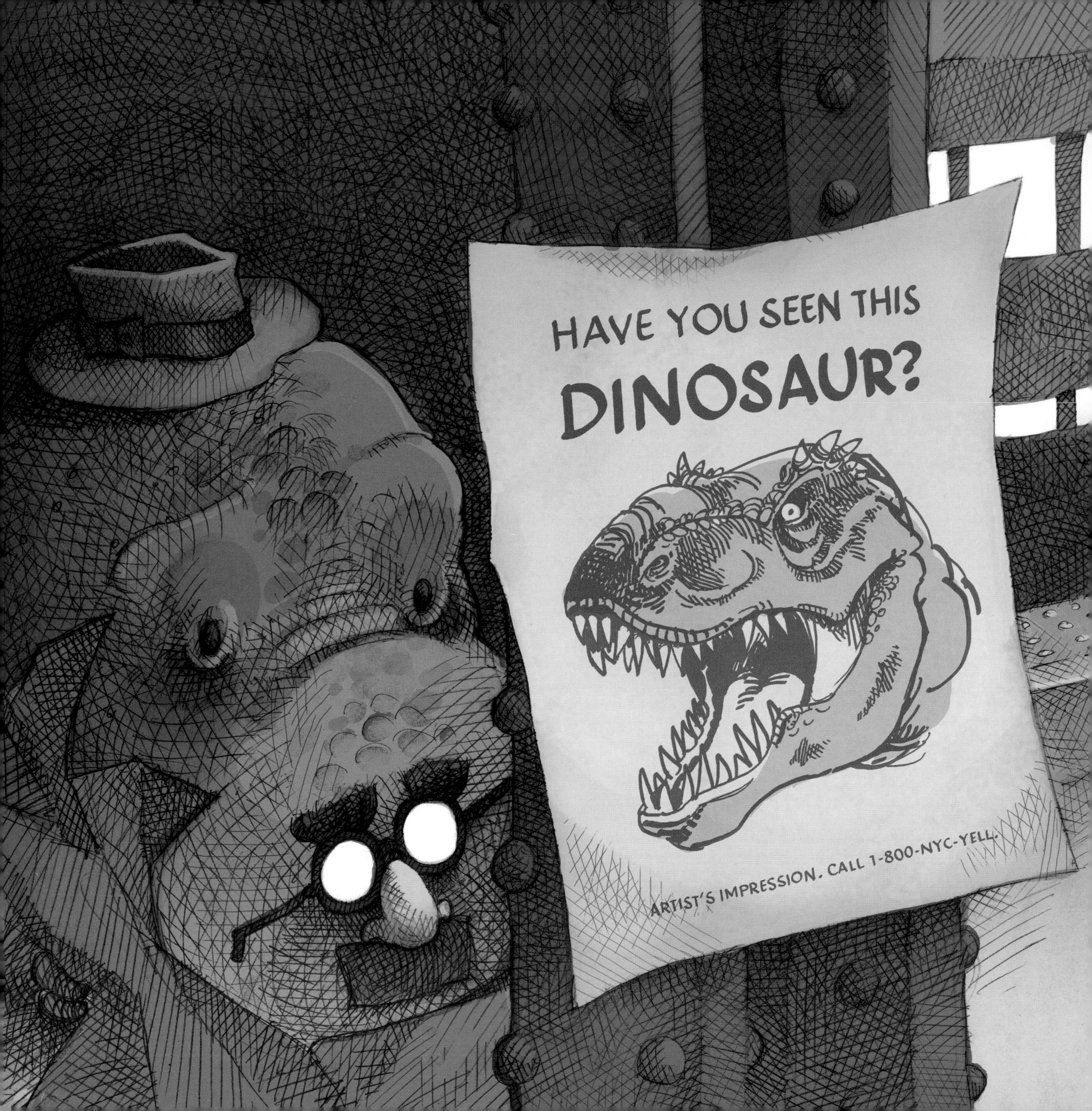
HAVE YOU SEEN THIS
DINOSAUR?
ARTIST'S IMPRESSION. CALL 1-800-NYC-YELL.

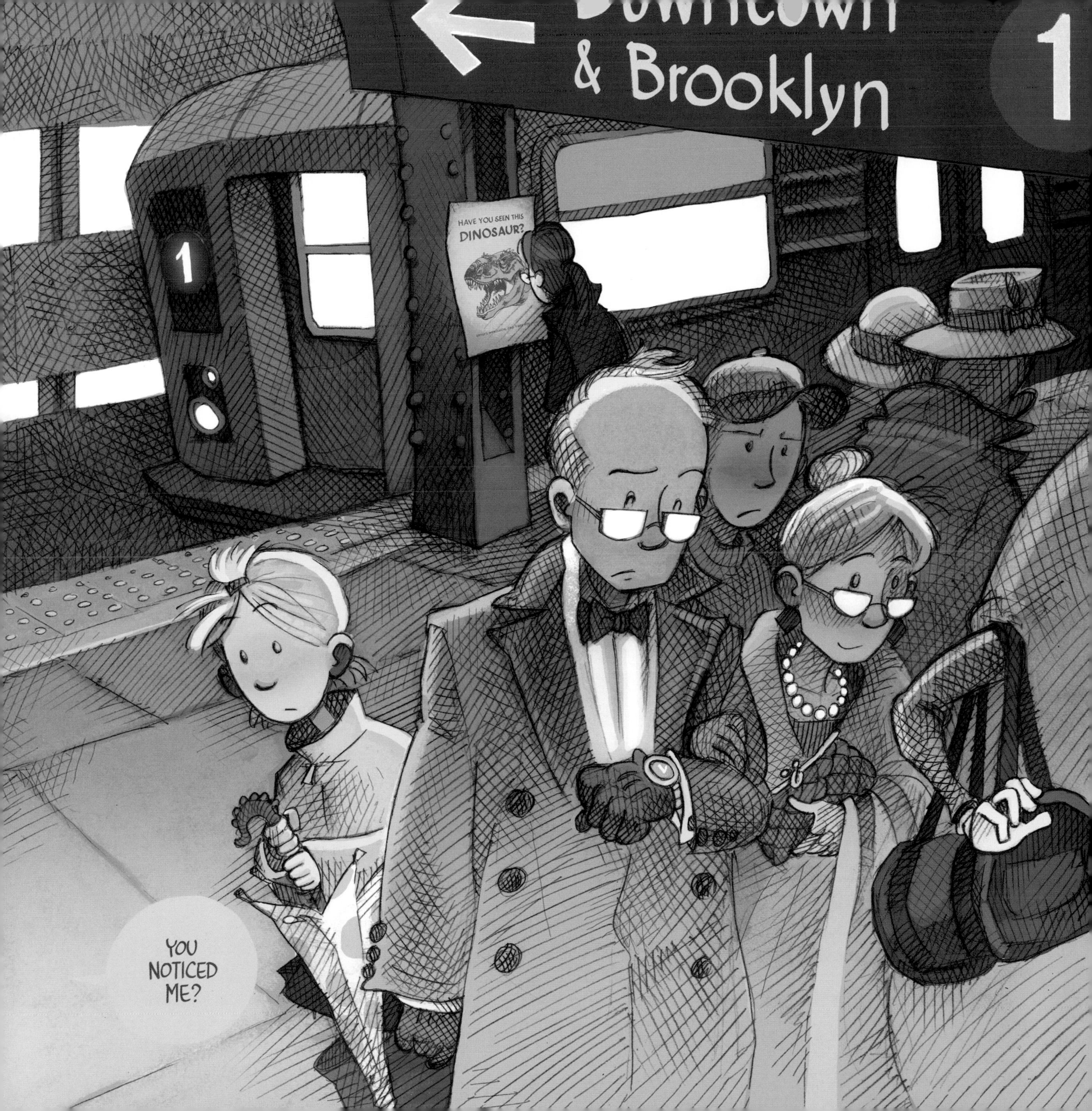
& Brooklyn
1
HAVE YOU SEEN THIS
DINOSAUR?
1
YOU NOTICED ME?

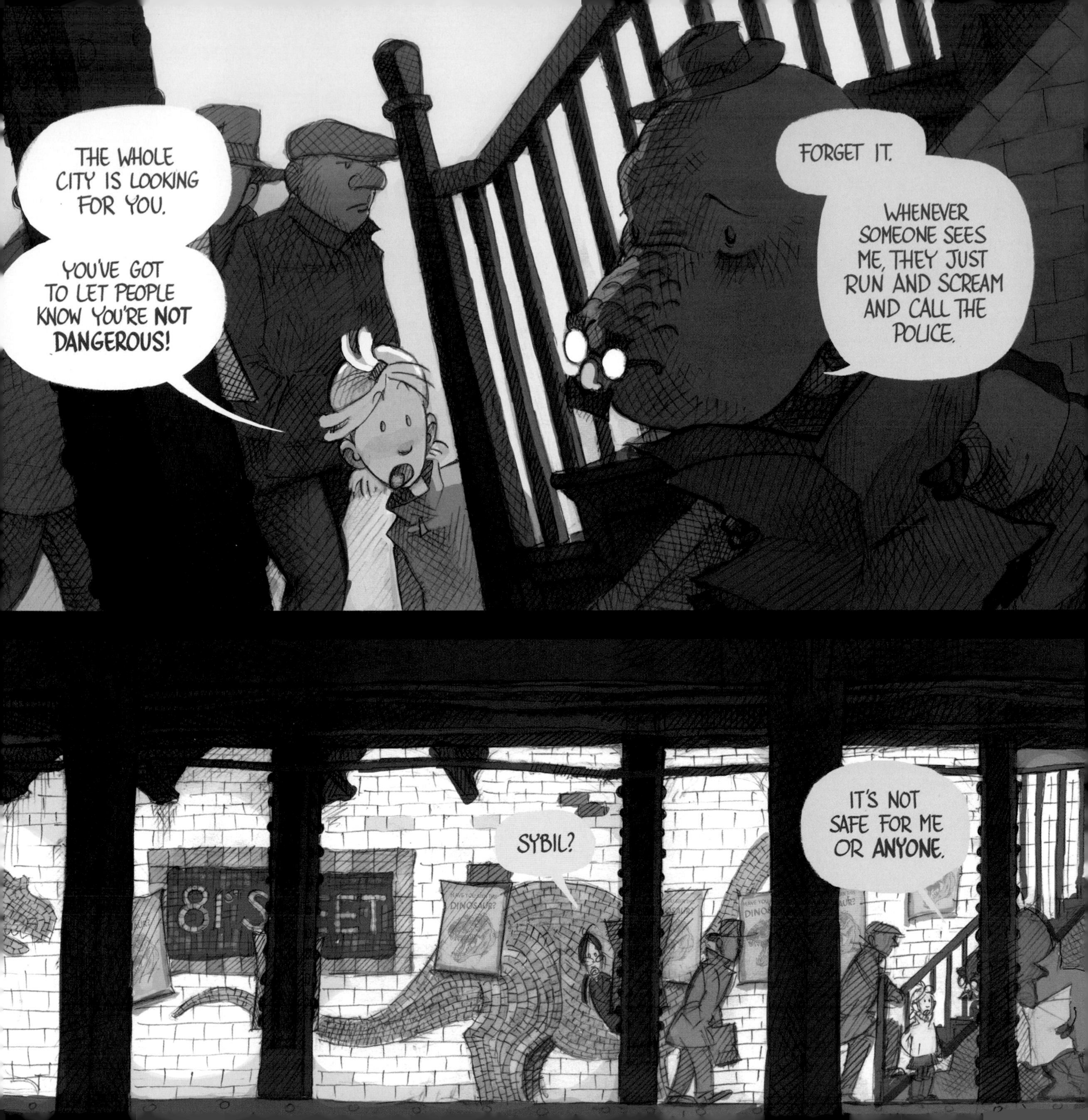
THE WHOLE CITY IS LOOKING FOR YOU.
YOU'VE GOT TO LET PEOPLE KNOW YOU'RE **NOT DANGEROUS!**
FORGET IT.
WHENEVER SOMEONE SEES ME, THEY JUST RUN AND SCREAM AND CALL THE POLICE.
81ST STREET
SYBIL?
IT'S NOT SAFE FOR ME OR **ANYONE.**

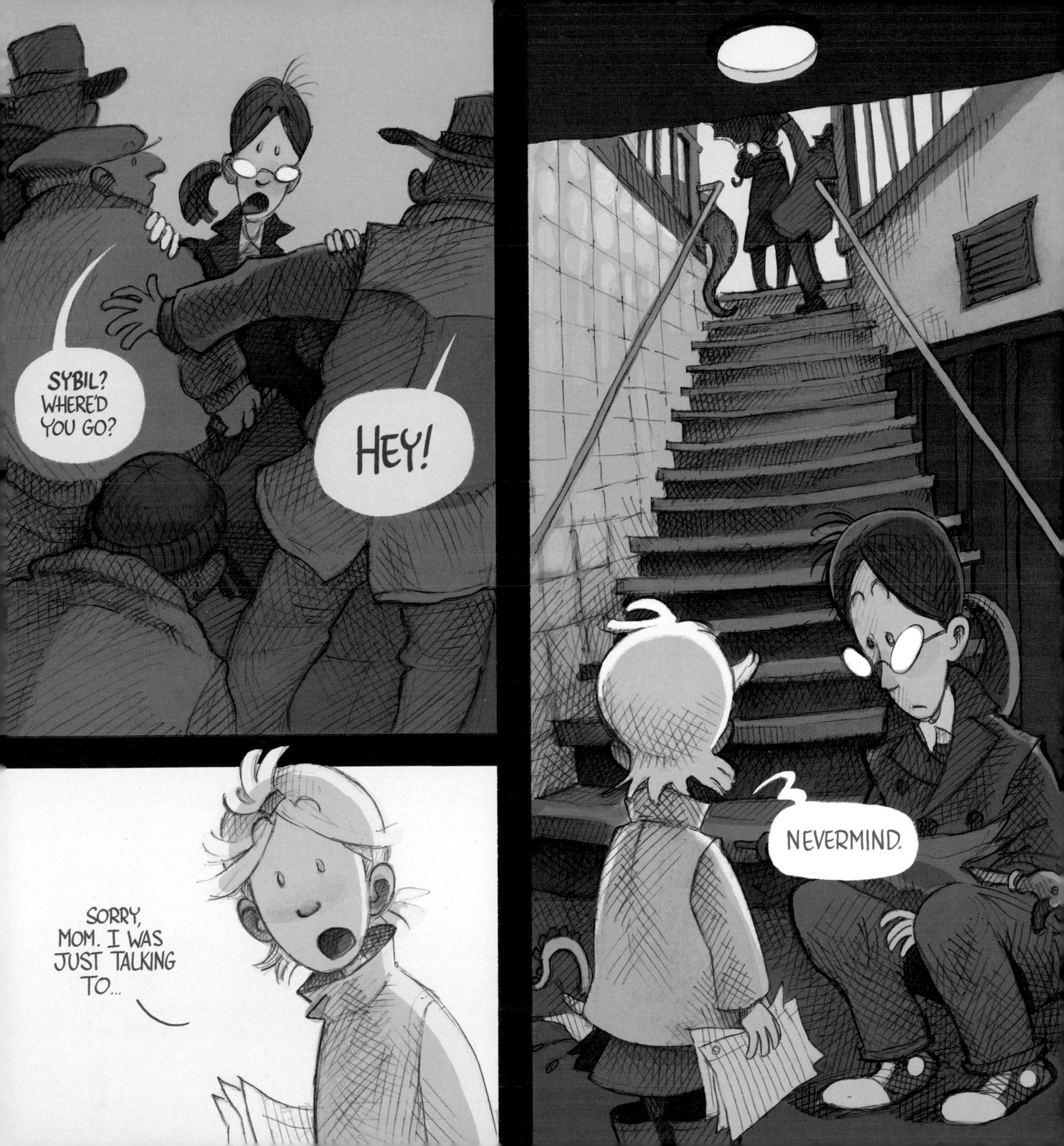
SYBIL? WHERE'D YOU GO?
HEY!
SORRY, MOM. I WAS JUST TALKING TO...
NEVERMIND.

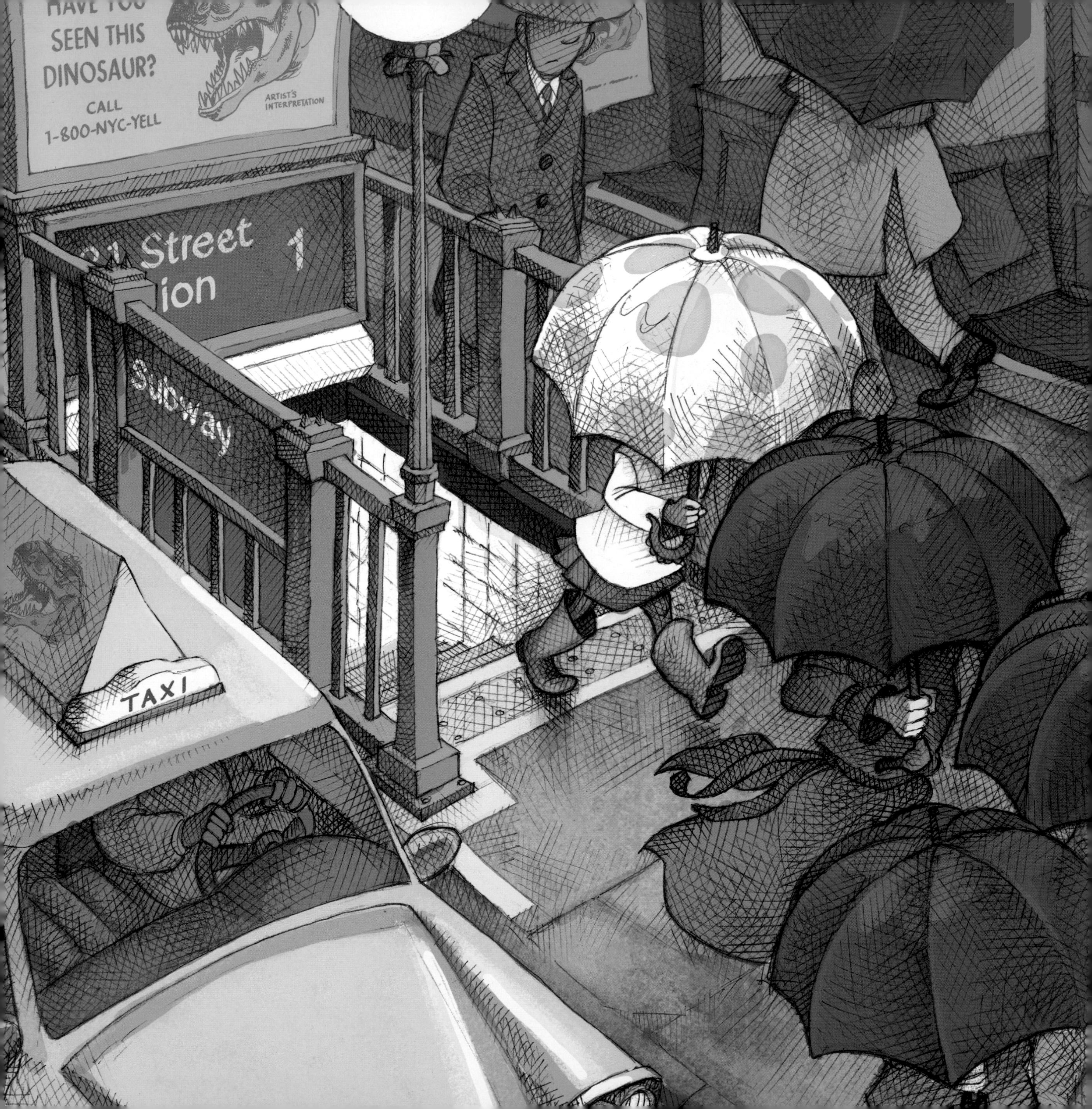

HAVE YOU SEEN THIS DINOSAUR?
CALL 1-800-NYC-YELL
ARTIST'S INTERPRETATION
Street
ion
1
Subway
TAXI

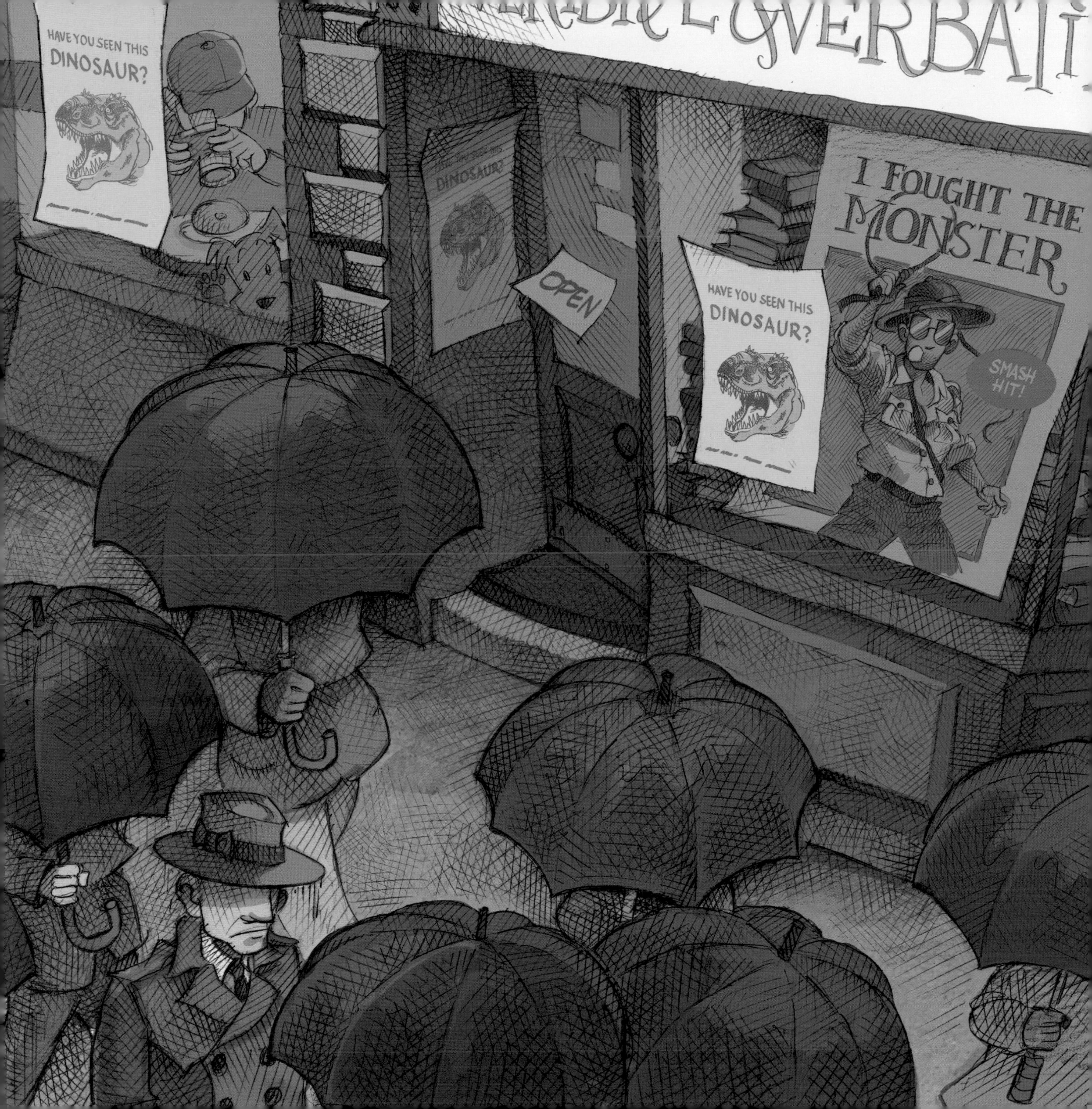
HAVE YOU SEEN THIS
DINOSAUR?
DINOSAUR?
OPEN
HAVE YOU SEEN THIS
DINOSAUR?
I FOUGHT THE
MONSTER
SMASH
HIT!

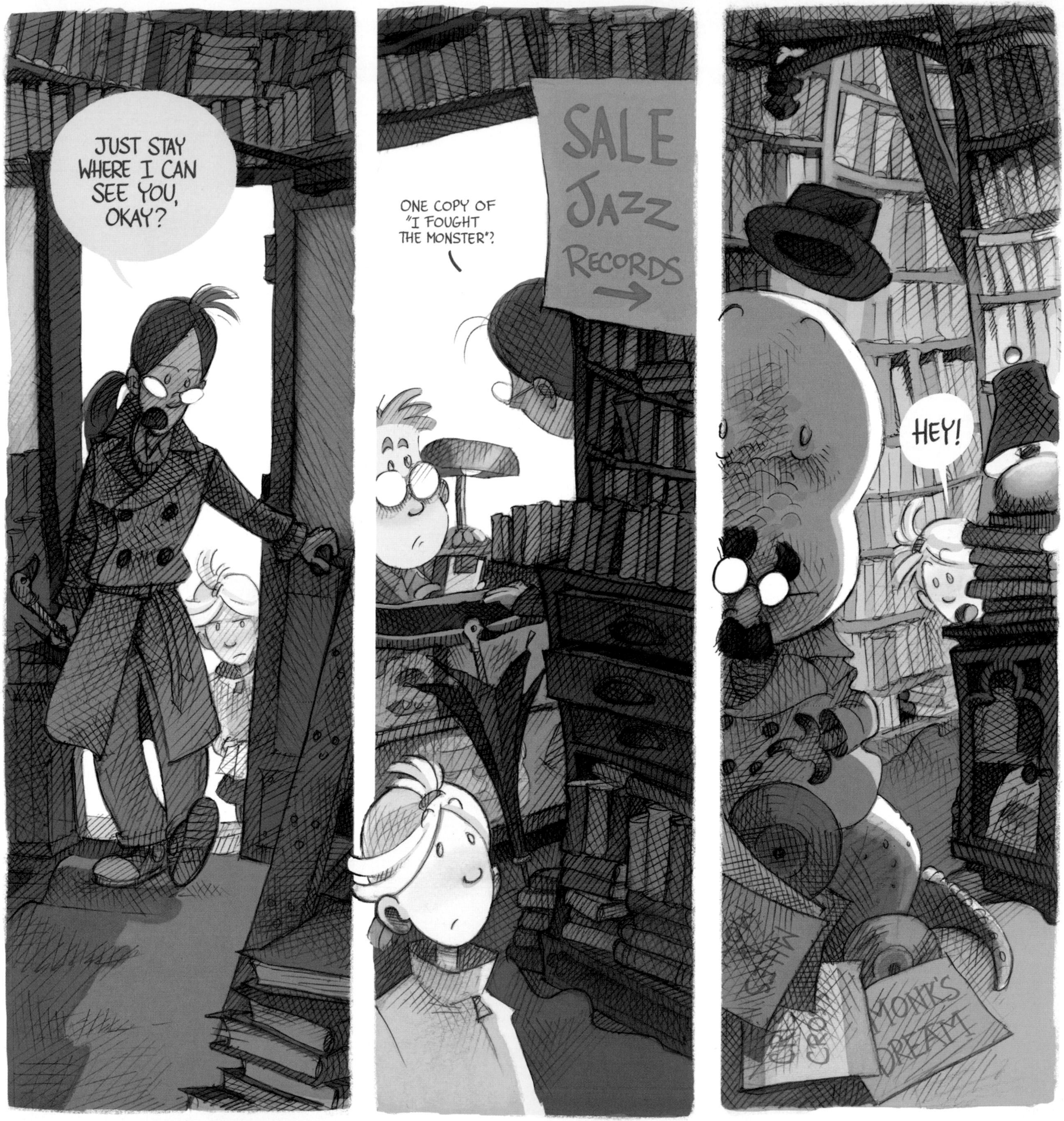

JUST STAY WHERE I CAN SEE YOU, OKAY?
SALE
JAZZ
RECORDS
ONE COPY OF "I FOUGHT THE MONSTER"?
HEY!
MONK'S DREAM

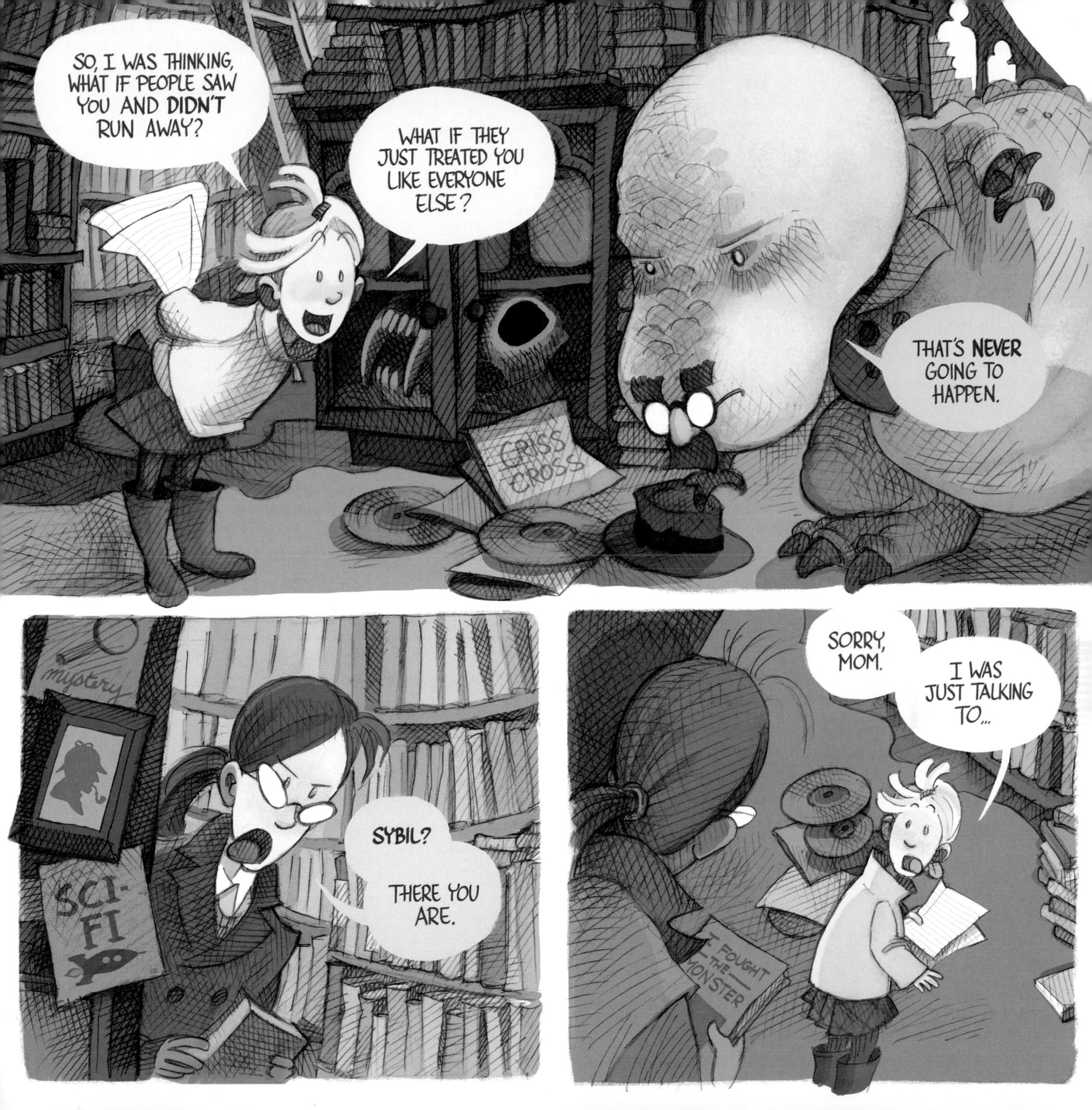
SO, I WAS THINKING, WHAT IF PEOPLE SAW YOU AND DIDN'T RUN AWAY?
WHAT IF THEY JUST TREATED YOU LIKE EVERYONE ELSE?
THAT'S NEVER GOING TO HAPPEN.
CRISS CROSS
mystery
SCI-FI
SYBIL?
THERE YOU ARE.
SORRY, MOM.
I WAS JUST TALKING TO...
I FOUGHT THE MONSTER

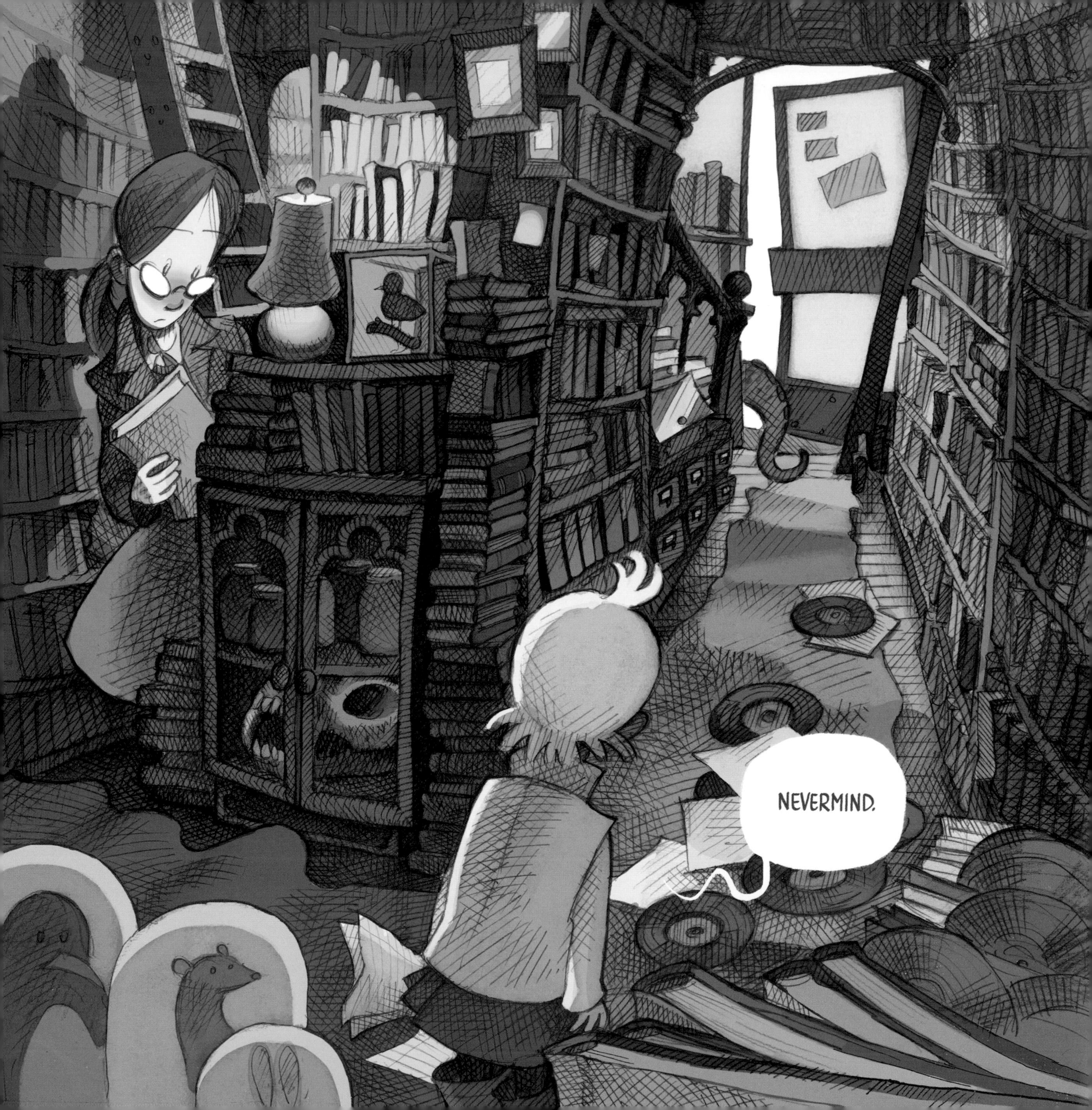
NEVERMIND.

Bolivar had to be more careful than ever
if he wanted to avoid detection.

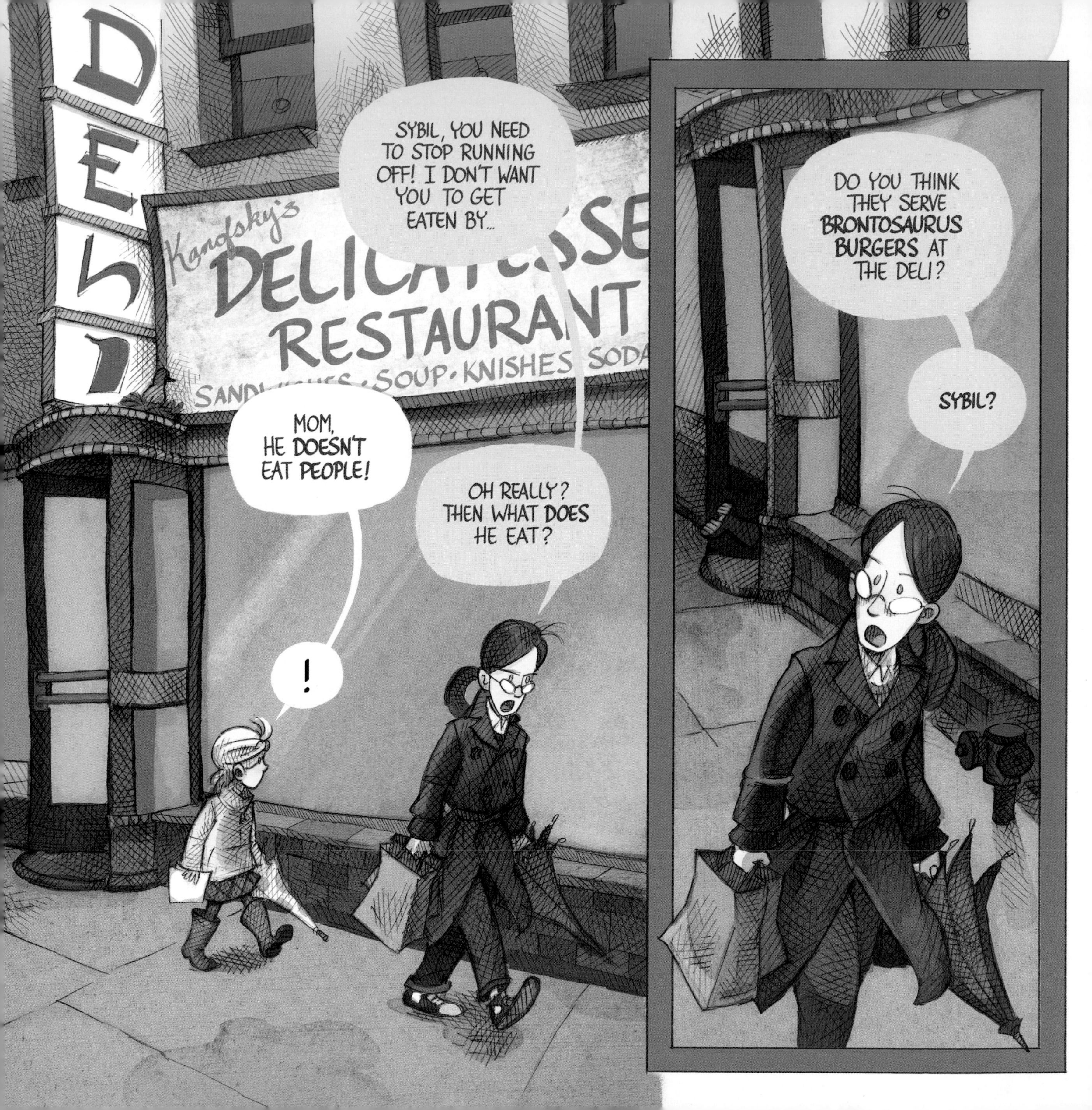

Kanofsky's
RESTAURANT
SOUP • KNISHES
SYBIL, YOU NEED TO STOP RUNNING OFF! I DON'T WANT YOU TO GET EATEN BY...
MOM, HE **DOESN'T** EAT **PEOPLE!**
OH REALLY? THEN WHAT **DOES** HE EAT?
!
DO YOU THINK THEY SERVE **BRONTOSAURUS BURGERS** AT THE DELI?
SYBIL?

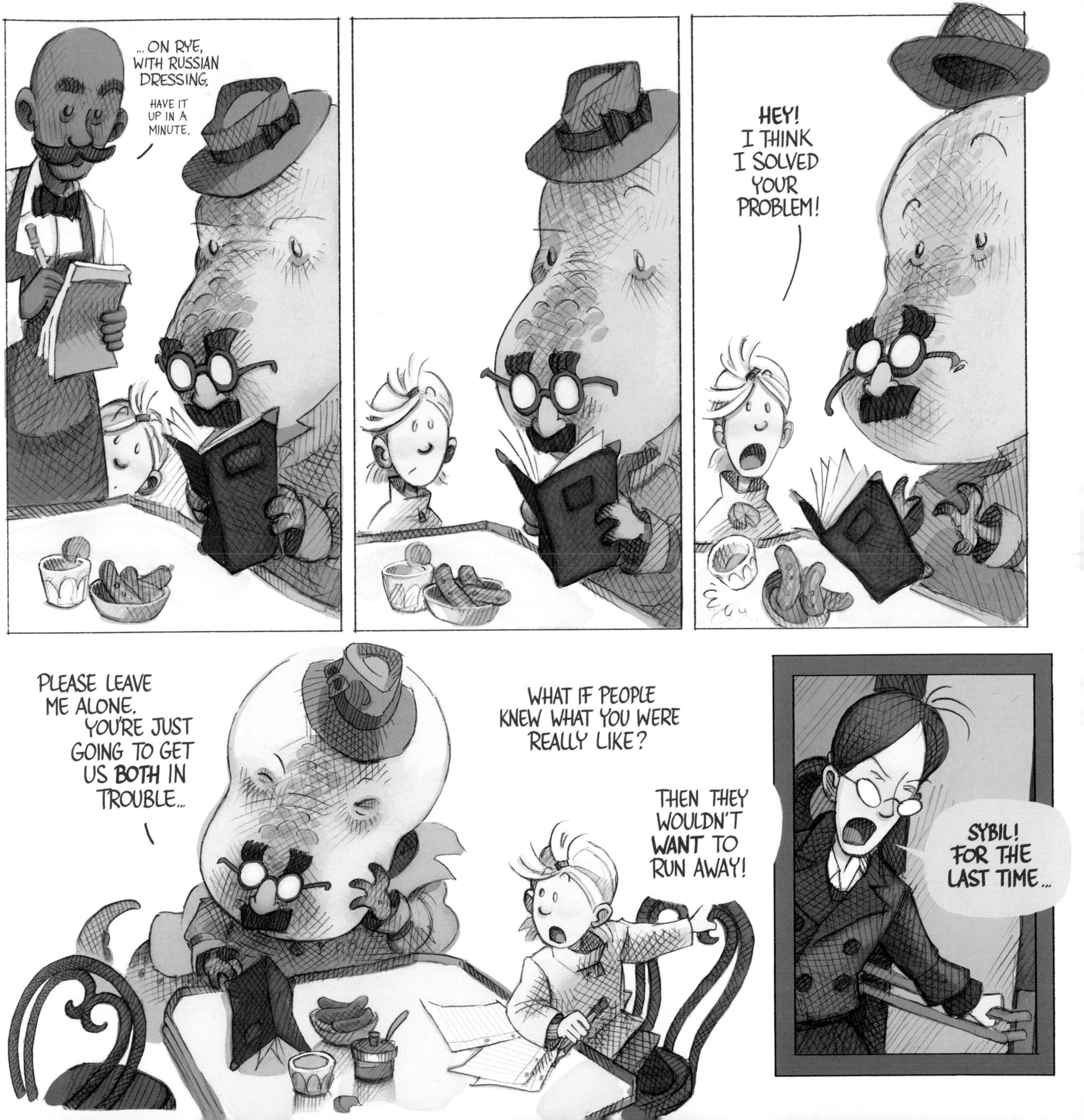

...ON RYE, WITH RUSSIAN DRESSING.
HAVE IT UP IN A MINUTE.
HEY! I THINK I SOLVED YOUR PROBLEM!
PLEASE LEAVE ME ALONE. YOU'RE JUST GOING TO GET US **BOTH** IN TROUBLE...
WHAT IF PEOPLE KNEW WHAT YOU WERE REALLY LIKE?
THEN THEY WOULDN'T **WANT** TO RUN AWAY!
SYBIL! FOR THE LAST TIME...

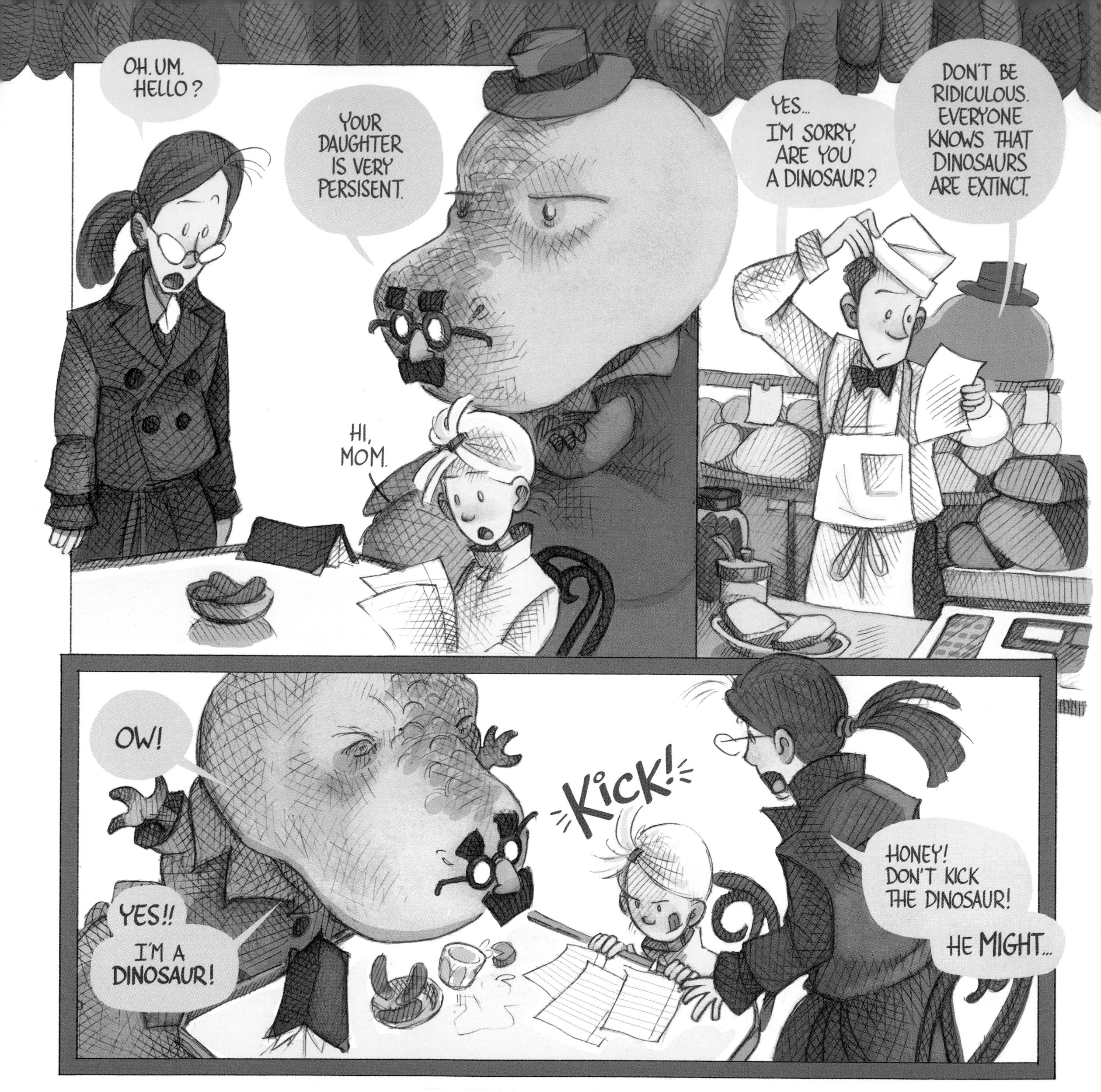
OH. UM. HELLO?
YOUR DAUGHTER IS VERY PERSISENT.
HI, MOM.
YES... I'M SORRY, ARE YOU A DINOSAUR?
DON'T BE RIDICULOUS. EVERYONE KNOWS THAT DINOSAURS ARE EXTINCT.
OW!
KICK!
YES!! I'M A DINOSAUR!
HONEY! DON'T KICK THE DINOSAUR!
HE MIGHT...

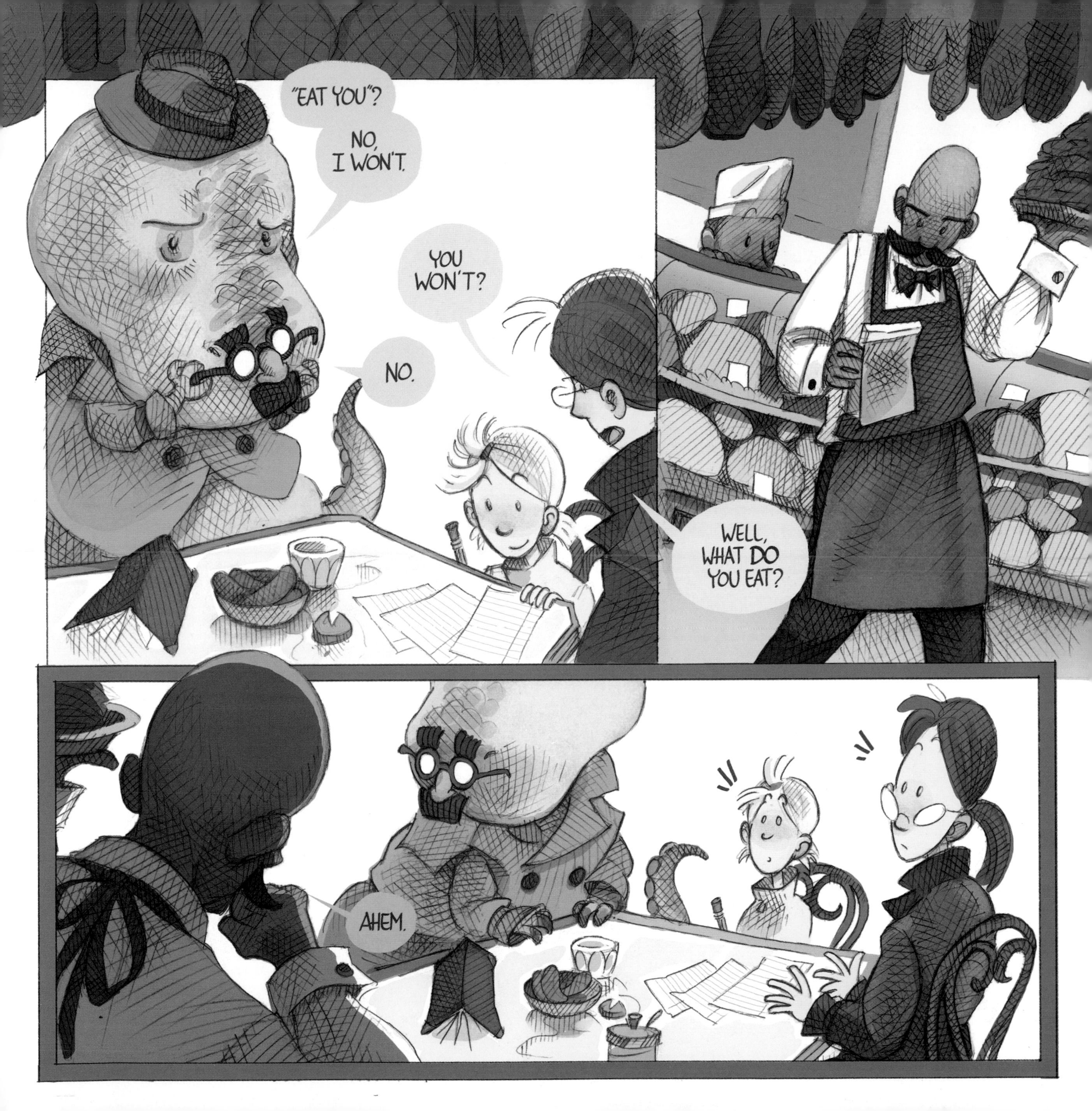
"EAT YOU"?
NO, I WON'T.
YOU WON'T?
NO.
WELL, WHAT DO YOU EAT?
AHEM.

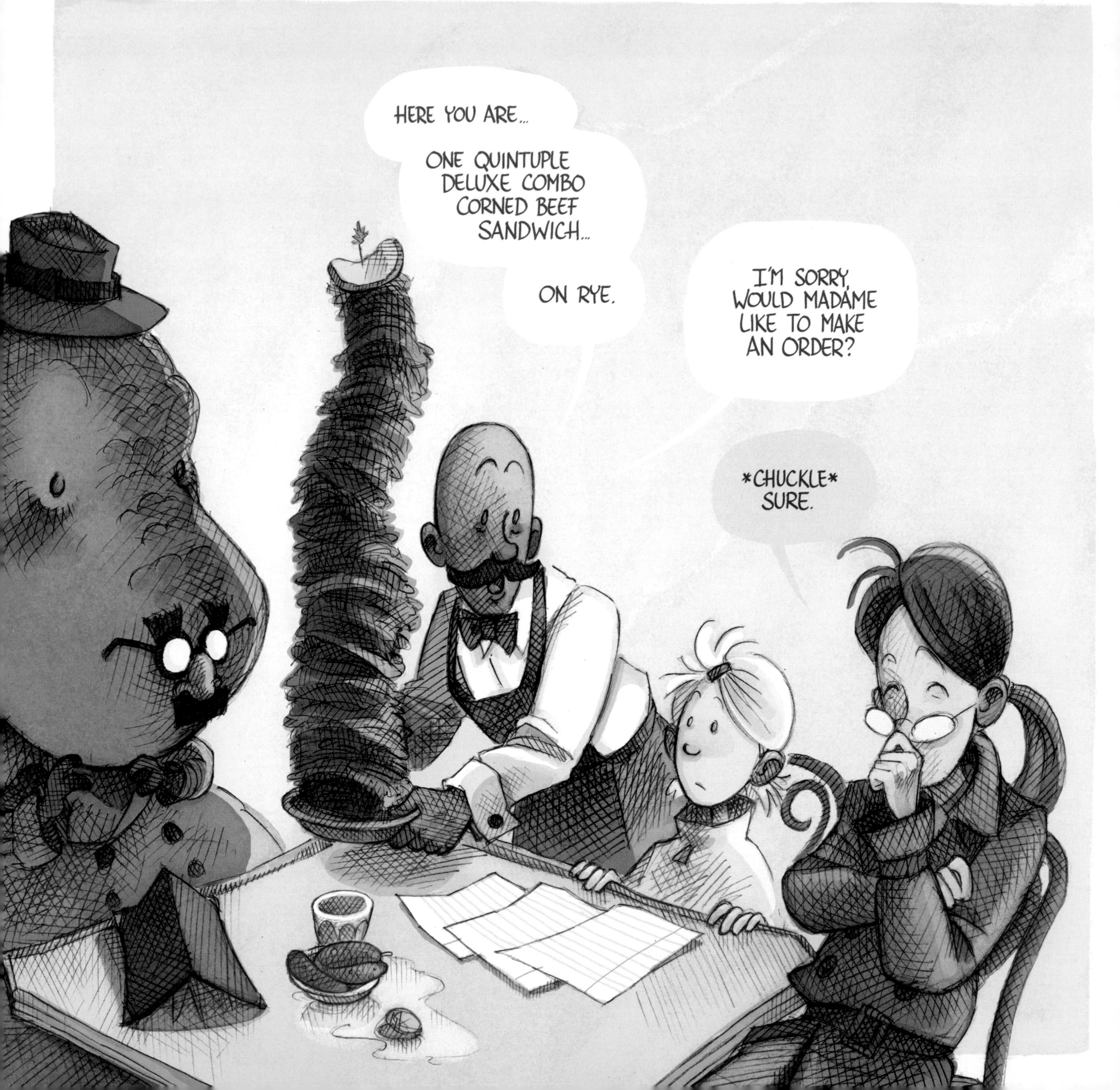
HERE YOU ARE...
ONE QUINTUPLE DELUXE COMBO CORNED BEEF SANDWICH...
ON RYE.
I'M SORRY, WOULD MADAME LIKE TO MAKE AN ORDER?
CHUCKLE SURE.

And that's how Bolivar remembered what he loved best about New York City.

He loved the museums, he loved the parks.

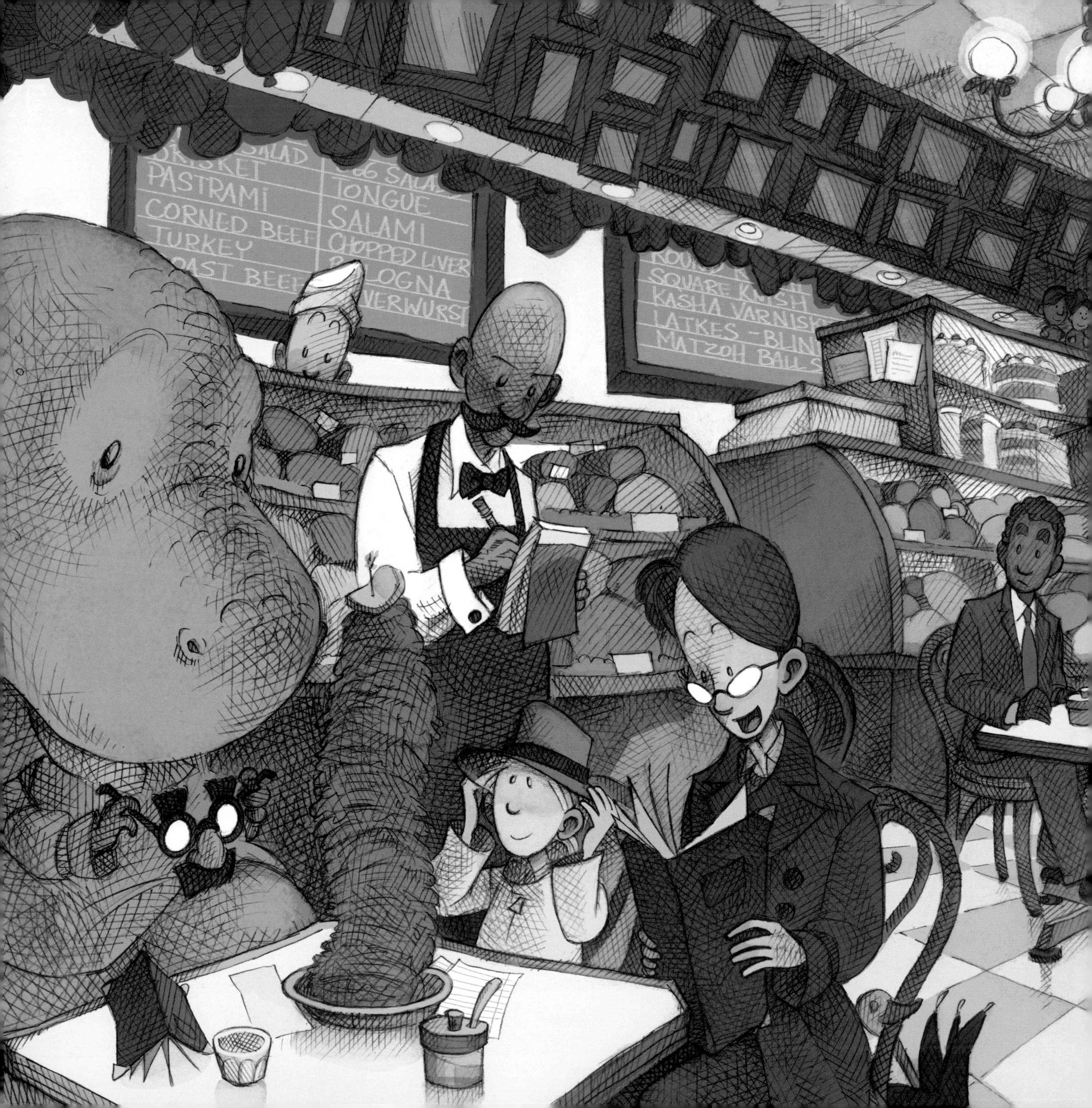
BRISKET
PASTRAMI
CORNED BEEF
TURKEY
TONGUE
SALAMI
CHOPPED LIVER
SQUARE KNISH
KASHA
LATKES

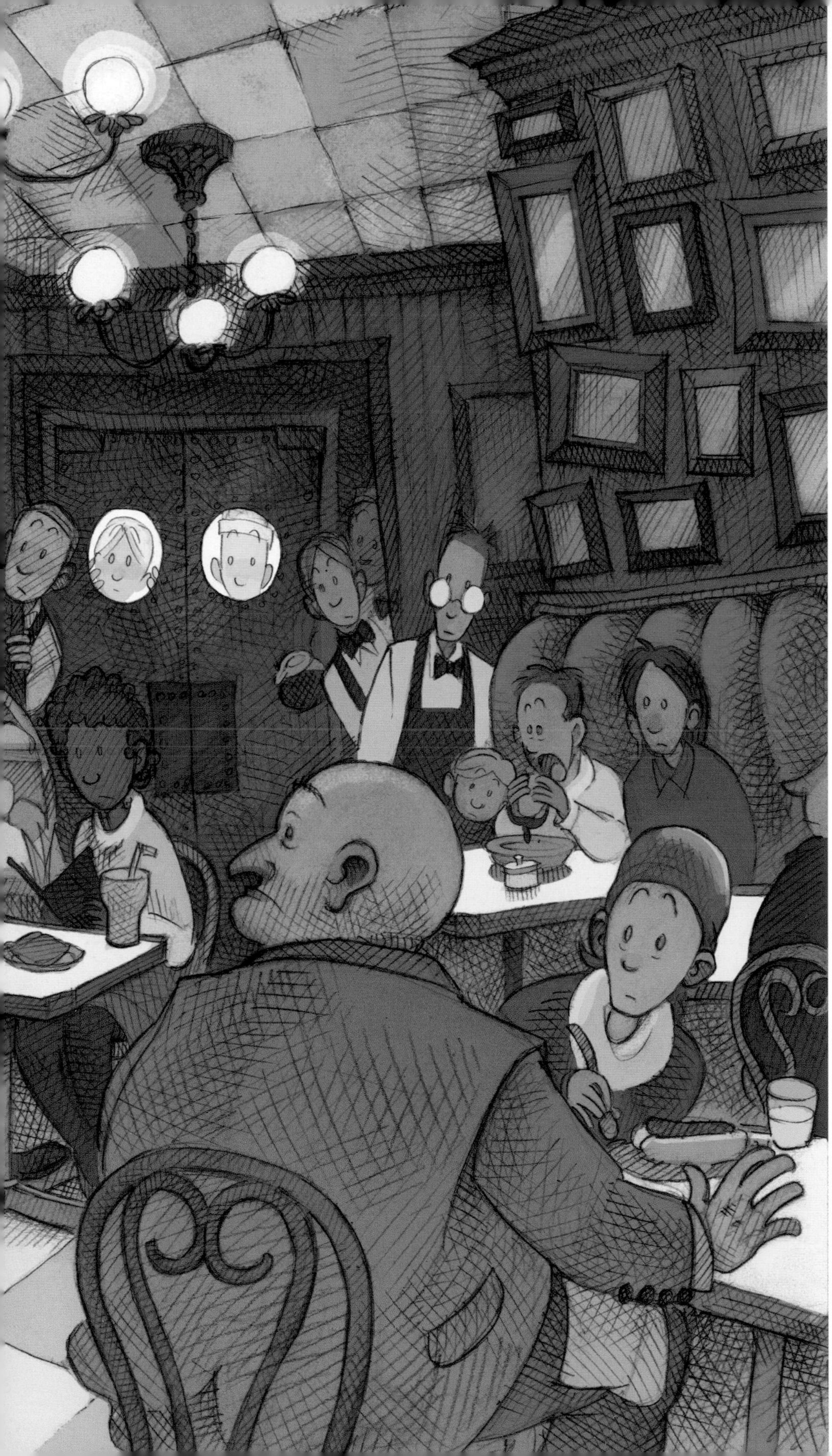

He loved the music,
he loved the food.

But Bolivar loved the people most of all.

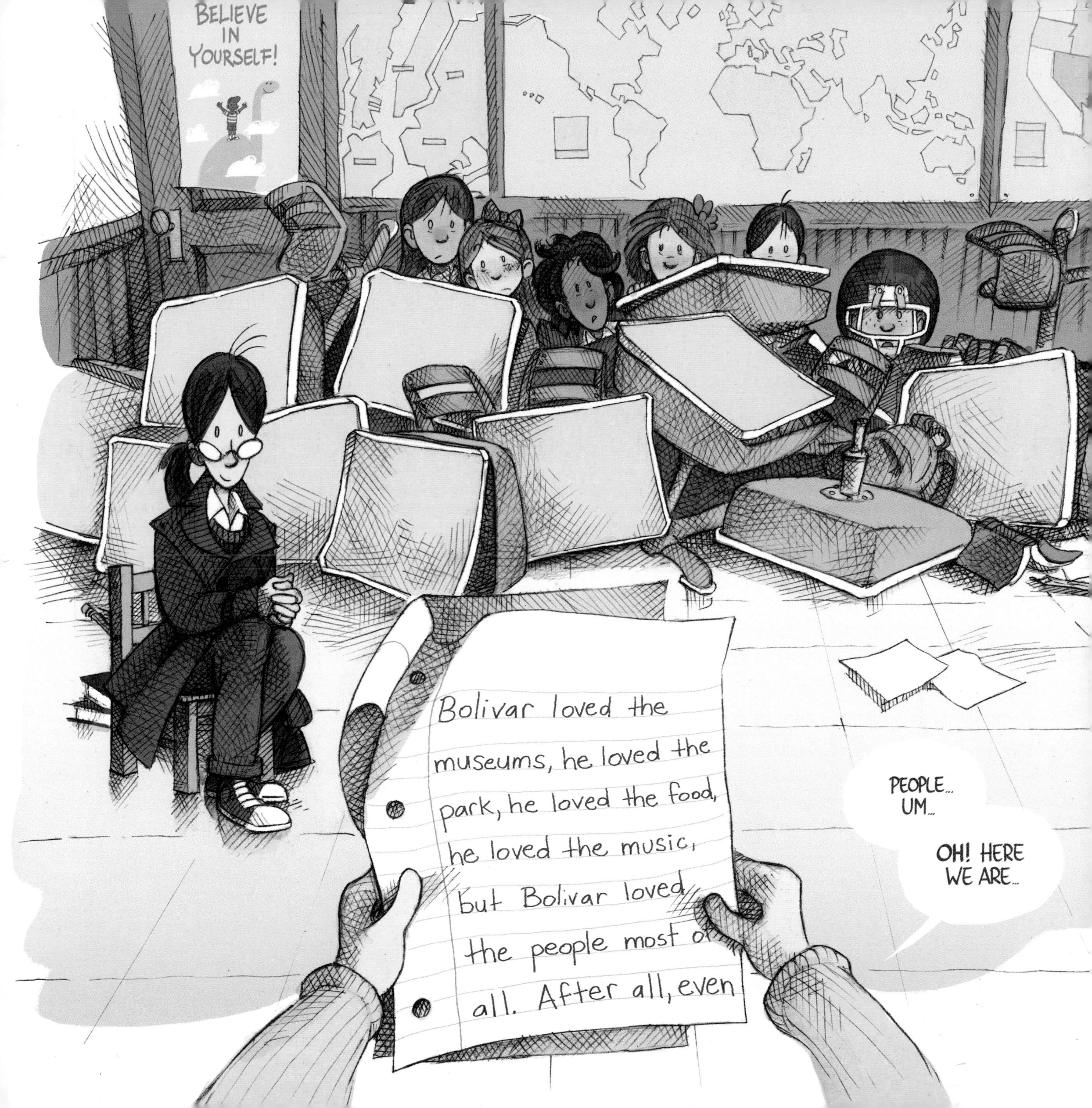
BELIEVE IN YOURSELF!
Bolivar loved the museums, he loved the park, he loved the food, he loved the music, but Bolivar loved the people most of all. After all, even
PEOPLE... UM...
OH! HERE WE ARE...

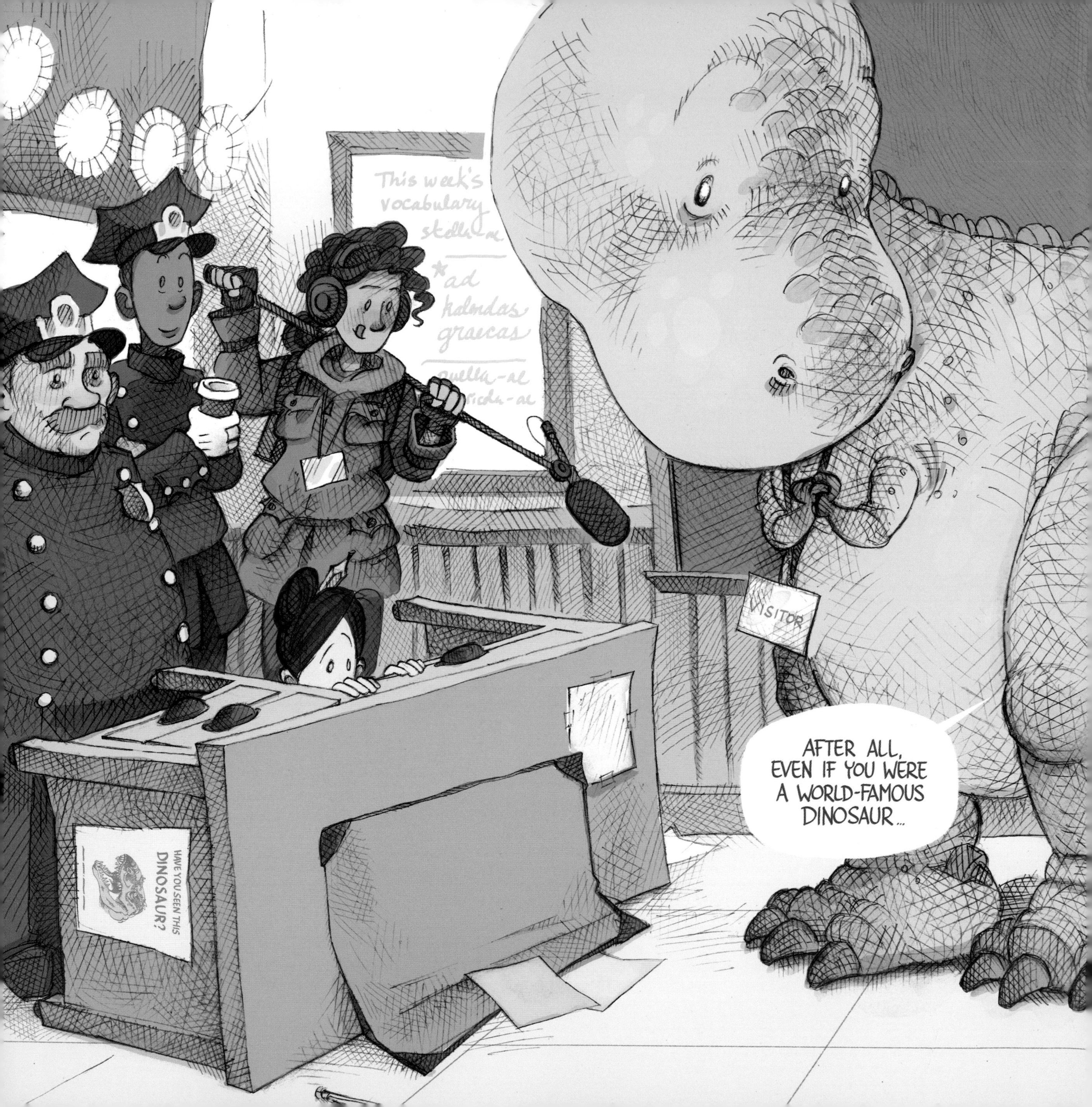
This week's vocabulary
stella-ae
*ad kalendas graecas
VISITOR
HAVE YOU SEEN THIS DINOSAUR?
AFTER ALL, EVEN IF YOU WERE A WORLD-FAMOUS DINOSAUR...

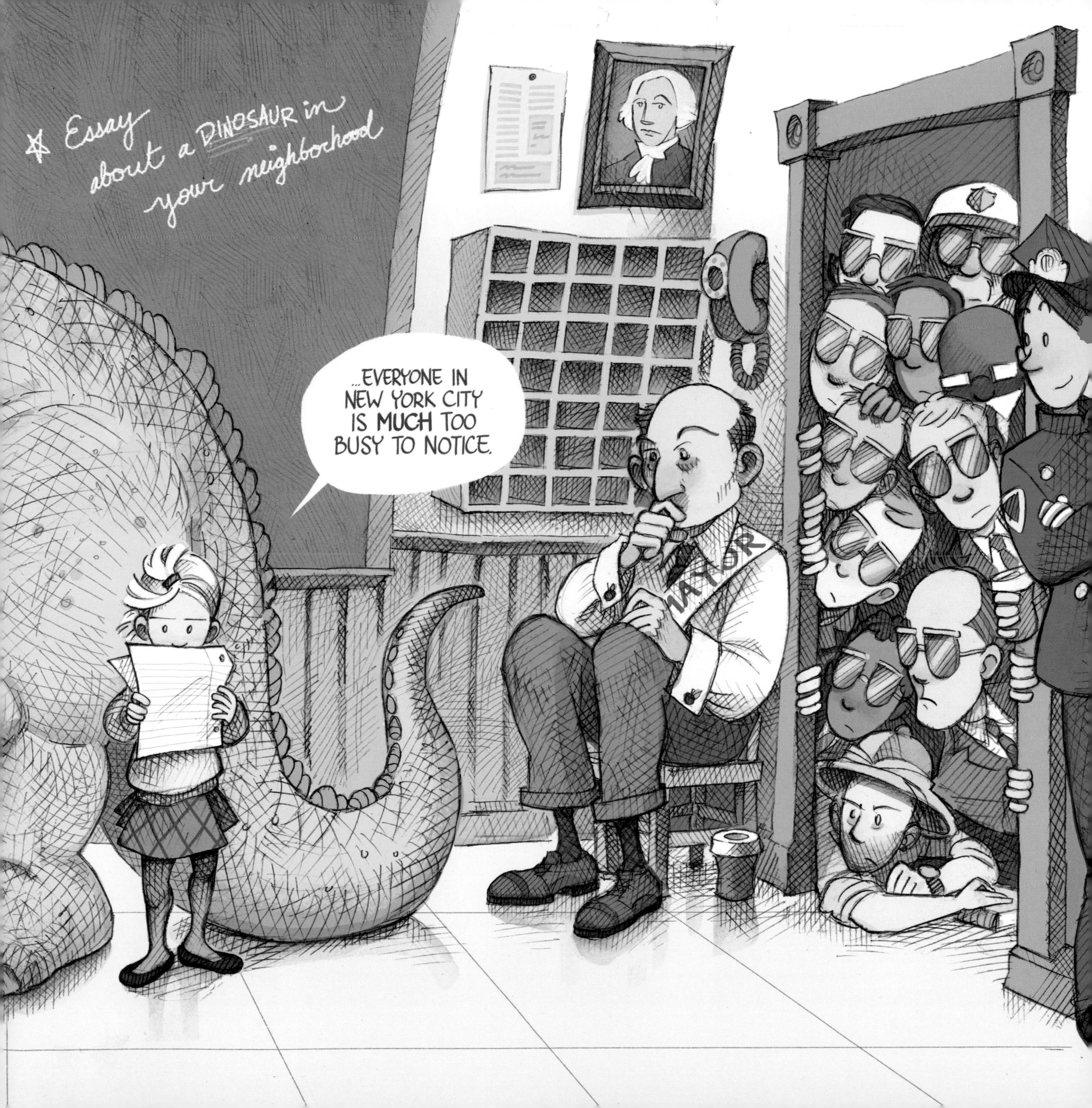

* Essay about a DINOSAUR in your neighborhood
...EVERYONE IN NEW YORK CITY IS MUCH TOO BUSY TO NOTICE.
MAYOR

...most of the time.

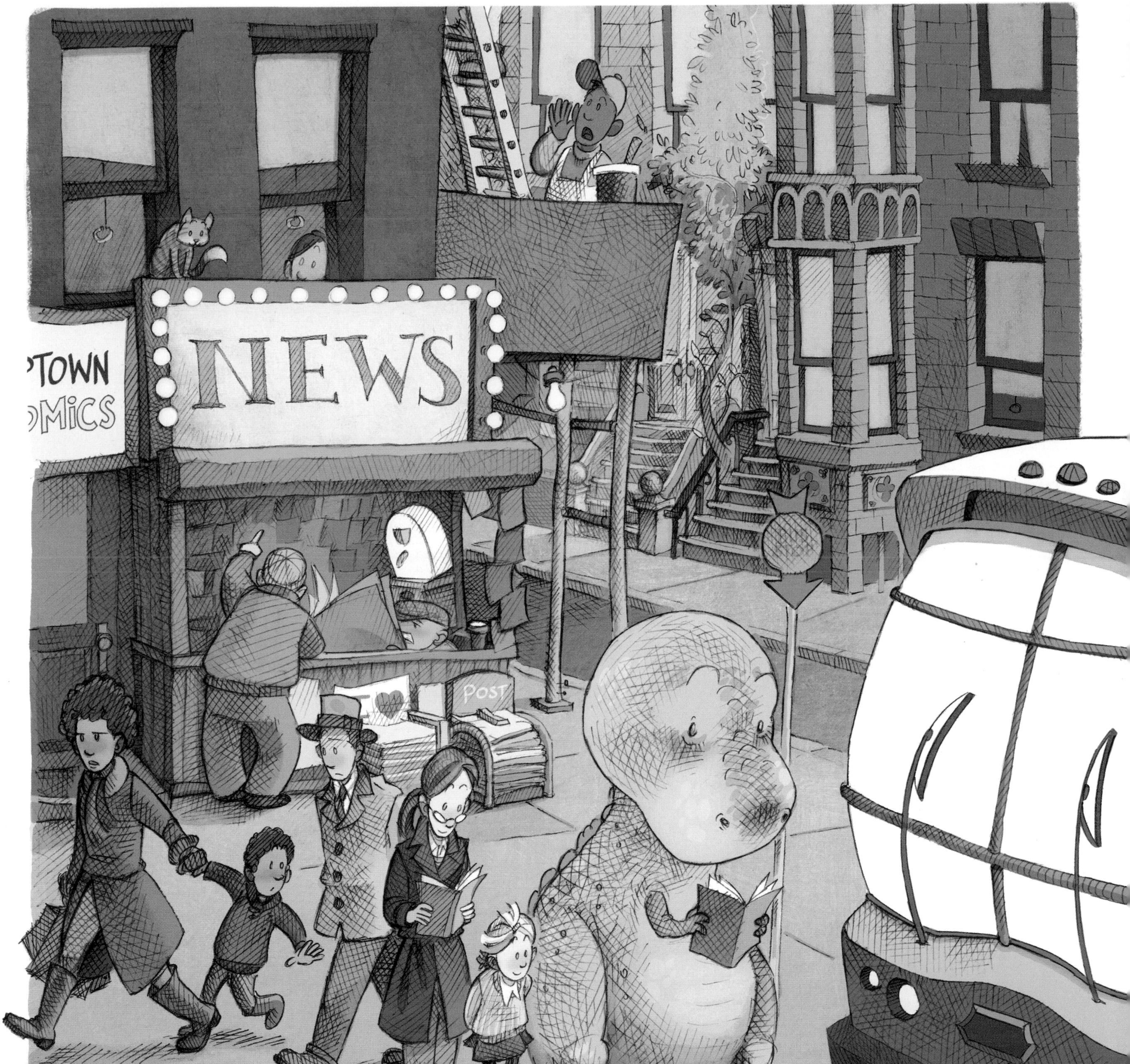
PTOWN
OMICS
NEWS
POST

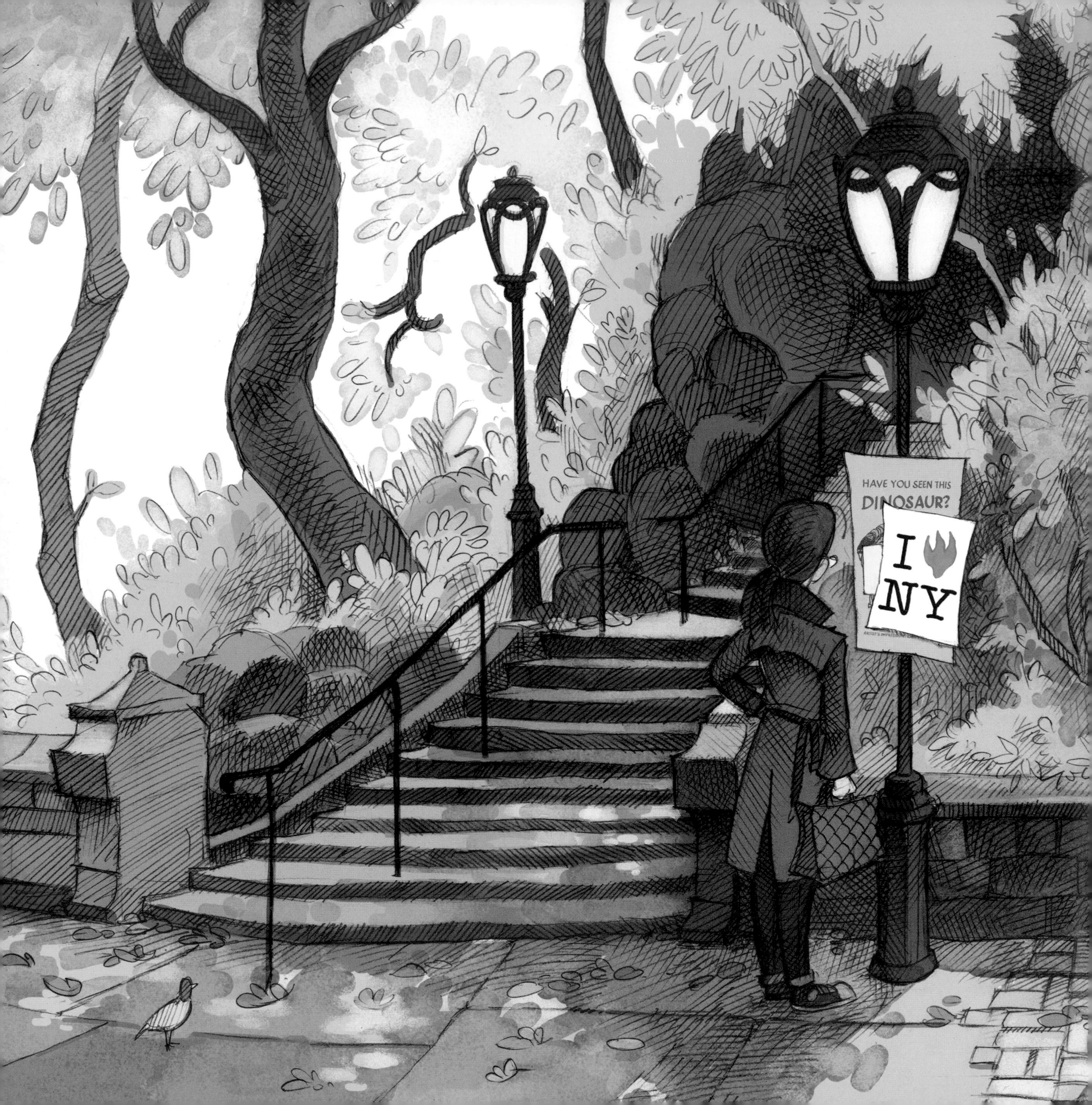
HAVE YOU SEEN THIS
DINOSAUR?
I
NY

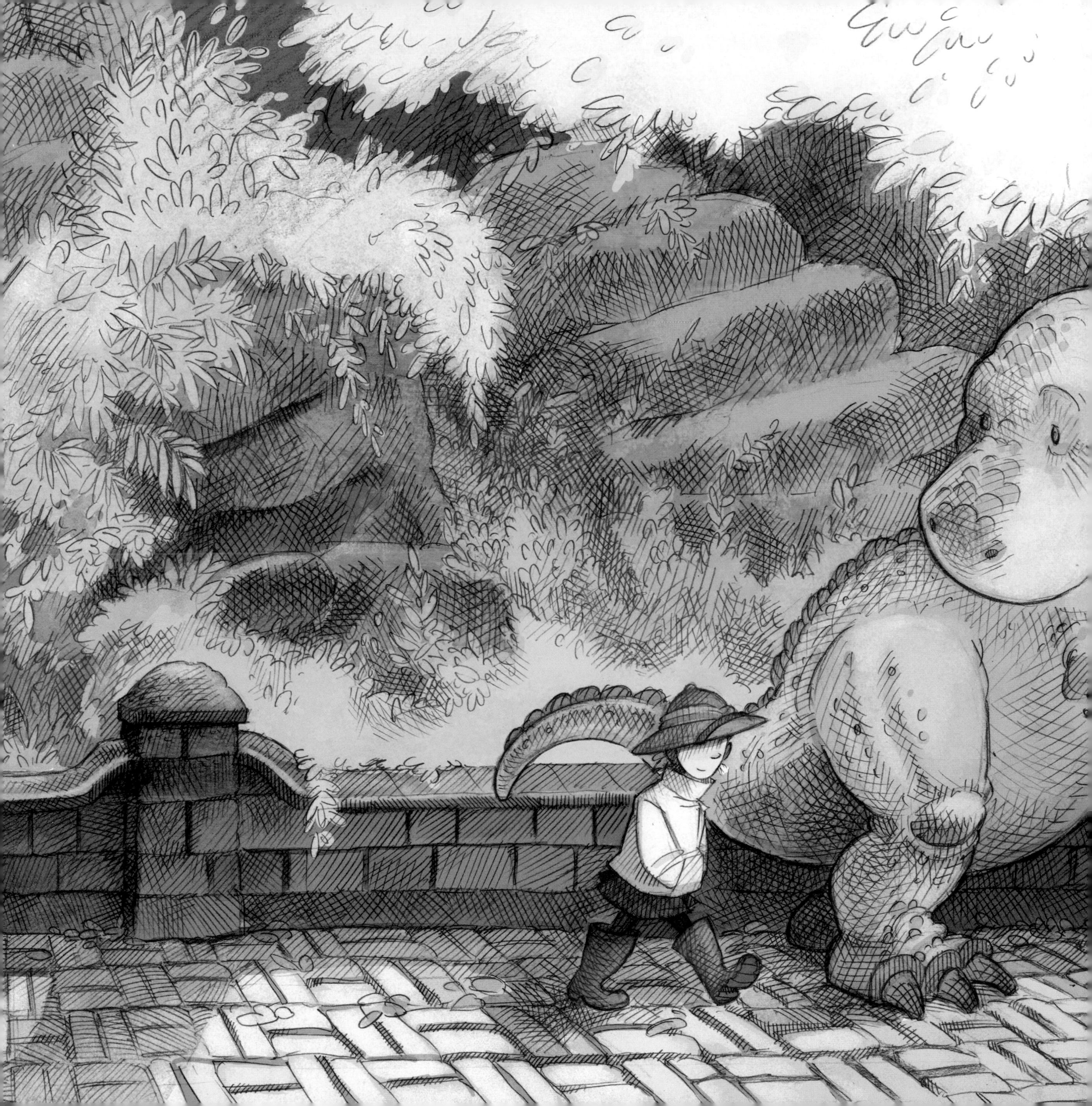

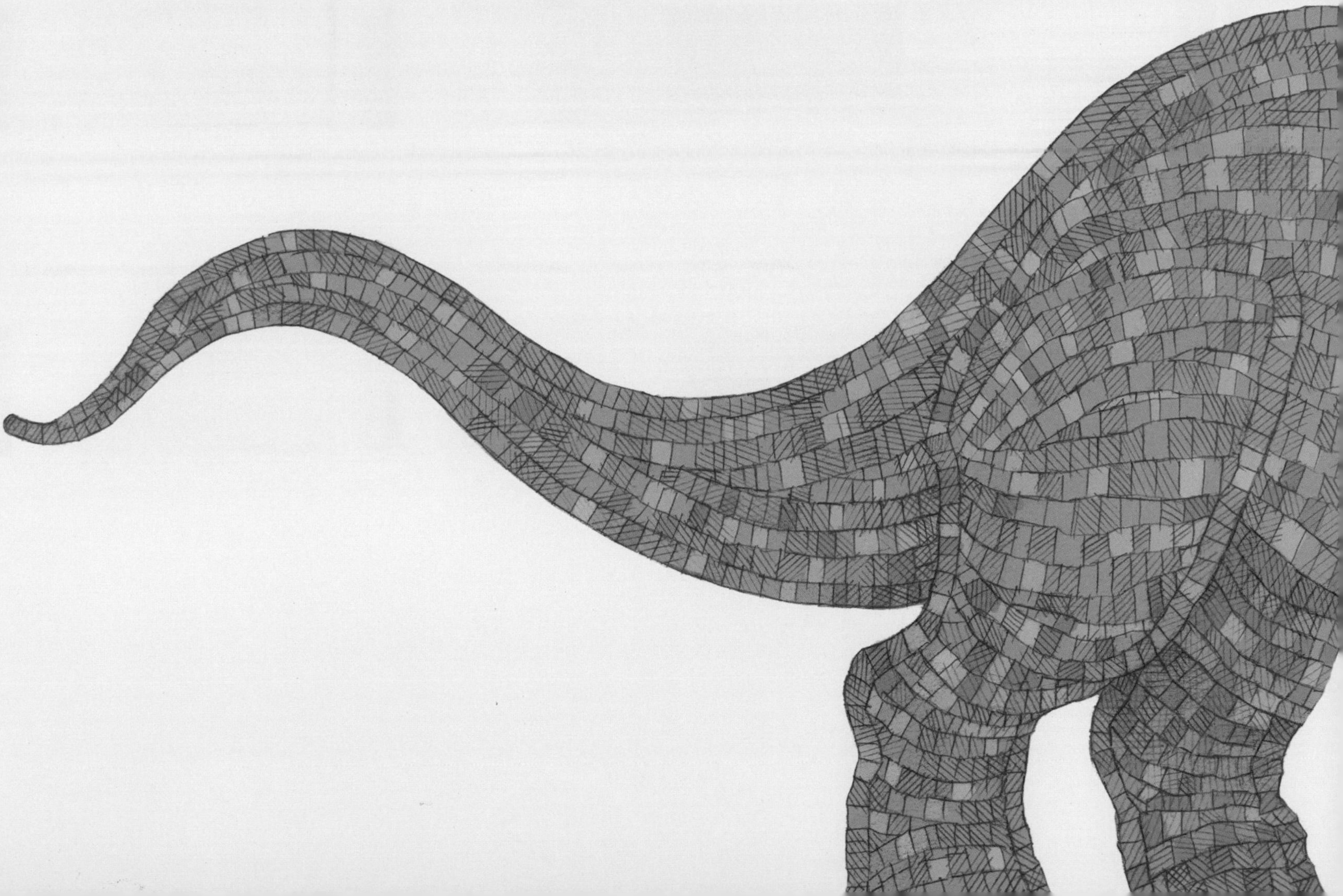

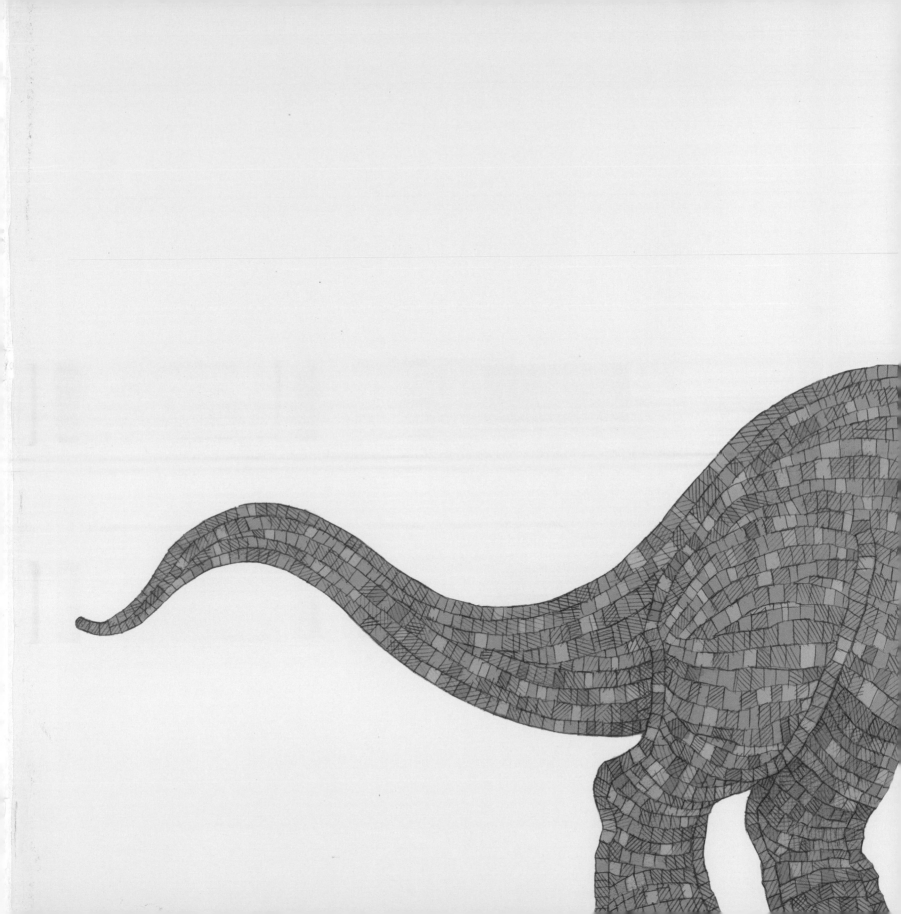

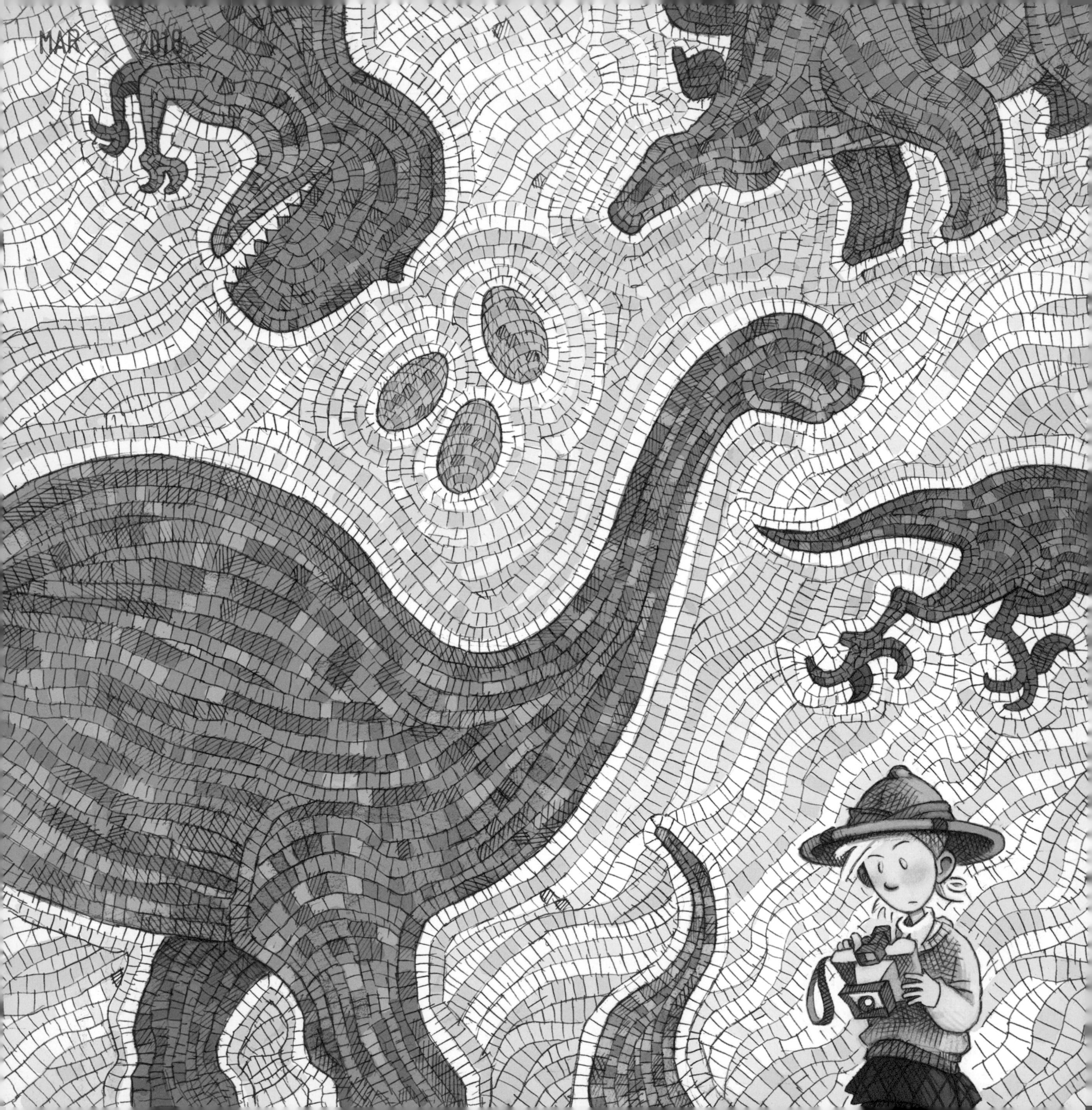
MAR 2018

ACKNOWLEDGEMENTS

This book took over five years to illustrate and, in that process, wreaked gentle havoc on a number of very patient and supportive people. Here are a few of them.

Bolivar was illustrated in studio spaces rented or borrowed from Nathaniel Angell, Eliot Samuels, and Mark and Lois Zollinhofer, and during an artist residency at the Haven—a day shelter in Charlottesville, Virginia. Thanks to New City Arts and the staff of the Haven for facilitating that residency.

Thanks to the team at Life Floor, especially Jonathan Keller, Spencer Howell, Jason Bahrke, and Gwen Ruehle for being supportive no matter how many leaves of absence I requested. Thank you also to Keith Glutting and the crew at the Cloisters Museum. Special thanks to Alison Dixon, Elizabeth Slater, Annie Colquitt, Sasha Young, Laura Adams Schulhof, and Kelli Grobe for being really good sports.

Drafts of this book were read and commented on by a number of generous friends, including Drew Dixon, Alex Kain, Virginia Scharf, Wade Bradshaw, John Lin, and Thomas Guarnera. Inspirational words and music were provided by Jesse Clements. Research, mainly walks in the park, was completed with the irreplaceable Jason Murphy.

Thank you to all the editors who have worked on this book, including Paul Morrissey, Rebecca "Tay" Taylor, Whitney Leopard, and Sierra Hahn. Thanks to my friends at Archaia who first believed in *Bolivar*, including P.J. Bickett, Jack Cummins and Mark Smylie, and to Ross Richie and the team at BOOM! Studios for patiently shepherding this project to completion.

I am indebted to a number of artists for inspiration, including my cousin Edward Addeo, who named Bolivar and sent him on his first adventures. This book is dedicated to him. Thanks also to Brian Jacques, David Petersen, Eve Aschheim, and Bill Watterson. Profuse apologies to Edward Hopper.

Over the course of this project, I relied on nearly daily support and encouragement from Stephen Christy, *Bolivar*'s first editor and original biggest fan; my dear friend and assistant Heather Simone; my parents David and Denise Rubin; and my incredibly funny and creative extended family.

Finally, thank you to Lucy, Sammy, and now Charlie for pulling me out of my apartment on the Upper West Side and into a richer life together than I could have ever imagined.

Fry's Spring
Easter 2017

ABOUT THE AUTHOR

SEAN RUBIN was born in Brooklyn, New York. As a city kid, he entertained himself by collecting interesting things, learning about obscure subjects, and drawing characters from books. He is an illustrator for the *Redwall* series and a contributor to the Eisner award-winning *Mouse Guard: Legends of the Guard* anthology.

Sean studied Art and Archeology at Princeton University, where he met his wife, Lucy. They have two sons and live in Charlottesville, Virginia.